SANDS
of *Zulaika*

Acclaim for Kathryn K. Abdul-Baki's Previous Books

Field of Fig and Olive

"A promising debut collection.... Place and character are vividly evoked and the distinct flavor of a different culture well caught...."
Kirkus Reviews

"It is difficult to heap enough praise on this author for her astonishingly vivid depictions of landscape and her ability to evoke spirit of place."
Seattle Times

"The stories offer insights into the cloistered world of Arab women...how women find means of expressing themselves in severely circumscribed settings."
Los Angeles Times Book Review

"In her Middle East world, sexual roles are sternly defined and jealously protected. But you don't have to be antediluvian to love the exotic settings and the humanity of the people in the 14 stories by Abdul-Baki. She has been blessed with the ability to make foreignness familiar."
Chicago Sun-Times

"An excellent 'translator' of Middle East sensibilities, particularly those of women. Her politics are feminist, her theme is human ethics, and her writing is finely honed."
Ms. Magazine

"This collection is truly a breakthrough in the world of Middle Eastern literature...written in English by someone who has a foot planted...in both the West and the Middle East."
Rocky Mountain News

"She challenges Western ways of thinking about the nature and behavior of Arab women and men and causes us to question some of our assumptions about the intricate relationships of families and lovers."
The Trenton Times

"Abdul-Baki's skillful and realistic presentation of characters, along with her masterly use of flashback and other narrative techniques, contributes to making her collection one of the most successful of its kind."
World Literature Today

"She does what every Arab leader would like to do – humanize the people of Arab descent, something long overdue in American Literature."
Former U.S. Senator James G. Abouresk

Tower of Dreams:

"She is a skilled craftsman…. The spirit of place and landscape are palpable…she shines in her ability to penetrate the psyche of young Arab women."
Seattle Times

Ghost Songs:

"A tranquil and beautiful novel…[it] gradually heats up into a thorough and tense examination of culture mores – both Arabic and American – without ever becoming judgmental."
Philadelphia City Paper

"She presents Arab culture…in narratives of exquisite technique, deep insights, and beautiful English…it bids fair to establish her as an Arab-American fiction writer worthy of wide recognition."
World Literature Today

OTHER WORKS BY KATHRYN K. ABDUL-BAKI

Fields of Fig and Olive:
Ameera and Other Stories of the Middle East

Tower of Dreams

Ghost Songs

SANDS
of Zulaika

Kathryn K. Abdul-Baki

An Original from Passeggiata Press

First Edition
Passeggiata Press
420 W. 14th Street
Pueblo, Colorado 81003

Library of Congress Cataloging-in-Publication Data

Abdul-Baki, Kathryn K.
  Sands of Zulaika / Kathryn Abdul-Baki. -- 1st ed.
     p. cm.
  ISBN 1-57889-115-9 (hardback) -- ISBN 1-57889-114-0 (pbk.) 1.
Middle East--Fiction. I. Title.
  PS3551.B269S36 2007
  813'.54--dc22

                                    2006039403

Table of Contents

Acknowledgments

A very loving thanks to all members of my family for their tremendous love and support while I was writing this novel. Your steadfast encouragement is a well of inspiration.

A special thanks to all members of The Group who patiently and generously contributed invaluable insights on the manuscript.

Thanks to my editor, Margaret Herdeck, for being there for me, and for her talented editing which made this a better book. A sincere appreciation to Donald Herdeck for giving me, and many others, a chance.

And thanks, as always, to my muse....

1

Prologue

Turquoise and chartreuse – this is how I remember Abu Samra – the color of the sea against the sand and yellowish gypsum houses. A landscape painting which draws me deeper into the canvas than I want to go, suspending me between two worlds, making me wonder which one was real.

Yes, certainly, my time in Abu Samra had been real. As real as the taffeta desert and fluid date palms. Green against magenta sunsets above the warm Gulf. Yellow-brown for the earthen alleyways cooled by black shadows. And there had been that other life, the heartbeat beneath the surface, overshadowing the life I was living in the canvas of the visible world.

Two worlds. The West and the enticing East. Two cities. Abu Samra and ancient Zulaika – a metropolis two meters under the sand. One reality attempting to blot out the other just as the blue of the sea fought all day to extinguish the blinding heat of the crystals of golden sand.

Abu Samra. No single canvas could contain it.

How to sketch the dusty market without painting in the bright aqua of the wooden doors and benches that awakened the drab streets? How to describe the dark silence of a village evening without painting in the translucent, gold-flecked shawls that lit the faces of the village women, the clinging crimson loincloths of the fishermen pulling in the sunset catch? The midnight of the city women's 'abayas against the men's long, white thobs. It was a spectacle that cannot be handled by oil or watercolor alone. Henna, kohl and indigo stain the canvas along with the greens of acacia, tamarisk and frangipani.

I am placed within that frame, along with my husband, Derek, and...

2

The Succulent Heat

The succulent heat embraced me first. A cocoon of intense warmth wrapped around me, followed by a moist wind whipping across my face and legs the moment I stepped out of the airplane to descend the metal steps to the sizzling tarmac. The wetness sucked the air from my lungs. When I reached the large, air-conditioned terminal, my free hand instinctively reached to cover my belly as if to shade it. Once inside, I glanced around for a glimpse of Derek who had arrived in Abu Samra ahead of me by several weeks.

Abu Samra. Even though, as a New Yorker, the unusual and even outrageous presented itself daily, the name aroused an exotic feeling in me. Here it was, finally before me.

Men in white robes and Arab headdresses strolled alongside women swathed from head to foot in silky black that swept the speckled, tile floor and concealed all but their amber faces. The white headdresses of the Arab men, held in place with a black cord, made them seem as opaque and unknowable as the women. The terminal echoed with a fervent, incomprehensible chatter and a pungent scent hung in the air as seductive as the women's wide, black-rimmed eyes. I felt abnormally pale by comparison, my blond complexion wan after thirteen hours of flying, and my hair stuck to my neck from the heavy air which pierced me on the short walk from the plane. I glanced around me, expecting Derek to come forward and claim me. Still no Derek.

Several dozen men wearing turbans and supple pantaloons lay asleep on the floor, propped up against overstuffed duffel bags. Indians, perhaps, or Pakistanis rather than Arabs. Expatriate workers seeking their fortunes in the oil-rich Gulf countries, no doubt, as Derek had described them in his letters. Some were barefooted, others had newspapers spread over their faces to shut out the din and bright lights of the terminal. Only one was awake, staring straight ahead as he smoked a cigarette, a shield of apathy across his face.

Bits of details that Derek had forwarded arranged themselves in a mosaic in my mind's eye as the realities of the place emerged. Abu Samra, a peninsula at the tip of the Persian Gulf, a last outpost of the British Empire and one of the first spots to have been drilled for oil early in the twentieth century. An oil state whose modest reserves were nearly exhausted, eclipsed by the larger, oil-rich Saudi Arabia and Kuwait. Yet, just as the peninsula had begun to settle once more into the blissful obscurity of a quaint Sheikhdom of fishermen, farmers, and pearl traders, a new surge of growth had erupted. The tiny Sheikhdom had reinvented itself as an offshore commercial center, a haven for banks and foreign businesses not permitted to operate freely in the more powerful Gulf states. This development had led to a quadrupling of the demand for electricity last year. Derek's New York firm, USA Electric, had won a bid to build the new power plant on the peninsula.

I scanned the room. This was Derek's dream. I felt a shard of remorse, along with a sudden, overwhelming tenderness. Derek had languished these past years waiting to get out of the head office in New York and into the field. He was an engineer. Abu Samra was the break he had been yearning for.

My months of balking at the prospect of moving to a confining finger of land in the heat-baked Persian Gulf, erupted once

4

more. I had dreaded the effect a move would have on my fledgling art career into which I had plunged myself the past few years. I also feared separating from family and close friends and all that was familiar and loved. There had been little hope, however, of changing Derek's decision to uproot the two – soon to have been three – of us.

At first, he had been confused by my inability to plunge wholeheartedly into this venture, had accused me of possessing a New Yorker's provincial arrogance. Then he had, more benevolently, attributed it to my unexpected pregnancy, to hormonal changes and the maternal instinct to protect one's young from the unknown. Yet, as I now inched forward along with the other passengers, too tired to care about the hopelessly wrinkled condition of my clothing, aware of the clamor of foreign words pressing against me like slightly jarring music, I knew that the source of my seeming reluctance to uproot myself was born in the almost primal fear of what this enforced isolation with Derek would bring.

There was still no sign of Derek. The woman in line ahead of me having her passport stamped was wearing a bright yellow dress. Amidst so much black and white, the yellow startled me. Suddenly, I was drawn back to our wedding day twelve years ago when I waited for Derek to arrive on his motorcycle to pick me up from my Riverside Drive apartment. I had clasped a bouquet of yellow lilies and freesia all the way to the courthouse, thinking how unhappy my Italian-Catholic parents would be to hear that I was marrying a Methodist and not having a church wedding.

Derek had intrigued me from the start. Here was a man whose descendents included one Frederick Monroe of the Mayflower, a man whose degree from Columbia had landed him on the fast track in USA Electric's training program, yet who chose to ride a motorcycle to work.

It had been for just this sort of thrill, the unorthodox, that I had abandoned the Midwest college campus after completing my

Fine Arts program and had returned to New York. The job I found that summer doing clerical work for a bank on Park Avenue was across the street from USA Electric. I met Derek in the coffee shop where I often ate lunch and where, in those days when he smoked, he would stop to buy cigarettes.

I was especially drawn to the way he moved, in short spurts, a jaunty authority commanding his arms and legs. His smile and his brusque spontaneity held me; but it was the lines of his body that fascinated me, his tense, angular shoulders, the tight muscles of his jaw, the contrast of his black hair against the light skin of his face, so different from my own light hair and skin that blended seamlessly into each other. The first time I saw him I went home and sketched him from memory, in bold strokes with black charcoal. His powerful torso and aquiline nose. Then I had carefully smudged the angles, as if I could smooth that turbulent energy right out of his skin.

"Gina?"

I spun round. At the sound of my name, a stream inside me suddenly spilled over. My feelings of ambivalence vanished. Through the memories, the gurgle of sound, the press of bodies, a surging hope propelled me toward Derek's voice and the comforting sight of his sun-browned face emerging from the crowd.

3

Sunsets

"The back-boot of the world," Derek announced triumphantly, sweeping his arm out of the car window to claim the kingdom of sand surrounding us.

As I watched him, I was overcome by the odd feeling that I was sitting next to a complete stranger. In the time he had been here, Derek had lost weight and even some of the hair around his temples, though perhaps it was the suntan that made his brow seem wider, or maybe the white bandage above his eyebrow. There was also a new temerity about him, an abrupt tone with which he had ordered the airport porter to locate my bags, and in the way he spoke of our surroundings now.

My eyes followed his pointing finger. The sun dipped into a red and gold horizon, sinking into the muted green of the Persian Gulf. The *Arabian* Gulf, the Arabs apparently called it. I could not look away from the water – green, blue, yellow, and pink where the sun brushed it. There were several slender palms along the shore.

It was somewhat cooler than an hour ago, as if the sun were a magnet drawing the heat down into the water with it. The car's air-conditioner was not working and the sweltering, wet breeze from the open window blew against me in gusts.

Derek glanced at my stomach half-heartedly, almost self-conscious.

"How's it going?"

"Fine," I said, looking down myself at my newly emptied belly, reminded again of the internal upheaval that had taken place inside of me since we had last seen each other. We had found out about the pregnancy six weeks ago, just before he left. It had been a shock, so unexpected after so long. The numbing confirmation by the doctor, which should have filled me with joy, had instead left me bewildered by the sheer irony of it. A conception, the ultimate symbol of unity, at a time of our gradual pulling away from each other.

"It takes a bit of getting used to," Derek said, somewhat apologetically. I realized he was talking about our surroundings, not the loss of my barely-begun pregnancy.

"The first impression is always the worst."

"You should have called to let me know," I said, turning my focus on him rather than me.

He touched his eyebrow. "What? About this?"

"You could have been killed." I tried not to betray my frustration that he had not called me as often as he had promised, that he had been away during the miscarriage, although he had wanted to fly home to New York to be with me as soon as I told him. I had refused, knowing he had no one to leave in charge of the new office.

"How could you have kept something as serious as a car accident from me, Derek? Why didn't you call me?"

"I didn't want you to worry. You'd suffered enough. Besides, I'm fine."

"You had a crash –"

"The car turned over. I didn't hit anyone. Just skidded into the desert and flipped."

"Twice, you said."

He shrugged. "Twice. But I wasn't hurt. Just a small cut."

I winced as he described, again, how he had lost control of the car one evening last week and somersaulted into an empty patch of sand. Guilt began to gnaw at me. I could have been here with him, I *should* have been here instead of being so intent on finishing up my projects in New York. Perhaps if I had been here I wouldn't have lost — I stopped myself and reached over and touched his hand on the steering wheel. I wanted him to know how frightened I was at the thought that he could have been seriously hurt. I wanted him to *need* my care. Especially since he had been about to become a father.

"It was nothing, really, honey," he said, smiling reassuringly. "Enjoy the sunset."

I withdrew my hand from his and stared back at the sea, which had suddenly caught fire as the sun descended below the horizon.

Two months earlier, I had driven Derek to Kennedy airport. I was to join him once he found an office and rented a house. I agreed with him that it would be easier on both of us, and certainly cheaper for his company, if he went on ahead and got things ready without having to accommodate me.

"Are you excited?" I had asked at the airport.

He had shrugged. "Of course. And nervous."

I had tried to look cheerful.

"You've waited a long time for this."

For the past several years he had pacified adversaries, overlooked slights from superiors, even contented himself with less salary than he could have had at any of the other top engineering firms because he knew that USA Electric had several overseas projects in the works. Now that they had been awarded the contract to build the electrical substation in Abu Samra, they selected Derek to oversee the construction which was projected to take a year. Derek's unofficial title was "trouble-shooter," one who could be counted on to push things through, get things done, considered a critical skill for the Abu Samra job.

We had stood together watching from the terminal window as the planes dipped onto the runway and soared away through the overcast sky. I had felt a swell of tenderness, a renewed bond with the father of my unborn child. But when I hugged him, pushed against him as if to remind him that a part of him was taking root within me, that this separation was now more tormenting than it would have normally been, he seemed distracted, fidgety. I sensed that I was embracing an empty shell. It was clear that Derek had already arrived in Abu Samra.

As I had driven home from the airport, my arm aching from the cholera shot that we were required to take for the trip, I tried to envision the sandy plains, the blue sea, the mysterious place that had already devoured my husband. Now that he was gone, the stab of separation eased and I started to resent having to follow him. The old concerns flared up — with one addition: I was now carrying a child. I had no idea how adequate the health facilities or doctors were there. An illness or accident that would be considered minor in New York might prove catastrophic in such a remote, perhaps ill-equipped place. And there was the obvious problem of Derek and me, of how apart we had grown in recent years.

Still of foremost concern to me was the setback to my career. I had been hired to teach two art classes in the fall at the Arts League. More important, after years of trying to establish connections with New York galleries, my watercolors had finally been accepted for an exhibition at the Mason Gallery off Madison Avenue. The exhibition could be postponed for eighteen months, the next time when the gallery space was available. But the loss of contacts, and especially the presumed unavailability of art museums and galleries in our new home, depressed me. I half considered sending word to Derek that I could not leave. I would wait out the year for him in New York while he focused on the job in Abu Samra. A year was not too long. Marriages survived longer separations. Ours could. *But with a baby on the way?*

Then the miscarriage. The sudden cramps and bleeding, the frantic calls to the doctor, the confirmation in the hospital that the pregnancy was lost, had not adequately taken hold after all. The attempts of the emergency room staff at consolation: it was best this

10

way, spontaneously terminated from the very beginning. Obviously, unhealthy from the start. Yet the agonizing feeling of emptiness was not so easy to soothe, as if I had been an imposter pretending at motherhood, fooling everyone. I had not even begun to show, just a tiny thickening of my waist. Amazing, how a few short weeks can change your life. How an image of the unformed fetus can embed itself so indelibly in your mind that you feel you've known it all your life.

Derek, to his credit, spent hours on the telephone with me, more tender than I had felt him in years. This would be a new start for us, he promised, although I sensed a small note of relief in his voice. We would try for another baby when I got to Abu Samra, he said, as soon as I was ready.

So, I had followed him.

Perhaps it was my father's cautious enthusiasm when he called from home in Connecticut to remind me how much my mother would have wanted me to go that had spurred me on. Her death last year had left me rudderless and disoriented, and the thought that she would have urged me to embark on an overseas venture seemed to instill in me a childish need to fulfill her wishes.

In addition, my continued inability to conceive had burdened both of us. Now that I had lost the pregnancy — I could not bring myself to call it "the baby" — I had to be with Derek. We were still a family. Perhaps this loss was meant to bring us together in a new and vital way.

Several weeks after he left for Abu Samra, I began to forget the old problems. I even forgot the times recently that he had been too preoccupied to respond to a kiss, to smile, to enjoy an evening of fun. When I moved close to him in bed, he would instinctively move away, as if intimacy would drain him of the energy he needed to get through the work day. Even though I tried not to take these rebuffs to heart, his indifference to everything but his job had taken its toll on me.

Derek had already been packed when I learned of my preg-

11

nancy. A week of morning nausea, which I had at first taken to be food poisoning, sent me to the doctor's office and to the surprising, though long-awaited, diagnosis of a baby. I had immediately called Derek with the news. Despite his surprise, tinged perhaps with slight disappointment at the awkward timing of it, he tried to sound excited. We had been married ten years, he said, as if to justify it. It was time. Later, when he called from Abu Samra to say that he had found a house, one with plenty of sand in the backyard for a baby to play in, I felt his eagerness for fatherhood, and found that I no longer minded leaving New York.

Sorting through my portfolio of watercolors, collages, silk-screens and oils as I packed up the apartment and put the furniture and my art into storage, for the first time I began to look forward to joining my husband in this new venture.

Cars now passed us along the streamer of black tarmac that spread across the sand. Part of a man's white Arab headdress fluttered out of a car window like a novice nun's veil, like the delicate white mantilla I had worn to church when I was twelve. The cars all seemed to be heading toward a mass of faded buildings in the distance.

"That's the city," Derek said.

I fanned my face with my passport. "And I thought it was hot in New York."

He laughed. "Wait until noon tomorrow. Just walking out the front door in the morning is like wading through a sauna. August isn't great for first impressions."

I flapped my skirt. The backs of my knees trickled sweat.

"I tell you," he exclaimed, suddenly, as though not quite believing it himself, "we're at the end of the earth."

We passed a row of tall, concrete buildings along the sea.

"I'm wait-listed for space in one of these buildings," Derek said, pointing to a white complex with large windows. "Right now my office is in the middle of downtown, over a tailor's shop."

We drove through a wide, white archway and suddenly a clut-

12

tered, dilapidated town crystallized before us. Sand-colored buildings stood beside whitewashed ones with fluted, arabesque windows. Some of the buildings had tall protrusions from the rooftops that looked like small towers while others had rows of scalloped stucco along the ridges. Narrow alleys branched surreptitiously off the main streets. A small boy on the roadside was pushing a large wheelbarrow piled high with thin, yellow stalks of fruit. He crossed the road in front of us, barely glancing at the car.

"Dates," Derek said. "They've just been picked." Further down the street, a white-domed building stood at a corner of a square. "That's the new mosque," he said. "Just look at the minaret." The slender tower to the side of the dome had a silver ball at the top that winked like a diamond in the dying sunlight.

"Well," I said, almost to myself, still unable to realize that we were actually in Abu Samra, thousands of miles away from anything remotely familiar.

Derek looked anxious.

"What do you think?"

I shrugged. "It doesn't feel like the end of the earth."

His eyebrows knitted in surprised relief.

"My little New Yorker. The outside world is opening up to you."

I ignored his remark, growing impatient with his nervous attempts to cheer me, with his fear that I was disappointed. I was tired, that was all. The time change and too many hours in the air. My eyes burned and I was hungry. Besides, I had the right to feel any way I damn well pleased. He was the one who had decided to bring us here. He had no right to try to control my feelings about the place, even if he was in control of the other aspects of our lives for now. Although I felt guilty, I suddenly resented being so dependent on Derek. With this move I had become a corporate wife. A follower. I was in Abu Samra only because of him. Here, I needed him to guide me around, to explain what things were, how things were done, what was expected of me. And I had the feeling that he

13

knew this and was happy. Again, I had a sudden, sharp fear of being isolated with Derek in this unknown place, a sense that this exile would only magnify the widening rift between us.

We were soon out of the downtown area and driving along a road flanked by dusty pink and white oleanders. I shut my eyes and jerked my head away as a cloud of dust blew through the window. Derek veered around a gap in the unpaved road.

"This is a brand new neighborhood. That's why it's a mess."

I opened my eyes and held onto the dashboard as we bounced over the sand. At the end of the road, in the middle of what appeared to be a construction site with stacked cinder blocks and pyramids of gravel, stood a two-story brown cement house surrounded by a high, brown wall. Derek pulled to a stop. He looked at me, waiting for the sand to settle from around the car. Then he smacked the steering wheel and smiled, jubilant, his eyes almost pleading for me to understand.

"You'll see, Gina. This'll be worth the sacrifice. My work here will *mean* something."

Suddenly, he took my damp hand in his, as though to walk me through all of our years together in one brief moment — both the happy ones and those last lonely, confused ones.

"Welcome home," he said, the affectionate words striking an unexpected cord of terror in me.

4

Home

I awoke to a clinking sound from outside, like the sound of a spike being hammered into the ground. Despite the thick blue drapes drawn across the bedroom windows, the sun, like yesterday's heat at the airport, pierced the walls. Except for the whir of the air conditioner, the house emitted no other sound. I could not help listening for the daily sounds heard from our fourth-floor Manhattan apartment — grating bus engines, car horns, police sirens that made up the very air of New York.

Derek's side of the bed was empty, the covers smoothed over in an old habit he still retained from his years at boarding school. I listened for the sound of water in the shower, for objects being moved about the bathroom, any indication that he was somewhere nearby. But there was only the vast, dense hush.

It was already noon in Abu Samra, four a.m. in New York. My head and legs, still on New York time, ached.

I pulled myself out of bed and drew back the drape. The sunlight flooded in through the hot window pane, releasing pale prisms onto the walls. Below a pallid lawn of sand stretched away from each side of the house. Beyond the brown garden wall was construction. New houses going up on the left and on the right, with their respective piles of sand recently dug out of the earth standing guard. Outside our front gate, cinder blocks and wood planks were stacked behind an old cement mixer.

I let go of the drape, the fabric still creased from the factory, still reeking of fresh dye. The entire house had been furnished by USA Electric with traditional, American furniture from New York. The thickly lined curtain fabric was obviously intended to block out the sun although its broad, formal cornice seemed out of place in the desert. The blue color of the fabric, perhaps meant to compensate for the desert outside, was too bright to be quenching or even soothing.

There was a smaller bedroom across the hall. Another heavy drape, soft lavender, darkened the room which had a large, canopy bed in the center. Last night, I had immediately imagined this room as having been the baby's, and could almost see the little body curled up in its bassinet in the cool, purple shadows, its dark hair in soft curls about its face. I stood there, drawing the image again in my mind before forcing myself to erase it.

My mother's voice, as it had been those last weeks of her life, faint and hesitant, suddenly flowed through me, words urging, reproving, dispensing last-minute advice before she was gone.

"He's a good man, Gina. Don't ruin your life. Make do. You need each other." And my nodding at her, smiling, reassuring, not wanting to leave her with the fear that I would ever be so rash or so desperate as to leave Derek. I had squeezed her hand. I had not married in the Catholic Church. The least I could do was spare her the thought of a divorce.

A small sitting room with a television and a sofa connected the three upstairs bedrooms. From here, a flight of stairs led up to yet another small landing with a shiny, wooden door. I climbed the stairs and tried the doorknob.

For the second time since arriving, I felt my body contract from the heat which ignited the concrete under my feet and ripped

16

through to the tips of my fingernails. I stepped quickly into a cooler, shaded area of the flat roof and scanned the surroundings.

In the distance, from this height, trucks and cars moved slowly along a blue ribbon of sea. Patches of palm trees emerged between the empty areas of desert and clusters of square, flat-roofed houses. Shanties with corrugated tin roofs dotted my immediate horizon. Then came the sounds — the faraway clamor of cars and trucks, the ripple of bleating goats or lambs. From somewhere nearby the clinking sounds I had heard earlier started again, along with a man's soft singing.

At the back of the house, outside the garden wall, another cement wall encased a large, rectangular plot of empty desert. The walled property was barren except for a concrete platform in the center and four tall columns surrounding it. A horizontal concrete slab formed a roof over the columns so that the small structure resembled an open horse stable, although there were no signs of animals. This strip of land appeared to have been set aside, reserved for some future use. With all the surrounding construction, I hoped this meant it would not be built on. It would be nice to keep this one sweeping view of the sea, even if it were from the roof.

I wanted suddenly to sketch the scene from this very spot, to set up my easel and mix a palette of colors to match the ecru, magenta, lilac, and olive near the sea. I felt my hands twitch. I could work well in this light, despite the heat. Light was everything. If the light was always this good from the roof, I would paint a lot here.

I would make myself forget the pain and doubt of the last few weeks, will myself to move forward into a new horizon. Yet, I was also wary of starting too soon. The surroundings were still too new. Attempts to reproduce what was before me now would be driven by emotion, be a mere rendering of what I thought I saw. I had to be patient, let the light and atmosphere soak into my skin. I would sketch the scene at sunset, when the colors were denser and I felt more objective.

The sounds drew my attention again.

They were vibrations and tones rather than complete sounds, bare snatches of noise that climbed up to the hot rooftop. An animal's grunt, the gritty roar of an engine, all broken by the closer clink-clink that had started up again, accompanied by the same reedy voice of a man singing.

The house going up next door was half done, the building materials — cinder blocks, cement bags and other debris — lying on the floors of the roofless, downstairs rooms. The walls were so close to ours that when finished, one could conceivably leap onto the next roof from this one. Again, I felt grateful for the open space of the walled plot to our back.

The clinking that had awakened me was coming from directly below now. Stepping to the edge of the roof, I saw a man in a purple turban squatting next to a wheelbarrow in one of the unfinished rooms. He was dressed in a baggy shirt and pants, like the men sprawled on the floor of the airport yesterday, and he was pounding something in a bowl. In the sand beside him a small fire flittered. A breeze bent the fire's flames and blew the sand about like fine shards of glass. Then, the clinking and singing stopped and the man tipped the contents of the bowl into a pan set in the middle of the flame.

Now the fire leaped, almost swallowing the pan. The piercing aroma of garlic and onions rose up, followed by the tantalizing smells of ginger, coriander, cumin. A delicious scent of curry suddenly permeated the air. It was a strangely serene sight, this lone worker meticulously preparing a meal in the desert, as if it were some sacred act.

"Derek?"

My voice drifted ahead of me into the rooms downstairs where the sunlight spread across the floor like a net. The carpet was the discreet color of sand, but the rest of the furniture was upholstered in a deep red damask. Even the windows were draped in claret, giving the rooms an air of a New England country inn or a

18

wintry English drawing room.

Derek had explained to me last night that the house was built in the Abu Samra style, with a large, central foyer, two separate sitting rooms — one for men, the other for women — and a large dining room. The rooms had been decorated with Queen Ann tables and wing chairs, Chippendale sofas and cherry wood bookcases. The new wood glowed rich and hard.

"Why would anyone furnish a house in a desert like this?" I had asked Derek, running my hand across the glossy cherry dining table.

"People here love American stuff."

"Teak or rattan would have been more appropriate, considering the climate. Don't you think?"

"Does it bother you that much?" he had said, beginning to sound impatient.

I shrugged. "I'd have chosen different colors."

Derek had pretended not to hear this, obviously not wanting to get into a discussion of colors with me.

In the foyer, an elegant credenza was set against a wall under an oil painting of an English hunt scene. Dogs and horses glanced out of a lush countryside. It was a cozy corner if one forgot the sandy reality outside the front door. I could see myself sitting here to write Christmas cards or letters to my father describing the flat silence of the house, the shrill sunlight.

In the kitchen was an oak table and chairs. The window above the sink faced the garden wall and the construction next door. The appliances sparkled — a white stove and refrigerator and a dishwasher that Derek had warned me was useless because of the brackish water.

On the kitchen table lay a note on yellow drafting paper: *"Had to leave early. Cereal in the refrigerator, please return there away from the humidity. Wash any fruit or vegetable you eat with disinfectant. The driver will get you whatever you need."*

I glanced at the bottle of 'Milton' disinfectant near the sink.

Next to it was a stack of red and green bills, Abu Samran currency obviously left by Derek in case I needed money. There was a portrait of a portly man in glasses and Arab headdress in the corner of one of the bills. It was the Ruler of Abu Samra. I had seen his photograph in the guidebook that Derek had brought back to New York from one of his trips here several months ago.

A carton of Danish milk and a box of Corn Flakes were in the refrigerator along with some apples and Ritz crackers. I ate a cracker and then a bowl of cereal, enjoying the familiar crunch of the flakes. I ate slowly, savoring the quiet and staring at the gleaming, handicapped dishwasher. I glanced again at Derek's note, this time with a rush of euphoria. It felt good to be taken care of.

It was Madame Shams, the psychic back in New York, who had predicted this move from the start. She had foreseen a journey to a place with much water: verdant, lush, aquamarine.

I had sketched her that afternoon in her apartment, trying to capture the peaceful intensity on her face with which her Eastern roots imbued her. When I had asked her if the journey was the right thing for us, she had warned me that Derek would have to be careful. She had been silent a few moments, as if having to translate from some indecipherable language. "Stomach trouble," she had said, finally. "He'll get an ulcer."

I had leaned forward, almost rubbing foreheads with her.

"What should he do? Can't we prevent it?"

"We can't change things. We can only be prepared," she had said. "How old are you?"

"Thirty-two."

"You are just starting your seven-year cycle. Your husband is coming to the end of his. You must be patient."

"What do you mean?" I asked. "Should we not go?"

She had smiled. "We can't rob you of your free will. Only you can decide whether or not to go. But your husband should be careful."

20

I had not expected this warning, nor news of an ulcer. This had been just the sort of problem I wanted to avoid. Still, Derek seemed perfectly healthy. I reminded myself that psychics were not infallible. Besides, I had never been one to operate out of fear.

Yet riding up the elevator of our East 83rd Street building, her prediction had clouded my thoughts again.

"It wards off ulcers," I told Derek, scooping the cream custard into a dessert plate after dinner.

The two of us were sitting at our dining table that overlooked the park outside. The early summer leaves were expanding into a rich, supple green against the window pane. My throat caught at the thought of leaving the quaint park where I spent many afternoons sketching the children as they played on swings, or an unobservant vagrant or dozing grandfather.

Derek had stared down at the custard through his dark lashes. "Do you have an ulcer?"

I hesitated a moment, afraid that Madame Shams' warning would preoccupy him at this critical time. Knowing that Derek was much too practical to give credence to a psychic's prophecy, I went ahead and told him of my afternoon visit.

"Gina, a fortune teller? Come on."

"She's a psychic. It's different."

"A lot of baloney," he had said, smiling despite himself, spooning more pudding onto his plate.

"Derek, for once I wish that you would consider something with an open mind."

"Open-mindedness has nothing to do with it, Honey. When you go overseas you consult guidebooks or people who've been there. Not psychics."

I wanted to tell him that all Madame Shams's other predictions had been accurate, like the one about his last promotion, about my art show, even her hint of an unplanned pregnancy. But despite my frustration, I did not want to ruin the excitement that had gripped Derek these past months. It was too late, anyway, to alter all the plans that had already been made.

That night in bed as my fingers stroked his shoulders, searching for the man I once thought could tame that unsettled part of me, I could barely remember what it had felt like to be in love with him, that early desire to follow him anywhere simply to be near him.

A part of me had known all along how necessary this move was. I had woken up too many nights from the shuffle of Derek's footsteps in the kitchen when he was unable to sleep from frustration. Despite the setback to my own career that this move would bring, I had to put him first. I knew that we were living only half a life in Manhattan, pressured and isolated from one another. Most days I felt I was actually buried, struggling for air through a thin straw of constant rituals performed as a wife and artist. Perhaps, as Derek kept insisting, getting out of New York was what we both needed.

Yet even when this surge of hope flared this morning at the kitchen table in this expansive, unfamiliar house, I wondered what the future held.

I saw myself soon after we were married, Derek hailing a cab to go to the hospital after I had suffered a case of appendicitis. I had come home from the hospital the next day to find that Derek had washed and ironed the curtains — a chore that had obsessed me for weeks but which I had been unable to do before the surgery. Gazing at the soft, white fabric billowing in the breeze like angel wings, overcome by compassion for Derek for trying to make me happy, I had started to cry. The memory of those white curtains reaffirming Derek's love stabbed at me now. Their pressed brightness seemed to belong to some other life.

I ran my hand across my stomach, more out of habit than with a feeling of loss now, and read Derek's note again, tracing his hurried, slanted writing, the way that he omitted 'r' when he rushed. Last night seemed long ago. Last night, with the faint scent of dust throughout this new house, the cool breath of the air conditioner, the smell of salt in the water as I washed my face at the bathroom sink before bed. The roughness of the sheets and the salty scent of Derek's skin from the brackish water. Then his caresses as we lay in bed before my own sudden, almost willful, surrender to sleep. Yes, we should start trying for a new baby. When I was ready.

5

Flirting Shadows

The morning light blanched the colors of the desert.

A lackluster pallor settled over everything so that old and new alike seemed to be doused in a filmy rinse. Nothing looked spectacular from a distance. Only when one got right up to it could one appreciate the emerald of a palm frond, the sparkle of a freshly white-washed mosque, the lacy lattice-work of a crumbling, gypsum house. Arching windows, airy rooftop towers, doors of carved Indian teak — all seemed worn down, tired. The sun and heat of the desert did not preserve sharp beauty, as though there were some rudimentary law deriding vanity.

But while the harsh light of day subdued Abu Samra, the monotone of night brought it unabashedly to life, as I discovered my second evening there.

The entire town glimmered through the mist of dust — white light bulbs strung across the balconies of white government buildings, zigurat-shaped plaster trim jutting up from the rooftops. The town's streets, smoldering alleys during the day, became a carnival of activity after sunset. Men's white *thobs* swept the ground as they walked alongside women in black *abayas*. Entire families it seemed, invigorated by the cool of evening, strolled through the glowing market *souq*, parting in unison whenever a slow-moving car passed. Latticed balconies hung out over the street while tall protrusions rose up from rooftops — wind towers Derek explained, the old Arab system, before air-conditioning, of drawing the breezes into the house from an open chute.

Clearly, the night belonged to the pedestrians. Arabs, Indians, Pakistanis, Koreans, an occasional European or American, walked down the brightly lit streets. A group of tanned, blond men dressed in shorts and with boisterous British accents stood outside a pizza restaurant. Yet they had an air of aloofness about them, a weariness that had been so apparent on the faces of the expatriate Indians at the airport the day before, faces of men here alone, earning money and biding their time without their wives or children until their contracts were up. I wondered, briefly, whether Derek had looked this forlorn before I arrived.

We paused at a jeweler's window filled with bright golden bangles, earrings, diamond watches, and thick pearl bracelets. Gold chains linked together into glittering breast plates, like golden armor, were displayed over velvet busts.

"Are these necklaces?" I asked, mesmerized.

Derek smiled. "Twenty-two carat."

"Do women actually wear them?"

"I can't tell what they wear under those black sheets."

I glanced at him. "I find their robes interesting. My eyes want to penetrate the darkness to the beauty underneath."

"How can you tell if they're beautiful when they're all covered up like that?"

"I can tell from their eyes," I said. "They've got gorgeous eyes. And they don't all cover up. You can tell from the ones who don't how pretty the ones who do are."

"Well," he said, "as far as I'm concerned they can keep their beauty to themselves."

Again, Derek displayed an uncharacteristic cynicism. Yet I could glean something of his frustration. Although I was fascinated by the black cloaks of the women and white shirt-dresses of the men, I found myself straining to see through the fabric to the actual body shapes. Elbows and ribs, breasts, hips, and even to a level below the flesh to femurs, tibias. I needed to see the flesh to draw it, to know these people who lived behind these impersonal, cloth walls. Covered like this, they walked the streets fortified against intrusion. For a Western man, suddenly being barred from gazing at female bodies must have been immensely aggravating.

He moved ahead of me as though to cut a path through the crowd. Fabric shops were lined with bolts of bright polyesters, cottons, silks, and the most elaborately tinseled chiffons I had ever seen. I thought of Van Dyck's plush velvets, slippery silks and starched crinolines — how he brought out the crispness of silks by masterful shadowing. I would buy some of these fabrics one day and experiment. Even the booths crammed with household items such as aluminum pots, plastic strainers, or indigo teapots juxtaposed haphazardly together, cried out to be painted.

Neon Hindi letters flashed above a movie theater where Indian men, and women in saris and bright makeup, black hair braided down their backs, stood in line. Except for the lingering smell of curry, this street could have been Coney Island, windows resplendent with garish trinkets, the smell of food booths stacked with things to nibble.

Several Indian men in turbans sat on the pavement, eating something out of a paper bag. I remembered the morning smells from the man's cooking over the open fire next door.

"What are they eating?" I asked.

Derek glanced at the men. "Samosas."

A vendor in a nearby food stall was tossing something from a smoking cauldron into paper bags. Spices seemed to swirl about the people waiting in line. Absently, I moved toward the stall, as if under a spell.

27

"Wait a minute," Derek said, his arm swinging suddenly in front of me. He went up to the vendor himself. I watched him, not accustomed to this new, protective attitude of his. He returned with a paper bag and pulled out a flaky, golden pastry.

"They're hot," he warned, too late, as I bit into the triangle. The soft filling scalded my mouth — potatoes, peppers, coriander, cumin, green peas. I was ravenous, absorbing the delicious taste and smell, even when my lips started to burn from the chilies. I had been craving this taste since smelling the man's cooking from the rooftop this morning! Nothing had ever tasted so good.

All at once, and for no discernible reason, I sensed that something extraordinary was about to happen. The warm breeze, the flirting shadows on the balconies, the murmuring voices of the night shoppers, only compounded this certainty. It suddenly felt as if all this was merely the backdrop for something else, something greater that was about to take hold of us and control us completely.

Yet rather than trepidation, an exuberance seized me. An inexplicable joy of being in a new place where nothing was familiar, a place where I felt safely invisible to the humanity in the street who seemed to inhabit a universe entirely removed from my own. A place where I could become somebody new, where the two of us could embark on a new existence.

"Careful!" Derek's arm came out again, drawing me back onto the sidewalk just as a roar erupted behind us. The glaring lights of a truck shot down the street.

"Sanitation," Derek muttered, as if he were swearing.

My mouth still flamed from the samosas.

The truck slowly gained on us, screeching as it stopped a few yards away. Suddenly, several men in blue uniforms leaped off, scooped up scattered paper and debris from the street and hurled it into the back. The other pedestrians hardly seemed to notice as the men chased the rear of the truck with armfuls of litter.

"Every night they do this," Derek said. We watched the truck move through the cloud of dust. "Tomorrow it'll be just as dirty."

"Why don't they put out trash bins?" I said, amazed at the notion that men collected trash, piece by piece, by hand.

"They do. Doesn't do any good."

"They just collect it every night?"

"Every night," he said, as if we were hapless victims of some bizarre, Abu Samran plot. "Totally inefficient. Some things here just don't make sense."

A man in a turban abruptly stopped on the sidewalk in front of us, lowered his head, and blew his nose into his fingertips.

"Christ!" Derek protested, pulling back as if to shield me. "See what I mean? That's one thing I can't take." He maneuvered forward, his dark curly head above the crowd.

I stood transfixed. Then I began to laugh, filled with a curious relief. I could not remember seeing Derek react so sharply to his environment, not even on the worst days of subway commuting in Manhattan, as he had just done to this simple, vulgar act of hygiene. I fought off a smile as I hurried to catch up with him. Although I was surprised by his revulsion, by this hint that he was less impressed by Abu Samra than he wanted to be, I was secretly elated by this rare, public display of emotion.

Later, after I turned out the light, Derek snuggled against my back, pressing his face gently into my neck.

"Derek?"

"Umm." His legs circled mine, warming me in the cool, air-conditioned room.

"Derek, are you happy here?"

He did not answer, nudging down the strap of my nightgown.

A soft, dry sadness swelled in my throat. It had been six weeks. I knew I should have hungered for his touch. But somehow, tonight, I was not ready yet. Especially after all the fascinating things I had just seen, I wanted to close my eyes and bring it all back, savor it all again alone.

"I'm tired," I said, trying to sound more exhausted than I really was.

29

"It's only afternoon in New York," Derek said.

"I know."

He was still. Then he moved away slightly. "Are you O.K.? I mean, what did the doctor say?"

"Everything's fine," I said. "I'm just tired right now."

"Didn't you miss me?"

"Of course I did," I said, suddenly defensive.

He was silent a minute. "I thought you'd be excited to see me. I mean — it's O.K. to have sex, isn't it?"

"Of course," I said, impatient. "It's just been a long time. It's been hard."

"For me, too." He sighed and kissed me lightly on the cheek. "But I didn't forget you."

"I didn't forget you, either," I said, suddenly feeling foolish. I rested my head against his and tried to relax.

"You looked happy tonight," he said.

"I am," I said, remembering the smells and sounds of the strange small town, so foreign and provocative. Then as sleep overtook me, freed me of the resentment and confusion of being uprooted, of having to bury my own ambitions in order to cater to Derek's, I relented. I could still inhale the fragrance of the Indian women at the cinema, taste the trenchant cumin of the samosas. I could discern the arabesque carvings on the wind towers. Perhaps life here *would* be different.

I pushed against Derek's palms as they slid down my ribs, reached up to pull his head to mine. Perhaps *we* could be different.

And later still, after making love, I dreamed of the truck cutting into the crowds on the moonlit Abu Samra streets, moving like a slow, lonely bull. The men ran behind it, gathering up trash as if it were purposely coughed up from the earth each day to provide for this frenzied, nocturnal activity.

6

Dafna

The garbage collectors.

Along with the heat, the bleating of goats and the aroma of onions and cumin, they are what I remember most about that first week in Abu Samra.

I think back to those days, clinging to those singular first impressions because no matter what else happened afterwards, those first few days had been uncomplicated and happy. I am astonished now at how content I had been, happy in a way that I had not been for years in New York. The night of that first day in Abu Samra, the night of the garbage collectors, I especially remember as the night before I met Marwan Jassim.

It was in front of our gate on that second morning in Abu Samra.

I had just been driven home from the market by Derek's office driver, 'Abbas, an elderly man whose melancholy eyes and sunken cheeks seemed to have weathered more summers in Abu Samra than his claim of sixty years. It was my first personal contact with an Arab here, and while he continued to respectfully avert his eyes from my face whenever he talked to me, he also seemed to have absorbed my freckled arms, blond hair, and green sun-dress in

31

a single, disapproving glance.

The past evening, the market had teemed with families. This morning, however, the market appeared altogether devoid of women. Men alone canvassed the streets in their white *thobs*, their sheer, white headdresses spread across their backs like moths' wings. It was only eight thirty, but the heat beat down on the car windows despite the air-conditioning, and my mouth was beginning to feel dry. A traffic policeman wearing a white helmet and gloves and showing no discomfort from the heat, signaled simultaneously to cars and donkey carts at a crowded intersection, his prim uniform reminding me of the peninsula's former status as a British colony.

Once through the arched white portals of the town, 'Abbas inched Derek's blue Buick through the maze of traffic. A donkey carrying a large sack of radishes stepped against the car. 'Abbas rolled down his window and reached out, impatiently nudging the donkey to the side of the road. A gust of hot, dank air rolled into the car. We continued to wade through traffic and pedestrians, finally coming to an outdoor market where rows of green canopies shaded open crates of fruits and vegetables.

Men were doing the shopping, carrying plastic bags from stall to stall, examining the produce under iridescent bug-repellent lights. On the roadside next to my window was a large basket stacked with egg-shaped maroon fruit.

"Are those plums?" I asked the driver.

'Abbas looked to where I was pointing. "Fig," he said.

I rolled down the window to get a closer look. I had never seen figs this sumptuous, large and round, with skin that looked freshly dusted with powdered sugar. I wanted to touch them, caress their iridescent fuzziness. Keeping in mind what Derek had said about letting the driver do the purchasing, I handed 'Abbas a five-dinar bill. "Can we buy some?"

He shifted the gear to park, leaped out of the door, picked a fig from the basket and handed it to me, looking somewhat impatient.

"Oh," I said, embarrassed that he thought I was hungry, "I need a dozen, please. I want to draw them." I gestured as if I were holding a pen and sketching.

He stared at me a moment, then turned and went to the vendor, returning seconds later with a paper bag filled with warm, soft lumps.

We continued through a round-about and came to a street that I remembered from the previous night's stroll with Derek.

"Do men do the shopping in Abu Samra?" I asked, sensing that 'Abbas felt uncomfortable to be seen in the market with a woman.

"Women are busy," he said, reaching out the window again, this time to greet two men standing at the street corner. By his tone, it was clear that he was wishing that I, too, had stayed home to cook and clean.

The bookstore stood at the end of an alley, tucked between a dry cleaner and a travel agency. Besides books, the musty shelves were stocked with music cassettes, toiletries, and assorted embroidery thread, knitting wool, stationery. To my surprise, it also carried a few art supplies, including 'Winsor and Newton' oil paints. Ecstatic, I gathered up sketch pads and brushes along with a handful of paint tubes and even a child's water color set to last me until my own supplies arrived in our shipment from New York.

The books themselves were mainly faded British Penguin editions of classics as well as American bestsellers of two and three years ago. There was even a book on Japanese flower arranging. On a shelf crowded with volumes on history, geography, and religion, I spotted a slim volume with a glossy red cover and yellow letters splashed across the front: *Sands of Zulaika: the Pre-History of Abu Samra*, published by Oxford University Press. I flipped through the pages. It appeared to be a short, archaeological document or thesis on a local prehistoric city. There were thick footnotes at the back and several medieval maps, all with Portuguese captions. There was also an old woodcut illustration of a peninsula that was obviously Abu Samra with a wide, pear-shaped enclave and a Portuguese galleon sailing in the sea.

I held on to the red book, then began leafing through a novel by Edna O'Brien. It suddenly seemed hotter and stuffier in the shop and I was beginning to feel thirsty again.

The buzzing in my ears that I had felt the night I arrived started up. Suddenly my voice, even the sound of my breathing, came as though I were hearing it from underwater. I pressed my hands against my ears and swallowed several times, then leaned against the shelf for a moment and closed my eyes. The sound of the ceiling fan above me swished like a helicopter's propellers.

I began to move forward, handing the books, paints, and money to the clerk at the cash register, hearing myself ask him how much they cost. By now the buzzing, along with the musty heat, grew unbearable. I rushed out to the street and found the car parked in the shade. I placed my hands on the hood, steadying myself as I sucked in deep breaths through my mouth. Despite the heat, the air of the open alley was a relief.

"Madame!" The Indian clerk ran up to me, holding my change and purchases.

'Abbas, too, dashed forward from where he had been squatting in the shade nearby. He quickly threw open the car door and I slumped into the back seat.

The buzzing subsided a bit and I opened my eyes. 'Abbas was nervously frowning down at me.

"I'm fine," I said, to reassure him. "I'm sorry. Let's go home."

"Madame is sick?" the Indian clerk said, glancing first at me, then at 'Abbas.

I shook my head, afraid I might vomit. But the rush of nausea was subsiding. 'Abbas closed the car door and I rested my head against the window. The cool breeze from the air conditioner began to filter to the back.

"OK?" 'Abbas grunted.

"Yes. Thank you."

"Very hot," he said, gruffly. I recognized the distinct reprimand.

The car started to move. A few minutes later we pulled up to a grocer's booth where 'Abbas yelled out something. A boy came running to the car with two bottles of Coca Cola. 'Abbas handed one to me. Then he pounded the gear and sped forward through the wide, white-washed arcs that led out of town toward our neighborhood.

My head had cleared, but my fingers still trembled against the cold bottle.

I could see the distress in 'Abbas' eyes through his mirror. I could well imagine how unnerving it must have been to have a strange woman in his charge practically faint.

'Abbas turned down an unpaved road, immediately familiar in its disarray and scattered piles of cinder blocks and sand. Workmen were directing a tractor several houses away from our wall.

"Too hot," 'Abbas said, the relief at my recovery making him appear content for the first time this morning. I regretted putting him through such worry on our first outing. But I was equally vexed by the look in his eyes in the rear-view mirror. The look of a victor. *Women*, it seemed to say, *should be at home, not out causing trouble in the morning heat.*

Citrine.

It was the color of the mid-morning sun on the sand. Once the car had stopped and we got out, I noticed the yellow enveloping us. *Citrine.* Shreds of this pale light settled against the teal of the car's hood, against the silver framing the windshield.

A man was standing in the shade of our garden wall, his head back, swallowing water that poured like a fountain from a large bottle into his open mouth. He tilted the bottle back and forth several times, letting the water drench his face and blue-black hair, soaking his shirt and khaki trousers. We stood, the three of us, outside the wall – 'Abbas, this dark stranger and I. The man lowered the bottle

35

and gazed at us, looking surprised, slowly moving away from the wall as though realizing that we were going to walk through this gate.

"Hello," he said. He shook his head lightly like a happy dog, flicking off the beads of water that glistened on his face and neck. He smoothed his thick hair with his palm and seemed to be waiting for me to reply.

"Hello," I said, assuming that he was a foreman of some sort overseeing the construction next door. Despite his trace of a British accent, I was certain that he was Arab rather than Indian or Pakistani. Perhaps it was in the way he stood, his feet firmly set in the sand as if he had sprouted from this very spot. Perhaps it was that his eyes were bolder, more almond shaped than many of the Indians' I had seen.

'Abbas was watching me. He seemed surprised that I had spoken to this wet, disheveled stranger.

"Hot," the man said, smiling.

"Yes, it is." I was aware that my head still felt heavy, that I was still slightly dizzy.

"Better to go inside," 'Abbas said, somewhat sternly, pointing at the house.

"Yes," I said, staring at the house, not wanting to feel faint again or to disappoint 'Abbas a second time. But before going, I found myself turning back to the stranger. "Can I get you a drink or something?"

He looked somewhat puzzled, seeming to consider this a minute. Then, he held up his empty water bottle.

"You've just had one," I said, feeling foolish. I had just seen him empty half a bottle of water into his mouth. "I just thought — I can't seem to tolerate the heat yet."

"If you can spare another bottle, I'd appreciate it," he said quickly, as though to oblige me or perhaps to spare me embarrassment. Again, the British-laced accent as he pronounced the 'c' in 'appreciate' like an 's'.

"Just a minute," I said, regretting having offered. He was a complete unknown, after all. I was conscious, immediately, of my bare arms and shoulders compared to the modest, draped women of last night. Who could tell what this man was thinking at my having so casually offered him a drink? He might be assuming that I had just invited him into the house. And I was aware that I had made a poor enough impression on 'Abbas already without doing something as irresponsible as striking up a conversation with this man.

Confident that 'Abbas would ensure that the man did not follow me inside, I went to retrieve a bottle of water from the carton in the kitchen.

When I returned, both men were chatting in Arabic.

"It's warm," I apologized, holding out the bottle.

The stranger had combed his hair and dried his face while I was inside. His eyes, when he turned to me, had an outer rim of green around the brown irises, a delicate hazel. His nose seemed slightly large for his face, Arab and yet the bridge high, almost Roman. But my gaze returned to his eyes, wide and slanted, and the deep sense of peace they possessed.

"Busy neighborhood," he said, nodding toward the construction next door. "They're ready to start one over there, too."

I glanced at the other side of the house, not far from the shanties. Sure enough, there were stakes and string marking off an area the size of our house.

"It never stops," he said. "It'll be ridiculously overbuilt soon."

"There shouldn't be too many more on this street," I said, suddenly disappointed that the other side of our house would soon be closed off by construction.

"Too many ventures for the present without thought to the future."

"What?" I said.

"We don't dwell much on the future here. Whatever comes after this lifetime is irrelevant. Things aren't meant to last. Only *Allah* is everlasting."

37

I assumed that by "we" he was referring to Abu Samrans. Or perhaps to Arabs in general. Although he seemed to be voicing some frustration, his tone was one of sarcastic tolerance rather than criticism.

"You don't have anything to do with this?" I said, puzzled that he would be so critical of the work going on.

"What, construction? No, no. I'm only here because my colleague was supposed to pick me up on the main road to go south, but he hasn't shown up. I thought someone in one of these houses would have a telephone I could use."

I now felt almost obliged to let him into the house to use ours. I was also mildly intrigued by an Arab man's being so forthcoming and uninhibited with a strange women after the reserved behavior of the men in the market and especially after my morning with the taciturn, glum 'Abbas.

But before I could make the offer of the telephone the man said: "Your driver has kindly agreed to drop me down the road a bit."

He tipped the water bottle toward his forehead in a salute, or thanks.

I glanced at 'Abbas, surprised that he had agreed to this without asking me first. He was supposed to remain at the house in case I needed something. But 'Abbas gave no sign that he intended to ask me for permission. Instead, in a gesture he had repeated several times already that morning, he took out a limp rag from the front seat and started to wipe the dust off the gleaming hood of the car.

"That'll be fine, but I need him back soon," I said to the man, loud enough for 'Abbas to hear. I wondered whether Derek would be upset that I had inadvertently given permission to a stranger to take up the driver's time. But then, I had not exactly been asked.

"It shouldn't take longer than a half an hour for him to get back," the man said. "It's only to Saali. Zulaika."

Zulaika. Some twinge of familiarity told me that I should recognize this name.

"By the way," the man continued, "you need salt tablets. Any pharmacy will have them. In a day or two you'll be fine. You were probably dehydrated. Are your legs sore?" he asked, glancing down at my legs beneath the hem of the sun dress. I could feel my feet suddenly puffy in the tight sandals.

I had assumed the intermittent throbbing in my legs was due to jet-lag.

"Salt tablets," I said, nodding, not wanting to prolong the conversation, or to tell him that my condition probably had to do with hormonal upheaval.

Then, as I started back through the gate I thought of something.

"I wonder," I said, turning back to him, "if you have any idea what this area is called."

"You mean right here?"

"This neighborhood. If I need to give someone my address or something."

He paused a minute then said: "Tell them *Dafna.* They shouldn't have a problem."

"*Dafna?*"

"*Dafna,*" he repeated, grinning. He lowered himself into the front seat of Derek's car as if it were some grand carriage. "It means 'the burial.'"

'Abbas started the engine. Sand from the unpaved road flew up, fine as a mist. I turned to go back into the house before the man could see my shock at what he had just said.

Later, under the hot, brackish flow of the shower, I held my head back. The water pelted my face, my neck and breasts. My skin, despite a lathering with soap, felt still coated with sand. I ran my fingers through my tangled hair. Even after I washed it, my hair felt coarse and sticky. New York Hudson River water left it as slippery as corn silk but this brackish water, slightly brown and tasting like tears, matted it like straw. I rubbed conditioner into it, wondering if in a few weeks it would begin to look dull and shed as Derek's had.

Turning off the water, I stepped onto the speckled tile of the bathroom floor, the same tile as that of the airport floor and the bookstore's. I opened the small, square window above the toilet and felt the warm air drift in. I could smell the desert outside; the sand, even the suffocating heat seemed to have a salty odor. I thought of New York where our bathroom window overlooked the lush, willow-shaded park. I wished I could have taken a walk there now, stopped by our favorite bakery for a cookie and freshly brewed coffee.

Then the sight of the man outside, the way that he had lapped up the water, and the faintly smug grin when he had said, *"Dafna,"* came back to me. His hair, the blackest I had ever seen, had been threaded with gray at the temples. I could hardly remember his face, a nondescript face, it now seemed, with a too large nose. But his voice, deep and full, had lodged itself indelibly in my brain. A thrill jolted me at the memory of his voice. His voice, and the remarkable transparency of his eyes with their unexpected, yet unmistakable, warmth.

7

The Prettiest Woman in Abu Samra

October was fraught with an explosion of cocktail parties held at the half-dozen international hotels in town.

With everyone back in Abu Samra after long summers in the Mediterranean, Europe, or the United States, every foreign business, bank, and embassy proceeded to host receptions to launch the fall business season. Attended mainly by the expatriate business and embassy communities, there was always a sprinkling of Abu Samran Ministers on hand, moving confidently among the expatriates like gilt-robed deities.

I had been in Abu Samra over a month when the first of these receptions took place. Derek and I were standing in the lobby of the Intercontinental Hotel along with a German banker, Johann Krebs. The hotel stood in lush contrast to the meager desert outside. Ivory and jade-studded Chinese screens lined the walls behind rosewood chests, brocade chairs, silk sofas. In the atrium, china urns held lush palms and pink hibiscus.

Johann Krebs, a bachelor, was on his second whiskey, his broad face flushed and loose above the collar of his beige safari suit — a style I had seen on numerous other expatriate men here. He

41

patted Derek heartily on the back whenever he wanted to emphasize some point he was making about off-shore banking.

Outside, a white Cadillac slowly sailed up to the hotel entrance. There seemed to be a moment of confusion as hotel porters rushed out of the lobby to open the car's doors. Two men in white *thobs* and headdresses emerged, their camel-colored men's *abayas* draped over their shoulders like translucent capes.

The two men glided through the doors, their feet appearing to hover above the slick, white marble as they moved forward. Gold filigree at the necks and front edges of the long *abayas* that reached their shoes flickered as they walked by, the men's eyes alighting on us in brief acknowledgement as they continued down the hall.

"Ahmad and Saleh Mansour," Derek said. "They're twins."

I watched them head for the ballroom at the end of the hall.

"They look like princes," I said.

"They're more than princes," Johann Krebs said, as though issuing a warning. "The Mansours consider themselves to be descended from the Prophet. Their family claims a limb from Hussein, the Prophet's grandson."

"They also happen to be the ruling family," Derek explained.

Except for a Roosevelt family member I had roomed with for a year at Northwestern and random sightings of the mayor of New York, this was my first glimpse of anyone remotely connected to royalty.

I had already learned that the Mansours were descendants of a Bedouin tribe from South Arabia who, in the eighteenth century, had driven out the Persian governor of Abu Samra. The Persians had briefly ruled the peninsula after evicting the Portuguese colonizers a century earlier. The Mansours and several other tribes had settled along the fertile coasts of Abu Samra and established their rule over the mostly placid, indigenous mixed Arab-Persian populace of farmers and fishermen.

"Impressive," I said, watching the intriguing men disappear into the ballroom.

"They certainly are," Derek said, staring down the hallway, too, as if some vestige of the twins still remained.

"They own the country," the German said as he took another drink from a tray passed around by a waiter. "You and I would be impressive too if we owned Abu Samra, eh Derek? Most of the time they act like they own the bloody universe."

Derek smiled. "Maybe they do, Johann," he said, and steered me ahead of him and Johann down the icy, air-conditioned hallway to the ballroom.

The pulsing voices hovered overhead as I felt the familiar dread ripple through me at having to face a roomful of strangers. Although not generally shy, I was uncomfortable at large, impersonal parties and having to strike up multiple conversations with people I did not know. This room, obviously set aside for such occasions, seemed particularly vast and formidable. With my body acting with a will of its own these days, I was particularly worried I might have an unexpected bout of nausea at any moment. I told myself not to be paranoid, however. The people in the room had been around newcomers with salt deficiency or other conditions imposed on them by bodies stubbornly refusing to adapt to the heat. Besides, the American Embassy had recommended an astute, experienced Abu Samran physician, a Dr. Mustapha, who had assured me that in a month my current discomfort would be a mere memory.

"Try and relax," he had said gently, after examining me. "You will be fine if you drink plenty of water and yogurt with salt." He had handled hundreds of expatriates, he said, who had trouble adjusting to the severe climate.

"The essential part," he said, his eyes twinkling, "is the state of mind." His own brown eyes had seemed to hold a universe of knowledge and I knew I could count on the infinite skills of the nurturing Dr. Mustapha if either Derek or I ever needed anything.

I tried to focus on the bright swirl of color before me now.

43

Women, mostly expatriates, were dressed in chiffons and silks, some bare shouldered, some even wearing the fashionable short skirts that had appeared on Fifth Avenue shortly before we left. Although Abu Samrans seemed to tolerate the freer dressing habits of foreigners, I had not expected to see so many strapless cocktail dresses or bold, plunging necklines, as if the hotel were a temporary asylum from the stringent mores of the Muslim world outside. I almost regretted having worn the chaste red suit I had assumed would be more appropriate for our first public outing.

Johann Krebs had disappeared and Derek was perusing the crowd, his eyes prowling, targeting those he knew or wanted to speak with. I was used to this from previous Manhattan receptions — Derek forging into the throngs of business associates as though shielded by some remarkable armor from the terror that would grip me at the same moment. I hated having to introduce myself over and over, find subjects to discuss that did not have to do with business, in which I was not involved, or painting, which seemed too obscure for most. Here there was the added disadvantage of my being new to the country.

Before Derek could vanish into the myriad dark suits, however, a low voice broke in.

"Mr. Monroe."

Derek suddenly beamed with pleasure. "Your Excellency."

The young man shook Derek's hand, one side of his headdress slipping forward over his jaw as he lowered his head slightly. It was one of the Mansours twins who had passed us in the hallway.

He was handsome in a way that I had always imagined Arab men to be: aquiline nose, shapely lips, wide, dark eyes. Only his tawny skin was paler than I expected, almost ivory above the neatly trimmed black mustache and beard framing his mouth.

Derek turned to me. "Sheikh Ahmad, this is my wife, Gina."

I stood perfectly still, wondering whether to bow or to curtsy. But the man merely extended his hand, gripping my fingers lightly.

"You've just arrived in Abu Samra?" he said, with a glimmer of a British accent.

"Yes, Sir," I answered, not sure how to address a Mansour. He raised his eyebrows, as if surprised.

I waited for him to say something. When he did not, I added, "I'm really enjoying it."

"Ah," he said, his eyes skeptical. "Interesting."

"Is there some reason I shouldn't?" I ventured after a few seconds.

The air seemed to stand still the moment I said this. Derek's apprehension sliced against me. I knew that he was sensitive to protocol and might be afraid that I would say the wrong thing, perhaps humiliate him in my ignorance of Abu Samran etiquette. But I continued to look at Sheikh Ahmad.

The Sheikh flipped one side of his headdress behind his shoulder, revealing two small buttons of gold braid at the collar of his *thob* which seemed to subtly accent his royal status.

"I don't know," he said, slowly, as though he were lost in some private vision. Then, he broke into a boyish grin. "No, of course not. It's just that the heat, the desert. Many foreigners find that it does strange things to them."

I smiled back, aware of Derek's admonishing glance.

"I nearly fainted in the market one morning, but I'm learning to deal with the heat."

The Sheikh laughed, wagging a finger at me. "Yes, take plenty of salt and do as we natives do – stay *out* of the sun."

"That's a little hard to do here," I said.

The Sheikh smiled, again. Derek seemed to relax a bit.

"You must bring your wife to our farm, Mr. Monroe," the Sheikh said, draping one side of his cape over his arm as he started to move on. "There's plenty of shade there."

"I will, Your Excellency," Derek said, obviously pleased by the invitation and the positive turn the conversation had taken.

Once he was gone, I looked at Derek. "His English is flawless."

"He studied at Oxford," Derek said. "Most of them go to the

States now, but Ahmad's father hates Americans."

"Why?" I said, surprised.

"Abu Samra was colonized by the British. Most of the elite here still look to Britain for a Western education. They see America as inferior, vulgar. The new colonialist power."

I was shocked. The young man certainly had not indicated that he felt any animosity towards us.

My glance fell on a tall, dark woman a short distance away wearing a pink suit. Her jet black hair was pulled back into a loose bun at her neck and her dark-rimmed eyes met mine for a second, then flickered away, as though she had been watching us.

"That's Sheikha Mariam," Derek said. "Sheikh Ahmad's cousin."

"A Mansour?"

"Yes."

"She's very attractive," I said.

As though aware of our gaze, the woman turned away.

"The prettiest woman in Abu Samra," Derek said.

I looked at him, surprised by his candid admiration. Derek rarely praised another woman's appearance out loud. He used to say that he favored blondes with blue eyes, like me.

"It's what everybody says," he added awkwardly, as if suddenly regretting his comment about the woman.

"I can see why."

He nudged me. "Go up and talk to her. She studied in New York. Has some degree from Columbia, geology or something. Only remember to address her as 'Your Excellency.'"

"'Your Excellency?'"

"It's the way to address the Mansours."

I tried to picture myself uttering this salutation to the mayor of New York.

"I can't, Derek."

"Sure you can," he said. "In Arabic it's 'Long of Life'. Be glad you don't have to slog through that."

Everything was so simple to Derek. I would have liked to go up to this elegant member of the ruling family and introduce myself as an enthused newcomer eager to learn more about her country. As a Mansour, and educated in the United States, she undoubtedly spoke good English. She might even prove to be as casual as her cousin Ahmad had been a few minutes ago. But I felt suddenly paralyzed, afraid of saying the wrong thing.

I turned to Derek, "Would you introduce me?"

But he was gone.

I looked around, irritated with Derek for his cold departure. Feeling lost, I glanced back at the woman in pink. Talking to her would certainly be preferable to standing alone.

I was trying to think of a suitable subject to approach the Sheikha with, when I felt a presence behind me. All at once, in that brief moment before turning around, I suddenly grew acutely aware of myself, of the room, of the people's voices. It was as though I could hear each of the conversations taking place around me; as if I were in ten different places at once.

Then I did turn round.

"Did you find out about *Dafna?*" the man asked.

A cool tremor licked my spine. That voice. Those eyes. He stood before me in a slightly rumpled blue suit, carrying a plate of pastries in one hand and a glass of what looked like orange juice in the other.

I could feel the vessels in my cheeks warm as I took in the ebony hair, the green-rimmed eyes like a serene spot of calm set in the turbulence all around me.

"Excuse me?"

"*Dafna?*" the man repeated. "The name of your neighborhood." His smooth voice was similar to that of the Sheikh I had just met, though this man's British accent was less clipped, more identifiably Arab.

Dafna. Of course. He had been the one to tell me the name of our neighborhood. His face looked even darker tonight, the skin

47

above his brow deeply bronzed as though he had spent the entire day in the sun. His hair seemed to be combed differently from the last time, too, straight back and flatter against his head, somehow making the nose less large. But the eyes shone as lucid as they had in the sun.

I recalled the hot morning more than a month ago, the throbbing in my head. The throbbing seemed to have returned now, only lower, beneath my ribs.

I conceded a smile. "The burial? Yes, I asked the gardener."

He shrugged, raising his eyebrows. "I didn't want to upset you when you'd just moved into that nice house."

"I wasn't upset. My husband was, a little."

He seemed to look sympathetic.

"Actually," I said, resenting the flicker in his eyes, "it's rather interesting. How many people back in New York can claim to live behind a — a —"

"Crematorium," he finished for me.

"Crematorium," I said, as though this were something commonplace. I could feel a chuckle bubble up despite my nervousness.

"A Hindu crematorium. It's the only one in this part of the Gulf," he said.

I could feel the surprise coat my face.

"Does it bother you?"

"Not terribly," I said, truthfully. I was amazed, myself, at how quickly I had gotten over my initial alarm. Even our new Indian cleaning lady, Lhatti, a Christian, had slapped her own cheeks with her hands and cried, "Oh God!" when I had told her what the property behind our house was intended for.

"But I won't know for sure how I feel until they start using it," I added.

He nodded. "A little fire is sure to liven things up."

"I guess it's better than living next to an ordinary cemetery."

He smiled. "Ashes aren't likely to haunt you."

I smiled back, confused by his prodding and by his slightly

patronizing tone, but enjoying the lightness of it.

"I'm just hoping nobody builds on it. The view of the sea makes it worth putting up with anything."

"You have a point," he said. Then, as though I had just passed some sort of test, he offered me one of his pastries.

In a sort of truce, I took a tiny *samosa*, hoping it would not burn my tongue.

"I prefer the ones in the market," he said. "These are made for expatriates. No zing."

I held it a moment, wondering whether it would upset my stomach, then decided I did not care if it did. I tried a bite. It slid down my throat smoothly.

"I trust you're not suffering from the heat any more?" he said.

I was sorry that he had remembered that.

"Actually the salt tablets helped. I no longer disgrace the driver downtown."

"Good," he said.

Then, lifting the hand with his drink in a toast, he said, "I'm Marwan Jassim."

"Gina Monroe."

"Mrs. Chase Manhattan or Mrs. Bank of America?"

I laughed. "What?."

"Not a banker's wife?"

The din of voices engulfed us like a monsoon. "My husband is with USA Electric."

"Oh?" he said, as if this were particularly fascinating.

Something about him suddenly made me wary. Perhaps it was the way that he kept glancing about, not in the same way that Derek did whenever he surveyed a room for contacts, but more as if he were worried that he would be seen talking to me.

"Are *you* a banker?" I asked.

"Me?" Again, he looked around as though to see whether someone was listening, or maybe to find a waiter.

Finally, he placed his glass on his plate. "I'm an archaeologist."

"An archaeologist?" I said. "You're kidding."

"I'm not." He downed a *samosa*.

"What on earth is of archaeological interest in Abu Samra?" I blurted out, before realizing that I might have offended him.

He merely took a gulp of his juice, however, his eyes beginning to sparkle.

"Plenty, Madam."

I had not yet been to many places beyond town except to the beach, but I certainly had not seen anything so far to warrant the attentions of an archaeologist. The peninsula seemed to be sand, water, and a maze of new business and housing developments. Some of the older parts of town were charming, and certainly picturesque from a painter's point of view, despite the derelict conditions. Yet, nothing seemed remotely historical and I had not seen or read of any excavations.

Derek had pointed out several lofty, decaying buildings to me the first time we had driven through the desert to the western shore. Gracefully sculpted arabesque windows and towers had remained intact despite the ravaged walls. Like other neglected or abandoned buildings in Abu Samra, they had appeared old, though certainly not in archeological terms as I understood them.

"I'm ignorant about local ruins. Are you referring to the old houses on the way to the beach?"

"Those are the old Mansour palaces," he said. "Circa 1920s."

"They look a lot older than that."

"To us Muslims, homes, even palaces, weren't necessarily built to last. Ever been to the Alhambra in Spain?"

I shook my head.

"One of the loveliest palaces in the world, built with the most degenerative of materials, wood and plaster, partly because lasting an eternity was the furthest thing from the minds of the *Emirs* who built it. Amazing that it's survived this long."

"I do plan to go someday. Are there any *ancient* ruins here?"

He seemed pleased by my interest. "Not a likely place."

"It's just that everything seems too fragile to last," I interrupted.

"That's why people haven't caught on to Abu Samran antiquity like in the rest of the Middle East. There are no pyramids, and no preserved cities like Petra, Palmyra, or Ba'albek. Nothing above ground. There are some forts — Portuguese, Persian, Omani — but they're not very old. Nothing over three hundred years. Everything else is buried. Our vast Abu Samra treasures, that is."

Just then, a waiter passed with a tray of small, yellow dates. The archaeologist took a few and gave me some.

"*Rutab,*" he said. "One of the few native things here not flown in from Australia or Singapore."

The dates were sweeter than I expected, with a buttery silkiness that lingered on my tongue.

The archaeologist picked one up and said, softly, as if hypnotized: "O date palm, tree that gives wealth, my precious brother, endowed with all wisdom, you are as stable as the earth, but the plan of the gods is remote."

I waited for him to continue.

"It's a Babylonian poem," he said, "several thousand years old." There was an almost mystical mood that seemed to have come over him after the short recitation.

I nodded, as if I were used to people reciting the poems of dead languages.

"I'd like to know more about the local archaeology," I said.

He seemed eager to explain. "It's all under the sand, of course. But you're quite right. Unlike Egypt or Iraq or Lebanon, nothing survives in this climate, not with what they used for building materials. Take those Mansour buildings you mentioned. They're about the best preserved and they were built only sixty years ago. There are a few more like them and some mosques left from the last century, but almost everything earlier than that has to be unearthed. With the exception of the mounds, of course," he said.

"Mounds?"

"Burial mounds. Those funny lumps scattered across the desert. Don't tell me you haven't seen them?"

"I don't think I have," I said, feeling even more foolish. *Mounds?* I thought back to the drive with Derek to the beach. There had been an oil refinery in the distance and some little hills, thousands of little hills in fact, that stuck up like rounded cones from the flat plain. Derek had not said anything about them.

"They're some of the oldest tombs recorded," he said.

"How old?"

"Second millennium B.C. Close to four thousand years."

I was stunned. I wanted to say something that would not further betray my ignorance but could only ask, "Who built them?"

"Our ancestors. Prehistoric Abu Samrans, so far as we know."

Prehistoric Abu Samrans. So he *was* Abu Samran.

"Surprised?" he said.

"Yes. Everything here seems too new. It never occurred to me that there was anything that ancient around."

He smiled. "Abu Samra was a major trading center in antiquity between Mesopotamia and India. It was the major port city of the Gulf, the way Dubai is now. The pearl beds put it on a par with frankincense Yemen and the Indus valley. There were also cultivated date forests due to the large number of natural, fresh-water wells. We've always had a settled farming and trading society here. Didn't have to raid each other or resort to sea piracy like other desert Arab tribes."

He looked at me, as though I had just lost track of something he said. I felt my lungs flex, as if the air were being forced out. I realized I had been studying his mouth. It was perfectly drawn, a pale, maroon color against his olive skin. His lips grew thin with energy and then soft and full whenever he stopped to hear a reply. I was suddenly embarrassed to have been studying him, as if I had been caught staring at him naked.

It had been a long time since I had been surprised like this by a strange man, at once attracted to him and confused, almost irrationally irritated by him, and all too aware that this discord was a distinct warning.

I tried to push these thoughts from my mind.

"Are these mounds of major significance? Like the pyramids?"

He seemed to be watching me, too, amused. "They're certainly known. Though not to laymen."

Again, the slight arrogance in his reply, the way he had been that morning outside the house when he had 'Abbas drive him off without asking me.

When I finished eating another date, he held out his plate for me to set the pit on. It seemed like a surprisingly intimate gesture.

I was surprised to find myself warming to him compared to the first time we met when I had been preoccupied with maintaining my distance in 'Abbas's presence. Yet, something about him seemed different tonight.

"They haven't had the publicity that the Egyptian and Iraqi monuments have," he was saying, looking serious now. "Zulaika isn't as well known as Mesopotamia or the First and Second kingdoms of Egypt. At least not yet."

"Zulaika?"

"Abu Samra's ancient capital."

The book. *Sands of Zulaika.* I had misplaced it along with the other books I had bought that first day in the confusion of unpacking. I had found it again recently and it was still on the side table in the upstairs sitting room where I put it. I remembered the antique map of the peninsula on the frontispiece.

"I have a book about it," I said. "I haven't read it yet, but I do have it."

"Needs to be updated," he said, simply.

"You know it?"

"I wrote it some years ago when we first started digging the mounds."

I was silent now, shocked. *Zulaika.* It sounded almost eerie, like something out of a legend. So *he* was the author of the book. I reprimanded myself for not having read it.

"Is that why you're here?" I said.

"Why I'm at this party?" He paused, as though I might be trying to entrap him. "Why is anybody here? The food's good."

Then, evidently sensing that I was not convinced he added, "Basically, Mrs. Monroe, I'm here for the same reason as everybody else." He rubbed his thumb and index finger together.

"Money." Then, as if I might have misunderstood, he added, "For my dig."

"You're actually digging now?"

"Of course," he said, his eyes shining. "Had you been a banker's wife I would have asked you to speak to your husband about a loan for me."

I was taken aback, suddenly wondering if he were insinuating that he had hoped to get money out of me.

"November to March is open season for archeologists in Abu Samra. The French, Danish, and ourselves. All vying for the real find."

"And you are?"

"The local team. We started with the Brits."

My mind was suddenly cluttered with visions of worm-infested mummies, scarabs. "What is it, exactly, that you're looking for?" I asked.

He raised his eyebrows, as if I should already have guessed this. "The rest of Zulaika. It's in the book."

He seemed about to say something else, but then stopped, abruptly shifting his stare to something across the room. I followed his glance. It was the dark lady, the Sheikha in the pink suit. *The most beautiful woman in Abu Samra.*

"Sheikha Mariam," he said.

I looked back at him. "You know her?"

"Sheikha Mariam? Of course."

"My husband says she's a geologist."

54

"*Archaeologist,*" he said, dismissing Derek's claim. An invisible thread seemed instantly to connect the Arab woman and her lanky compatriot. They occupied an insular space bolted tight against the rest of us non-Arabs.

"We've worked together in the past," he added. "She's an excellent digger. Only, now she's been appointed Head of Antiquities and doesn't do lowly field work anymore."

Impressed that a woman would hold such a high position in this obviously male-dominated society I blurted out, "My husband thinks she's the prettiest woman in Abu Samra."

A slow grin spread over his face. "I'd say she has a bit of competition in this room."

I felt myself flush. I had not meant to betray Derek's private remark to me, or to fish for a compliment.

"If I were to guess," he said, as if to divert the conversation, "I'd say you're a writer."

"Oh?" I said. "Why?"

"The abstract look in your eyes, as if you're somewhere else, writing a script as we speak."

It was my turn to be amused. "You mean absent-minded."

He shook his head. "*Preoccupied.*"

I smiled. "I paint. And I do get carried away imagining how I'd draw something. Sorry."

"Ah, an artist. So, what will you paint here? Anything excite you yet?"

"Just about everything. The sunlight on the sand, the colors of the sea, the faded old buildings in town."

"Well, if you like landscapes, come to my dig. There's a village nearby called Saali you might find interesting."

"I'd like to see your dig," I said, amazed at how comfortable I felt saying this. "You've piqued my curiosity."

He seemed to stare at me slightly longer than necessary, as if he were confiding some delicate secret. Although I had not moved an inch, I felt something in me surging toward him.

55

Then I grew wary again. I had met his kind before, more than once. Men who find married women easy and convenient bait, who assume that a woman is starved for attention simply because she is married, men who even prefer a husband in the background so that there are no commitments involved. It annoyed me that I might have struck him as just the sort of woman to feel neglected and in need of his time.

As if sensing my apprehension, he said, "I've enjoyed talking to you, Mrs. Monroe," and extended his hand. I shook it, aware of the warmth of his palm despite its roughness. We seemed to hold onto each other a few extra seconds.

"Get to those mounds sometime. They shouldn't be missed," he said, as I slid my hand, almost reluctantly, from his grip.

"Sure," I said, trying to sound nonchalant. "Thanks for the information."

"You'll find another world out there beyond all of this," he said, quickly. "A world that links us all to each other, through time and cultures. It's a place that will truly show you how we are all one in this universe."

I looked at him, but said nothing, trying to understand the meaning of his last sentence.

When he drifted into the crowd I let go of the unease I had experienced earlier, not doubting for a second that I was in full control of the hot and cold stream of my emotions. I had nothing to fear from this man, or any other. On the contrary. I had an immense sense of my own strength and freedom suddenly. Freedom bolstered by a certain detachment.

Yet as I glanced about for a sign of Derek, I realized that I had not given him a thought during the past half hour. Instead of Derek, I again spotted the alluring Sheikha and found myself quickly turning away. The neutrality I had felt moments before faded. I suddenly did not want to see the look in her eyes, the eyes of the prettiest woman in Abu Samra, when the archaeologist, Marwan Jassim, walked up to her.

8

The Mounds

One morning in mid-October, while arranging the closet in the lavender bedroom, I glanced out of the window to find a large pile of wood stacked neatly on the cement platform in the walled property behind the house.

I opened the window. A dry breeze blew in through the screen. Below, the pink and white oleander bushes swayed against the garden wall. Lhatti was in the garden picking jasmine blossoms from a bush the gardener had planted for us. Each afternoon, after her housework was done, Lhatti sewed these blooms into a chain which she wrapped around her glossy black hair.

Since learning that the empty plot behind the house was a crematorium, we had yet to see a burning. We had not seen anyone enter the lot, nor had there ever been any smoke or any of the suspicious smells that Derek had anticipated. I had been almost disappointed to think that it might no longer be in use.

Derek had been more upset than I had expected by the explanation given to us by our gardener, Khalid, a young man from a nearby village, when we asked him a month ago what the word *Dafna,* the burial, had to do with our neighborhood.

"I'll get a letter off to the Minister of Health right away," Derek had said that evening as we stood on the roof looking down at the walled property in disbelief. The cement floor and columns I had taken for a stable were actually the platform for a funeral pyre!

Dusk had spilled across the sand in an amber mist. Down the road, the colorful tin shanties that emitted the sounds of animals in the mornings radiated with the squeals and laughter of children.

"Do you think there'll be a smell?" I had asked. Even though much of my early morning sickness had subsided, I was still very sensitive to certain smells and the mere thought of what I imagined was the smell of roasting human flesh made my stomach churn.

Derek grimaced. "I don't even want to think about the smell."

"The landlord should have disclosed it to you," I said, knowing that Derek was furious with himself for having overlooked this detail when he rented the house.

He scowled at the flat rooftops before us as if he were drawing up a battle plan. "I'll start looking for another place tomorrow."

"Let's just wait and see what happens first," I said, calmly pointing to the expansive view of the sea. "I'd hate to give this up."

It was, admittedly, a selfish thought. I had started to paint in the mornings after Derek left for work, before the sun was too strong. I would practically run up to the rooftop with its splendid view of the distant villages, the sea, the palms and frangipani trailing over the garden walls of nearby houses. I had done several watercolors of the shanties behind us and had just started an oil of an intricate, latticed window of an old gypsum house visible from one side of the roof.

"What if they start burning bodies?" Derek said. "We won't be able to go outside at all. It's right behind our garden, for Christ's sake."

I stifled a laugh, not wanting to further anger him. But it *was* absurd to discover that such a thing existed in our own backyard. I couldn't wait to send my father and friends photographs of our backyard crematorium. I knew that I should have felt the same revulsion that Derek did, yet I could muster up no more than an amused ambivalence.

"Maybe it's not used anymore," I said, trying to console Derek.

"*He* knew what it was. It must still be functional."

Derek meant that Khalid, the gardener, knew about it. Yet I had immediately recalled the mischievous look on the archaeologist's face when he had spoken of it that day outside the house. He, too, obviously found the proximity of the crematorium somewhat farcical.

I had stared at Derek, his mind at work, his jaw jutting forward, clearly puzzled by my indifference. I understood why the crematorium bothered him so much, yet I could not bring myself to share his dismay. Watching his face that evening, I wondered whether had we been faced with this same situation years earlier he would have taken it more lightly, as he had generally taken things then. It occurred to me that everything I had once loved in him — his strength, his vigorous stabs at life, even his tight, honed features — had been merely the veneer of youth. The youthful vigor that had once been so seductive had suddenly become a rigid, humorless intensity that seemed an unnecessary burden to have to bear, both on his part and mine.

It had surprised me suddenly, came upon me gently at first, then hit me like a cold shower, that this was the man whom I had chosen to spend the rest of my life with. I had attributed his growing, bleak sternness to the stringent corporate structure he'd had to endure the past few years. I often felt guilty that he had become like this because of *us*, because of his need to secure a financial future for the two of us and our anticipated children. His work had provided me with the necessary time and opportunity to create my art. Yet even this acknowledgment on my part of his hard work had become a burden to me. It saddened me, now, to realize how my feelings for him had changed.

"This should take a good chunk off the rent when I speak to

the landlord about it," he muttered as we went back down into the house.

I was suddenly impatient, remembering his disapproval days earlier of the ineffectual garbage service.

"Derek, you can't always be in control — can't always force other people's garbage into bins or tell people how to dispose of their dead."

"We're not talking about litter, Gina. This is ludicrous. They can burn their dead bodies somewhere out in the desert. We're trying to *live* here."

But Derek had to send off two letters, insisting that a functioning crematorium in the midst of a residential community posed countless health hazards, before he received a genial reply from the Ministry of Health saying that the matter would be looked into. This brief acknowledgment seemed to appease him for the moment, and he had ceased discussing the need to move.

The actual sight of the stacked wood this morning, however, alarmed me.

I promptly forgot my enthusiasm for peculiar anecdotes to write home about and, instead, shut the open bedroom window and drew the lavender drapes. They would not close all the way so I got some safety pins and loosely tacked the panels together.

I thought of the smell. I had no idea what a burning human corpse smelled like. What if the odor drifted in through the open bathroom window? I went to close it, wondering how we were going to go outside knowing that the roasting flesh we smelled had once been a man — or woman.

Lhatti was singing as she came upstairs. She often sang to herself in Hindi as she did the housework, and even when she sang in English, as she sometimes did, it sounded like Hindi in her high, lilting voice. I hurried back to the bedroom to shut the drapes completely before she came into the room, not wanting her to panic at the view, especially since she had expressed such horror when first told of the crematorium.

I was almost done when, through a gap at the top, I saw a gray pickup truck pull up to the property. Afraid to witness what might be about to occur, I nonetheless watched as the driver and two other men got out of the front of the truck. They stood a moment, staring at the high wall surrounding the property as though wondering how to get inside. Then they walked around to the back of the truck, lowered the flap, and slowly carried out a long, white swathed object and set it on the ground.

At my mother's funeral last year there had been so many flowers, in the church, under the green canopy on the cemetery lawn, even at the last moment when the coffin was lowered into the earth, it was wrapped in white gladiolus. Everything had been so fragrant, at once beautiful and disturbing, as though despite all the preparation during her illness the past year, we had been afraid to acknowledge her death, were actually attempting to camouflage it.

There was little chance of disguising the fact of death before me now, however.

The Indian men here continued to stare at the wall, the body momentarily forgotten. I took a deep breath, staring at the lump lying prostrate on the sand at their feet.

Another vehicle, a small red Toyota, pulled up alongside the truck. More men got out and stared at the wall before them, as if trying to figure out how best to scale it. Then, the two groups hoisted the swathed object off the ground and onto their shoulders and entered the compound through a back gate.

A pitiless yellow sun was midway up the sky. The men carried the body perfunctorily around the plot several times, as if it were a weightless shell; then they approached the shaded platform and lowered it onto the pile of wood.

They went to work immediately, sprinkling the pyre with something from a red container, placing objects at each corner of the platform. Then they began to cover the body with more of the stacked wood. When they were done, they all backed away.

One man now came forward and shook a can, which I

61

guessed held fuel, over the pyre. Then he lit matches and threw them onto the wood. There were several more dousings and more matches thrown by the other men before a loud crack shattered the air and shook the bedroom's window panes.

I pulled back from the glass.

Lhatti hurried into the bedroom.

"Madam? What's happened?"

"It's nothing, just some builders," I said. When she left, I peered back out through the crack in the drape. By now, tongues of flame were bursting through the wood. The men, apparently unharmed, were squatting nearby and smoking cigarettes. The flames leaped into the air, licking the breeze. The sound of flying sparks penetrated the closed bedroom window, occasional quick snaps like the pop of gunfire.

I continued to watch, feeling calmer now, almost bewitched, as the fire devoured the wood. Perhaps it was the composure of the men or the silent feeling of liberation that seemed to hover above the scene that made me lose my initial fear. *It will all be over in minutes, all evidence of this life will be diluted into ashes, will sink back into the sand,* the scene seemed to say.

As the heat waves simmered above the fire, I remembered what the archaeologist, Marwan Jassim, had said about Abu Samra's prehistory. It had all dissolved back into the sand, the sole preserver.

I was amazed to have thought of him now, during this solemn ritual. I wondered whether part of his startling appeal lay in his pursuit of some larger truth in his surroundings. He seemed to be infused in the peninsula somehow, not simply as a citizen, but to know it on some spiritual level and still be fascinated by it in a way that most others, even the Arabs I had met, were not. To imagine that there was something immortal buried beneath the sand, that all did not end with the unassuming, fragile-looking visible city and desert landscape. It was similar to what I searched for myself each time I began a new canvas or watercolor — the shape, the color, the true value of what lay hidden beneath the surface.

By now I had read his *Sands of Zulaika* and was impressed by his theories and his methodical deductions. He had tied the peninsula to the Mesopotamian and Indian civilizations of four thousand years ago, making the location a vital trading post midway down the Persian Gulf. He seemed convinced that the peninsula was the location of the fabled city of Zulaika mentioned in numerous Sumerian cuneiform texts found in Iraq during the last century. Yet he seemed to be convinced of this almost more out of some profound mystical intuition than from scientific research or patriotic bias.

I had continued to see Marwan Jassim at receptions after that first one at the Intercontinental, often in the same blue suit and looking a little bewildered that he was there at all, as though he had dropped into our midst purely by accident. He usually made a point of coming up and talking to me, in the beginning asking what my latest adventure in Abu Samra was — an awkward attempt at conversation or a barely disguised reference to what he perhaps assumed was the pampered life of an expatriate wife.

I began to suspect a seductive tactic I had seen or experienced with other men, one which slyly gnawed at the ego until the victim begged for some favorable recognition. An art teacher of mine used to stand over my shoulder, subtly ridiculing my work until I found myself inexplicably craving his criticism, destructive as it was. He had eventually been fired over an incident involving another female student. But to suppose that Marwan Jassim was using this ruse with me was to assume that he was pursuing me, and I had no evidence of that, did not even dare to imagine it.

He had not forgotten that I painted. After our first few meetings, once he was obviously more at ease approaching me, he began to ask about my work and about the New York art scene.

"Come to our site at the Portuguese fort and I promise you will find plenty to paint," he said, inviting me yet again. "We've got the best sunset on the peninsula for one thing."

He even admitted his own frustrations with drawing.

"I've been trying to document the strata, but the sand is so

63

porous it's hard to get it to stay put long enough to make a good sketch. And anyway, I don't have much ability."

"You do all the drawings yourself?"

"Unfortunately. My partner is even worse with a pencil than I am." He shrugged. "Maybe you could help us."

I smiled. "Are you offering me a job, Dr. Jassim?"

"Marwan" he corrected me. "Well, I can't pay you at the moment, but come have a look. We've found some fascinating things."

Another time, at a reception at the American Embassy, I introduced him to Derek.

"How'd you meet the archaeologist?" Derek asked me later in the car on the way home.

I had both anticipated and dreaded this question all evening.

"I found him outside the front gate one morning. He needed a lift to Saali and 'Abbas volunteered to take him."

Derek was quiet for a moment. "He's a little strange. Asked me lots of questions about the Saali project. Seems he has some theory he's trying to sell to the Mansours about some ruined city in that area."

"Zulaika."

"What?"

"Zulaika's the name of the city. He's written a book about it. We have it at home."

But if Derek was interested in knowing more about Marwan Jassim or Zulaika, he did not indicate it.

Yet after that night, the archaeologist ceased approaching me so readily as he had before, as if his meeting Derek seemed to place a barrier between us, proving in a concrete way that I belonged to someone. I was annoyed that between men there was an understood rule about not infringing on another's territory, like tomcats marking their respective domains. Yet in a way I was grateful that some space had been put between us.

One day not long afterwards, 'Abbas pointed a stubby, gnarled finger out the car window at a lone tree in the distance. It was the only significant tree in sight on the flat plain.

"The 'tree of life'," he said, matter-of-factly.

"The 'tree of life'? What is it?" I asked.

The driver shrugged at my question as he often did when he had to explain some evident truth he deemed I should already know. Yet, I had come to discern the note of pleasure in his voice at sharing his time-worn knowledge with me, and could detect the warmth that escaped when he let down his guard and simply forgot that I was his boss's wife and a foreigner. "It came to Abu Samra in the beginning. Allah planted it."

'Abbas gazed grimly into his mirror at me, relinquishing a twinkle in his eye before looking back at the tree, at the grayish branches that rose faintly into the air. It seemed to be a very large acacia, but it was too far away to tell.

"Allah planted it?" I asked.

"Allah planted it," he confirmed. "The leaves make good medicine."

"What kind of medicine?"

As if to illustrate the tree's powers, he held up his hand, the joints and fingers rough and swollen. "For skin. For eyes. For stomach."

"You've used it?"

"Yes."

"And it works?"

"Allah be praised," he said, holding up his hand again, as though in proof.

We were driving along the smooth carriageway through the desert on our way to the beach. I liked to go swimming on Thursday, before the Friday Sabbath when the beach was crowded. In October, the warm Gulf water was much more refreshing. I had been disappointed on my first trip to the beach in August to find the water a warm, extremely salty bath, despite its exquisite aqua color. Now the water was just right, crisp without being uncom-

65

fortably cool; and its extra saltiness did, in fact, make swimming easier.

The road to the beach cut across Abu Samra's vast Riyadhi oil field. It was Abu Samra's oldest, having been drilled by the British in the 1920s and named for the then Ruler, Sheikh Riyadh Mansour. It was said to still produce a substantial amount of the country's exported oil.

Suddenly, a yellow steel giraffe on the side of the road bowed its head up and down as though to take lazy, cool drinks from the earth. Several more followed.

"Oil pump," 'Abbas announced.

"They look so real," I said, staring at the painted eyes on the yellow drills, which made the dozen or so giraffe-like machines a welcome mirage against the flat, lifeless stretch of sand.

It was only when 'Abbas finally turned onto the dirt road that led to the beach, however, that I glimpsed the actual mounds in the distance.

At first it appeared as though the horizon were moving slightly, like a rippling, white-capped ocean. Then, as the car continued forward, I realized that the horizon did actually undulate, rising and dipping in a series of graceful, rolling hills.

"'Abbas, what are those?"

The driver craned his neck to hear me better.

"Can you pull off over here?"

He turned his head, warily, to where I was pointing.

"Those hills, see?" I leaned forward. "Can we go to those hills?"

He pulled the car to the side of the carriageway as a truck loaded with sand barreled past us. He shook his head. "No road."

"Is there no way to get there?"

"No road," he repeated, resolutely. "Bad for car."

I knew that 'Abbas would be looking for any excuse to go on to the beach as originally planned in order to be back home by six o'clock to pick up Derek with minimal dust accumulation on the

66

car. Yet feeling that my request was not as unreasonable as he tried
to make it seem, I persisted.

"'Abbas, there are tire tracks on the sand. I'm sure we can get
there. We'll forget about the beach today."

The driver shifted gears impatiently, waiting for an oncoming
car to pass. Then very gently, as though driving across cartons of
fresh eggs, he acquiesced to my unexpected demand, lowering the
Buick's wheels onto the sand.

Despite his reluctance, the car crunched easily across the desert toward the hills. I grew nervous suddenly, wondering whether
the tire tracks I had seen might belong to Marwan Jassim's vehicle,
afraid that we would find him working out here. Within minutes,
however, as we became virtually surrounded by a forest of wide,
round mounds, I saw that we were quite alone. Nearly all of them
were perfect spheres the height of a single-story house, and they
stretched all the way to the horizon in ripples. One after another,
they spread before us, resembling huge rounds of rising dough.

I could feel a childish excitement welling up inside me. These
were undoubtedly the ancient mounds. The prehistoric necropolis I
had read of in the book.

"Can we walk on them?" I asked 'Abbas, suddenly remembering that we were technically in a cemetery, and that this might be
considered hallowed ground in Abu Samra.

But 'Abbas waved me on, impatiently. Then he smiled. "Go,
yes. Go. Walk."

I went up one of the smaller ones, scattering sand and pebbles
behind me, then I chose a larger one, approximately fifteen feet
high, and climbed carefully to the top. Unlike the porous sand of
the desert, the surface of the mounds was hard, littered with pebbles
and what appeared to be broken bits of limestone that crunched
under my sandals. *Tumuli.* I had seen a picture in the guidebook, but
I had not imagined that they would be so many or so easy to find. I
went down the mound and up another like a charmed sleepwalker.

About a mile away, off to one side, was a small village. Among the cluster of houses and palm trees seemed to be several more mounds, larger and higher, the size of two-story houses. They did not seem as perfectly honed as these smaller ones, more as if a bulldozer had pushed the sand up into jagged hills and incorporated them for some other purpose. One of them was emitting a stream of smoke like a small volcano.

The sudden quiet deafened me, throbbing and palpable across the plain. It was infinitely more quiet than Dafna now with its vehicles trekking up and down the coast and the vibrant sounds of animals from the nearby shanties. I could almost hear Marwan Jassim's voice telling me again of the existence of a wealthy, prehistoric city on the peninsula. It was hard to believe that this was it, that I was standing on "an empire of history," as he referred to the mounds in his book.

Finally, I sat down on top of one and scanned the hills, so unlike the rest of the flat peninsula. The sun was starting its descent and a gentle breeze fanned my neck and face.

I was glad I was not swimming. It was getting late anyway, and 'Abbas would have to get back for Derek. Only now I wanted to rush straight to Derek's office and bring him here instead of going home. He *had* to see the splendor of these mounds, to forget about the office and his work for a few minutes and realize that it was worth putting up with all the inconveniences of the peninsula, even with the crematorium in our back yard, for this. It was not something that could be described. It had to be felt by stepping on the same sharp debris that gnawed at my shoes, by breathing in the same dust. History lay remote and dead beneath my feet and yet, emphatically alive. I wanted Derek to see it with me, to open himself to it all.

Below, behind several mounds, was the blue car. 'Abbas was leaning listlessly against the hood, his eyes closed, his arms folded over his chest. He seemed distrustful of the hills, choosing to remain on the predictable, flat ground of the desert.

I felt lonely as 'Abbas retrieved his rag and began to blow and gently sweep the sand off the car. Irritation glazed his brow as he worked, apparently untouched by the marvels that lay around him on this primordial field. I was amazed by his apathy, for I could practically feel the hills vibrate beneath me, as if they were pregnant wombs, about to open and give birth at any moment to some mysterious, unseen life. Seeing the driver so indifferent, guessing that Derek would probably react the same way if I brought him here, made me feel as though 'Abbas were actually an extension of Derek.

I watched the diligent, sulking sweeps of 'Abbas' arm against the car's hood, cleaning relentlessly. Round and round. Then I looked back at the serene plain and endless mounds. It seemed as though a thousand women had lain down and bared their breasts to the sky.

All at once I was filled with such bitter pleasure that I stood up. I felt the heat rushing to my face and heard my blood pumping, just as I had at that first cocktail party when I turned round to face him. This was Marwan Jassim's domain.

His image began to ripen inside of me — the sweaty face, the stiff brush of hair, the mouth recklessly awaiting the stream gushing from a bottle of water, eager to be quenched. I wondered what it would be like to be with a man so entranced by things beyond the surface, beyond his control. A man who purposely sought out what was hidden and unknown and uncontrollable. A man who sought unity in everything, who saw everything in the universe and all of us in it as "one", as he had put it the other night

I glanced around me, shielding my eyes from the afternoon sun. I wondered how long it would be possible to keep this image of Marwan Jassim inside of me, intact, separate and safe from my daily life. I knew now what it was that had drawn me to him outside our house that day so soon after I arrived in Abu Samra. It was a certain recognition, a delectable, yet unsettling knowledge that my world was about to change. I had felt it that first night walking with Derek in the marketplace. Yet I had not perceived the danger before. The world, however, was no longer the terrain I knew so well. From now on, it could be a hazardous place, one that was richly, brilliantly, fraught with possibilities.

9

The Garden Club

My mother had died the year before we left for Abu Samra.

At the time, her death seemed to have taken with it most of my youth. My father and I had attended her, watched her slowly burn down like a candle before our very eyes, yielding bit by bit to the breast cancer.

Several times a week, in what had turned out to be a poignant, year-long vigil, I had boarded the train from Grand Central to my parents' Norwalk, Connecticut home to see her. During these joyless rides, transitions that carried me from the frenetic world of the living to the lulled resignation of death, I often thought of my mother in terms of a candle, a pale, wax flame that diminished with each passing week.

Occasionally, a trace of her old infectious smile flashed across her lips, giving me and my father hope that she would recover. In a sort of macabre consolation, her smile that year had seemed to grow richer and more encompassing than ever, as though in a body that was shrinking, a spirit was blooming, thriving, freeing itself of earthly boundaries.

As 'Abbas drove me along the peninsula's fertile north shore one November morning to the first season's meeting of the Abu Samra Garden Club, I thought back to those long train rides to Connecticut. Many were made on early autumn mornings as dying leaves had whipped past the train's windows, yellows and tangerines that by their very brightness had soothed me. I felt a similar comfort now in the soft, autumn green of Abu Samra's palms and oleanders and by the faint scent of sand and eucalyptus.

I thought of my mother, the effervescent woman who would have flourished in this expatriate life of cocktail parties and ladies' coffees. In the past few years we had grown closer — she becoming almost the sister I never had — and how often I wished, since coming here, that she was with me to share in the excitement of a completely new place. She could have helped me see it in her own unique way, so willing to share her high sense of adventure. She should have been here in Abu Samra in place of me, she who had always dreamed of living in some far away place, but never had the chance.

I could not help making the connection during those morning train rides between the candle that was my mother and the faint wick that was my own life and marriage. Each seemed so strongly bent on consuming itself. Just as I had watched her waste away, powerless to intervene, I had felt my marriage shriveling, burning itself out. She had seen it too. It pained me now to think that she might have feared the troubles in my marriage even more than her own death.

Today's Garden Club meeting was being held jointly with the American Women's Auxiliary at the Agricultural Center twenty minutes north of Dafna. The Agricultural Center itself was located in an old, tree-lined compound that had once housed British civil servants in the 1930s and 40s. The compound still reflected a genteel harmony as though the gardens had all been planted and were lovingly tended to by a single gardener sent over from England by the Queen herself.

We drove through an archway of palms that gave way to a frangipani-lined street with large houses on either side. Unlike other compounds, this one seemed stuck in the colonial era, the houses sporting large porches shaded by flaming mimosas, with date-laden palms growing high between the gardens. Pink petunias and orange nasturtiums lined concrete walkways and mauve bougainvillea vines clung to garden walls. The homes were built, as were many of the older homes in Abu Samra, with local gypsum — a clay that turned the walls a warm golden-brown and made them appear to melt into the sand.

At the end of the street was the Agricultural Center. 'Abbas pulled up behind a flotilla of black Cadillacs parked outside a large house with a blue gate.

"Mansour," he said, nodding at the shimmering cars. *"Sheikhas."* His tone was tinged with an ambiguous mixture of the apprehension and irritability I had come to notice in him whenever there was any mention of the royal family.

"The Mansours?" I was surprised. The invitation had come from the American Women's Auxiliary. I had assumed that there would be only expatriates attending.

"Sheikha Budur," 'Abbas said, pointing to a rose-colored Mercedes parked ahead. Sheikha Budur was the First Lady of Abu Samra, the wife of the *Emir* Sheikh Salim Mansour.

I gazed at the watery sheen of the pink vehicle. Evidently, there were no casual outings in Abu Samra. Anywhere one went one was likely to meet someone of consequence. Although I was dressed formally enough in a lavender blouse and skirt, next to the darker, glittering Abu Samra women it was difficult not to feel too tall, too blond — practically transparent. Even too skinny.

I shut the car door and 'Abbas abruptly drove off, calling out, "one o'clock," as though it were a command and not an agreement to return for me at the time I had myself requested.

Two expatriate women sat at a desk inside the open door wearing labels on their chests with "AWA hostess" stamped in red

73

ink. They looked familiar from the dozen receptions Derek and I had already attended.

"Gina Monroe," I said.

"Monroe, Monroe," murmured one of the women whose red hair was several shades brighter than her orange lipstick. She rifled through a stack of name labels. "Monroe. Here we are."

The other hostess offered me a peach orchid from a bowl of water. This woman had soft, brown hair which was cropped short at her neck and ears, accentuating her round face. Her smile was pleasant.

"Bank or oil?" the red-headed woman asked, with grating, throaty congeniality.

"USA Electric," I said, pinning the flower over my breast. Drops of water turned the lavender fabric a dark maroon.

"New blood!" the red-head exclaimed. "Mary and I are both oil. From Texas. I'm Carla."

I shook the extended freckled hand with orange nails.

"Almost everyone this year seems to be a banker. How'd you get here?" Carla asked.

"My husband's working on the Saali electrical project. We're only here for a year."

"Saali? The new power plant?" she said.

"Yes."

"Did I meet your husband?" she asked, tapping her nails on the table top. "Tall? Dark hair?"

I smiled. "Sounds like him." Women usually found Derek attractive, his dark eyes and brows penetrating in an unusual way for an American of such untainted English background.

The other woman, Mary, nodded at me. "That power plant is important. Those villages are finally going to get air-conditioning."

"The locals don't care about air-conditioning," Carla said, crisply, pronouncing it *lowcals*. "They want the TVs." There were wet crescents under the arms of her silk blouse and her forehead was beaded with moisture despite the rotating ceiling fan overhead.

"You look familiar," Mary said to me. Her eyebrows lifted above misty, gray eyes. "Do you, by any chance, live in that new neighborhood off the hospital road?"

"In Dafna," I said.

"The street with the two pea-green houses?" she said.

"Yes," I said, surprised that she knew it.

"Well, say *hi* to your neighbor," Carla cut in.

"You?" I tried to look cheerful at the prospect of this brash red-head being my neighbor.

"Me," Mary said. "I live down the street from you. The sand-colored house wedged in between those two green ones."

I looked at her in disbelief. I knew it at once. It was an odd-shaped beige house that seemed to have been originally built as a wing to connect the two green houses. When I had first seen it I had remarked to Derek that I doubted it ever got any sunlight. I remembered him saying that was hardly a tragedy in Abu Samra.

"Two years ago when we moved here, there was a housing shortage," Mary explained. "I wish your house had been ready when we were looking. You have that nice expanse behind you."

There was no sarcasm to indicate that she knew that the "expanse" behind the house was a crematorium. I found myself immediately liking her.

"Come by for coffee," she said, shaking my hand. "I'm home most mornings."

In the next room, a waiter was serving glasses of pastel-colored drinks. I chose a glass filled with a whitish liquid that tasted like almonds.

In New York, with neither the time nor inclination to join clubs or women's groups, it had been a rarity for me to attend coffees. I was surprised now to find myself eager for this ambiance of female camaraderie and chatter. I was amazed, too, at how much I suddenly missed home. The caress of American voices was comforting. Even Carla's Texas lilt and raucous laughter was strangely soothing.

Along the wall of the inner sitting room sat some dozen Arab women draped in black '*abayas*. I presumed they were the Mansours. Their '*abaya* cloaks hung limply from their shoulders, exposing sable hair. Several of the younger women had stylish chin-length cuts, in almost brazen defiance of the solemn braids of the older women. A few wore the thick gold necklaces and earrings I had seen in the market windows, and the air seemed filled with the perpetual soft jingle of bracelets. I was struck by the animated way they talked to one another, more like giggling schoolgirls than grown royal women.

I recognized the one wearing a chic beige pantsuit and no *abaya*. Her hair was loose about her face today, which made her appear younger than the first time I had seen her. It was the archaeologist Sheikha I had seen at the reception some months ago. *The prettiest woman in Abu Samra,* Derek had called her. Next to her sat a dignified, homely older woman with glaring circles beneath her eyes. She seemed slightly removed from the rest, and merely nodded gravely through the peals of laughter. From the deferential way the other women treated her, I assumed she was Sheikha Budur, wife of the Emir.

A robust, elderly expatriate woman who had been sitting with the Mansours now stood and went to a podium at one end of the room. She clapped her hands several times and approached the microphone.

When the guests were quiet, she introduced herself in a clear British accent, as President of the Abu Samra Garden Club. Then she proceeded to welcome the *Emir's* wife, Sheikha Budur, thanking her for attending the year's first meeting under the patronage of her husband, His Highness Sheikh Salim.

There was a general round of applause. Sheikha Budur glanced round the room and inclined her head slightly, covering her mouth as though to suppress an embarrassed giggle.

"This is Her Highness's first visit, and we are most grateful for her support," announced the President. "With her are other ladies of the Mansour family. We are indeed honored that the Sheikhas

76

could make it this morning." There was more applause from everyone, although the Mansours seemed slightly bewildered by the accolades.

The President surveyed the room happily. "We've got surprises for you this year, but before discussing plans for the upcoming show in March, I want to report that we've been able to obtain papaya trees from Thailand. They're just off the plane, and with the long growing season here, they should produce fruit in a year's time."

The President then began to read from a list in her hand: Mesquite bean trees and Gaillardias from Iraq. Indian Lilac, Myrtle, Frangipani, and Jatroba from Karachi. There were annuals to be grown from seed — Sweet Sultans, Linum, Sunflowers, Hollyhocks — as well as established Dahlias, Mignonettes, Verbena, Zinnias, and Pansies. For those without gardeners or those who felt they were hopeless when it came to growing flowers, there were Oleanders and Bougainvillea, which needed little tending.

The best vegetables to grow with any success, she said, were Beetroot, carrots, celery, onions, cauliflower and lettuce. I was trying to remember the titillating names of the flowers she had just mentioned, *Linum, Jatroba, Sweet Sultans,* when I heard a voice behind me whisper, "That's Sheikha Budur?"

"I can't believe it," someone whispered back.

"I thought *he* was a cad but after seeing her, I forgive him," the first woman said, emitting a quick gasp.

"She's so — well, you'd think he would have the pick of Abu Samra."

"She's his cousin. He had to marry her."

"He's got dozens of cousins."

There was a pause, then the first voice came again. "She's quite highly thought of. Besides, he didn't have a choice. They tell him whom to marry. He has enough going on outside, though. You can't exactly pity him."

"You can't exactly *blame* him," the second voice said. Again, the muffled laugh.

I moved away slightly. I had heard this talk before, how members of the ruling family, like many traditional Abu Samrans, relied on matchmaking elders to choose mates for them. The rumor was that the *Emir*, though far from a handsome man himself, had a roving eye. He had apparently carved out a section of Abu Samra's fertile North as a game reserve and where he had also built a palace to discreetly entertain foreign female guests.

Although I found all of this fascinating when I first heard of it — it seemed that it was not uncommon for expatriate wives to receive invitations to tea at the Emir's remote palace — I felt sorry that this dignified woman was so neglected. Although plain, she had an elegance and an appealing, penetrating gaze.

The President of the Club was giving advice on growing grass, telling newcomers to cover new seed with sand to insure a thick, green lawn in the spring. Cow manure was at a premium now due to the demand, she said, but a cart-load could be obtained from one of the villages if ordered early enough. We were told that our young flower seedlings would be crushed by the winter's strong north winds and the leaves become spotted with salt from the brackish surface soil splashed onto them during the rains. The flowers, though, would bloom just as gloriously in the spring, she assured us, and concluded her speech by saying that if we were patient, we would reap richly. For Abu Samra, though a challenge to the casual gardener, would prove a delight to those who persevered.

Her talk of the fragility of the local plants seemed to highlight our own transience, and the fact that as expatriates we were alien to the peninsula. I found myself suddenly thinking of Marwan Jassim and what he had said outside my house that first day: how in Abu Samra only Allah was regarded as everlasting, everything else being temporary.

Even now, the archaeologist and his thoughts invaded my morning. Less than a week ago we had seen each other at yet another reception. Although, since introducing him to Derek, I sensed a hesitance on his part to talk to me as freely as he had before, we had an uncanny ability to spot each other across crowded lobbies and ballrooms, the way mothers distinguish their child's voice from myriad others. Last week he had come up to me soon after Derek and I arrived at the Indonesian embassy.

"You're here too," I had said.

He smiled, looking happy to see me. "How could I stay away?" Then he added, "We're all here for the same reason."

"Money?" I asked, disappointed and yet relieved that he had quickly moved the conversation onto neutral ground.

"Of course."

"You make us all sound like scavengers."

"But we are, Mrs. Monroe."

I wondered if he was joking. "I don't see it that way."

"Everyone here is working for their own benefit — not Abu Samra's. Neo-colonialists, if you like. No different from the English and Portuguese who controlled this region in the past. Only instead of guns, they rule with dollars."

I was shocked by this blunt accusation. "But these banks bring in business. Derek's firm is going to provide more electricity. How's that scavenging?"

He smiled. "That's a Westerner's way of justifying things. You might ask how much his American company is going to make out of the deal? USA Electric, right?"

"I don't know what you mean about justifying anything. I certainly don't think his company means to do any harm."

"I meant the West in general, certainly, not just his firm," he said, more gently.

"What about the benefits of new business? All the building that's taken place since the country became a banking center?"

"You mean the business profits that are siphoned back to the home countries, the Great White Mother? All that'll be left here in a few years are these ridiculous hotels, not that they'll be needed any more once the oil runs out. We're simply being provided with con-

79

venience. The West's technology at the expense of our *essence*. Our intrinsic spirituality. And for what? So we can get hooked on a morally bankrupt consumer civilization."

I was quiet for a moment. I had read in his book that he had obtained his doctorate from the University of London. I wondered how he could be so cynical in person and yet write so optimistically, even poetically, about Abu Samra in his book.

"What about you?" I said. "Are you as morally bankrupt as the rest of us?"

I saw the spark in his eyes that had seemed to target me the first time we met in Dafna. But now there was also an affection in his gaze, as if my opinion mattered to him in some way.

"I'm as much a scavenger as anybody else, Mrs. Monroe. Perhaps even more so since I do it less obviously. Only, I like to think that I work for all of us, not just for myself or my country."

"Then, how are *you* harming Abu Samra? I've been to the mounds and I've read your book. I think enhancing knowledge about the peninsula's history is important."

He smiled. "I see. I don't steal artifacts, I just uncover them. I don't destroy, I merely find what was lost. And I'm a *local* at that. Well, you're right. I didn't set out to harm anyone. But I always ask myself whether I'm preserving or exploiting. Who gave *me* the right to dictate what our history was? And what if I make a mistake, make an assumption that's incorrect? I'm writing our history each time I go into the ground. Since we're all linked, in a way I'm writing man's history. That's a risky business. And, in the long run, Mrs. Monroe, I suppose I *am* doing much of it for myself."

I was taken aback by the persistence in his tone. What about our all being "one"? Certainly, he was enriching global knowledge. I was puzzled that he seemed to downplay this.

"Only you know your intentions," I said. "But I think you're being unfair. Give yourself credit for the contributions you're making. Do you Abu Samrans really resent foreigners that much?"

"I think people here were a lot happier before oil was ever

discovered. Now foreigners swim in our sea, explore every nook and cranny of our tiny peninsula more than we ourselves do, build their Western buildings and factories which will eventually pollute the entire area — an area that, by the way, survived just fine for thousands of years left alone. I'm sorry to disappoint you, Mrs. Monroe. But none of what's being done here is really going to benefit Abu Samrans in the long run. *None* of it."

I was not sure how or whether to even reply. Had he simply had a bad day or were we really destroying this place like he said?

I had looked around for a sign of Derek, both to reassure me that our presence here was not entirely an abomination and also because I felt that I had been standing with Marwan Jassim far too long.

"I think you're being harsh, Dr. Jassim. I'd like to continue this sometime, but..."

"I'm sorry to have kept you," he said, backing away to let me through the crowd.

I smiled. "I hope I can visit your dig sometime. I'd like to see for myself what horrors you're inflicting on Abu Samra."

He chuckled. "I've been waiting for you."

I felt surprise cross my face at this unexpected comment.

Over the next few days I had thought of little else but Marwan Jassim's words. *I've been waiting for you.* Had he really been waiting? And for what, exactly? I also wondered whether his resentment at what was going on in Abu Samra with the deluge of foreigners was reasonable. I was piqued that he thought I had, as he put it, a 'superior' attitude toward the Abu Samrans when nothing could have been further from the truth.

When I had asked Derek whether he thought foreigners were inadvertently harming Abu Samra by modernizing it too quickly, he looked annoyed.

"Do you think they can keep up with the rest of the world in these medieval conditions?"

"But isn't that just our way of looking at things? Technology isn't necessarily the answer here."

"*They* think it is. They *want* to join the rest of the world. We're only here to help."

"Maybe they don't realize what they'll be losing, though."

He laughed. "What's to lose?"

"You know what I mean."

Derek, obviously, did not share Marwan Jassim's view. I wondered how many others did actually agree with the archaeologist. After all, he had struck even me as a bit peculiar, definitely unconventional, in the beginning. A thing, it was becoming clear to me, I was oddly, helplessly, drawn to.

Following the club President's talk, we were shown a film on English gardens and then there was an orchid raffle. After that, the meeting adjourned and waiters reappeared with trays of fresh strawberries, cucumber sandwiches, and pots of tea and coffee.

I glanced at my watch. It would be another half hour until 'Abbas returned.

The guests seemed to have suddenly forgotten about gardens and were talking about which stores sold the latest French clothes, which the cheapest gold or the cheapest bottled water, and whether to choose a lake in Kashmir or a trip to Kabul for an R&R. I tried to discern which of the women belonged to the voices in the conversation about the Emir's wife, Sheikha Budur, that I had overheard earlier, but everyone had moved around by now.

Across the room, waiters hovered around the Sheikhas, offering them glasses of juice and tea sandwiches. Although the women gesticulated elaborately, their voices never rose much higher than whispers, making them sound like a cluster of happy birds. Seen in a group like this, their resemblance to one another was uncanny — the wide eyes, the slightly rounded noses, the slope of the eyebrows. Even the level glance of Sheikha Budur seemed to run through the group like a stamp.

Someone tapped my shoulder. It was the Club President.

"Mrs. Monroe? Someone would like to meet you." She led me toward the seated Mansours.

"Your Highness, this is Gina Monroe. She's new. Her husband is with the American electric company."

Derek had explained that whereas one addressed the other Mansours as 'Excellency', 'Highness' was the title conferred upon the Ruling Sheikh and his wife.

Starting with Sheikha Budur, I shook the row of extended hands, trying to greet each one appropriately as well as not stare at the several slender palms painted in intricate, dark henna patterns as though they were wrapped in lace. The last Sheikha I greeted was Sheikha Mariam, the archaeologist. Her wide eyes shone within their rims of *kohl*. Her lips were full and perfectly shaped. *The prettiest woman in Abu Samra.* I could not help wondering if Marwan Jassim felt this way. She was indeed beautiful, an ideal artist's model with such assertive, sculpted features. Only her expression — gentle yet strong — would be a challenge.

After I expressed my pleasure to be in Abu Samra, the elder Sheikha Budur said something to Sheikha Mariam.

"My aunt wants to know how many children you have?" Sheikha Mariam translated. Her voice was huskier than I imagined it would be, her accent not the fine British of her Oxford-educated cousin Ahmad.

"None, Your Highness."

The women glanced at one another, Sheikha Budur looking skeptically at my flat belly. Then she nodded approvingly and said something to Sheikha Mariam.

"My aunt says that God willing you will soon have them."

I flushed at the Sheikha's polite concern. Was she voicing her intuition? Perhaps I *would* have them soon, as she said. There was an uncanny wisdom in her demeanor that was both startling and pleasant.

"Thank you, Your Highnesss. I hope so." I understood that pregnancy and motherhood was something obviously revered and

83

respected in this community, and to be somehow brought into this female fold by a total stranger was touching.

Sheikha Mariam's gaze had not left my face.

"Are you a friend of Dr. Jassim?" she said suddenly.

"Dr. Jassim?" I was surprised by the abrupt change of topic.

"I saw you talking with him. I thought you were friends."

"We've only met a few times," I said quickly, the blood throbbing in my temples. In a small place like Abu Samra, nothing, apparently, went unnoticed. I remembered the tinge of admiration in Marwan Jassim's voice when he had spoken of the Sheikha's digging.

The Sheikha stared at me, unflinching. "Are you an archaeologist?"

I was not sure whether I was being questioned or whether, since I was a newcomer, the Sheikha's inquiries were simply out of politeness.

"No," I replied. "I don't know much about archaeology, although I find it fascinating. I'm always interested in what Dr. Jassim has to say about Abu Samra's history." By now I had reread most of *Sands of Zulaika*, although much of the technicalities were still confusing. "I'm a painter, Your Excellency."

"An artist?" Sheikha Mariam said, then translated to Sheikha Budur who nodded. Sheikha Mariam looked back at me. "We have many fine artists in Abu Samra. We admire art."

I could not help wondering at this point how all of these royal women regarded this room full of expatriates, whether they saw us as scavengers as Marwan Jassim did, or whether they saw benefits to the foreign presence in their country.

"I hope to see the work of your artists," I said, encouraged to hear of an art community.

"We have several galleries," she said, then added, "You must also visit our excavations. They're quite extraordinary. Dr. Jassim is good at putting people to work."

"I've never dug," I said. "He has great admiration for *your* work, Your Excellency."

She did not seem surprised that I knew that she was an archaeologist. She shrugged. "I'm not digging now."

There was an awkward silence until other expatriates came up to shake hands with the honored guests. I backed away, somewhat relieved to be free from the Sheikha's scrutiny.

I spoke with several other American and British women who introduced themselves to me, then, when I glanced back to the couch and chairs where the Mansours had been sitting, they were empty.

Several minutes later I too left, armed with bags of fresh mint, aubergine, and broccoli plants with which to breathe life into my new garden in Dafna.

10

Saali

By November, the soggy heat of summer was a memory. A cool, dry breeze carrying tiny particles of sand and dust, replaced it, drawing them up and dispersing them as a reminder that the desert was still there; hibernating beneath this sudden reprieve, perhaps, but still there.

I steered the Renault through a round-about and onto the carriageway leading to Saali, carefully shifting gears, making way for the cars and trucks that impatiently careened past me as though in some ruthless affirmation of their drivers' immortality.

At the Garden Club meeting I had heard of the Renault being for sale and convinced Derek that 'Abbas's time was too valuable to spend driving me to and from the growing multitude of social functions that I was obliged to attend.

Yet this was the first time I had driven alone on the carriageway. Over the past few weeks 'Abbas had stoically taught me to shift gears, his gnarled fingers frantically grabbing for the gear stick whenever we approached a round-about, and uttering "Allah, Allah," as he braced himself for the frenzy of jolts whenever I removed my foot too quickly from the clutch. Yet, despite his hours of training, now that I was driving alone, the roads seemed as unfamiliar as when I had first arrived.

Although at first I could not help missing the driver's sullen company, his occasional betrayals of a covert smile or softening in his eyes, it felt good to drive again, to plunge in and out of traffic, to decide on a whim to go somewhere without having to ask 'Abbas to take me. I had forgotten how good it felt to be mobile again without having to rely on anyone.

Not only the roads, but the very landscape of the peninsula seemed to have undergone some elemental transformation before my eyes. On previous rides with 'Abbas or Derek, I had felt my thoughts and feelings censored. Derek's aloofness to the environment, like 'Abbas' sorrowful grimaces, kept my emotions in check. Neither of them seemed to notice the translucency of the sea in the mornings, the extraordinary shadings of the desert, the reflection of the brown fishing dhows as they rocked on the water like huge, ungainly geese.

On my own now, I immersed myself in the sparkling aqua and yellows of the Gulf, the water so shallow in places it seemed that one could wade all the way to Saudi Arabia. I absorbed the shimmer of amethyst sand, for 'Abbas representing a scourge of dust on Derek's car, suddenly growing vivid and fecund before me.

It was no longer a mystery to me why 'Abbas judged the desert so harshly. According to Derek, the driver's forefathers had been among those Abu Samra traders who had plied the Gulf to Southern Iran and back, marrying Persian women from the Iranian towns of Ahwaz and Abadan. 'Abbas himself admitted not being certain whether his ancestors had actually been Arabs or Persians — it had been too long ago. Yet, his apparent lack of interest in the desert was perhaps rooted in some deep affinity to a more verdant, bounteous land, an innate longing for the mountains of Iran, of which he might not have even been aware.

Derek's indifference to the landscape, on the other hand, had perhaps more to do with his growing disillusionment with work than with any particular dislike of the desert. For it was becoming increasingly apparent to me that everything he saw in Abu Samra was tinged by the frustration of having to function quickly and efficiently in an environment as languid as this, a place whose fundamental rhythms were so out of step with his own. This ceaseless strain seemed to blind him to the rugged beauty of the place, to the unexpected charm of our surroundings that had completely captured me.

Though Derek and I had driven out to the mounds together soon after I first saw them with 'Abbas, he had not exhibited any particular excitement at seeing them. We had trouble finding them at first since I had mistakenly directed him down the wrong road, so it had been past sunset when we finally spotted the rippling plain.

"Isn't it late to go exploring?" Derek had said when I leaped out of the car to show them to him.

"Just for a minute, Derek. You have to climb them to see the view. They extend for miles."

When he followed me up one, I noticed for the first time that he had not changed out of his office shoes before coming.

"Isn't it incredible?" I blurted out.

"So these are the famous burial mounds," he said, scanning the view.

"Thousands of years old, Derek. *Thousands.*"

He picked up a jagged piece of stone from the ground. "Take a look," he said, handing it to me, then stooped to pick up another.

"What is it?"

"Worked flint," he said.

I stared at the stone. "How do you know?"

"I collected Indian ones on camping trips in Arizona as a kid. This one looks like an arrow head."

The small oblong shapes with chipped edges scattered on the mounds hardly looked like genuine tools or arrow heads, but I was eager to believe that they had been fashioned by human hands millennia ago, and I was thrilled that Derek had connected them to a positive memory.

"I never knew that you went camping in Arizona. Did you

89

enjoy it?" I asked, hoping that he would find even more on this spot to interest him.

"Sure. When it wasn't too hot."

"Doesn't this make you feel insignificant, Derek? Look how many centuries it took for this cemetery to become this huge. I feel like I'm connecting with the souls of the people who lived here, like I knew each one of them."

Derek continued to search the ground, picking up and discarding various pieces of rock or flint.

I pulled a sketch pad out of my purse and began to draw the rolling horizon and village off to the right. A thin spiral of smoke seemed to be coming from one of the larger mounds in the village, as if it had been transformed into some sort of bakery.

Derek began to dust off his hands. "We need to get home to catch the evening news."

I had looked up, not believing that his interest had worn off so quickly.

"Just a few more minutes," I said, hurrying to fill in the details of the sketch that I had started. I could build on it later.

But now, on my own, I was driving along the southern shore to Marwan Jassim's dig in Saali, which was located at the site of an old Omani fort. He had briefly described its location to me. Derek, too, had shown me on a map how to get to the carriageway going south, wanting me to get to know my way around the peninsula. For even to Derek my need to be driven everywhere by 'Abbas had begun to be a burden.

A municipal project was underway along the carriageway. Hundreds of palms and pink oleanders had been planted on the beach interspersed with brightly painted, corrugated-iron shelters. The newspaper had reported a government campaign to make Abu Samra 'as green as Hawaii and as clean as Singapore,' and the stunning number of transplanted trees and yellow refuse containers seemed to confirm this. There were also several food stalls with signs advertising *kebabs* and *samosas*.

After I passed the last shelter, the road veered slightly away from the coast. A large blue sign announced 'Saali' in both Arabic and English, and seconds later, the road began to snake through a village of cement houses.

Saali bore little resemblance to the peninsula's other mud-brick villages that blended into the surrounding landscape, like the one nestled among the desert tumulii. There was a certain flashy exuberance displayed in this village, newer wealth that put it at odds with its quiet surroundings. The cement houses were sharp-angled boxes painted garish green or maroon, without the old-fashioned wind towers of the traditional homes. Instead of the subtle plaster work of the mud-brick or gypsum walls of the old houses near Dafna that I had already painted, these were plain, flat cement slabs that rose into unfinished second-story rooms with protruding iron beams. The front doors too were made of smooth iron rather than carved teak or painted wood. Only the dome of the Saali mosque was the traditional vibrant blue, as were the cluster of aqua benches under some mimosa trees that served as an outdoor men's cafe. I was surprised that Marwan Jassim had suggested that this particular village would inspire me.

It was almost noon and the road through the village was deserted except for a few small boys, the smallest ones naked below the waist. They briefly chased the Renault, waving frantically and sticking out their tongues. The boys, I noticed, had uncommonly light skin compared to the children in town. A few had sun-bleached hair and light eyes. It was known that the indigenous villagers had extensively intermarried with lighter-skinned Persians over the centuries. In his book, Marwan Jassim had even suggested that the villagers' fair complexions also had to do with the presence of Portuguese soldiers stationed here three hundred years before.

The village, however, was not my destination. Once past the gas station at the end of the street, past the mosque and the vegetable fields on either side of the road, I detected the faint outline of a

91

hill in the distance against the line of sapphire sea. This had to be the Omani fort.

I started to lift my foot off the gas as an unexpected rush of giddiness gripped me. I knew I should turn back. I *had* to turn back. Coming here was a mistake, even if I had been invited to take a look. But despite my hesitation, my toe resolutely bore down on the gas peddle as if with an energy all its own.

A blue pick-up truck and a white jeep faced the beach. I pulled up next to the jeep, parked, and stepped out onto the sand. There was nobody in sight and no sounds except for a faint rumbling of engines somewhere in the distance.

The sea was choppier here than in town, with whitecaps snapping at the shore. Debris littered the sand — Pepsi bottles, pieces of wood, a black plastic shoe. Seagulls flew overhead in a slow, silent glide.

On the slope of the hill that faced the sea was what appeared to be the ramparts of an ancient wall. It vaguely resembled a large, abandoned sand castle. This was, I guessed, the fort, considered to be Abu Samra's oldest remaining Omani military structure. It was built early in the last century when the Arabs of Oman, a country adjoining Saudi Arabia and then a major maritime force in the Gulf, had set up strategic garrisons on this peninsula. The hill seemed to push right into what was left of the fort wall, the sand filling in the fort's chambers. At the foot of the hill was a broad trench with crumbling protrusions which looked like low, meandering walls. Gradation-like steps led down to a pit of rubble where there were more discarded cans and bottles.

Glancing up from the trench, I saw a head abruptly appear at the top of the hill. A dark man in a vivid purple tunic and baggy trousers was pushing a wheelbarrow. He stopped and stared down at me. Then another man appeared beside him. This one wore only khaki trousers. His bare chest was like the pale shadow of the man in the purple tunic. I stood perfectly still, the seagulls strutting along the sand at my feet. Finally, I raised my hand and waved up to Marwan Jassim.

"So, you've found us," he said when I reached the top of the hill.

"It was easier than I thought. I hadn't expected so many signs for Saali."

He smiled. "Hard to get lost here." He pointed to a table behind him. "Drink?"

The folding metal table was spread with bottles of juice and beer, half-eaten loaves of bread and small cartons of yogurt. A young man with red hair and a thick, red beard got up from a stool at the table, put down his bottle of beer, and brushed crumbs from his thighs.

"This is my colleague, John Reese," Marwan Jassim said, nodding to the young man. The man, about twenty five, came forward and smiled slightly, extending a large hand. He wore a black and white checkered head cloth like the ones Arab men wore, but instead of a black cord to hold it in place, he had tied the edges at the back to fit his head making him look like some long lost deserter of the French Foreign Legion.

"John's from Oxford," Marwan Jassim added, "but as you see, he's gone native."

I smiled, still feeling like a trespasser.

"I've interrupted your lunch," I said, sensing again that I should not have been there. I had acted in haste and in poor judgment.

"We're just done," Marwan said, amiably. "Besides, you add color. *Movable* color."

He pulled a frosty bottle of beer out of a cooler. He popped it open on the edge of the table, licking the snowy froth off his hand, and handed it to me.

"Sorry you missed lunch. We get hungry early, starting at five in the morning. This should quench you though."

93

"Australian," I said, glancing at the green and gold label.

"Almost as good as ale, John says — certainly outdoes the American variety."

"Aren't you having any?" I said, as he reached for a small carton of juice. I felt odd to be the only woman at the site and to be drinking beer at that. I suspected that as a Muslim, Marwan Jassim did not drink any alcohol and I wished that I had declined the offer.

But he waved off my hesitancy, as if guessing my thoughts. "I never drink when I'm working," he said. "I'd fall asleep."

Despite the cool weather, the Oxford Reese also wore only khaki shorts. Only, whereas his shoulders glowed a painful, burned pink, Marwan Jassim's hairless skin was a deep yellow-bronze. I remembered the way I had seen him that first time, drinking, drowning his face against the heat, casually stepping aside for me to enter my front gate, as if inviting me to enter into his world.

Several Indian workmen, including the man in the purple tunic who had first appeared on the crest of the hill, were squatting a short distance away, sifting sand in large, wooden sieves. I sensed their glances although they did not look directly at us.

"Welcome to Saali," Marwan Jassim said, waving his arm as though the entire hill and plain beneath us, including the mute village, belonged to him. White streams of sweat had dried on his stomach and arms. I had drawn a model once whose similar lean body and hairless chest had throbbed with the same nervous energy. He had also been lanky, like an El Greco Christ, and I had trouble bringing out the strength of his limbs without making them look fragile.

I glanced back toward the village. "My husband has a project near here. I've been hearing him talk about Saali for a long time. I've also been curious to see your evil work."

Marwan Jassim laughed.

"I apologize for my insufferable mood the other night. I'd spent the day haggling at the Ministry of Education. Each step you take here has to receive written permission from the government

94

which sometimes takes weeks. Most of the time I feel my hands are tied in innumerable knots."

I nodded, surprised that a native Abu Samran would say this.

"I read in the newspaper that you're starting a new dig," I said.

"Right here. But it's hardly new, as you can see."

"You're not working on the mounds?"

He threw his head back and swallowed some juice. "The tumuli? That's just for fun. We've documented most of what there is to know there, for now."

He stared about him, somewhat with pride. "Something new has come up here, although this is an old site — the oldest in Abu Samra." He walked a few feet ahead and beckoned to me.

John Reese left us and went over to the Indian workmen, but I followed Marwan Jassim to the edge of the hill. I knew better than to stand beside this man, enjoying the sensation coming over me, the thrill along with the sharp blade of panic. I suddenly felt as I had that first morning standing on my roof, looking down at the workman cooking over the fire. I was once more totally aware of confronting something so new and vigorous that it would change me forever.

Marwan Jassim pointed to the pit. "Whatever you see on the surface, these rocks and low walls, are the remains of the Omani fort which is only about two hundred years old. That was built on the ruins of an existing Portuguese fort built in the sixteenth century." He smiled. "The Portuguese controlled these parts long before the Brits ever set foot here."

I looked at him. "Why did the Portuguese come all the way out here?"

"They were the major sea power at the time. They had to control the Gulf if they were to control the shipping trade to India and the African slave trade. They were good builders, as you can see. Over the years their walls have simply been plastered over and repaired. They eventually lost the Gulf to England, of course."

There was no trace of emotion in his voice this time as he said

95

this, simply a scientist's dry, observation of fact.

"So this really is a Portuguese fort?"

"Partly. Under it are earlier remains of a medieval Islamic palace. There are quite a few scattered along the coast. There are some minor Helenistic remains under that."

"Greek?"

"Alexander the Great, or remnants of his army, passed through here. There are Helenistic graves throughout the peninsula."

I had read that in his book. "O.K. But why *were* the Greeks here?"

"And the Romans later on, looking for riches and more routes to India. They all wanted control of the frankincense trade from Yemen and the spice trade from India. They were usually disastrous expeditions, but ones Europeans couldn't resist. *Money,*" he said, again with that rubbing together of his fingers that I had found disturbing the first night we talked. "But even Alexander is late. Before him were the Babylonians and the Cassites."

"Zulaika?" I said, trying to recall the theory he had argued in his book, although I had forgotten how Zulaika fit into all that he had just mentioned.

"Any Zulaikan remains will be the most valuable, of course. They're the earliest significant settlements."

He squatted and pointed to the trench. "This was first excavated twenty-five years ago, then most of it purposely reburied to preserve it. Most of the artifacts and potsherds have been taken back to England for further study."

I stared down, starting to focus, beginning to discern the remains of possible walls and even steps. It was like spying on someone's private plunder. "Were you always interested in archaeology?"

"It was the farthest thing from my mind. I wanted to be a barrister."

"You studied law?"

"I'd planned to. But once I got to Oxford I decided to study man. To find out why we tick, do the idiotic things we do."

He was still squatting, his back and shoulders rigid in the autumn sun. I watched the tensing of his back muscles as he softly scraped at the sand near his foot with a trowel he took from his pocket. It was the most sensual movement I had ever seen a man make.

He glanced up at me. "When I was growing up, I was taught not to question. I swore to myself that the rest of my life would be different. I would question *everything*. Piecing together human history entails endless questioning."

"That's an interesting reason for taking up archaeology."

He laughed. "A lot of people do it for even more bizarre reasons, and most of us start notoriously late. It seems to be the trend. You have to reach a point in your life where you can live with the long hours and months and years of slow work. There's no instant gratification in this."

He took out a smaller tool, like a dentist's, and probed a hard, dry patch. "Except maybe in places like Abu Samra. Just about anywhere you poke around you find stuff."

I squatted beside him and watched him work on the small spot. "Sounds like art," I said. "Long on hours and short on rewards."

"At least you get to see your creations immediately. You can hang up your work and put beauty back into the world," he said, looking up at me, shielding his eyes from the sun. He gazed at me, holding my own gaze as if it were something fragile and fascinating.

He went back to scraping. "We have to get to the minutest detail of an artifact without disturbing or endangering what we're looking for." His voice was stable and deep and more relaxed than in the ballrooms where we had met the past month. It was easy to see that he was far more at ease in his own element.

"You don't ever want to destroy the context because you achieve stabilization by saving the site as is. Even if you have to bury it again to preserve it. Above all else, you need to preserve it

97

just as you found it in order to photograph and draw it," he said.

"So just how old is this site?"

"It's been dated back to 1800 B.C., when this peninsula was a large urban center."

I stared at the broken wall below. "This goes back four thousand years?"

He nodded. "We know from the strata, the different layers of earth. We also know the dates from the burial style and the pottery sherds found inside the graves. And from the skeletons, of course."

He got up and walked a few feet away from me, looked around on the ground, and picked something up. He held it out. It was flat and lightly caked with dirt. "The archeologist's best friend. A pot sherd. This piece of pottery tells us more about their civilization than anything else."

He gently rubbed away the dirt, blowing the dust off the piece of pinkish clay. Now that he had pointed it out, I realized that I had seen similar ones on the surfaces of the burial mounds. Derek had picked up a few himself.

"Some of this was unearthed about twenty years ago," he said. "Bones were found below where you're standing, buried within the clay floor rather than under it. That's typical of the Cassite Age. So is the pottery. Then, they found some of the seals which had been used for commercial transactions. Those were earlier, assumed to be Zulaikan."

I stepped back, suddenly sensing I was trampling bodies beneath me. I was flattered that he was taking the time to tell me about it, as if he expected me to be able to pick up his train of thought with no problem.

"That large chamber, there, was probably a depot," he went on, his voice growing higher, more urgent. "Ships anchored out there. This was the port authority of Abu Samra three thousand years ago."

I stared at the trench below us, trying to imagine what he had described in his book: rooms with coffers of gold from India and pearls from the Gulf's rich sea beds, merchants from Mesopotamia, India, and Egypt haggling over the price of precious metals or wheat.

He suddenly reached for my arm. "And over there," he said, pulling me slightly toward him, "was the business office. The place is littered with coins bearing the seal of Sargon."

I tried to think through the firm touch of his fingers on my skin, tried to remember: Sargon, Mesopotamia, Babylon. Half-forgotten high school history lessons starting to take root in the sand. I tried to recall the other details I had read in his book, but it was hard to focus on anything but the way my arm seemed to turn limp above my elbow where he held it.

"Who discovered it?" I asked, moving slightly away from him.

He let go of me. "British team. Headed by John's father." He nodded back toward the other men. "Now, John's with us, instead. He's a bio-archaeologist, a bone man. He's the one who knows about the people who used to live here. Burials are critical. From the bones we get to know how old the people were when they died, what diseases plagued them, their sex, their ritual practices. Without bones there would be a tremendous gap in the excavation. With them, we can resurrect these people. So far, it's been frustrating for him this year," he said, with a chuckle. "All we've found are the remains of goats, fish, and a few cattle. If he's lucky, he'll find a few camel bones."

I moved farther back from the edge, almost not wanting to know, as though to learn more would draw me closer to this man. For a moment I felt, absurdly, that some force was about to suck me down into the pit, or into some new, uneasy association with him that I had been secretly longing for these past weeks.

The sun had grown stronger. I took a few sips of the beer, the malt scorching my throat.

Marwan Jassim shifted his weight, lifting both hands to his head, running them through his thick hair. His breathing was as distinct to me as carefully played notes on a piano. I avoided looking at him, at his bare shoulders and belly with a faint line of black hair disappearing into his trousers. Again, I felt it was wrong for me to be here beside him.

Then, I saw something flickering in the trench. I pointed it out to him. "Would that be a coin?"

He looked pleased by my interest, as if he had been waiting for me to notice. "That's glass. Glass fragments and potsherds. Helenistic terra-cotta. Most of the coins are in London."

I was hooked. "If that was the depot down there, what was this hill?"

Now, he grinned, broadly. "*Tel.*"

"What?"

"This is a *tel,*" he said, scraping his foot gingerly, as though to avoid crushing something underfoot. "It means 'hill' in Arabic. Millennia of man-made debris that has grown into an elevation. It appears to be a hill, but it's really a large mound. Below your feet are at least two cities separated by a time span of some eight-hundred years from each other and two-thousand years from us. That's what we know. I'm beginning to think, however, that it may go back even a thousand years earlier."

A breeze ruffled my hair, cooling my damp neck, my arms. Only now did I realize how much I had been perspiring.

He took my arm again and pulled me toward the edge. "It's all here. There's enough material to fill five lifetimes. If I look long enough I'll find some of it."

I wanted to say something to mark my feelings in some way. But I said nothing. It was best to say nothing. I moved back and he looked down at my arm which he still held, as if wondering how his hand had come to be there. Then he released me, this time more reluctantly.

"If this is an old trench, why are you working on it?" I said, trying to overcome the blush that I felt rushing to my face.

He stared at me a minute, looking as confused as I by what

seemed to have just passed between us from the touch of his hand on my skin. "It's not the trench I'm here for," he answered quickly. "We're going to dig the *tel* this time."

I looked at the ground near my foot, puzzled. "There's grass growing on it. I mean, how do you know there's anything under it? Maybe it's just a hill."

He smiled, but gave no indication that he thought the question stupid. "In these parts, no hill that juts up from an otherwise flat plain is just a hill. Ever tried digging?"

I shook my head, suddenly wishing that I had read more on archaeology in the past or that I could discern worked flint the way Derek could.

"It's generally assumed that this *tel* itself goes back no further than the Helenistic period when it was a fort. That anything of *real* consequence having to do with Zulaika has been excavated in the surrounding trenches or will be found at the other Portuguese fort in the northern end of the peninsula. But I think this *tel* will prove to be the real treasure."

"Why?"

He shrugged. "A feeling. Just a feeling."

All at once, the workman in the purple tunic appeared behind him. The man hovered silently, a trowel in his hand.

Marwan Jassim turned around. The workman stared at him from dark, sunken eyes. The red-headed man and the other workmen some ways off were kneeling over something.

"Mr. Reese wants you, Sir," the workman said.

Marwan Jassim seemed to grow tense. "Yes. I'm coming, Pardi," he said, then turned back to me. "They want to start."

"I have to go, too," I said, suddenly sure that the workman had been sent so the red-headed man would not have to interrupt us himself. I wondered whether he had seen his colleague's hand on my arm.

"You're welcome to stay and watch, or even dig, Mrs. Monroe."

"Thanks. Not today."

101

He wagged a finger at me. "Come back before the others descend like locusts to see what we've found. Once they see us churning up relics, they'll be merciless. Especially the press. This hill, as you call it, will be bubbling with potsherds, slivers of bones, seals."

"I've never dug before."

"We'll teach you.

"I'm also — well, I don't know how much energy I have. I was pregnant," I said.

His eyes seemed to glaze over at my words. I had no idea why I had mentioned that. Although his feet had not moved, I suddenly sensed that he was further away from me.

"Well — how are you now?"

"I mean, I don't think I should be kneeling a lot."

"Of course. I understand."

"Maybe I could draw some of the things. Take photographs for you."

He nodded and smiled, as if to humor me. "That would be very helpful."

"All right, Dr. Jassim," I said, not quite believing I had offered to do that.

"Marwan" he corrected. "And you'd be very accurate. I can tell by the way you observe things. You look through them and beyond. It's an annoying trait of artists," he said, smiling.

"But we could use someone with a discerning eye. John and I barely have time." He reached out and shook my hand, holding my gaze comfortably. "Have a look around," he said. Then he walked off toward the others.

I stared at his back, dark and slim, his shoulders taught above the light, boyish gait. I glanced down at the trench a moment longer before starting down the hill, my shoes sliding over the gravel. Or *was* it gravel? I bent to pick up a piece of green glass. Its edges were worn smooth, like a small translucent stone. I turned it over in my hand, wondering whether it was part of a broken beer or 7-Up bottle or a centuries-old glass fragment. I slipped it into my pocket.

At the bottom of the hill, out of sight, I emptied the rest of my lager onto the parched rubble, the liquid washing over more broken fragments of pottery. I picked up a piece. It was like the reddish one Marwan had just shown me. Then, I walked on to my car, without looking back.

Again, I rebuked myself for coming. I had been afraid of pain all my life, avoiding the risks that lead to unhappiness. Perhaps this fear had stopped me from searching for more, had led me to stay with Derek and the safe haven of his stability these past years, despite my discontent.

Yet, I was beginning to confront life in a different way now, had started to question things, just like Marwan Jassim said. For ever since our first meeting, I had been seized by a sense of freedom such as I had never felt before. From that day outside my house, this man's spell had trapped me in its web. I could already imagine the emptiness and pain that the end of this type of infatuation would bring. Yet despite these doubts, I had begun to hope — with a surge of guilt — that my web was being equally spun about him.

11

The *Tel*

Some days, to escape the panic that would suddenly consume me as I realized that my life now tied me to Derek far more than before, I would simply go out in the car and drive aimlessly. I drove along the streets of Abu Samra, pretending to myself that I was familiarizing myself with the town, slowly making my way through the cluttered market where latticed balconies jutted out over the streets like watchful mothers and wind-towers crowned old houses like steeples. Then on to the newer neighborhoods still adrift in cinder-blocks and bags of cement. I drove along the sea where the fishing dhows swayed above their luminous shadows and into palm gardens where village men scaled the trunks to harvest the burnished fruit.

But my mind, though fascinated by what lay before me, could barely focus on the landscape. I was like a confused young girl drunk on her new-found power to attract a man. Thinking of Marwan Jassim drove me out of my world and into his with such force that sometimes I grew oblivious to everything around me until I suddenly found myself driving down a street with no memory of how I had arrived. At times, I actually envied that other woman back in New York, that artist and wife who, though feeling suffocated, had been safely buffered from such emotional upheaval.

I had been attracted to other men during my marriage, but never this much. I barely knew Marwan Jassim, had not even found him particularly appealing at first. Yet he now invaded my every thought. It was as if I had been desperately searching for a new path in my life and he had been sent to guide me there. Perhaps it had been his ease at the site — his encouraging me to dig and to sketch his work, his apparent trust in my abilities — that had so disarmed me.

At cocktail functions he would ask me things Derek never did, such as what I hoped to achieve from my painting, where I looked for inspiration, whether I painted from my soul. He seemed surprised when I described my frustration in New York trying to find a gallery to exhibit my work. He asked me what exhibiting would do for me that the actual act of painting did not, told me that one had to learn to enjoy the act of the work itself, *for itself*, rather than for the results.

"Why not just *be?*" he said. "The act of producing is as rewarding as the completed project. Appreciate the rose when it's still a bud."

Certainly, I knew what he meant; yet I rarely worked from this premise. It was always with the final result in mind that I set out on my day's work, not just the pleasure of painting, the *exploration*, as Marwan Jassim described it. Like Derek, I seemed to be always bent on a mission, thinking ahead to the finished endeavor, planning the next one. Otherwise, I thought, I would accomplish nothing. And was not every goal meant to lead or fit into some larger one?

I imagined Marwan Jassim going from trench to trench on the *tel*, investigating, charting. His voice was still clear in my mind from the other day: *You don't want to destroy the context, you want to save the site as is, even if you have to bury it again to preserve it.* I could not imagine reburying a season's work in order to preserve it anymore than I could imagine destroying a canvas in order to save it. Yet *he* could.

Some days I tested my resolve to stay away from the site by

heading straight for the carriageway that led to Saali. I would go through the roundabout to tempt myself, to prove that I could contain this urge to continue on to the village and to the *tel*. When I turned and started back down the same road I had just come up, resisting the temptation, it was a small, but sad victory over myself.

There was a daily English newspaper in Abu Samra. The paper itself was a snowy white, the newsprint inking onto my fingertips like soft tar. Published for expatriates, it included a skeleton of international news and general Gulf news along with local stories — a chronicle of business transactions and bids that were taking place on the peninsula, the official travels of the Abu Samran Sheikhs and ministers, the newest coveted office space available for rent. Sheikh Salim, the Ruler, was frequently mentioned as were the elegant Sheikh Ahmad and his twin, Sheikh Salih. Sheikha Mariam was referred to whenever there was anything pertaining to archaeology or to the museum. Sheikha Budur, apparently out of deference to her status as the Ruler's wife, was never mentioned.

I would peruse the pages at the kitchen table after Derek left for work or when I took a break from painting. I was shocked, at first, to read of the catastrophes that seemed to occur with alarming frequency on the peninsula. An eight year-old boy killed when he fell down an empty well; a mother and her thirteen year-old daughter electrocuted as they cleaned the kitchen refrigerator; a British diver stung by a giant stingray one morning while repairing the jetty; a dhow ferrying women and children to picnic on an island off the coast capsizing and all of the passengers drowned, despite the shallow water, because they could not swim. How could that be, I asked myself. People living on the sea, yet who could not swim? In one horrific incident, Indian laborers from Calcutta who were being smuggled by boat to Abu Samra by a ruthless recruiter were thrown overboard to drown in the middle of the Gulf.

Since the miscarriage, I had become particularly vulnerable to loss, especially the violent taking of life. The gruesome image of

107

poverty-stricken men seeking their fortunes far from home, only to be scavenged by sharks in the crystalline Gulf, lingered in my mind in obscene detail. Since Abu Samra was so small, these incidents seemed all the more tragic. I knew the horrible stories of illegal Mexican, Haitian, and Cuban immigrants in the United States. I had volunteered in a shelter on the lower West Side where some of these people ended up. Yet in the vastness of New York, I had been too removed from their tragedies to dwell on them for long.

Here I saw such men every day, workmen next door squatting over cooking fires, pushing wheelbarrows full of sand, queuing for the cinema in the evenings. In death, I saw them burn on a wood pyre behind our house. I imagined their screams from the sharks, these men whose dreams for a better life had come to such an abrupt, brutal end. I read about them as I sat in the kitchen surrounded by shiny, white appliances designed to content a Western woman so far from home. I felt both ashamed and lucky to be so pampered, and was well aware that it was Derek to whom I owed this comfortable existence at this moment.

Sometimes, the horror of these incidents made me think of what Marwan Jassim had said about expatriates polluting the peninsula. I wanted him to explain to me what it all meant, how it could be that so much suffering happened to such luckless people. And did we "scavengers" have anything to do with it?

One morning, I read the word *Muharram* in the newspaper. It was a word I had heard uttered a lot lately at receptions and dinner parties — a word mumbled, as if giving it prominence in conversation might be risky. The newspaper article was illusive, mentioning only that *Muharram*, the first month of the Muslim lunar calendar, was only three weeks away.

I had already learned that *Muharram* was considered a holy month by *Shia* Muslims who made up the majority of the Peninsula's population. It was a time during which *Shias* grieved the martyrdom of the Prophet Mohammad's grandson, Hussein, who had

108

been slain in a battle that had resulted in Islam dividing into its two sects, *Sunni* and *Shia.*

My neighbor, Mary, whom I had met at the Garden Club, had explained *Muharram* to me. From Huntsville, Texas, Mary had worked briefly as a journalist before coming to Abu Samra with her husband two years ago. In the time she had been here, she seemed to have amassed considerable knowledge about the Gulf and I was impressed by her affection for the Peninsula. Unlike some of the other expatriates I met, she never referred to the Abu Samrans as 'locals' and seemed totally at ease in the downtown *souk* market, as if she were simply strolling down a street in Huntsville. She was considerate in other ways, too. During the first rain storm, when the electricity had gone off in Dafna and Derek had not yet returned home from work, she had knocked on our door and thrust a battery-operated lantern into my hand. "I know you're alone," she had said, as she ran back toward her house in the downpour. We had since become good friends.

Over coffee in my kitchen Mary told me of *Muharram.*

"During the first ten days of the month, the *Shias* mourn not only Hussein but the transfer of the Muslim leadership from the Prophet's kin to the elected *Sunni* Caliphs. Most of Abu Samra's villagers, who regard themselves as the Peninsula's original inhabitants, are *Shia.*"

"What about the Mansours?"

"The Mansours and most of the wealthier merchants migrated here from Saudi less than two hundred years ago. Probably persecuted by other tribes. They're *Sunni. Muharram* is commemorated only by the indigenous *Shia* and it's a time when the villages are immersed in religious and political fervor."

"Why?"

"Both in grief over the ancient martyrs and to mourn their loss of political power to the current rulers. It's a time when outsiders — expats as well as non-*Shia* Arabs — stay away from the villages."

109

"Does it get violent?"

"Everybody's on edge."

I was intrigued. "Have you ever seen these processions?"

She puffed on her cigarette and nodded. "It's a cross between a funeral entourage and a miracle play. It's somewhat sad, but there's an exhilaration too. Like the relief after an exorcism. The men march, beating their chests with their fists. The next day they swing at their backs with metal whips. The last day is the most important. That's when they strike their foreheads with swords."

I winced. "Swords?"

"They don't hurt themselves, but its bloody. The women cheer the men on, since only the men and boys participate. Some carry children on litters to symbolize the wounded in the original battle. Others carry wooden models of tombs. But it's the raw emotion that's so incredible. To watch it as an outsider gives only a small indication of what the participants must feel."

"It sounds ghastly."

She shrugged. "Actually, its fairly peaceful despite the blood. But it *is* shocking. Especially since you don't usually see such high emotion displayed here."

"And they do this every November?"

"It comes two weeks earlier each year, like everything else on the lunar calendar."

Mary spoke softly of the event, much as the other expatriates had. But rather than be frightened of it, she seemed to see it as an expected part of life in a foreign posting. She lit another cigarette. "The ruling family hates it. It's a challenge to their authority, a show of strength by the *Shias*. On the other hand, Abu Samra is one of the few places where the *Muharram* processions are still allowed to take place. But, it doesn't mean the Mansours like it."

"Why do they allow it?"

She smiled. "It keeps down the population's frustrations better than prohibiting it would. Same reason they allow the Indians to cremate despite their own abhorrence for it."

110

I nodded. The outdoor crematorium had grown to be a topic of lively discussion for our visitors. The expatriates found it fascinating, the Arabs, revolting.

I was intrigued by this apparent friction between *Sunni* and *Shia* Abu Samrans that Mary talked about. It was a revelation to me. I had not detected resentment among the Abu Samrans toward anyone. On the contrary, they seemed uncommonly tolerant. I remembered Sheikha Mariam's confident smile, her pretty cousins at the garden club, Sheikha Budur with her artless laugh beneath the dignified gaze. But Marwan Jassim had referred to himself as a 'local'. I wondered if that meant that he was *Shia*.

"Is the ruling family in danger of being overthrown?" I asked.

"It could happen. The government's wary of everything — a coup right here, Saudi Arabia on their flank, Iran's interest in the Gulf."

"Iran?"

"Not a serious threat, but it's there. They wouldn't mind extending their influence over the oil-producing Arab nations." She tapped her ashes into her saucer. "Abu Samra's really a latent volcano. Haven't you noticed?" Smoke rose above her as if to prove her point about the volcano.

"To be honest, I haven't felt any of the problems you're talking about."

"You're still new." She smiled, then put out her cigarette. "You're lucky you don't smoke. Bad habits are easy to get into. Stay a good girl."

There was a mock regret in her voice as she gathered her cigarettes and lighter into her purse. *Stay a good girl.* Was it a warning? Had she already gleaned my troubled feelings?

"Mary, you've lived away from the States a long time."

"Yes."

"Don't you miss Texas?"

She seemed to debate this a minute, staring out the kitchen window. "I miss the actual fact of Texas. But I don't miss the life

111

we had there. Especially not Huntsville."

I laughed. "You're happy here?"

She took a deep breath. "I'm excited by life here. It may be a dreary, small corner of the earth to some folks, but I get to meet fascinating people I'd rarely get the chance to in Texas. Last year we met Thor Heyerdahl when he stopped by on his latest voyage. We met Prince Charles on a state visit. He came to the Garden Club. A lot of — expats — don't get involved here, of course, and miss out on things. Some of them isolate themselves and go a little crazy, I think."

"Crazy?"

"They seem to get reckless being so far from home. They go and do things they'd never ordinarily do. Some people just can't take being out of their own environment too long."

I was silent.

She smiled. "It's like they're in the theater, suspension of disbelief or something. Their whole stay seems unreal to them, so whatever they do doesn't seem to count."

I knew she could have been talking about me. Since first arriving I had felt rewired somehow, straddling a precipice.

"By the way, do you and Derek play bridge?" she asked, obviously unaware of my discomfort.

"A little. We took lessons once."

"Good," Mary said. "I'll call you when the cocktail season's over and we'll play."

"I'd like that," I said, thinking how relaxing it would be to spend a casual evening over a bridge game instead of dressing up to go out and be on display.

As I walked her to the front gate, she turned to me. "Be good," she said, again, as she stamped her cigarette into the sand. I watched her walk back down the dirt road to her own house.

Next door, the ever-present bulldozer was lifting gravel from a heap. Several workmen were mixing cement. Although we had been here nearly three months, the house next door was still not finished.

The bulldozer let loose a torrent of gravel, the dust rising in gusts toward my gate. The grating sound of the huge mouth lifting the rocks reminded me of Marwan Jassim's dig, as if the two were somehow interwoven — Marwan's digging downward to rebuild an ancient city, and this machine building upward. I went back inside, trying to envision Marwan's face, how I had first perceived him standing only a few feet away.

I thought of what Mary had said about watching the *Muharram* procession from a rooftop. She had watched it from somewhere close to Saali. It seemed impossible to envision Saali embroiled in religious frenzy in a few weeks. I wondered whether Marwan would have to stop his dig or whether he would work through *Muharram*.

A weight settled over me as I returned to the house. Despite all my previous efforts to avoid it, I felt that I had to go back to the dig before Saali got caught up in the religious passion Mary described, and all work was forced to stop.

The newspaper article sat in the Renault for several days before I actually veered out of the roundabout and started down the Saali road. The article describing the upcoming month of *Muharram* was mainly a news item about the Abu Samran police and rescue squad preparing for the self-inflicted injuries that would be incurred during the processions. There seemed to be a hint of unrest even in the journalist's dry, dispassionate words. I needed to find out from Marwan Jassim whether he would be stopping his dig.

Reaching the village, I drove along the newly paved road that divided Saali neatly down the middle. My breathing quickened as I passed the cement houses, the mosque, the café with the lush Indian almond trees shading turquoise benches. Although at first I barely noticed the change in the village since a week ago, when I reached the end of the street I caught sight in my rear-view mirror of the green flags draped over the edge of the rooftops. It was like a bleak version of some Irish festival in New York. Green shamrock and clover.

113

But my eyes quickly returned to the road for the first sign of the sea and *tel*. I could not justify my going back to the *tel*, to Marwan, except my natural curiosity about the work he was doing and the fact that I had volunteered to draw for him even knowing it had been a mistake to do so. Moreover, although I was sure that he would be pleased to see me, I hoped he could not detect how much I wanted to see *him*.

There were no cars parked on the beach this time. No breeze. Just a slight bite to the air. A grand silence seemed to crouch above the water which today was as smooth as a sheet of cellophane. I got out of the car and stared up at the hill, disappointed. There was no one in sight. The previously excavated trench at its base that Marwan had called a depot seemed even less defined than when I had first seen it, as if it had been newly coated with a layer of sand. I tried to see it as it must have been thousands of years ago, the crumbling stairs leading into chambers where merchants bargained and laborers hauled in cargoes of local pearls, Mesopotamian grains, Indian gold and ivory. I was continually amazed that such an important, vibrant society had existed on this modest peninsula only to disappear and be forgotten for millennia.

I climbed to the top of the hill. The dig looked abandoned. Wheelbarrows were scattered haphazardly, some tipped forward as if standing at attention. One was filled with dirt-encrusted tools while another sheltered the blue cooler from which Marwan had retrieved the Australian beer the last time I had been there. The table where he and his assistant John Reese had been eating lunch that day had been moved. In its place was a neatly cordoned-off, partly dug square. In one corner of the square the sand was a dark gray.

I looked around, walking to the edge where Marwan had knelt and pointed out the lower trench to me, explaining how meticulous the system of digging was to preserve things as they found them.

I picked up one of the trowels from the wheelbarrow of tools and walked over to an untouched patch where some grasses protruded. I knelt and carefully scraped at the sand. The earth was hard, resisting the metal. I pressed a bit harder on the trowel, scattering small pebbles.

As the earth gave way under my hand, I thought of what I might be disturbing. Marwan had said that he suspected that a grave-complex lay nearby. I stopped scraping, despite the irresistible urge to feel what Marwan did when he explored these depths.

Then I heard the rattle of a motor. From the edge of the *tel* I could see two men, Marwan and John, getting out of the jeep. An Indian workman was with them, carrying a large carton. Marwan looked up, as if assuming all along that I would be there.

"You have to keep it light, confine yourself to this space," he said, demonstrating in delicate strokes the scraping I was to do in a corner of the cordoned trench. "The potsherds are extremely fragile here, so be alert to any hardening under the trowel. Also be aware of animal bone, scraps of metal. Anything."

"You're sure it's O.K.?"

"Of course. We can use the help. I see you've already done a bit," he said.

Although his voice was cheerful, his eyes flitted away from mine, as though he was not sure how to respond to my unexpected appearance.

I knelt down, the pebbles pressing into my knees through my jeans. I scraped the trowel lightly back and forth across the dirt as he had done, my movements feeling awkward compared to his confident strokes.

He squatted beside me. "Don't be afraid. Like this."

His own trowel grazed the sand like a chef skimming flour off a slab of pastry. He watched me a few minutes, blocking the sun from my back. I tried to focus on my hand. The careful emphasis on the motions and muscles of my fingers was like learning to write for the first time.

Across the *tel*, the Indian workman, Pardi, was squatting and scraping a different area. He seemed accustomed to doing this, for his rhythmic movements looked effortless and he seemed to have an infinite ability to remain in this cramped position. Now and then he picked up a large wooden sieve, filled it with the sand that he had just scraped up, and casually shook it about. Dust, in glittering golden flakes, rose above the sieve. His eyes darted away from me whenever I glanced at him, as though he had been secretly monitoring me.

"Remember — potsherds," Marwan said crisply, still squatting beside me. "One of our most valuable artifacts was found a few feet away from here seven years ago. A cuneiform inscription on a small stone altar. It proved the Zulaikans were in contact with peoples outside the Peninsula, in Mesopotamia and India."

My hand stopped. "What if I crush something?"

"You won't."

"Was that the oldest thing you found here?"

"The oldest so far from this *tel*. Part of an older pottery vessel was found near the mounds. It dates to about 2500 B.C."

I scrutinized the earth before me, afraid to continue. Then, before I realized what was happening, he had covered my hand with his, moving it firmly back and forth. "You'll do fine," he said.

I watched our hands guide the trowel against the dirt, sometimes in short spurts, sometimes in gentle sweeps. My hand seemed to burn under his now, although I could barely feel his skin against mine, aware only of his breaths close to my face as I watched our hands, my light fingers covered by his darker ones, angle back and forth.

All at once he said, "It's all a dream, some muddled film, this life in Abu Samra."

"What?"

"The expats' inane cocktail parties, we Arabs with our *In sha Allahs* and interminable thimble-fulls of coffee. The closest thing to real life is buried right here beneath the sand. History. We think we're lucky to have the oil. We don't realize that our moment of glory vanished three thousand years ago."

He spoke as if he personally were responsible for this lacka-

116

daisical attitude of his countrymen, which he felt was becoming a damnable nuisance.

"Wouldn't you call that a superior Western attitude?" I asked.

He stopped scraping, lifted his hand off mine. "How is that?"

"Maybe we value history too much for its own sake. Maybe your people's faith in God's will and their pausing to drink coffee all day is what keeps you sane, what's sustained your culture for so long. What gives you that spirituality which, you say, the rest of us have lost. At least it's good therapy."

He smiled sheepishly. "I'm tripping over my own theories."

I resumed scraping. "You said that people here seem to live for the moment rather than plan long term. They seem satisfied. Maybe they've acquired a certain peace of mind by not pushing too hard."

He smiled again. "You're catching on."

Later, we sat on the ground on the edge of the *tel*, each sipping from a bottle of 7-Up. The sea was turning a deep copper. The water was beginning to smell in the still of sunset, a rich, rotting fish smell, the stench of centuries of living and dying. A month ago I vomited from this smell. Now it was a familiar part of my growing attachment to this old world.

Below us, John Reese was loading tools into the back of the white jeep. Pardi was squatting some distance away on the beach, seeming to stare at the horizon.

"He's meditating," Marwan said, following my gaze.

I felt my own knees ache from having knelt all afternoon. "I can't believe he can crouch comfortably like that."

"Pardi's got infinite patience. He meditates each day before work and every afternoon when we're done. It's second nature to him. He's from the Brahman caste, the highest in India. Used to be mainly priests. His family fell on hard times several generations ago. That's why he's a laborer. He's obviously capable of a lot more, but he never went to school."

117

"Maybe that's why he seems so confident," I said.

"That, and we had a good day," he said. In the morning, John had found two small beads that appeared to be part of a necklace of Islamic vintage which, Marwan explained, could be dated from anywhere within the last thousand years. The dark gray sand in the corner of the cordoned square was probably ash, he said, most likely the remains of a stove or kiln. I had brushed up a bit of bone myself that looked like a chicken's wing.

"See those fishermen over there?" Marwan pointed to two men further down the beach who were examining their fishing nets. They were bare-chested with long loin clothes wrapped around their hips. "I used to help my uncle mend his nets as a child. My family fished for many generations."

"Really?" I said, finding the idea of Marwan Jassim spending his days pulling in nets with the day's catch oddly conceivable. "So you might have been a fisherman?"

"No, I could never have been a fisherman."

"No?"

"My father was a school teacher — the first of his generation to be fully educated. He would yell at me for helping my uncle. It was always books, books, books for me."

"He must have been delighted to see you go on to Oxford."

"He was dead by then."

"I'm sorry."

He shrugged. "He knew I'd get there eventually. But he also knew, I think, that I would have been just as happy fishing."

"Would you?"

His eyes twinkled. "Of course. I'd be happy no matter what I did. Happiness isn't hard to attain. You just make up your mind to be happy. In fact, I *am* a fisherman. I check my nets, my sieves and tools each night for that one special little fish that will solve a piece of the riddle."

"Will *Muharram* interfere with your work?" I asked, finally bringing up the newspaper clipping.

118

"*Muharram?*" He stared at the horizon through the green glass of the 7-Up bottle. "The tenth day, maybe."

"Do you work during *Muharram?*"

"I've always timed my digs so as not to coincide with it, or with the *Haj* which involves endless festivities in the villages. This year it was impossible. So I'll work, discreetly."

"*Muharram* is different from the *Haj*, though."

"Oh yes. The pilgrimage to Mecca is a very positive event."

"Won't it be dangerous to be out here during *Muharram?*"

I envisioned the processions that Mary described, the men flagellating themselves, drawing blood from their backs and foreheads.

Marwan drank the soda in long gulps, then rolled the empty bottle between his palms. "We'll just have to play it by ear. We'll keep John's beer out of sight," he said, winking.

He stood and held out his hand to help me up. "Will you be back tomorrow?"

"I promised to go to the beach," I said, hoping he would not hear the disappointment in my voice. I wanted to come back and work, but it would soon be too cold to swim and Derek had been wanting to go swimming.

"I suppose you go to the foreigner's beach?" he said.

"We go to the one beyond the mounds."

"That's the foreigner's beach. No Arabs allowed."

I looked surprised. "I didn't know that."

He smiled. "Only select members of the royal family are permitted."

"Why?"

"Don't tell me you don't know."

"I *don't* know," I said.

"It's purpose is to keep the Arabs out so that the expats can feel comfortable," he said. I did not have to guess at his underlying meaning. "Be careful," he added. "Some of the Mansours have roving eyes."

"Everyone tells me to be careful here," I said, knowing that he was referring to the rumors that some of the young Mansour Sheikhs propositioned foreign women on the beach. I had never seen it actually happen, though. "The only Sheikh I've actually met, Sheikh Ahmad, is perfectly charming."

"Ahmad's a different kettle of fish, although chasing foreign women isn't entirely beneath him either. Anyway, just thought you should know."

"You think I go for that reason? To meet a Sheikh?"

"Of course not. But be careful, all the same."

We walked down the hill. As he said goodbye, he reached out and shook my hand. Then he leaned down and formally kissed it. "Thanks for your help," he said, as if to apologize, to justify the spontaneous kiss. Then he added, "It's hard not to touch you."

I turned away, despite myself. For he must have known, now, after this afternoon, that he need not worry about the Mansours usurping the claim he had made on my heart.

12

Dinner Party

In November, I suggested to Derek that we invite the two Arab engineers in his office to our home for dinner and I gave him invitations requesting them to bring their wives.

Derek looked amused. "You've got to be kidding."

"I'm not," I said, surprised that he thought so.

"You're wasting your time. Abu Samran men don't take their wives to the homes of foreigners."

"Why not?"

"Local women don't attend social functions with men who aren't their relatives. Have a tea for the wives, instead."

"But we've only invited expatriates since we arrived. Shouldn't we extend the courtesy to your Arab employees? You're their boss, Derek."

"They don't expect an invitation from their employer," he said. "Only the rich elite you see at cocktail parties go to mixed gatherings. Most of the men here never mention their wives to strangers."

I was shocked by Derek's condescending tone and by his lack of interest in getting to know his Arab employees better. Though not senior enough to be invited to the hotel cocktail parties, both of the engineers seemed to be congenial and open to Western ideas. I could not imagine that their wives were so vastly different from them, or that they would refuse a dinner invitation just because men would be present.

"It would be nice to engage with the *real* people of Abu Samra for a change, Derek. How else are we going to know them?"

"I told you — it's not done here. If you insist on inviting the women, tell the men yourself."

Despite Derek's skepticism, I wanted to know Abu Samrans better. Especially since meeting Marwan Jassim. The more I understood his people, the more I would understand him.

Derek's office was still on top of the tailor's shop on the main street of the market. Having given up hope of leasing space in the newer office buildings, Derek had rented three more rooms, expanding into the entire second floor of the old building. It was now a maze of angles and freshly painted walls with three separate offices and a large computer room. Along with the two Arab engineers, there was an Indian accountant and a male secretary from Goa who, Derek complained, spent more time brewing cups of cardamom coffee for the engineers than anything else.

The town was more crowded than usual and I had to park in an alley behind the produce stalls. A salty breeze carried the smells of ripe tomatoes and cantaloupe. Behind the stalls, boxes of mangoes from Thailand and crates of apples and pears stamped with "LEBANON" in large, black letters were stacked into neat pyramids. Once inside the glass doors of USA Electric, however, the medicinal smell of new carpet flushed out all sensual memory of the market.

The head office had commended Derek for finding qualified local staff and the reports sent back to New York by the auditors who had come to Abu Samra cited Derek's operation as exemplary. One of these New York auditors was Peter McCrae. Pete. A short, plump, bald man from Queens, Pete had been in Abu Samra the week that I had arrived and had just returned a second time.

When I entered the office now, he was hunched over the secretary's desk studying data on the computer, his bald pate abnormally pale next to the secretary's thick black hair. He straightened up when he saw me, then bowed, ceremoniously, tipping his hand to his head with a flourish as if to remove an invisible hat.

I smiled at the gallant gesture and, for a moment, considered inviting him to the dinner I was planning. He had a knack for telling jokes and it would be good to catch up on some New York news. But I remembered what Derek had said about the Abu Samran women and mixed gatherings and since I wanted the wives to come, I knew I had to limit the number of men. After chatting with Pete for a few minutes, I went down the hall to look for the engineers.

In their pristine white *thobs* and headdresses, the Arabs gave the room a just-laundered look. I shook hands with them and handed them the invitations, saying that I would very much like to meet their wives. To my surprise, and almost in spite of Derek's warnings, both men accepted immediately, nodding and uttering *In sha Allah*, God willing. I could hardly believe it at first, and repeated that I wanted them to bring their wives. When they assured me that they would, I excused myself and went straight to Derek's room, anticipating his disbelief when I told him how easy reaching out to these men had been.

As the date for the dinner approached, however, I grew nervous. I knew not to serve pork or liquor, both forbidden and offensive to Muslims, yet I was uncertain how to entertain Arabs and even less sure about their food likes and dislikes. I wanted to present Derek as a generous host, as well as to indicate to his employees that he understood and respected Abu Samran traditions of hospitality. Lamb *shish-kebab* and roast chicken were safe choices, with an eggplant casserole and plenty of rice, which I knew to be a staple of Abu Samran meals.

Having heard of the lavish food prepared in Arab households, I planned for twice the amount I would have served to a similar group of expatriates. Still, on the day of the dinner, it did not seem enough. To make things worse, the aroma of cooking spices all day long, usually so agreeable, made my faded morning sickness flare up again so that I had to leave the kitchen at regular intervals.

Until the last minute, Derek insisted that I was fretting for nothing, that the women would not come. "*In sha Allah* means just that. God willing. Maybe yes, maybe no."

"They said they would bring their wives."

"They said *In sha Allah*. Don't be disappointed."

I tried to ignore Derek's cynicism, telling myself that it had been worth the effort of inviting them, even if we did end up having dinner with the men only. However, when I answered the door that night and found the two men standing before me with two young Arab women, I could hardly contain my excitement.

The wives had the trademark Abu Samran blue-black hair and almond eyes and both wore knee-length silk dresses. One had her hair in a ponytail and seemed slightly older and spoke better English, although the other woman could easily manage a conversation. They sat together on the red couch, silently gazing at the dark wood furniture and red drapes. I explained that the furniture and colors had not been my choice, that I would have chosen pastels and lighter wood to give the rooms a cooler look. They nodded, as if agreeing that a blue or green upholstery would have been more suitable for a hot climate.

Although neither woman seemed bothered by Derek's presence, they did not exhibit the carefree joviality that I had seen the Mansour women display at the all-female Garden Club gathering. The older woman bore a striking resemblance to Sheikha Mariam with her delicately sculpted jaw and small nose tapering off in a rounded point. Her name was Awatif and she had a Sociology degree from the University of Baghdad. Currently, she told us, she worked at Abu Samra's juvenile delinquent rehabilitation center. She was newly married and had no children. The younger woman, Alia, was more reserved. She said that she stayed home with her two small boys.

Awatif was so slight and delicate-mannered that it was hard to imagine her supervising delinquents. When I asked her what it was like to work with troubled boys and girls, she corrected me, softly. "All of them are boys. Girls here are protected by their families. They seldom get into trouble."

"Are drugs a problem for the boys?" I asked.

She looked shocked, but kept her same, soft manner. "Never. That is not a problem in Abu Samra. Only some small thefts, running away from home, or not going to school."

"Drugs are a *big* problem in America," I said. "You're lucky."

"If the proper care and attention is provided, a child is never delinquent in Abu Samra," Awatif said. "Ours is a peaceful society." It was hard to contradict this statement, especially when it was uttered in such a hushed, polite tone.

It was evident that she enjoyed her work. There were some twenty boys in the center at the moment, she said, almost all of whom were victims of parental abuse or neglect, or of simple ignorance on the parents' part. The center's program was aimed mainly at helping the boys to readjust to outside life. Nobody ever stayed beyond sixth months. If they could live with their families and be supervised at home, that was preferable.

I was about to ask the younger woman about her children, but Lhatti called me to the kitchen to check on the food. When I passed Derek, he was engaged in a discussion with the men, lecturing them on the crematorium behind the house and the ways in which he might still persuade the Ministry of Health to close it down. Not used to conversing with his employees outside the office, he seemed ill at ease, as if he might lower himself in their eyes by shedding his authority now. I was surprised to see that while he was pouring 7-up into glasses for the women, the two men were already sipping from tumblers of Scotch.

Lhatti set out the roast chicken, eggplant casserole, and grilled *shish kebab* over a large tray of saffron rice. Triangles of Arabic bread were wedged into a basket with a lace napkin, and oleanders from

125

the garden gave the table a sweet, pink fluorescence. In deference to the Muslim guests, I had placed jugs of water and Pepsi on the table instead of the wine we normally served to expatriates.

Then, as the guests began to serve themselves, the doorbell rang.

In the yellow light of the bulb above the front door, looking even shorter and plumper than ever, stood Pete. Behind him, half-hidden by the dark, were three other men. The one closest to Pete had only one arm, the other ending above the elbow. The sight of the man standing further back, a man whose red hair seemed ready to catch fire under the yellow bulb, gave me a start. It was John Reese. Behind him stood a darker man — Marwan Jassim.

Before I could say anything, Pete was ambling towards me. Enveloped in a pungent swirl of whiskey fumes, he took my hand and brushed it to his lips.

"My dear lady," he said.

John Reese and the one-armed man seemed to be slightly embarrassed, as if this had not been their idea. John looked at me, attempting a smile. I nodded, politely, pretending to be meeting him for the first time, feeling an immense, consuming weakness run through me. I glanced behind him to Marwan Jassim who seemed perfectly at ease.

Derek had come up behind me. I waited for him to ask them all to leave, to explain that we had a situation that did not allow for extra men. But instead, to my utter surprise, I heard him tell them to come in.

In the kitchen, retrieving extra plates, I could barely breathe. I turned to Derek who had followed me to help. "You didn't tell me you invited Pete," I said.

"I didn't. He must have overheard the men in the office."

I took Derek's arm. "Can't you get rid of them?"

"Not now, they're already here. Don't worry. There's plenty of food."

"You *must*, Derek. Pete's drunk."

Derek brushed past me. "Gina—"

"Derek, the women!"

He turned back to me. "Believe me, honey," he said, his eyes almost pleading, "these fellas'll be the life of the party."

It occurred to me then that Derek was secretly relieved by the unexpected appearance of the expatriates, happy that he would not be left to entertain the Arabs alone.

In the dining room, the guests were circling the table, filling their plates. The women and I returned to the sitting room to eat while the men remained standing around the dining table listening to Derek talk about the Saali project.

Derek had explained to me, beforehand, that the custom was for the women to sit separately from the men and I was relieved for the excuse to stay away from Marwan Jassim. I began to worry again, but this time not about the Abu Samrans. I tried to hear what Marwan and Derek were talking about, afraid that Marwan or John might say something about my going to Saali. My greatest struggle tonight would be to act as if Saali meant absolutely nothing to me.

The women ate quietly, then returned to the table and refilled their plates. This time, they ate only a few bites, leaving their plates half full. I was puzzled, wondering whether something was wrong with the food. Finally, I helped Lhatti gather up the half-full women's plates along with the half-full ones of their husbands, and carried them to the kitchen. Only the expatriates had finished off their food. Lhatti brought out the tray of grapes and melon and another filled with Abu Samran sweets. Again, the women and I filled our plates and went to the sitting room.

I was beginning to enjoy Marwan Jassim's presence in our dining room. An almost delicious moment of danger gripped me before sanity returned. Derek himself seemed more relaxed now with the expatriates present. Although Marwan made no attempt at conversation with me, he frequently glanced in my direction. Pete and Derek, meanwhile, were discussing the home office in New York.

127

All at once Pete left the men and came into the sitting room, lowering himself into a red velvet wing chair and closing and opening his eyes several times as if trying to concentrate. He began to softly hum what sounded like "Danny Boy," as he picked up a crystal ashtray from a side table and twirled it on his fingertip.

"My dear lady," he said, finally, putting down the ashtray and drawing me into focus. "You and I have met before."

At first I pretended not to hear. The Arab men had followed him into the sitting room and were sipping their coffee in silence, their eyes swinging from Pete to me and back to Pete who had continued to fix me with his stare. I could not believe that Pete, who had been to Abu Samra before and must have been aware of the protocol regarding men's behavior toward women, was acting so callous. Awatif seemed slightly amused, as if Pete were simply an overgrown, Western version of one of her delinquent boys. I took heart from her placid demeanor and tried to shrug off Pete's bold glances.

"We've met before — " he began, again.

"Yes, a few days ago in the office," I said.

His smile grew. "No, no, no." I felt his eyes travel across my face and down to my breasts. "We have met in some other life."

The Abu Samrans looked intrigued. I swallowed, my anger turning to a fiery lump in my throat. I glanced at Derek who was still in the dining room. The Abu Samrans, too, looked at Derek, as though wondering how he was going to handle this man's behavior. I could see Marwan staring at us, watching Pete.

The lamps felt too bright. The room seemed too hot. I could almost hear the mocking thoughts of the Arab women and their husbands. I was sure that to the Abu Samrans I must have seemed shameless to even tolerate Pete's presence at this point. I wanted to explain that I was innocent, that I had not asked for Pete's attention. Yet I felt as guilty as if I had made a pass at him myself, knowing that my role as Derek's wife in this large, expatriate house was a charade. Perhaps I had no right to be offended by Pete's unwanted lust. In my mind, I was already an adulteress. For even now I was thinking of a man other than my husband.

Pete mumbled something in his whiskey-drenched voice. I tried to smile, hoping he would leave before he said or did something completely bizarre.

Finally, it was Marwan Jassim who appeared behind Pete. He prodded Pete on the back, saying that it was time to leave. My eyes met Marwan's for a moment. I thought he might say something and I felt my eyes go blank with fear. But he simply thanked me for the dinner. I tried to smile, as if nothing uncomfortable had occurred. Then, the four men left, John and the one-armed man supporting Pete as they walked carefully toward the garden gate.

Later, after Lhatti had cleaned up and gone home, Derek and I remained in the kitchen as he finished a glass of wine.

Never again, I thought, rinsing a silver tray. I was baffled. The guests seemed to have liked the food, but the Abu Samrans had left plates of *shish kebab* and rice practically untouched. Derek, seeming to sense that something was wrong, put his hand on my shoulder. "I told you not to bother, Gina. This isn't the sort of gathering they're used to."

I swung around to face him. "You should never have allowed Pete to stay."

Derek looked surprised.

"He was *drunk*," I said.

"He's just homesick."

"You didn't see how insolent he was to me! In front of your employees and their wives!" I dropped the tray into the sink. Metal clashed against metal. I wanted to break something, just as Derek had destroyed my attempt to host a cordial dinner by allowing Pete to stay.

"Forget it, Gina."

"I was humiliated, Derek. He insisted that we knew each other romantically in some other life."

Derek chuckled. "Take it as a compliment. So, he finds you sexy. A lot of men do."

"He's an arrogant fool," I said, in no mood to joke or be given compliments. "I was ashamed of him, ashamed that those people had to see an American behaving that way." My fingers circled a crystal goblet. I squeezed hard, suddenly breaking the stem. Surprised, I dropped it onto the floor.

Derek came to me, looking confounded. I shrugged him off and knelt down to pick up the glass. I started to cry. Although I tried to move away, Derek put his arms around me and lifted me up. "Gina. He's just a lonely man. You're probably the best thing he's seen since he's been here."

"You don't understand, Derek. Damn it, you don't even care!"

He looked at my face, as if to avoid the jagged fragments of crystal in my hands. "How can you say that, Gina?"

Of course, there was no way Derek could have understood at this point that my humiliation in front of the guests was not the real cause of my fury. He had no way of knowing that the grief I felt was not because Pete had made such brazen advances with his eyes all over my body, but that I wanted it to be Marwan. Derek took the brunt of my anger. For he was unable to do anything, unable to stop me in any way from wanting Marwan so much.

Then, I heard him say something, his voice so low that it took a moment to understand what he said:

"If he ever does it again, I'll kill him."

I looked at Derek, startled by the sudden harshness in his tone. But instead of being happy that he was vowing to protect me from Pete, I selfishly felt trapped instead, as if he had brought me back to a reality I was desperately trying to escape.

The next afternoon I drove to the *tel* again. Marwan was not at the site when I arrived, so John told me to help Pardi scrape a corner of the trench at the bottom of the hill, an area first excavated, apparently, by his father. An hour later Marwan arrived. At first, he seemed to avoid me, keeping off to the side and going over papers with John. Later, however, he came over to where I was digging and leaned on an overturned wheelbarrow nearby to jot things in his notebook as he did each evening, recapping the day's activity.

Finally he spoke. "We surprised you last night."

I looked up.

"It wasn't intentional. Pete met us in town and insisted everyone was invited to dinner with him. It wasn't until you opened the door that I realized whose house it was. They've done some work on your street. I hardly recognized it."

"I'm afraid I didn't hide my disappointment when you walked in. I was worried that the women would be embarrassed with so many men present."

Marwan chuckled. "Abu Samran women can handle men. They just appear shy and vulnerable. They're not at all."

"Really?"

"It's all an act. Maybe to make the men feel good. They're really very strong-willed, bossy, even," he said.

"I didn't know they were that independent."

"That depends on your notion of independence. Women here think they live better than anyone. Labor is cheap so they can afford cooks and chauffeurs and nannies, even the poorer housewives have family to help them out. I think they pity Western women. They certainly wouldn't trade places with you."

"They may have a point." I stood up and stretched my legs. I thought of my harried life in New York which had seemed to start as soon as Derek left for the office each morning and end when he came home, often late, without my remembering much of what had gone on during the hours in between when I painted or took a class. That life seemed to belong to another person now, the years rolling into one long blur of days spent gearing for the weekend when the routine of the week would temporarily halt and Derek and I could enjoy an outing to a restaurant or museum together. But in the last

131

years Derek had lost interest even in short recreational activities, bringing home more and more work from the office even on weekends.

"How do you know Pete?" I asked Marwan.

"John met him in some hotel bar."

I wanted to ask what he and Derek had talked about last night, but could not bring myself to.

"The food was delicious," he said, suddenly.

"Everyone seemed to leave so much on their plates. I thought something was wrong."

He laughed, blowing some dust off his notebook. "They were just being good guests," he said. "A guest's duty here is to indicate that the host has fed him well. To finish everything on our plates suggests that we're still hungry. Old Bedouin custom."

"Are you serious?"

"Oh yes. We always serve ourselves generous second helpings and then leave some of it uneaten. It's the polite thing to do."

I laughed in relief. "I was so embarrassed."

"Don't be. It's all new to you."

After a moment I said, "You seem to fit into your traditions so well despite your being so modern in other ways."

He shrugged. "My roots are here. I actually belong everywhere. But I can't imagine not being in Abu Samra at least part of the year. I'd go mad confined to London. Here I see people who are actually happy. I rarely see that in England anymore."

"Things *are* different here. I'm learning to see color a new way. The extreme light does interesting things to it."

"Yes," he said, as if he understood perfectly. He added, "One man couldn't pry his eyes off you last night."

I knew at once by his amused expression that he was talking about Pete. "He was drunk."

"Actually it didn't show until he saw you."

"I was afraid he would do something awful and embarrass those women," I said.

"You handled him expertly."

"I don't know about that."

"I would have interfered, but I could see you didn't need any help," he said.

I guessed that he had been watching Pete the entire time. I wondered what he really thought, whether he was puzzled that Derek had not intervened and whether he had any idea how I had wished *he* had been flirting with me instead of Pete.

Suddenly, the scratching on his notebook stopped. "John was impressed by your husband," he said. "I suppose you haven't brought him to the site yet."

"No, I haven't."

"Perhaps you should."

"Why?" I was surprised and disappointed that Marwan would suggest Derek be included in what I regarded as our private scenario.

"If he sees the work we're doing, he might accept your coming here."

"He doesn't mind that I'm here," I said. "He knows I like prowling about ruins, as he puts it. I try to get him to go look for flint heads. He's very good at recognizing them. Sometimes we go to the mounds and I sketch — "

"Then why do you always act so tense," he interrupted, "get that scared look on your face when you feel you've stayed a bit later than you should?"

I was not aware that he had noticed my discomfort each afternoon as I started for home, anticipating that Derek would be asking me about my day.

I turned my attention back to where I had been scraping, not expecting him to understand my guilt at being away from the house for long lengths of time just to be here, even though Derek was gone all afternoon. I wondered whether he was disappointed by my answer, whether he wanted me to say that Derek was jealous of the hours I spent here.

All at once Marwan came and stood over me as I brushed at the spot that I had been digging earlier.

"The colors of the sand, the bits of bone, they remind me of Georgia O'Keeffe's paintings," he said, suddenly.

I looked up. "Are you a fan of hers?"

"Of her desert landscapes. How about you?"

"I like her work. But I think of her as singularly American. I don't picture you in the Southwest," I said, instantly feeling a grin spread across my face.

"I like what she does with bones, their scorched whiteness filling up those arid spaces on the canvas. It's a work of genius."

"Derek never liked her work," I said. "I guess I assumed that most men don't. Especially her flowers."

"Men aren't supposed to like flowers?" he said.

I thought of their intense sensuality that supposedly did not appeal to men. "I just meant he was never eager to go to any exhibitions of her work."

"Perhaps it has to do with the desert. I like the desert."

"Maybe it does."

"Tell me," he said abruptly, as if something just occurred to him. "What is it exactly between you two?"

I ceased brushing. "What do you mean?"

"Well, he seems a reasonable enough chap, gives you a good life, a big house. Provides you with security. Isn't that what women want?"

I felt as if I had to tighten my fingers by force around the trowel to keep it from slipping out of my grip. "You think the only thing women want are big houses and security?"

"So, there *is* something wrong," he said.

"Did I give that impression last night?"

He shook his head. "I've seen you two together. And not just last night. You never connect. *You* always seem to be searching for something, for *someone* just over the horizon, and he seems unaware that you even exist. A damn fool, if you ask me."

I stood up. "I didn't ask you."

He put out his hands. "Sorry. I've trespassed."

I stared at him coldly. He had just ripped away the warm bond I felt earlier working so close to him. I suddenly felt exposed.

"Forget it, please," he said. "I had no right."

"It's really nobody's business."

When I started to pick up the tools I had been working with, he said, "Please don't go."

The honesty in his voice surprised me even more than what he had said earlier about Derek and me. I stood, holding the tools in my hand as if desperate to get rid of them.

"Have you ever been married?" I asked, suddenly.

The question obviously surprised him. "Briefly. After I got back from studying in England."

"What happened?"

"We had nothing in common. Didn't last a year. Some ten years ago."

I was relieved to have finally asked him this. "So you know marriage can be difficult sometimes."

He nodded. "She wanted more security. More money. She didn't undertand that the wealth I was looking for was right under my feet."

I took a deep breath. So, even half the globe away marriages ended up being mistakes. I relaxed a bit. His own marital failure made mine and Derek's seem somehow less so.

Then he said, "I've been wanting to tell you how much I liked the painting of the shrine on the beach you did the other day. The one with the smashing sunset. That's really what reminded me of O'Keeffe."

"Thank you."

"I'm impressed by your ability to create something so completely beautiful in a matter of minutes," he went on. He looked sorry, almost like a small boy trying desperately to get on his mother's good side after some transgression. I had to fight a blinding urge to go and hug him and tell him that he was forgiven.

"If the light's right, I sometimes get lucky."

"I want to buy it from you," he said.

"You don't have to buy it. I'll give it to you."

"But I want to buy it," he said. "It's my favorite view of the beach and you caught it perfectly."

"Consider it sold then."

The silence thickened around us until I thought I would choke. I was confused, and yet not sure if Marwan was causing it or if my conflicting emotions were the cause. At times, he acted like a lover, flattering me, guiding me as I dug, hovering above my shoulder so that the heat from his legs seared my back as though he were actually touching me. Other times, such as when he had brought up Derek, I felt as if my feelings meant nothing to him at all. He seemed to have put me into a sealed box, one which he was tempted from time to time to open in order to peek inside or perhaps caress its contents, before quickly locking it again for fear that something might escape.

I sat back in the dirt, staring at the sea, wanting to be let out of that box so that he could really see me, understand all that I felt for him. But I knew I had to change the subject.

"So why were settlements as important as Zulaika abandoned forever?" I asked.

He squatted down beside me, scooping up bits of earth and lightly sifting the dirt through his hands, feeling for anything. I felt his body loosen, as if he too were freed by this diversion. "In these parts, usually because a major well or water source had dried up. Streams changed course, or climatic conditions became intolerable. Sometimes there was a severe economic drought that literally killed a thriving civilization."

I watched as he brushed at the dry ground as though to check something. I loved his intuitive skill, how he instinctively knew when something of importance lay beneath his touch. He had told me himself that the sound of the trowel on the earth was different when there was pottery below.

136

Earlier, John had apparently found fragments of a clay storage jar several feet away. Embedded in the hard dirt, the red clay handle sticking up from the ground, it turned out to be part of a larger oil jar some fifty centimeters long. Marwan had immediately speculated that it was 'Zulaikan.' They had pieced together its perfectly round handles, its graceful mouth and broken cone base. A torrent of optimism flooded over the two of them. Even the workmen stood by mesmerized as John and Marwan carefully chipped and brushed at the dry mud, holding the fragments as if they were precious gems.

They had poked and dusted to dislodge the dirt, talking all the while about Middle Bronze settlements. When they had looked at it more carefully, however, both had concluded that the jar bore stronger resemblance to Hellenistic work.

"Were Hellenistic jars like the one you found today actually imported from Greece all those years ago?" I asked Marwan now.

His whole body seemed to relax, as if his formal knowledge fortified him, made him safe from the strain his own personal views on my life had brought us moments ago.

"Probably copied," he said. "Alexander's armies passed through here more than once, trying to gain control of the incense trade. Arabia was injected with Hellenistic customs and practices and goods even in the short span of his life. His silver *drachma* was used, even Greek building styles and earthenware items were copied. You can see some of the wells built by the Greeks and perfectly lined with stone still in use today in the north of the peninsula."

I shook my head, amazed.

Finally he stood up and sighed. "What I would give for a good surveyor."

"Won't the government provide you with one?"

"Wishful thinking." Then he pointed at the shards of the jug of that morning that they had placed on some blankets while they drew and cataloged the pieces. "Priceless," he said, almost sadly.

He slipped the trowel into his pocket. "Let's call it a day, Mrs.

Monroe. It's getting late. I have to give you up to your husband now."

I smiled, as if this were a joke.

"Let's get it over with. Don't torment me further," he said, his voice suddenly flat.

I continued to smile, despite the emptiness that churned in me. This time, as we parted, there were no polite, impromptu hand kisses from him.

I drove home through Saali. With *Muharram* only days away, more green flags hung outside the houses. The village had become unusually congested in the afternoons, people gathering in the street, the grocery store, the barber shop. Men sat on the blue benches of the cafe beneath the trees, some with their feet tucked under them, absorbed in talk. Women tended more than usual to turn their heads away when I drove by now, drawing the rims of their shawls across their faces. I had grown accustomed to this display of modesty, however — the village women's instinctive need to shield themselves from the eyes of a stranger, even a female stranger.

In the evenings, the impulse to stop the car in the village and make a few sketches was almost irresistible. Unlike in the mornings, once the sun dropped beyond the rooftops, the colors of the village walls grew sultry by nightfall, the entire scene soaked in a reddish incandescence. Yet I never stopped until I was well past the main street when I could pull over to the side less noticeably.

This afternoon, however, my thoughts stayed with Marwan, to what he had asked me about Derek and me. I hated the thought that he knew something was wrong, that he might somehow think that I was looking for romance.

I suddenly thought of Madame Shams back in New York, of her warning that Derek should be careful. There had been something about another man. Had she been referring to Marwan Jassim? Had she known about him, even then? I wondered what expla-

138

nation she would give for his entering my life, now, and for causing such chaos.

But I did not need Madame Shams to explain what I already knew. Marwan had shaken me from a deadly sleep and ruthlessly exposed me to an entirely new world. I had not felt so alive in years, with the brilliant taste of life on my tongue.

How far was I willing to take this? When I was beside Marwan, the risks of such involvement were swallowed up in the exquisite pleasure of the moment. It was only when I was alone again, driving home through Saali, that I was able to focus on the full threat of his presence in my life.

13

Sheikha Mariam

Looking back, I am amazed at the scenes which I had completely missed or ignored. The tremors began to shake the peninsula even then. I recall how the village women averted their eyes from my passing car, the slight, curt motion of the hand as it drew the thin shawl across cheeks and nose. It was no longer simply a gesture of feminine modesty. It was a gesture of separation, a stone wall erected between an indigenous woman and a foreigner in that delicate piece of cloth.

Certainly the other expatriates must have felt the shifting sands underneath our feet. There was talk of the mounting tension between Iran and the other Gulf states, of the Mullahs in the streets of Teheran protesting against Saudi Arabia, reckless fervor that I now see was carefully edited and briefly televised each night on the news. But none of it had seemed to threaten our reality in Abu Samra. Even when my father called from New York to ask if we were all right, it had taken me several moments to realize that he was worried about the unrest in Iran.

Despite the upheavals elsewhere, it appeared to me at least that a certain calm coated the peninsula, folding us into its protective wings. We were moving from the dense heat of summer and fall into the pleasant cool of winter. In Abu Samra, even my feeling for the seasons was changing. It was the first time in years that I was eager for winter. There was a different life-cycle now, winter no longer signifying death, spring and summer a rebirth. Instead, winter with its copious rains meant new life, a reprieve from the asphyxiating heat. Flowers, dead beneath the hot sands of summer, nudged routes through the porous, rain-drenched earth. November through February became the months of renewal instead of hibernating slumber as they were in North America.

The desert beyond the crematorium joined enthusiastically with this new life, erupting in a carpet of dandelions. The flaming yellow flowers, weeds in my other life in New York, were a welcome sight here in the desert, a harbinger of cool weather, of blooming gardens and abundant crops. Each time it rained, the dandelions unfolded further, reaching for the horizon. As I painted from my roof early in the morning, Manhattan faded in memory taking my loss with it. Instead, my eyes sought out Saali and its now fertile sands and the *tel* further on, skirting the sea. And Marwan on top of his mound, his profile reminding me of a Babylonian god.

In town, though, the rains halted everything. Alleys quickly flooded from the frenzied showers, causing deep pockets of water to accumulate. For days afterwards, cars would ply the drenched streets like dazed alligators, often abandoned in the middle of a lane, their wheels completely submerged in water. Women hoisted up their *abayas* to cross streets, baring previously hidden calves and ankles. Men leaped over the puddles, daintily lifting the hems of their winter *thobs* to keep them from getting wet.

After a rain, 'Abbas always insisted on driving me downtown himself, claiming that only Derek's Buick could tread the water safely. I had sensed that the driver secretly resented the independence the Renault had given me these past months. Nevertheless, I was almost happy for the diversion of his cranky presence, bringing back as it did the memories of my first days in Abu Samra when things had been blissfully tranquil. As reassuring as his presence was, however, I didn't hesitate to dismiss 'Abbas the moment we got home to Dafna where, within minutes, I got into my work clothes and headed the Renault toward Saali.

The villages clearly thrived on the rain. Instead of the muddy onslaught on the town's alleyways, the rain quenched the thirsty fields. Village men tilled the soil alongside the road, heavy sweaters pulled over long, cotton loin wraps. Even the village women were more visible in the cool weather, striding from village to field and back with baskets of greens on their heads.

I warmed at the thought of Saali each time I approached it. The village, despite its lackluster newness, had come to be linked with the hours each week I spent with Marwan. Sometimes, to hold back my eagerness to see him, I would stop just where the village's mina-ret and the first house with its maroon wall came into view. With colored pencils, I would quickly draw the lucid browns and grays of the street, the ecru of the sand, the purple shadows of damp houses, the dusky green of the palm trees; the *tel* in the distance. Having done a sketch or two I would begin to relax. Then I would get back in the car and drive the rest of the way to the beach to help Marwan document the strata.

Even the cocktail parties had dwindled in late October, allow-ing us the newly discovered luxury of evenings in front of the televi-sion. With our nights freer, Mary and her husband, Frank, invited Derek and me over to play bridge. We met Thursday nights before the Friday weekend, and although they were the better players, they seemed to enjoy playing with us as much as we did with them. I even had time at the end of the month to unpack my sewing ma-chine and make a Halloween costume for myself, stitching bright *sari* fabric into a gypsy skirt. Derek put on his usual Charlie Chaplin hat, pasted tufts of blackened cotton above his lip, and we went to the cocktail party at the American Embassy.

I made a few trips to the *souq* downtown where I bought cop-per pots to use as planters, and beige silk *sari* fabric for cushions.

The cushions toned down the red of the living room drapes, considerably lightening up the room. I also had several of my watercolors of Saali framed and hung in place of the English hunting lithographs ordered by the New York decorator. Although Derek objected to altering anything in the original house decor, a few days later he admitted that the watercolors were refreshing and that he much preferred them to the hunting scenes. Perhaps he was encouraged, too, by my obvious attempts to relate to our new home.

October and November were also filled with ladies' luncheons, lavish affairs given by the French, American, and Japanese embassies, as well as by American and British members of the Garden Club. There were teas at the homes of the Arab women too — Lebanese and Syrian wives of diplomats and businessmen as well as a few prominent Abu Samran ladies. I received an invitation to one such tea given by Sheikha Mariam, a *henna* party for one of her female relatives.

It was an honor to have been invited by the Sheikha, Derek had said, with obvious pride. The Mansours were apparently selective when asking expatriates to their homes, especially newcomers.

Even Mary, when she heard that the invitation was to a *henna* party, a women's ceremony held days before a wedding and during which the bride's hands and feet were decorated with *henna,* gushed, "Now I'm downright envious, Gina Monroe." I was surprised myself by the invitation. For except for our brief conversation at the Garden Club, I had not seen Sheikha Mariam often enough to consider myself a candidate for such exclusive consideration.

'Abbas drove me to the Sheikha's palace in the secluded Mansour compound. We rode into the desert, past the distant ruins of the older palaces with their shadowy, ornate arches and decaying wind towers. The current palaces, which I had seen only from a distance when Derek had pointed them out to me, towered above the dunes even further into the desert. They seemed to have purposely been built far from the beach, as if from some tenacious, primal need of the Mansours to retain their lofty Bedouin origins rather than ally themselves with the peninsula's indigenous sea-faring and farming population.

From the outside, the Sheikha's palace was a simple, two-story villa of white-painted cement. The interior, however, presented a much richer image. A robed female servant ushered me into a grand, marble salon awash in bouquets of lilies and orchids. Gold encrusted chairs lined the walls of the room and were already filled with seated women. Most of the guests appeared to be Abu Samrans, dressed in the traditional gold-embroidered chiffon gowns that hung to the floor. Even the older ladies shone in glittering pink, green, azure, magenta.

I followed several women down the line of guests already seated, shaking hands, watching as the Arabs greeted one another with kisses on either cheek. As at the Garden Club, the resemblance in the faces of the Mansour women was evident in the crescent curve of the brows, the slight droop of the eyes, the small, fleshy noses. All indelible family traits. The Ruler's wife, Sheikha Budur, was seated in a large arm chair. Next to her, covered from head to ankles by a transparent white veil, sat the bride. I could see the outline of her wide eyes and rouged mouth under the veil and wondered if she were one of the young Mansours I had seen at the Garden Club meeting. Beneath the hem of her white gown peeked two small, bare feet propped on a cushion, painted in lacy swirls of black-orange dye. The only other visible part of her body were her palms, which were being decorated by a woman seated on the floor beside her.

I shook hands with Sheikha Budur and greeted the immobilized bride. From the Ruler's wife, I thought I detected an involuntary yet distinct glance at my belly, as if she remembered me and what she had wished for me at the Garden Club meeting.

When I reached an empty chair at the other end of the room, I sat down next to a young Arab woman in a business suit. An attendant in a bright flowing shawl immediately appeared and poured me a small glass of tea.

145

"Welcome, welcome," came a voice above the murmuring. Sheikha Mariam, wearing a radiant blue gown, was walking toward me.

"Your Excellency," I said, mesmerized, "this is lovely."

Her eyes glowed, mischievously. "Our version of your 'stag party.'"

"I'm sure none of our stag parties compare to this," I said, picturing the usual bikini-clad woman springing out of a cake for the groom, or a jaded male-stripper for the bride.

The Sheikha glanced fondly at the veiled figure. "She's my niece."

"Congratulations."

She chuckled. "We will celebrate for the next weeks until her wedding, until she is so tired she will beg to be taken to her groom's house for some rest."

I smiled. "Such beautiful patterns on her feet."

Sheikha Mariam nodded. Then, after a brief pause she asked, "How is work?"

"Work?"

"At Saali."

I was surprised by her change of tone and that she knew that I went there. "I'm not actually working. Dr. Jassim simply tolerates my curiosity."

She continued to smile. "I mean your painting. Marwan tells me that you paint the villages."

"I do mostly watercolors, your Excellency," I said, even more surprised that Marwan had talked to the Sheikha about me. "I've been sketching parts of the excavation for Dr. Jassim, but I find the villages charming."

The Sheikha cocked her head. "I've not heard anyone praise Saali for its charm before, but foreigners seem to find things of interest in Abu Samra. Sometimes they point out places we've never even noticed ourselves."

"I see new things every day, Your Excellency."

146

Her eyes narrowed, slightly. "Will you show me sometime? I would like to see your paintings, even your site drawings." She glanced across the room at some arriving guests, then turned back to me. "I am at the site many evenings."

I felt as if I had just been slapped on the wrist although there was no change in the Sheikha's gracious manner. She had certainly never come when I was there. Did she purposely wait until we all left?

"I'm too busy to go during the day," she continued, as though reading my mind. "Digging, however, is my first love, not the administrative work of the Ministry."

She moved away now, extending her hand to another guest. I took a sip of tea, savoring the unexpected cardamon flavor, watching as Sheikha Mariam exuded the same courtly welcome to several other expatriate women who had just entered the room. I recognized them. Like me, they seemed awed by the shimmering swells of chiffon and fresh blossoms. Meanwhile, the attendant came up again to refill my tea glass.

I sketched the room in my head — the rounded shapes of the elder women as they sat hunched in their chairs, their gowns sweeping the shiny floor; the ebony hair of the younger women spreading across their faces like veils whenever they bent to kiss one another; and the mysterious figure concealed in white, patiently being adorned. Smells and colors as hypnotic and aromatic as a roomful of rose petals.

My thoughts returned to Sheikha Mariam's trips to the site. I wondered whether she went simply to check on the excavation's progress or whether she was looking for something more specific. I assumed Marwan knew of her visits although he had never mentioned them to me. And they obviously talked about me. I began to wonder if I had been invited this morning because of Marwan, or the Sheikha's interest in learning more about me for what reason I could not immediately discern.

We were soon ushered into the dining room where an exquisitely set table held silver platters of food. Indian *samosas*, meat and cheese pies, French pastries, *baklava*, dates, and a seemingly endless array of tiny Abu Samran cookies arranged like mosaics on glimmering trays. I helped myself, remembering to take a few extra savories to leave on my plate.

I watched the uninhibited gaiety of the Sheikhas. In sharp contrast to their usually reserved appearance in the streets, in private gatherings Arab women obviously felt free to behave with the abandon of elated schoolgirls. It was as if an individual's true feelings had to be hidden from public scrutiny in a country so small and insular.

We were presently summoned back to the sitting room where the bride had remained, still totally concealed except for her slender fingers which she now held splayed apart for the lacy henna to dry. It was already afternoon, and I thought it was probably time to leave. Yet there seemed to be a sudden air of anticipation that made me hesitate.

Sure enough, an elderly woman draped in a white shawl suddenly appeared and seated herself in the middle of the floor. On a tambourine the size of a drum, she began to beat out a slow, haunting rhythm that instantly brought a hush to the room.

Some of the women closed their eyes and began to keep time with nods of their heads as the beats grew louder. The old woman began a crooning chant, like the pounding of waves on some distant shore, accompanied by the thudding jingle of the tambourine. Women began to clap while others, including Sheikha Mariam, joined the singer in the center of the room. Lifting the hems of their gowns, they began to rock from side to side, swaying their hips, moving in slow circles around the singer. They shook their shoulders flirtatiously, approaching each other as if they would touch, then moving apart again. Every so often a woman would throw her head forward, letting her black hair cascade to the floor, while another would shuffle over to the bride and shake her own hair about her as if anointing her with some special blessing.

Finally, the singing and dancing stopped as unceremoniously as it had started and the singer left the room.

Female servants now strolled in carrying trays with brass coffee pots.

I knew that the pale, cardamom coffee served in tiny cups signaled the end of a party, so I was surprised when more servants followed the first group in, with what appeared to be trays of smoke. Plumes of burning incense swirled alongside assorted bottles of French perfume that were now being offered to the guests. Intrigued, I patted a few drops from a bottle of Chanel onto my wrist. When the trays were offered to the Arab women, however, they reached first for the incense burners, passing the clouds of smoke over the loose folds of their clothes and wafting it into their hair. Sheikha Mariam herself held a burner above the head of the bride, fanning the aroma about her.

I suddenly saw ancient Zulaika before me, the Sheikha a priestess performing a sacred rite over the bride. As I rose with the others to leave, barely able to look away from the few remaining women still dousing themselves with smoke, I felt like laughing out loud, both at my own ignorance of this intricate society, and at my own previously limited life. I could understand, suddenly, Marwan's ridicule of the arrogance of expatriates who assumed that Abu Samra was a backward place needing the skills and experience of the West.

"The idea is to leave smelling as good as when you came," Marwan said the next day, amused by my fascination with the passing of the perfume and incense at the end of the party.

"It was like a dream," I said.

"*Henna* parties are exclusive events. To be invited means that you're well liked."

"I feel lucky," I said.

"It's not a matter of luck. You make your own luck, your own opportunities. The Sheikha likes you. She's very intuitive. She knew you would appreciate such an event."

"She seems so wise."

"She is wise, but she doesn't let her mind rule her feelings. She listens to her instincts."

I glanced at him, wondering what the Sheikha's instincts told her about Marwan's dig. To my surprise, however, when I related to Marwan what Sheikha Mariam had said about coming to the dig in the evenings, he looked neither shocked nor cross.

"The Sheikha supervises all the sites as part of her job. Sometimes we go over the work together."

He was rinsing the tools in water poured by Pardi from a heavy plastic jug. He did this with the same delicacy he used when brushing a potsherd, rubbing the hardened dirt from the trowels as though he might break the tools or miss a small bead or perhaps a tooth if he used force. I wondered what it would feel like to be touched and caressed by such caring hands.

"You told her I paint here," I said.

He looked at me. "Did you not want her to know? She was curious about you. I didn't think you'd mind." He stood and handed the tools to Pardi who took them back to the wheelbarrow. "I also told her you were getting to be a pretty good digger."

Despite being upset that my privacy had been invaded in my absence, I realized my pique was due to the obvious fact that the Sheikha and Marwan had many private talks about work or other matters.

If Marwan had been aware of the true source of my resentment, however, he did not let on. I felt foolish, suddenly, for being so sensitive. "She seems interested in art."

"She is," he said. Then, after a pause he added, "She's engaged to be married."

"Sheikha Mariam?"

"To her cousin, Sheikh Ahmad. They've just announced it."

"The one from Oxford?"

He nodded. "Surprised?"

"A little," I said, trying to hide the lift in my voice.

"Cousins marry here. It's almost unheard of for a Mansour woman to marry outside her family."

I could see that he had mistaken my relief at the Sheikha's interest in a man other than himself for surprise at an unfamiliar cultural tradition. Yet I was happy, again, that he did not detect the true source of my consolation.

I thought back to my first and only conversation with Sheikh Ahmad, how gallant I had found him. "They'll make a handsome pair," I said.

"Oh yes. Ahmad's quite the dashing prince."

"Sheikha Mariam never said a thing about her engagement," I said. "She seemed more concerned about the dig."

"Her worry's the same as mine."

"Worry?"

Marwan watched Pardi wheel the tools down the *tel* to the jeep. "That they'll tear up this hill before we can finish."

I turned to him. "What are you talking about?"

He paused, seeming to scan my face. "You don't know?"

"Know what?"

He kept staring at me as though I were hiding something. "The electric sub-station in Saali. There'll be a mad scramble to get it finished before the heat of next summer sets in. They want to run cables through this entire stretch of beach."

"Here?"

"Sheikha Mariam has finally gotten the Public Works Department to provide us with a full time surveyor to photograph and map the finds and to provide extra laborers to finish the excavations within the next month. But that's as far as we can go in preserving the *tel.*"

"You — you can't be serious."

He stared at me, again as though not quite believing that I was not aware of this.

151

Stunned, I scanned the mound, the trenches, the piles of sand. "They would sacrifice *this?*"

Marwan wiped his palms on his pants, staring out at the water. "They have before."

"But can you finish in a month?"

"Even at a furious pace and working two shifts, we'll never finish in a month."

"What then?"

"Then? The engineers'll move in."

For a moment, I thought that he was goading me, trying to test my reactions, my loyalties. He knew that Derek was the engineer in charge of the power plant.

I stared out at the blue sea sheathed in orange. It was getting late.

"Splendid, isn't it?" he said. "This is the best sunset on the peninsula. Is it any wonder the Zulaikans chose this spot for their capital?"

But I could hardly admire the sunset now.

"Can't you do anything?" I asked. I wondered, suddenly, whether Derek was responsible — at least in part — for the decision to use this beach as the location for the cables. Derek had been advising the Public Works Department. USA Electric would be supplying Abu Samra with most of the design and implementation of the peninsula's new electrical plant. But I could not believe that an electrical station would be given more weight than history.

I felt a tautness in my throat. "I can't believe the government would sacrifice this place." Then I blurted out, "Does my husband have anything to do with this?"

Marwan did not answer.

"Does he?"

"I don't know."

I was suddenly angry without knowing exactly why, except I clearly felt caught between Derek and Marwan.

"But you think that this *tel* will yield substantial archaeological finds," I said.

"I'm more sure each day. I think it'll prove to be the most important excavation in the Gulf since the dig in Yemen for *Saba*. Ancient Sheba."

"Haven't you told them?"

"I've practically been screaming about it for the last two years."

"Talk to Derek," I said. "Maybe they can delay the work until you've done what you need to do."

"Why would they do that? How could a delay possibly be to their benefit?"

"But I'm sure they'll understand what you're trying to do. Derek would. You should speak to him."

He sighed.

"I can come next week. I'm not too busy."

"It's *Muharram* next week," he said. "I don't know how much work we'll get done."

Muharram. I had forgotten. "Will you be here?" I asked.

"John and I will be. The workmen get spooked and prefer to stay away."

I had heard that some people did not report to work during this time. Derek had practically ordered me to stay home, away from the beaches and villages. "So, it *is* dangerous."

"No, of course it's not. Nobody attacks anybody, if that's what you mean. The whole thing blows over in two weeks."

Two weeks. I felt my breath stop. How could I stay away from Saali, from *him*, for that long? Simply knowing that I would see him each day, if only for a few minutes, kept me breathing. *Two weeks*. It sounded like forever.

"Since you'll be short of help, I should come," I said.

"Don't if you're uncomfortable. A lot of expats prefer to leave the peninsula during this time."

"Why?"

He shrugged. "An excuse for a holiday. No reason to. The marchers aren't psychopaths. I don't know why everybody makes such a bloody fuss over it, getting neurotic over something that has nothing to do with them."

"Have you ever participated in the marches?" I asked, not sure how far I could tread into his religious beliefs — whether or not I would offend him.

"Of course. As a child I waited all year to watch my older cousins and uncles march. My father would have nothing to do with the ritual. It's dramatic to watch, but it's certainly not dangerous."

We walked down the *tel* in silence. I sat in my car, hesitating before starting the motor, wanting to tell him that, *Muharram* or not, I would come.

For a moment he stared at me, looking as if he might be about to ask me to do just that. Instead, he got into his jeep and started the motor, turning the wheels toward the sunset as though to drive straight into it. Then, he slammed his palm on the gear, jolting the jeep into reverse. He yelled out to John and Pardi to hurry up.

The kitchen door let in the cool November air as Derek and I sat at the table eating cheese sandwiches in pockets of thin Arabic bread. Derek brought the flat rounds of fresh bread home from the market, and we filled them with cheese and tomatoes and toasted them. He especially enjoyed going to the bakery on Friday mornings to buy the savory pies as they came out hot from the oven. At first I used to go with him. However, the bakeries on Friday, like the produce market, seemed to be the men's domain. Women patrons, even expatriates, seemed to be regarded as intruders.

"Is the Saali project going to be built on the beach?" I asked.

Derek looked up from his plate. He seemed puzzled by the question. "We'll be laying those cables along that entire stretch," he said.

"Why there?"

"What do you mean?"

"There's the Portugese fort, and much older remains. It's a historical site. Maybe the most important evidence of the country's ancient history."

154

Although I had talked about the Saali fort to him several times, he looked at me as if he were unaware of this. "The location has been studied. It's the best possible place," he said.

"But there's a *tel* there."

"A what?"

"A *tel*. It's not just an empty piece of land. It's a site. An archaeological treasure."

"The entire peninsula's a damned museum to be encased in glass if you look at it that way," he grumbled.

"Don't exaggerate, Derek."

"Gina, we couldn't do a thing if we worried about every relic. The Saali station was designed and begun before I took over. It's impossible to change plans that are several years old."

I heard the grudge in his voice, the tone he adopted whenever he felt that I did not appreciate his work.

"But this place is special, Derek," I said. "If you just go see it you'll know what I mean. There are three or four thousand years of history. Babylonian, Greek, Arab," I said, hearing my voice grow strained. "You should care more about what you're going to destroy."

"*I'm* not destroying anything," he said. "And just why are you spending so much time out there anyway? That oddball archaeologist has brainwashed you. He's obsessed. Everybody says so. That fellow working with him told me the same thing the night they showed up here."

"John Reese said that?"

"He told me they were both practically married to that dig. Same thing."

"Well, he's certainly not crazy. If anybody's crazy, it's people who don't acknowledge what he's trying to do, who are willing to tear up an entire heritage, *his* heritage, just for an electrical plant that can be built somewhere else."

"You don't know what you're talking about," he snapped.

"*You* don't know either!"

155

I stood up, tears in my eyes, hating to argue with Derek like this, yet hating even more the thought of spending the rest of my life with someone with whom I had so little in common anymore. Was I being unreasonable? Was he? Had we both changed so much, become so different from each other that everything had to be some sort of contest between us?

Now, Derek stood up and patted my shoulder. "This is *nuts*," he said. "I don't want to fight. Just don't go anywhere near that place next week. Not with *Muharram*."

Yet despite his conciliatory gesture, I moved away from his touch. "It's not dangerous the way you think," I said. "It's not like I'd be attacked or anything."

"I don't want you in Saali, period. No telling what could happen."

"It's only a march."

"It's more than that."

"*You've* never seen it."

His voice rose. "I forbid you to go, Gina."

"You *forbid* me?" I said, my voice surprisingly calm. "I can't believe you said that. I know you want to protect me, but you're simply using this as a way to keep me home."

"Shit," he muttered. "You're like a God-damn leaf, Gina. You can be blown any which way by the slightest puff. Anyone can tell you anything and you'll believe it."

He left the kitchen. I got up, too, wanting to yell after him that he was right, that for years I had listened to what he told me about what was good for us and what was not, had let him map out our life without a second thought. I *had* been like a leaf, blown around by his singular view of things. But no more.

Marwan had been right. It was no use trying to talk Derek into delaying the work schedule, or into doing anything that would reflect poorly on his and USA Electric's ability to complete the Saali project in the time planned. Abu Samra was Derek's testing ground, I now saw. Perhaps he had been told as much in New York before

156

we left. If this project proved to be a success, there would be more in the future, maybe promotions, other overseas assignments. I should have been supportive, should have encouraged him to go ahead and finish the project as fast as possible. Instead, I had dared to suggest moving the very location from Saali. How stupid and disloyal I must have sounded.

I rinsed the dishes and put them in the strainer to dry, thinking of Marwan in the jeep facing the sunset. Everything seemed new and fresh and strange when I was with him, from the smell of his skin and his spicy after-shave cologne whenever he knelt beside me to see if I had come across anything, to his slightest movements which I could practically sense before he made them. Each time he stood near me my flesh would erupt as if I had just been caught in some magnetic field.

On the other hand, I could not blame Derek for losing his temper with me. We had been distant for weeks, rarely touching, barely making love any more. And we both knew it was not the miscarriage. Giving in to his occasional advances only made me feel empty, making things worse. I could barely remember our passionate love-making during the beginning of our marriage. When we were intimate now, I could not help imagining that it was Marwan, and wanting *him,* not Derek, with me, whispering to me, making me gasp in delight as his image grew inside me.

I gazed out of the window into the night, trying to dispel my anger at Derek. Things were not entirely his fault. But I could not even focus on him for long. Marwan flooded my thoughts again. And again. For even a fleeting thought or vision of him crowded everything else out of my mind. And right now, I needed to forget.

14

Muharram

Religious *Shia* notables and pious men began to arrive in Abu Samra by plane and by boat from the holy cities of *Qom* in Iran and *Kerbela* in Iraq, and from Oman, Kuwait and other countries in the Gulf where the *Muharram* ritual processions had been banned in recent years. Many of these men were Abu Samran nationals who came home to be with their families during the holy month and to take part in the religious ceremonies and marches. But some were foreign nationals, *Shia* brethren, who came in a show of political force and support.

According to Mary, the marches in Abu Samra were used by militant *Shias* for political rather than purely religious reasons as they were in Iran, for instance. In Abu Samra, they served as a reminder to the immigrant *Sunni* Mansours that their days of rule over the peninsula were numbered. Since the occasion resurrected the ancient enmity between the *Shias* and *Sunnis*, this sudden swell in the numbers of *Shias* on the peninsula over the following weeks was apparently worrisome to the *Sunni* Mansour government. Especially with the recent unrest in Teheran.

New elections in Iran had brought to power a moderate Prime

Minister, Ali Mohammad Akbari, who had upset many of the Mullahs by advocating establishing ties with the United States and Britain and taking a more lenient view of Sunni Saudi Arabia, a constant target of the fundamentalist *Shia* Iranian government since the overthrow of the Shah. Any unrest in Iran was anticipated to affect the political mood in Abu Samra because of the disgruntled *Shia* population who continued to look to Iran for support whenever it sought more representation in the Mansour government. The Abu Samrans thus anxiously tracked each turn of events in Teheran.

From Dafna we heard *Shia* preachers orate the story of the murder of the Prophet's grandson Hussein twelve centuries earlier from the loudspeakers of the mosques and religious meeting houses. The sermons continued all day, encircling the landscape in a single, long monotone which eclipsed all other sound, while growing louder and more urgent toward evening as men returned home from work. All other activity appeared frozen as the orations lingered late into the night. Afterwards, the congregations left the mosques and marched through the village streets in processions which built up over the next few days until the ninth and tenth days when *Muharram* reached its peak.

On the first day of *Muharram*, I stayed home. Derek had wanted me to stop driving for the entire ten days, but I insisted that was unnecessary. Even 'Abbas said that driving in the city was perfectly safe. Derek relented only when I agreed to let 'Abbas drive me the first few days, convinced that a foreign woman alone in a car would be a target for some crazed religious zealot.

"There's never been that kind of violence against women here," I said.

"That English woman was stoned in front of her own house," Derek said, looking exasperated by my lack of concern.

"She was wearing shorts in a village, Derek, and she was pelted with pebbles by some kids."

Derek nonetheless insisted that I not drive near any villages nor sketch or take photographs of anything or anyone. Although rare, there were reported incidents in the past in which participants in the processions had been so aroused by the re-enactment of the murders of the Prophet's descendants that they had injured their fellow marchers as well as bystanders.

In the past, being confined to the house would not have bothered me, giving me an excuse to paint or read. But the thought of not seeing Marwan was pure agony. Also, since learning that the beach around the *tel* would be dug to lay those cables, I had thought of little else, feeling it my personal duty to help Marwan and John document as much of the work as possible before they had to stop. As Derek's partner, I felt partially responsible for USA Electric's plans. I could not fathom how the company, or the Abu Samran government for that matter, could have overlooked such a vital detail as the existence of an archaeological site in its vicinity. I was infuriated that Derek was not willing to consider changing the path of the cables in light of the obvious historical importance of the dig site.

Marwan said that he would be working through the next ten days despite the shortage of workmen. He and John would be there, and Pardi. Faithful Pardi who did whatever asked of him diligently and without protest and who, because he showed more initiative than the others, had made himself an indispensable foreman. He made sure the other workers arrived early and worked until it was time to quit for the day. His co-workers respected him as did Marwan and John.

I often spotted Pardi at the end of an afternoon, squatting on his heels a little apart from the others, silently watching the setting sun. Once when I had picked some small flowers at the base of the *tel* before going home, he appeared visibly shaken and told me that in the future it would be better to wait until the morning to pick flowers, since at night they slept. Surprised and somewhat ashamed by what he obviously saw as my ignorance on such matters, I thanked him for enlightening me and promised not to pick flowers after sunset. Lately, however, I sensed that Pardi had come to resent the attention Marwan paid me. I could not help detect a sulk behind his otherwise docile gaze as he stood patiently listening to Marwan's instructions as each sifted carefully through the contents of the wheelbarrows. It was not difficult to imagine Pardi's happiness on the days that I was not there to distract Marwan from these one-on-one lessons.

I went up to the roof. I had set up my easel and began to sketch the distant line of yellow-green sea, the forest of palms, the sand, the remaining shanties and crematorium. Soon, however, I forgot the immediate scenery and began to draw from memory the flat-roofed houses of Saali, the iron doors and grilles on the windows, the thin, exposed metal beams on the rooftops, the village road wet and shimmering from the rains. If I could not go to Saali, drawing the village would bring me closer to Marwan.

Before I could finish the sketch, a pickup truck pulled up outside the crematorium. I was no longer alarmed by the occasional burnings. I watched silently as several men carried a shrouded corpse from the truck into the lot. Still, feeling like a voyeur, I put away the easel and carried the painting into the house to wait until they were finished.

Two more days passed. It would be a week or more until I could go back to the *tel*. Although I had dreaded the days I would spend away from the site, I had not realized just how desolate they would be. At times it seemed as if I had almost forgotten how to eat or sleep. Although I understood Derek's concern about my safety, I resented more than ever his insistence that I stay close to home, and even more his lack of interest to witness any of the processions.

"The marches aren't put on for our benefit," he said, clearly puzzled by my curiosity.

"But it's a unique event. I'm sure we could watch discreetly. Others have."

"Snoops," Derek muttered.

"I wouldn't call Mary a snoop. She just likes to see things for herself instead of learning about them secondhand."

162

"You can't photograph or sketch them Gina. The police will confiscate any cameras and film. They're very strict."

"I'm not going to photograph them. But if I *see* them, I can paint them later."

"Why would you want to paint a *Muharram* march?" Derek asked, a look of aversion sweeping across his face.

I could find no answer to give other than genuine interest. Whenever I heard or read of this *Sunni-Shia* rift, I imagined Sheikha Mariam's face, her upward sweep of bronze cheekbones, the sheet of black hair against the blue gown she had worn at the *henna* ceremony. Could such a woman be hated because of her family lineage? I thought of Awatif and Alia, the wives of the engineers who had come to dinner, their gentle, confident manner betraying no trace of bitterness at being *Shias* in a *Sunni*-ruled country. It was hard to imagine these women being capable of such enmity for the Mansours or for someone as capable and charming as Sheikha Mariam. Neither could I see Marwan, nor 'Abbas or our gardener, Khalid, also *Shias*, harming anyone.

"If these marches are so threatening, is it wise for the Mansours to allow them?" I asked Mary as we drove to the downtown supermarket together.

"Permitting the marches gives them less importance than banning them would," she said. "With this new Akbari situation in Iran, the *Shias* here are going to be listening to the anti-Western rhetoric of the Mullahs and flare up against the Mansours. The government will bend over backwards to avoid antagonizing *Shias*. It'll let them march to Kingdom Come just to show tolerance."

"But, what does everybody else do at this time? Stay indoors for two weeks?"

Mary seemed unperturbed by the idea. "A lot of people take their R&Rs. Have you thought of going away for a week? Renting a houseboat in Kashmir? Camping in Kabul?"

For many in Abu Samra, a fully staffed houseboat on the glassy

163

lakes of Kashmir was the ultimate luxury. More adventurous expatriates preferred trekking in rugged Afghanistan.

"Derek won't take time off now," I said, knowing that even if he could take a vacation, I did not want to go anywhere with him. I could not leave Abu Samra so long as Marwan was here. Every minute here seemed precious, even if I could not see him.

"Are *you* going away?" I asked.

"No. I'll needlepoint and bake my pies. Thanksgiving's only a couple of weeks away."

"I forgot all about Thanksgiving."

"The supermarket flies in everything fresh that week. Turkeys, sweet potatoes, even fresh pumpkins."

I smiled, not particularly inspired by the idea of baking pumpkin pies.

On the third day of *Muharram*, I knew I had to get back to Saali. Yet, I did not feel comfortable driving out to the village by myself. I thought of Mary and wondered whether she would go with me. Maybe we would even see one of the processions. She said that she had watched them a few years ago from the house of a friend — a former Peace-Corps worker still living in Abu Samra — which was located on the outskirts of Saali. Perhaps we could watch the marches from this friend's house. If Mary agreed, we could first go to the site. Just seeing Marwan for a few minutes would be enough. I would not even tell Derek.

Muharram did not seem to faze Mary, and having done her Thanksgiving baking, she seemed as eager as I to get out of Dafna. She contacted her Peace Corps friend and arranged for the three of us to meet. Her friend advised us to wait until the tenth day when the festival reached its zenith and the day the marching would be the most interesting.

To make my confinement at home easier until then, I invited Mary to join me on the roof while I painted. She brought over a large bag full of needlepoint and I brought up a chair and put it in

164

the shade so she could work comfortably while I painted in the light. Over the next few days, Mary worked on a tapestry while I finished a painting of a black-robed woman entering the arched portals of Saali's mosque. Occasionally Mary got up to watch me work, peering quietly over my shoulder. Although I had never spoken to her of my longing to be with Marwan, I felt that she saw it all in the painting. The sense that I was inadvertently sharing this secret with her through the canvas brought me a measure of peace.

Finally the tenth day arrived. To my relief, when I asked Mary if we could stop at the *tel* on the way to her friend's she agreed at once, curious to see the site that I had told her so much about. This time, instead of driving through Saali to get to the *tel*, Mary directed me along a different road so that we got directly to the beach without passing through the village. My heart pounded as we approached the *tel* in the distance against the backdrop of gray sea. Only the incessant sermonizing voice from the mosque's loudspeaker indicated that something in Saali was different.

I parked beside Marwan's white jeep, trembling as I stepped onto the sand. For a moment, I had a frantic change of heart, ashamed of having used Mary to get here and almost wishing that she was not with me now so that I could start up the engine and be gone before Marwan spotted us. But it was too late. Mary was already out of the car, looking up at the *tel* and at the lower trench near our feet.

"So, this is it!" she exclaimed, a look of amazement spreading across her face. She pointed at the cordoned-off square at the base of the *tel* where we had been working the last time I was here. "Incredible. I never knew you had gotten this far."

"It's *they* who've gotten this far, Mary, I'm mostly in their way."

"I'm sure you make yourself useful," she said, glancing about with genuine admiration.

I felt a curious rush of pride at how much had been done over the past month. I also noticed the evidence of new activity. There was a newly marked square and piles of freshly-dug sand, extra

165

wheelbarrows, and a tripod ready for a camera.

My eyes darted to the top of the *tel* for a sign. Spotting no one, I quickly turned back to Mary and pointed to the foundations of the medieval Islamic palace on the left and the layer where the Islamic period ended and the Helenistic graves began. Then I showed her the less defined, suspected Zulaikan period.

"Zulaika," she said, nodding.

"The earliest period," I said. She knew something about the third millennium Zulaikans having been strategically located in the Gulf to control the flow of goods between Mesopotamia and India; how they had fished their famous pearls even then, and how the Sumerian king-hero *Gilgamesh* was thought to have undertaken his legendary exploits on this peninsula.

"You've certainly learned a lot," she said.

I smiled, but not because of what she said. For I had suddenly sensed Marwan's presence even before I saw him on the *tel*.

I resisted looking up at first. Perhaps he would be concerned and upset that I had come. He had not encouraged me to. Had he been waiting for me, missing me as I had him, I wondered. His mere existence had become a drug which circumstances had forcefully withdrawn from me these past few days. Seeing him so near now, a rush sped through my entire system. I felt faint and incredibly alive at the same time.

I tried to keep Mary's attention on the pit, chattering on nervously. When I did pause, daring finally to glance up at the *tel* and praying that Marwan would signal us to come up to where he was working, he was already descending towards us, recklessly sliding down the rocks.

His hair was blown back as if he had worked against a strong wind all day. The dried sweat at his temples was gray from the dust and his shirt was covered with a chalky film. Only his eyes shone like sea crystals behind the dark lashes.

Marwan did not possess the standard handsome face which

166

might appeal to me in New York. Yet here, with his rich, earth tinted skin, surrounded by history and legend, radiating the exuberance of a man totally happy with his work and himself, I could not take my eyes off him. His was simply and suddenly the dearest, most beautiful face I had ever seen.

"Mrs. Monroe," he said, his voice dropping slightly.

It was all I could do to keep my own voice level. "Dr. Jassim, this is Mary Reynolds. She's been wanting to have a look at the site."

They shook hands, Mary expressing admiration for the trenches. I watched Marwan's face brighten as he listened.

"Are you here alone?" I said, seeing no sign of anyone else.

"Pardi's up there. John's sick."

But I could have come and helped, I wanted to insist, feeling a surge of disappointment that he had not tried to contact me. But in front of Mary I said nothing.

I did tell him that we had come to watch the procession from outside Saali.

He looked surprised. "You shouldn't go alone."

I thought he meant we should go back home. Then, without explanation, he called out instructions to Pardi to put things away.

He turned back to us. "I'll go with you."

I glanced at him. I had not anticipated his coming with us. I looked at Mary.

"Ellen won't mind," she said. "It's probably better to have a man around."

He went off to rinse his face and hands and returned wearing a clean, pressed shirt. Then the three of us got into my car and drove toward Saali.

The normally active village was dismally quiet now, with only the wail of a child coming from inside a house and the background hum of a sermon from the mosque. Green flags graced every doorway.

Ellen Swayne, it turned out, had come to Abu Samra as a

167

Peace Corps volunteer, but now taught English at a girls' high school downtown. Middle-aged, with a bird-like face and curly, graying hair, she had the same serene demeanor I found so appealing in Mary. She looked happy to see us.

Before leading us up to her roof, she switched on the coffee machine. "We'll need this later," she said.

"Is this the route they still take?" Mary asked.

"The marchers pass down this street as they leave the mosque and head to town," she said.

Marwan looked at his watch. "It won't be long now."

Although her roof was somewhat lower than the others along the road, we could clearly see the people on the rooftops across from us. They were mostly women and girls, some of them carrying green flags, some carrying babies or small children. A few old men stood with them.

We waited some twenty minutes before I heard the first echo of drums in the distance. Then came a muted *pfit* that I later realized was the sound of fists pounding naked flesh. The thuds grew clearer with each passing minute, and soon we could hear excited shouting in the distance. The women on the roof across the street broke into shrill, happy cries.

We continued to wait in silence.

"Once they're past Saali, they're ready to march downtown," Ellen said.

"Do they ever try to attack the Mansour palaces or a police station or anything?" Mary asked.

Marwan smiled, it seemed to me, with a scientist's dispassionate detachment. "It'd be foolish. Insurrection isn't really on their minds."

Marwan gripped my shoulder when I stepped too close to the edge of the roof, pulling me back firmly to remind me to stay out of view of the street. "Better be discreet. But watch carefully, it'll be worth remembering," he said. "It's likely to be banned in the future, even here."

I was grateful for his hand on my shoulder, glad that he had come with us. I *did* want to remember it all, to go home and paint it immediately. But I was blinded by the warm pressure of his fingers and barely able to focus on the street.

Later, I would remember the strange sounds. Like those first ones of the sheep and honking horns from my own rooftop in Dafna. They would be stamped just as deeply on my consciousness, perhaps all the more so because of my connection to Marwan through his hand. I could practically breathe in the first throbs of the drums, and then the men's hoarse chants: *Ya Ali, Ya Hussein.* The sounds of men crashing their fists against bared chests, the snap of metal whips against backs as they flagellated themselves, the clashing of cymbals by the boys running alongside to cheer them on.

Finally, the men appeared. They approached slowly in rows, stopping according to the cues from the flag-bearers in front. Some men pounded their chests with one fist, others whipped at their backs in rhythm with metal chains. A few were bare-chested, but most of them wore white shirts that seemed to have been ripped open in the back by the chains striking the exposed skin. The smaller boys ran beside them, clapping as the men whipped themselves. Just as Marwan had described that he had done at their age.

Once this group had passed, we could see the criss-cross of red blood, like a wire mesh, against the men's backs.

I shuddered.

Sensing this, Marwan squeezed my arm slightly.

"Each group is a different nationality," he whispered to me, as though to divert me. "Over there are the Iranians and further back the Saudis. You can tell by their banners. The litters those men are carrying on their shoulders represent the coffins of the slain."

The jubilant yet sorrowful wails of the normally reticent village women started again, as if they themselves had just lost loved ones in the centuries-old massacre of the Prophet's descendants.

"Look," Marwan said. A small child was being led down the

169

road on a white horse which had been splattered with red paint. "He symbolizes the slain children of the Prophet's grandson. And the man on the camel is supposed to be Zain al-Abdin, the sole adult male survivor of the slaughter."

I watched the little boy on the horse, probably not yet in first grade, holding himself erect and looking as serious as the men. The man on the camel — the only camel we had seen in the procession — had his eyes closed as if in contemplation or prayer. As the boy passed below us, the women on the rooftop renewed their wailing.

"It's seems so sad," I said.

"It's mostly conjured up for the ritual," Mary said.

"It's not really conjured up," Marwan said. "There *is* tremendous sadness at this time. It's almost bred into us. But it'll all be over tomorrow."

Ellen nodded. "Everyone will be back to work as usual and those women will be cheerfully hanging out laundry and sweeping their doorsteps. Each year I'm stunned by their resilience and ability to bounce from one mood to another."

"But the preaching will go on for another three days," Marwan said, "the three days that Hussein lay slain on the battlefield in *Kerbela*."

Just then, another group of marchers rounded the bend. These men carried swords. I drew back at the sight of the first few men with red foreheads. Every few steps they stopped. Then with the drummers directing them, they tapped their foreheads with the long, unsheathed swords. It was a grave, silent act, the men staring ahead, trance-like, slow drops of blood dripping from their foreheads on to their snow-white shirts.

A soft whistle escaped Mary's lips and I could feel her grow tense.

"That must hurt," I said.

"Pain isn't the goal. It's all symbolic," Marwan said. "In their mental state they can't feel anything anyway."

The men passed slowly below the house, halting and striking

themselves with their swords in time with the drum beats.

I suddenly felt my body grow rigid. One of the bloodied marchers seemed to be looking right up at me. I stepped back quickly, bumping into Marwan, sure that the man was someone I knew who had recognized me. The features of the other men were barely discernible from the blood trickling down their noses and temples, but even in its contorted state this face was familiar. I wondered whether it was one of the engineers in Derek's office, both *Shia*.

Marwan put his hand on my shoulder again, misunderstanding my fear. "Would you rather go inside?"

I shook my head.

All at once a marcher near the end of his row slumped to the ground. For a few seconds nobody around him seemed to notice. Then, when the others started to move forward, it was obvious that the man had fainted. Several men bent down to help him up, one wiping the blood from his head.

Marwan turned to Ellen. "He'll need ice. And water." They both hurried into the house.

I started to go with them to help, but Mary stopped me. "We'd better stay here."

I realized that she was right. I could not risk being seen by someone who knew me, perhaps had seen me with Marwan, and would get word to Derek that I was at Saali today. I stood further back from the edge of the roof, hidden from view, but close enough to see Marwan come out of the house, carrying a bowl of water and a cloth.

The drumbeats had not wavered and the procession was moving steadily forward despite the prostrate man who had been pulled to the side of the road. Several marchers were kneeling around him as Marwan bent down and placed the cloth on the man's face. One of the marchers undid the man's shirt while Marwan resoaked the cloth and applied it again. Then, two men hoisted the injured man

171

up from below his arms and helped him cross the road to a house with an open door. A third man ran after them carrying the man's bloodied sword. Seconds later, an ambulance pulled up to the house where the man had been taken.

"He seems to have lost a bit too much blood, but it may be more nerves than anything," Marwan said as he and Ellen returned. "The medics will see to him."

"It's like those people who spoke in tongues at my aunt's church that I used to have to go to when I was little," Ellen said. "We had our share of fainting in North Carolina, too."

By now most of the men, boys, and stragglers had passed beneath the roof and the chanting had died down in the distance. Even the medics soon came out of the house where the man had been taken and drove away in their ambulance.

Ellen led us back down the stairs to her sitting room where we sat without speaking for a few minutes. I felt empty, as if the marchers had dragged away a part of me with them. I also felt a vague disappointment. I realized that I had been expecting some sort of tragedy to occur, some thoughtless act of violence that surely would have erupted in New York under such circumstances. But despite the man fainting, it had all passed uneventfully.

Ellen served us the coffee and we talked about our own rituals in America and England: Mardi-Gras, Ash Wednesday, Palm Sunday. No processions I had ever watched, however, had the same haunted fervor we had just witnessed on the faces of the men, or the frenzied glee on the faces of the small boys running beside them.

Mary turned to me. "Have enough material to paint?"

Still shaken by the serenity on the stark faces of the chain and sword-bearers, I nodded. "I'll have to wait a few days and see."

"This is the side of Abu Samra most expats never know," Ellen said.

"Different from anything *I've* seen anywhere," Mary said.

Finally, Marwan stood up. "I'd better be going."

I looked up, having dreaded this moment. Then, to my surprise, Mary asked if I could drive Marwan back to the site while she visited a little longer with Ellen. I could pick her up on my way back, she said, so we could drive home to Dafna together.

I was surprised by her suggestion that I go out alone, considering the emotional climate of the village. But I also guessed that she had noticed Marwan's behavior toward me on the roof and might have suspected my main reason for coming to Saali this afternoon.

"I won't be long," I said, at once grateful for and overwhelmed by Mary's generous intuition. I followed Marwan out.

As we drove back through Saali, I felt I was seeing everything anew. The streets had more people than before, but all was quiet, as if the entire town had just been put to sleep.

Marwan, too, seemed to have forgotten all that we had just seen, and began to talk of their finds these past days, of the new trench at the foot of the *tel* that he was sure would yield Helenistic potsherds. I listened intently, as though being sung a lullabye, realizing how much I had missed his voice recounting the details about the work.

The sun had just set, leaving a wreath of gold between the gray sea and pink sky. The last traces of light were dissolving into the sand and water on the shore. Marwan's jeep was still on the beach, but there was no sign of Pardi.

"He's probably left on the workmen's truck that passes by," Marwan said. "Come up and look at the sunset."

We climbed to the top of the *tel*. The tools had been neatly put away. From a distance, I thought I could still hear the drumbeats and chants of the marchers. But Marwan seemed to have totally shifted his focus back to the site.

"About 2300 B.C., Sargon of Akkad sent his trading agents to Zulaika to work out a deal with Indian merchants to sell him gold and ivory. Those agents might have stood in this very spot, looking out at the fading sun." He said this as matter-of-factly as if it were

173

an account he had just read in the morning paper.

"God, how can you accept that this might be destroyed?" I said, abruptly. "It's been driving me nuts."

He looked at me. "I don't think about it, I just continue the work each day. I still have a few connections at the Ministry of Public Works. We're waiting for their answer."

"Will that change anything?"

"Sheikha Mariam has been talking to them too."

"But, I don't see—"

"Shhh," he said, suddenly, "Let's not talk about it. Just enjoy the quiet of this place."

I allowed myself to be pulled into his vision of a moment four thousand years ago. I stared at the sunset over the water. "Was it as beautiful then, do you think?"

He nodded. "More so. No pollution or refineries to dilute the colors."

"It feels strange to think that they saw with their eyes exactly what we're seeing now."

"Umm," he said. Then he stretched out his arms in front of him as if to gather in the entire *tel* and the few palms along the sea. I wished that I could have drawn him this way, knew exactly the color I would use for his skin, for his eyes. "King of the mountain," he called out lightly.

I smiled, despite the emotions racking me. "I wonder what he was like — your Zulaikan king."

He dropped his hands. "We may just find out."

We walked back down the mound. I told him that I might come the next day to sketch the dig. When we reached the cars I put out my hand to thank him for coming with us to watch the procession. He took my hand and held it a few moments. Then, without warning, he pulled me toward him.

"Why do you keep walking into my life?" he said, his voice suddenly cracking.

I gasped in surprise as his arms folded me against his chest.

"Marwan," I whispered in disbelief, feeling I was saying his name for the first time. Saying it in private like this, freely, was like speaking some new, secret language. I felt my arms going around him, felt him hug me tighter, and I shivered, grasping onto him as if I might be sucked out into the dark, cold water behind me.

Then I heard the sounds of the waves, felt the cold, wet sand give way to our weight, molding itself to my back, to my thighs. The chill seeped through my clothes to my skin. I kept hearing the waves lap the shore, flicking drops of cold salt water onto my legs. Rhythmic, lolling waves that seemed to wash away the last dregs of my own fear and guilt that lay wedged like a barrier between us.

I studied his face, recognizing the same despair in his eyes that raged in me. I wondered whether he guessed that I had thought of him all these weeks, mutely crying out his name over and over.

"Kiss me," I heard him say.

I arched my back straining to rise into his body as his mouth slid across my face. The gently surging water reached the tips of my toes, then receded. I wanted to devour him.

In the dark I could feel his mouth move against my cheek. "I wanted to kiss you that very first day I saw you in Dafna," he said.

I smiled in disbelief.

"I did. Desperately. But it would have been inappropriate with your driver looking on. And he made it immediately clear that you had a husband."

I laughed. "But you'd never seen me before in your life."

He ran his fingers through my hair. "Oh yes I had. Maybe not consciously. But I knew you existed. And there you were, materialized before me. You looked so sweet standing there in the heat, looking at me suspiciously and then offering me a drink."

"I was sick. You told me I needed salt pills."

"Sick or not, you were irresistible."

I did not admit to having been inexplicably drawn to him at the same time, and wondered whether I had been reacting to his own

175

feelings or whether I had, extraordinarily, known of *his* existence before too.

He pressed against me again and I tasted the length and heat of him through our clothes. His hand came down and slid over my stomach, down to my thighs. He said nothing. I sighed, then I kissed his lips, hard, closing my eyes as if I could drink him into me and keep him forever.

We held onto each other a long while in the darkness, until I could no longer tell when we had fumbled with buttons and he had entered me. It all felt so natural and familiar in the cool sand, in the dark. Finally, his words found me. "My God, we're like caged birds waiting to be freed."

15

The Chest

I began to look at winter as I never had before. It was a balmy, breezy coolness that brushed the peninsula, not quite cold, more like one of New York's ripe Indian summers. It brought on the same sense of well-being that the thought of a week with no school used to bring me as a child, a soothing foreshadowing of gentle days to come.

The winter also seemed to reflect the discreet Abu Samrans in a way that the charring heat of summer did not. The mellow good-nature that I had come to expect from the vendors in the fruit market, the innate poise of the women, including the Mansour Sheikhas, at morning coffees, all seemed to be genetic traits, as inevitable a part of Abu Samra as the tepid, damp winds that blew across the Gulf. Hearing that New York already had its first frost, I was thankful for these extra months of warmth as I climbed the steps to my roof and set up my easel and paints. But as I sorted out the tubes, squeezing cadmium blue, green, ecru, burnt sienna, and white onto the palette, my mind drifted to the chill of the sand and the elusive moon over the water that night on the beach at Saali.

I could still feel the crystals crunch against my back as Marwan's weight drove me into the sand. And I could hear the crazed, lost sounds of our voices, and knew that I could not hide behind the mask any more. He knew how I felt now, what I had felt for him all along; and he confessed how he had wanted me, not daring to let on all these weeks, afraid that I might reject him. I was a married woman, after all. I had recently been pregnant. What hope could he have of sparking my interest?

"Do you realize we're lying on a necropolis under a full moon?" he had asked in amazement, trailing his fingers down my face.

I had imagined the thousands of past lives trapped beneath us, extinct voices rising to the surface, longing to be heard. I had clung to him even tighter so as not to be dragged into those depths, fusing myself to the coarse material of his trousers and the muscles of his thigh through my slacks. Once I had been startled. Something seemed to move further down the beach where the Saali fishermen pulled in their nets each night. Afraid of being discovered by someone from the village, remembering the familiar face of the one bloodied marcher earlier, I kept glancing out to where the moonlight settled on the water like a wad of cotton.

Marwan had rolled onto his back and I leaned over and kissed his closed eyes and mouth, surprised at how soft and new his lips felt under mine. Yet when his tongue brushed my mouth it was as familiar as if I had always known it. Just as his hand felt where it cupped my breast, as if marveling at its roundness. His palm rested there, unflinching.

When we had readjusted our clothing, he held my face in both hands. "Damn it. I wish you were free."

I was silent.

He sat up, then he stood and put out his hand to help me up. "If you weren't married, I could take you home with me right now and start all over."

"I *want* to be with you," I said, leaning against him.

178

"Come with me."

"Where?" He had told me once that he lived with his mother and unmarried sister just outside of town.

"We'll go to John's place."

John had an apartment at the *Oasis*, an old hotel in town originally built for visiting British dignitaries. It was now mostly patronized by expatriate workers in Abu Samra on extended assignments. But going to the *Oasis* was out of the question. Somebody would see us. Marwan knew that. Besides, the last thing I wanted was for John to know about us.

Studying his face, I wondered why it was that he always seemed so young to me. He was forty-two, he had told me. Yet he seemed much younger, light years younger than Derek, who was forty.

"Marwan."

He stepped back, perhaps anticipating what I was going to say and not wanting to be interrogated about what all this was supposed to mean to us both. He seemed to be waiting, expecting me to demand something of him.

"What is it?" he said, softly.

I looked up, deciding there was nothing *to* say. Even if he denied that he had intended this evening to happen or to amount to anything, that he had not meant any of it and that I should now go home to my husband and forget him, I would say nothing.

Then, he spoke. "Gina, I'm going to Cairo in a few weeks. There's some business I have to attend to at the Antiquities Department there."

I stared at him. "What about the *tel*?" I said, quickly.

"John'll be here. I'll only be gone a few days."

"A few days," I repeated. At least it was not a month, or longer.

He reached out and grasped my shoulders. "Can you get away for three days?"

I wondered whether I had heard him correctly.

179

"Will you come with me?" he said, more urgently.

I felt as if I had suddenly been lifted off the *tel,* off this very earth, and put on some other planet. My hands tingled. Then I pulled myself back — back to the salty air, the ground under my feet, Derek waiting back home. "How can I do that?"

"Find an excuse to leave."

My mind was already scaling the mountain of reasons that I could give Derek for going to Cairo for three days without him. "My husband."

"You can leave your husband for a few days." He knew that I had a housekeeper. He must have thought I could pack and leave without a thought because of Lhatti.

"I've no idea what I'd tell Derek."

"Tell him you're taking a tour with some ladies. Women are always jetting off to Delhi or Kashmir together. You'll be going to Cairo."

"I can't."

He seemed baffled, as if it had not occurred to him how ludicrous the idea was. Then, he said, "We need to get away."

"Marwan, stop."

"We need to be together, to talk about this. We can't do it here."

I touched his hand, ran my fingers over the work callouses on his palm. I glanced at my watch in the faint light. We had been gone nearly an hour. Mary and Ellen would be wondering what was keeping me. "I've got to get back," I said.

He sighed, but was silent as we walked to my car. Once I was seated he shut the door after me as tenderly as if he were tucking a baby into bed. He ran his fingers along the chrome of the car's open window. "Come with me."

I covered his hand with mine. "I *want* to go with you, I just can't."

He reached into the car and lightly touched my chin, my cheek. I grasped his hand, unable to conceive of spending the rest of the night, or my life for that matter, without him.

I waited until he was in his jeep before driving off ahead of him, past the palm trees where earlier I thought I had seen someone. The slim, long trunks seemed to bow and twist in the night; beyond them, the water glittered under the moon like scattered pearls. I glanced back to the road and wondered whether I had actually seen a figure lingering among the trees on the shore. I knew we could not afford to be seen together like this, even if it were only by someone from the village.

When I drove through Saali, I kept my eyes focussed on Marwan's jeep's headlights behind me, afraid that I would lose my way if I lost sight of them. The silence of the village shrieked at me. When I finally pulled into the driveway of Ellen's house, Marwan slowed down behind me, then passed me and waved. I thought I heard him call out "Cairo!"

There had been no questions from Mary, never a mention of the time it had taken me to get to the *tel* and back, nor about my slacks being wrinkled and damp or my face flushed. By now, however, I was certain that she knew, at least must have deduced something from the protective way Marwan had been acting toward me on the rooftop. She said nothing about it on the way home, however, talking instead, about Ellen's disappointment with the Peace Corps and why she had decided to leave. Instead of helping the needy in Abu Samra, she told me, Ellen had been assigned to tutor the children of one of the Mansour Sheikhs.

"It's ridiculous," Mary said as we approached the lights of Dafna. "You come all this way, thinking you're going to do good for poor people, but you end up teaching rich people's children."

I barely followed what Mary was saying, however. All I could feel now was Marwan's urgent weight on me, my entire body still raw, my lips and cheeks burning as if my face were a canvas he had painted a bright red.

When I got home, Derek was sitting in the kitchen eating dinner.

"Where's Lhatti?" I asked. Although it was almost seven, she never left before I got home.

"I let her off early because of the situation," he said.

"Situation?"

He looked at me. "The marches. There was a clash between some marchers and the police in town. Several people were wounded. Shops closed early. Where were you?"

"I was with Mary. Visiting a friend of hers."

"I told you not to go out this late. Tonight of all nights."

"This was the only time we could go. We didn't see anything unusual."

"Shit, Gina! Are you living on the moon? Look around you. I told you it's dangerous."

"I'm sorry," I said, trying to sound calm, sensing that he was staring at my face, that he knew I was lying. I stepped slightly away from the glare of the kitchen light on my skin. "How was your day?" I said.

"Gina," Derek said.

I looked up.

"How can I make you understand that things aren't as safe here as they look? *Shias* all over the peninsula are feeling restless, cocky. No telling what could happen, especially after the incident in town this afternoon. I'm asking you to be careful."

"O.K.," I said, turning away from him.

"You should've been in before dark, at least." He sounded angry and frustrated by the fact that I had not obeyed his orders to stay close to home.

"I'm all right, Derek," I said. When he left the kitchen I went to the sink and rinsed my face in cold water over and over, to put out the fire in my skin.

It had been two days since that night on the beach. The *Muhar-*

ram marches had ended and Abu Samra seemed to have rebounded to its normal complacency. Yet I had not dared to go back to Saali. I did not know whether Derek suspected that I had been there that afternoon and I did not want to anger him if he were to find that I had gone to the village after he had clearly expressed his concern. But I was also not ready to face Marwan. Part of me feared that all that had happened that night had been due to the extraordinary scene of the marching. What if he did not acknowledge what had happened between us, or if he even regretted it?

I poured my energy into the new canvas now.

The cool, salt wind swirled about me as I tried to concentrate. In the canvas's foreground, two men in white *thobs* sat on a bench at an outdoor café, Saali's cafe with the broad-leafed Indian almond shading the benches. A languid, fuschia sunset melted in the background. The bench and wooden door behind the seated men were the bright aqua of the Gulf at mid-morning and the color used to paint front doors in Abu Samra. I had worked hard the past two days, wanting the canvas to fill my life the way painting once had. But I could not get absorbed in this one. Every minute of it was forced work, unlike the sheer pleasure that digging with Marwan gave me. And it showed. Although the drawing was good, even if it was the sort of nostalgic native scene that an expatriate might paint, something in the colors and spirit was missing. The sunset lacked the drama of the real ones, the way the sun would lower itself into the sea like a flaming, pink candelabra. Even the water was lusterless. I had to keep adding yellow to reflect the pale greens above the sandbars; but rather than capture the Gulf's translucency, the water looked dull.

I stood back, not so much appraising the painting now as smelling and listening. Ever since the house next door was completed, the scents of the curry and *chapatis* prepared each noon by the workmen had disappeared. Most of the shanties behind the crematorium had recently been torn down and the land been leveled to build more houses. It was not clear where the shanty dwellers had

183

gone, only that the sounds of the children and animals that had laced the humid mornings of my first days here were now absent. Instead, the air carried the gurgle of trucks fetching sand from the desert along the carriageways to one of the construction sites on the reclaimed land being expanded into the sea. This was being done up and down along the coast where the shallow waters of the shore were covered with sand to expand the land into the sea. The speed with which a five-story building would go up on newly reclaimed land, that only weeks ago had been under water, was astonishing. Equally surprising was how solid this new ground was, although I could imagine these buildings slowly sinking and finally disappearing once again into the soft, wet sand. Like Zulaika. Like the temporary state of my present life here.

Suddenly, so quietly that I barely heard the motor, a pick-up truck drew up to the crematorium. I glanced down at the crematorium platform and noticed for the first time that a stack of wood had been piled there. Four men got out from the cab. After several minutes of discussion, the men carried out the mummy-like bundle from the back of the truck.

Damn, I thought, gathering my paints together, almost as annoyed at the corpse as I was at the men conducting the funeral.

As the men arranged the sticks over the swathed body, I lifted the painting off the easel and placed it out of view in the shaded section of the roof. As usual, the men did not seem particularly upset by the occasion, as if these burnings were merely business matters that had to be attended to as quickly as possible. Still, it would be a few hours before the burning was done. I went back into the house.

Later, when I returned to the roof, another truck was parked near the first one. A different group of men had gathered near the wall and seemed to be waiting their turn. These men wore turbans and looked somewhat more dignified than the first group, their tunics blowing in the breeze like crisp flags. The first fire had died to a

184

long, low mound and I thought I could sense an elongated shape still in the embers. I had the sudden, peaceful sensation of a spirit floating above the coals, as if the flames had freed it once and for all from the limits of the body and from all that had circumscribed its earthly existence.

Out of view, I cleared away my paints and carried the canvas back down into the house to dry until the next morning.

Not being able to paint made me restless, however, since a new canvas was already taking hold of me, one of Saali on the day of the procession. I needed to start it while the images and colors still throbbed within me. For now that I had seen Saali with its tranquility ripped away, I had lost interest in painting its quaintness. I wanted to paint men drawing their own blood, paint the women's anguished chanting as they waved their green flags. The grey light on the street, the men's browned shoulders and bloodied foreheads. I wanted to show it all, the actual scenes as well as my raw feelings during the march and afterward on the beach. I had to seal that day inside me, forever.

Derek came home later than usual that evening. He usually went upstairs after dinner to watch the televised news in English. Sometimes he would also watch an American sitcom or police drama to relax. Tonight, however, he come down to the living room where I was reading and asked if I wanted to go downtown.

"We might as well take advantage of the weather before it gets any colder," he said.

I was surprised by the idea. It had been weeks since we had gone into town at night to walk. He was obviously restless. Something had changed between us since the other night and he must have felt my distance these past few days. Afraid that he would ask me what was wrong if I refused, I agreed to go.

Nights in Abu Samra still mystified me. Instead of an abrupt ending of the day, the evenings were more like beginnings, the stores staying open until past ten o'clock, the pungent street smells beckoning us to the *samosa* and *kabab* stalls. The nocturnal life of the market reminded me of Manhattan. Unlike Norwalk where life seemed to shut down after dark, Abu Samran shoppers appeared in the darkened streets of the *souq* as if they had been waiting to do so all day. Only the produce market, bustling in the mornings, was deserted after dark. Elsewhere, amidst the barrage of Arabic, Farsi, Hindi and Urdu, throngs of young men sauntered down the streets, some in white *thobs* that glowed lavender under the neon lamps, others in billowy tunics and pantaloons. Women huddled in front of jewelers' windows or slinked along the streets like coquettish phantoms.

I was now beginning to understand and even appreciate the magic of the flowing, shapeless, black *abayas*. Like the mystery of an elaborately hennaed foot peeking out of a sandal, the concealing wraps ignited the imagination. So little visible suggested so much.

As soon as we parked and started toward the market, the grating sound of the garbage collectors rumbled up the street. The men ran behind the truck as usual, holding pieces of cardboard like mitts to scoop up stray papers. People barely glanced up as the truck and frenetic collectors invaded the evening calm. To escape the noise, Derek and I turned down a side road not far from his office. It was one of the old alleyways that was accessible only by foot or donkey cart and there was a row of small dilapidated shops where brass and copper were worked. Mary had first brought me here, where the best copper merchants in town sold their wares. She had told me their goods would not flake or discolor like some of the cheaper, imported variety, and I had bought my brass pots from a vendor she had recommended.

This same elderly vendor now sat on the floor of his shop, his legs spread around an enormous cauldron that he was hammering. He was apparently one of very few brass workers left in Abu Samra, having learned the trade from his grandfather, and he was the only one in his family to carry it on. I had paid the higher prices for his

186

pots once I saw the difference between his work and the rest. Everything in the shop clearly had a unique touch — reddish brass etched with palms and flowers, camels and gazelles.

When the man saw us at the window he stopped his work. "Yes? Come in," he called, the same humorous scowl that I remembered from last time commanding us to enter.

Although at first Derek resisted, typically disliking to haggle with the market merchants, he finally followed me in. The man immediately poured us each a small glass of tea, then led us to the back of the shop where he turned on a light bulb, and gestured to something in the corner. When my eyes adjusted to the glare, I saw that he was pointing to a chocolate-colored wooden chest. Its top and sides were worked with flat pieces of yellow brass and bright yellow nails. Its squat, round legs were also studded with shiny nails.

I ran my fingers over the cool, smooth tops of the nails. "Is this an Abu Samran style?"

"Yes, Abu Samra, yes," the man said, adjusting his headdress, throwing the white flaps over either side of his head to get them out of his face. He patted the wood as though it were a prize horse he was showing. He held up his thumb. "Only one. Year. One."

"Your work?" I asked.

The man inclined his head. "Of course."

"I think he means he only does one a year," I said.

"That's Indian teak," Derek said. "Probably costs a fortune."

Overhearing Derek mention India, the man said, quickly, "No India. Abu Samra." Then, he went back to his mat and resumed his hammering as if we had suddenly disappeared from the shop.

I caressed the top of the chest, the slippery brown wood like Marwan's smooth skin. The brass curved around the edges and the nail heads met in straight rows up and down the sides. I moved back slightly to admire it. "I've never seen anything like this."

"They have them in all the Sheikh's offices," Derek said, with the detached fondness with which one talks of a painting that is safely in a museum and not for sale.

187

"One a year," I said.

"Let's go," Derek said. "He knows we're looking at it. He'll want us to buy it."

I tapped the chest. Again it reminded me of Marwan, its beautiful bronze color, its elegance. I knew that it had to be expensive, but I also resented Derek's dismissal of it without even examining it. "Don't you like it?" I said.

"It's a little gaudy. Anyway, it'll be here tomorrow."

"I don't think it's gaudy at all. This could be our one special Abu Samran souvenir."

Derek looked impatient. "Can't you see how hard he's trying to sell it? You can't decide to buy it just like that."

"Why not?"

"You're expected to bargain. It's part of the deal to sell you something. He'd be disappointed if you just snapped it up."

"But this is good work. Anyway, you don't like to bargain."

Then I noticed the green flag propped against the wall behind the chest, like the ones the Saali women had been waving from their rooftops.

I felt my breath halt. The man was obviously *Shia*. I glanced back at him. I immediately thought of the marcher I had seen from Ellen's rooftop who had looked so familiar; the one I thought had recognized me. Was this the man?

I suddenly wanted to leave the store, sure it was he!

"You're right," I said to Derek. "We'll come back some other time."

Derek followed me out of the shop, obviously relieved that I had not been more persistent about the chest.

All at once, the fervor of that afternoon on the roof came back as if it were occurring before me right now, the melancholy marchers, the faint stench of blood in the air, Marwan's hand pulling me back from the edge. And what came later.

Back on the main street, the garbage truck was gone, though

the dismal echo of its motor could still be heard. A heady smell of cumin abruptly filled the air.

"Want a *samosa?*" Derek asked.

"Sure," I said, absently.

I waited at the corner while he disappeared into a nearby shop. Some blond men looking like oil rig workers stood across the street. Despite the cool breeze, they were wearing shorts. One of them, catching me looking at them, whistled. I looked away.

Then, there was a stirring behind me.

"Madam?"

I turned. The shy, boyish face was almost unrecognizable in the dim street light.

"Pardi?" I said.

He was wearing an orange tunic and trousers and looked taller and bolder than the slight, khaki-clad workman of the site. Behind him were several other Indian men I did not recognize, standing in line for a movie.

Pardi brought his palm to his chest in a familiar gesture. "Will you not be coming anymore, Madam?"

For a moment, I did not know what he meant. Then, I realized that he was referring to my recent absence from the site. "Oh, yes. I'll be coming, Pardi."

"You don't have car?" he asked.

"I do. I've just been busy. I'll be back in a few days."

It was like Pardi to be concerned with whatever went on at the site. He was a loyal workman. But I suspected that he was disappointed to hear that I would be going back. The last few times at the site I had noticed him in earnest discussions with Marwan and heard Marwan repeat, in an annoyed tone, that Pardi was not to wander off the site, that the work should be completed on the *tel* before they followed up other ideas. After that, Pardi seemed to be more sullen than usual.

But tonight he looked almost jovial. He even seemed somewhat heftier, his neck creased where it met his chest of curling,

189

black hair. I became aware of my own light jacket and skirt. I felt diminished somehow, without work clothes and tools.

Suddenly, I stepped closer to him. "Pardi, would you do me a favor?"

Pardi's eyes seemed to sink further into his head. "Madam?"

I had never asked him to do anything before and I had no idea how far I could trust him, but I had to get word through him to Marwan.

"Could you give Dr. Jassim a message for me?"

"Dr. Jassim?"

"Tell him that I said, *yes.*"

He raised his eyebrows, looking unsure.

"Will you see him tomorrow?" I said.

"Yes, Madam."

"Just tell him 'yes'."

"I'll tell him, Madam."

I backed away from him toward the *samosa* booth. He watched me from where he had rejoined the other men in line for the movie theater. I knew I should not have trusted him to tell Marwan anything. Still, it could not hurt to say one word.

We were walking past a row of fabric shops displaying *saris*. The gold-embroidered borders were pleated and fanned up on the wall like the luminous wings of Monarch butterflies.

"Derek?"

Derek looked at me. In his face I thought I saw a deep, visceral knowledge of what I was about to say.

"Derek, I'd like to go to Cairo."

He let out a surprised laugh. "When should we go?"

I tried to smile. "There's a short trip I can make with some lady friends, just three days. I want to go."

"I'm due for an R&R. If you give me a few weeks, I can plan it."

190

I was silent a moment. "It's a ladies-only trip. Mary told me about it."

I had said it. I could lie. I had even dragged Mary into it again.

Derek looked ahead as he ate the *samosa*, gulping in breaths of air to cool his mouth. "By yourself?"

"Yes."

"Can't you wait for me to go?"

"It's a special trip for ladies," I repeated.

I was angry at myself for this deception. But I could not give in now. I wondered if he knew this, felt how compelling my need to escape him was. I wondered whether he knew that I had already left him in the most essential way possible.

16

Cairo

The plane tilted suddenly, the engines sounding as we began to descend. I studied the vastness of the desert, isolated pyramids startlingly clear from this height, black highways stretching like spindly spider legs. Luxor, Memphis, Thebes: land of Nefertiti, Akhenaten, Re. In my purse were brochures on Karnak and Aswan where the Nubians were said to flock to the tourist boats to dance as they had for the Pharaohs. Perhaps I could fool myself, and everybody else, into thinking that I was a mere tourist here to witness these ancient wonders.

Then we landed, the plane bouncing lightly, and I plunged too deeply into my vision of meeting Marwan to think of anything else. He had called from the airport the day he left to make sure that I was coming.

"I don't know," I had said.

"I'm waiting for you."

The sound of his voice, so sure, had filled me with the intense, squeamish desire I felt the moment I saw him at the site each day. I knew that I could buy a ticket and go if I chose to. I had already told Derek that I was going with two other women from the American Women's Association for three days. It had not been difficult to convince him, especially since the New York auditors were back in Abu Samra and he would be busy working late with Pete the next few days to help them finish reviewing the accounts. He would hardly notice that I was gone. And I had told Mary that I was going, just in case Derek asked her about this trip, whether she knew about it and why she had not gone along as well. I told her that I needed to get away from Abu Samra for a few days and she had not asked with whom I was going. I suspected, nevertheless, that she knew.

With Lhatti to care for the house, I had no need to worry about the practical matters. Still, the sound of Marwan's voice over the phone several days earlier urging me to join him had dazed me, making me more acutely aware than ever what it would mean if I went.

It was cooler than Abu Samra in Cairo's crowded airport. The customs hall was dusty and chaotic, the tall, burly Egyptian porters alarmingly boisterous compared to the quiet Koreans and Indians who were contracted to run Abu Samra's airport. This joviality appealed instantly, despite its jarring nature, so different from the reticent aloofness of the Abu Samrans. The chaotic ambiance acted as a loosening agent and, for the first time in months, my spirits soared as I anxiously searched the faces behind the glass partition for Marwan.

Then I spotted him waving, smiling as if to say, "I told you you could do it," and I felt a sudden shyness, as if I were a mail-order bride waiting to be claimed by a stranger.

"On your left is the City of the Dead," Marwan said in the taxi. I looked to where he was pointing. Hundreds of domed mausoleums, like small mosques, were enshrouded in the late afternoon haze. Children darted in and out of what looked like crypts that seemed to have been turned into squalid dwellings. It was a slum. Not a joyful sight, although I could tell that it delighted Marwan. He was in his element in any cemetery and he seemed to have grown more relaxed here, the furrows on his brow smoother, his eyes glowing with both pleasure and disbelief to see me.

"Nothing subtle about Cairo," he said. "Not its history, its beauty, nor its poverty. Different from Abu Samra in every way you can imagine."

I nodded, eager to understand it all as I sat so close to him, so far from my other life and anything that bound me to it. I reached out and touched his hand, something I would never have done in a taxi in Abu Samra. But I had entered the freeing anonymity of a big city now, as if I were back in New York.

He smiled and squeezed my fingers. "Soon, if the smog's not too bad, you'll be able to see the pyramids."

The pyramids! I peered ahead, although I was unable to detect anything in front of us but the endless traffic and pale, massive huddle of buildings in the distance.

The Hilton loomed over the Nile, it's striped blue and white awnings fluttering in the breeze. In the lobby, European-looking men and women were dressed in evening clothes. A tall, dark-haired man in a gray suit had his back to us.

Derek! I could feel myself draw back. But when the man turned, linking his arm to that of the woman next to him, I saw that it was not Derek at all.

"All set," Marwan said, presenting me with a paper to sign. Then we followed the hotel porter into a crowded elevator.

"I've booked you a separate room in your name. I thought it would be best that way," he whispered, almost apologetic.

"Yes." I knew that I had to have my own room in the event that Derek called.

The porter unlocked the door of my room and went to the window and drew open the drapes. We were on the fifth floor. Through the glass doors I could see cobalt water below.

"Our rooms overlook the river. Yours has the better view," Marwan said, closing the door after the porter.

I went to the glass and stared at the scene beyond the balcony, the tall buildings across the water, the rows of Eucalyptus and willows brushing the somber river bank. I knew this had to be expensive for Marwan, knew he was thinking of my comfort rather than his in booking us rooms here. I was embarrassed that he probably assumed that Derek would have booked us in sophisticated accommodations and that he could not possibly do less. I wanted to tell him that I would have stayed anywhere with him, would have slept in a tent or alleyway just to be with him. But all I could do was watch him draw the curtains of the room, shutting out the light, Cairo, and the rest of the world.

He came and took my hands and for a moment we simply stared at each other, as if still not daring to believe that we were actually here, together. Then he led me to the bed and drew me down onto it with him. I buried my face in his shirt, pressing my nose against the hollow of his neck, sniffing the familiar aftershave I smelled under the sweat and dust of the site each day. He felt vulnerable there, the skin tender, almost feminine. I kissed his throat.

His hands slid over my wool sweater down my breasts to my waist and my stomach, as if he knew my body as he did his own. I closed my eyes.

"Is it safe?" he asked. I knew that he was referring to protection from pregnancy.

I nodded, not caring about anything now but feeling him inside me forever.

He pulled my sweater up over my arms and head as I stared straight into his eyes, the irises with flecks of yellow in them.

I undid his shirt and slid it off his shoulders, feeling the warmth of his chest against my ribs, as if he had seasons of sunlight stored within his skin. I explored the hard, slender length of his arms and back with my fingertips, imagining how I would paint them, where I would put the shadows and smudge the edges to bring out the tough muscle against the softer indentations of flesh.

"You drive me crazy," he whispered.

I held his face in my palms. "Marwan — " I said, hesitant.

196

"Just enjoy this," he urged softly. "Enjoy what we have now."

"Don't you worry?"

He kissed me on the forehead. "No. Just rejoice."

We slipped off the rest of our clothes and he rolled onto me carefully, as though concerned about my comfort. Our angles and curves seemed to melt effortlessly into each other's empty spaces, my breasts fitting against the flesh of his chest, my leg wrapping around his. It was like seeing him all over again for the first time, this acute and wonderful feeling of freedom.

Kissing my eyes, my mouth, my neck, he gently pushed into me. Soon, a slow stirring began to move through me, spreading from my thighs up to my neck, growing steadier and stronger until I no longer seemed to inhabit my body. Gasping, he buried his face in my hair on the pillow.

We lay in the peace of the dark room as if no other time or place existed. I had never felt I had given myself so completely to a man before, never felt so enriched, so in love, and so safe at once. Marwan lay dozing, his chest barely rising and falling. I bent close to make sure I could hear his breaths, the way a mother might check on her newborn. In sleep he *was* oddly childlike, a look of assured serenity coating his face. I wondered whether I had been unconsciously drawn to that when I first met him. That crystal awareness that exuded from deep within himself, that everything would be just fine.

I could not yet relax, nor shed the disbelief at having him so close, of being in a strange, distant place where nobody could find us or keep us away from each other. I only knew for sure that I was with the only person in the world I wanted to be with.

Later when we showered together, I opened my mouth to the water's soft, clear sweetness as though I had never tasted such water before, marveling at how easily the soap lathered over my body. The shampoo worked itself into a dense foam, my hair feeling clean and silken for the first time in months, with no trace of the hard brackishness of Abu Samra's water. I closed my eyes, wrapping my arms around Marwan's soapy back as the shower rained down on us.

When I had dried my hair, I came out of the bathroom and saw Marwan standing on the balcony, gazing at the river.

"Do you need something?" he called as I picked up the telephone receiver.

I shook my head. "I have to make a quick call."

He turned away, as if understanding that this could not involve him, and I regretted my promise to call Derek immediately after I arrived in Cairo. On the other hand, I knew that if I called early enough he would still be at work and I could leave a message with Lhatti instead of having to talk directly to him.

It *was* Lhatti who answered the telephone and told me that Derek had come home early and gone out for dinner. Everything was fine, she said. Although Lhatti had meant to reassure me, I still felt a remorseful guilt.

I slipped on my skirt and sweater and went out to the balcony. The sun had disappeared beyond the distant buildings, but a pink halo clung to the river as it moved below us in a steady flow. The banks were strewn with the bright lights from the stream of traffic on either side of the water and across the giant bridges. In the distance, across the river, hovered the looming shadows of several buildings.

I touched Marwan's back and his neck where the hair was still wet. "It's chilly," I said.

He kissed me quickly then smiled, any annoyance or ambivalence he might have felt over my calling Abu Samra obviously gone.

"What do you think?" he said.

"About what?"

He seemed suddenly shy, as if wondering whether our lovemaking had been satisfying to me. "About Cairo."

"It feels good to be in a big city," I said, hungrily absorbing the sounds of car horns, motors, a clattering distant din I had not heard in the months I had been away from New York. The crowds, the pace, even the river seemed to be hurrying somewhere. "This could almost be the Hudson," I said, suddenly nostalgic.

"The Hudson?"

"Our river, in Manhattan."

He raised his eyebrows in mock horror. "You'd better not let an Egyptian hear you compare the Nile to the Hudson, or to the Thames for that matter."

I laughed. "Sorry."

"This river is the very reason for Egypt's civilization. A mixed blessing, actually, since the beginning of time. If the yearly flood was too abundant, whole villages were destroyed. If the flood was too low, it meant famine. Only the Egyptians could handle such a harsh life for so long."

I gazed out at the water. A barge docked on the other bank had just turned on a row of decorative outside lights. It appeared to be a floating restaurant. I turned to him. "I've always wanted to come here, Marwan. I just never could have imagined that it would be with you. And yet it's so perfect that it is."

He pulled me closer. "Dream it. Believe it. That's when you make it a reality."

"You're totally unconventional Marwan."

"In what way?"

"You don't seem very Arab in your way of thinking. At least not in the traditional sense."

"We're not so different from Westerners."

"But *you* are. You're different from anyone I've ever met. You're certainly not a traditional Muslim, are you? I mean, seducing a married woman."

He laughed softly. "What is a traditional Muslim? What is Islam? It's a submission to the will of the world. Allah can be a traditional God, or the natural flow of the universe. I try not to fight that flow. In that way, I'm very much a traditional Muslim." He reached over and held my hand. "When you came into my life, I simply accepted it. I was grateful and thanked Allah. And now look how happy I am."

I lay my head on his shoulder, loving him for saying that.

"But look at where we are, Marwan."

He stroked my hair. "We're in a wonderful place, Gina."

I could not deny that, despite the reality of the situation.

After a few minutes I said, "I can't wait to see the pyramids."

"Tomorrow," he said, cryptically. "You'll see everything to-morrow."

Back inside the room, while he leafed through some papers, checking the names of people he needed to contact, I hung up my clothes in the closet. Under the glare of the hotel lamp I noticed for the first time how threadbare the carpet was, noticed, too, the deep stains on the dark drapes. I felt a surge of guilt again, realizing where I was and with whom.

"Hungry?" Marwan asked, when he was done.

"I'm famished," I said.

"There's a nice restaurant upstairs."

"Are you sure it's all right to be seen together?"

He chuckled. "In a city of fifteen million? I don't think anyone will care."

During the night I opened my eyes and looked at my watch. It was past midnight. I had been dragged from sleep as if someone were drawing me up by a chain. I vaguely remembered that my dream, which had vanished too soon, had been about the baby.

Awake now, I thought I heard someone knocking. I got up and peered through the door's small viewer. The hallway was empty. I returned to bed, the reflection of the outside lights invading the darkened room like a spotlight in a prison cell.

I slid open the glass doors to the balcony. There were more lights and noise than earlier. I watched the cars drift along the street, their lights a parallel, twinkling tributary of the Nile. Deep down, I had somehow come hoping to extinguish my fascination with Marwan. I had hoped that seeing him out of Abu Samra, away from the *tel* whose myths and secrets imbued him with the mysticism of a

200

prophet, would force me to see Marwan as he really was. A restless, curious, brilliant, man, but a mere man, not a magician with the power to grant me the happiness I longed for. I had even hoped that making love to him would finally free me to resume coasting in the stale reality I had lived in for years.

Only this had not happened. Now that I had truly experienced him, I was drawn to him even more.

When I got back into bed, he roused slightly, and put out his arms. I slid into them comfortably. Again, that look of infinite peace settled on his brow.

Next morning he bent to kiss me, handing me two long-stemmed white roses. I sat up in bed, pressing the petals to my nose. Though he had barely touched me, my body eagerly responded to him, remembering all too well each grain of pleasure from the day before.

"I ordered breakfast," he said, and began to wheel the table set with food out onto the balcony. He looked handsome in a crisp blue shirt, and I wanted to pull him back into bed beside me, but I remembered that he had an appointment.

I washed my face and slipped on my robe and joined him on the balcony. He smelled of the cloves-scented hotel soap that I had just used myself, and for a second it seemed as if we inhabited the same skin.

Below us, the river glided slowly under bridges which were already congested with cars and buses. There were tall, ornate apartment buildings and grand villas on the opposite bank, shimmering in the morning light. Further away, nestled in a forest of willows, were the large buildings I had seen last night.

"That's the museum," Marwan said, turning to kiss me in full daylight.

I quickly stepped out of view of any possible observers.

Laughing at my fears, he scooped my hair up off my neck and kissed me again.

"Can we go to the pyramids when you're done?" I asked.

"Of course. But not today." Seeing the surprise on my face he chuckled. "There's a special way I want you to see them. Today we'll go somewhere else."

"Where?"

"You'll see. Now let's eat. You'll need your energy."

Breakfast — laid out as beautifully as a banquet — was warm croissants and buns, butter and jams from Rumania, English tea bags and foil packets of *Nescafe*. Although it did not resemble anything remotely like I imagined an Egyptian breakfast to be, it looked delicious. I offered Marwan a tea bag. He shook his head and ripped open a coffee packet instead.

"I thought all Arabs liked tea," I said, putting a tea bag in my own cup and pouring hot water over it.

"Can't stand the stuff. Never did. Thank God for coffee."

I laughed. "So where are we going today?"

"Downtown."

I suddenly remembered that Derek had asked me to bring him back an Egyptian robe.

"Marwan?"

"Yes?"

I felt my face change at the thought of Derek.

"What is it?" he said, reaching across the table.

I shook my head. He stood suddenly and bent over and kissed my forehead, as if he knew that there was nothing he could say or do to solve our predicament. We both knew that we could have each other only for these brief few days.

He came over to me. "It's all right. I'm with you. I just need to meet someone for half an hour. I'll be back by ten. Meet me downstairs."

He hugged me and we kissed. I told myself not to cling to him, not to be a burden. But when he left, I felt totally abandoned.

From the balcony, I watched the Nile shimmer under the layers of diffused light. Through the diesel fumes below, businessmen, women, and school children in navy-blue uniforms waited to cross the street. A young vendor was balancing a mound of plastic kitchen baskets on his head and crowing loudly above the din of traffic. I tried to take comfort in these small daily tasks carried on in this city, activities that went on despite the ache inside me. I went into the room, opened my suitcase, and took out a sketchbook.

I was a different woman from the one who had looked out over this river yesterday. I had changed in a way I had never thought possible. No longer merely a wife, I had made a choice now. Coming here had been the first step, had released me from the notion that I had to be tied to Derek forever. Marwan had made love to me last night in a way that I thought I would never know again, as if my every thought and breath was a part of him. I could still feel his smooth, boy's chest on mine, his taut stomach, his legs darting playfully between mine, his lips grazing my skin, his smile against my cheek.

Yet it almost made me sad this morning just to think of last night. I wanted to enjoy the moment as fully as he wanted me to, as he was able to, but I was unable to forget about what would come afterwards. Simply knowing that in two days I would have to go back to Derek was terrifying.

With more than an hour to spare before meeting Marwan, I decided to go for a walk.

The hotel entrance was blocked by a group of smartly-dressed young Arab men and women who I assumed were Egyptian. As they spoke, they laughed and gesticulated elaborately, politely parting for me to pass. As in Abu Samra, I was immediately conscious of my light skin and hair, feeling almost frail compared to their darker hardiness. Yet I also felt stronger than I ever had in my life.

Across two streets was the Nile, blue and calm, yet aloof, as though millennia of history had rendered it dispassionate to the problems of mere mortals. I walked along a sidewalk running parallel to the river, passing palatial villas with vast lawns. Government ministries, the signs said. I felt like a trespasser, strolling the ancient banks. It was just a river, but I could not help feeling that its waters held the story of the world — held the answers to what lay ahead in my life.

Egyptian sailboats skimmed the water around clumps of stiff reeds. Bulrushes. Moses. One of the boats had a dog on the prow that barked loudly. I was suddenly filled with tenderness for Marwan for having brought me here. Even for Derek for not preventing me from coming.

When I got back to the hotel Marwan was waiting at the reception desk.

"Ready?" he said. As if preparing to excavate, he had removed his tie and rolled up his sleeves. As he ushered me out to a waiting taxi, my earlier ambivalence at being here lifted. I eagerly and gratefully surrendered to his infectious enthusiasm and to the smoggy Cairo morning.

The Cairo bazaar of *Khan Khalili* emitted a suffocating concoction of scents and colors. Awakened with new love, I took it all in thirstily. Ground cinnamon, cardamom, reddish sumac and turmeric were piled into tall cones in open burlap sacks. The sharp aroma of salted fish barely masked the stench of blood from butchers hacking at carcasses in nearby stalls.

The men in the market seemed both brash and friendly. Many of the market women wore traditional long dresses and fringed head scarves, their *kohled* eyes staring out with bold curiosity. Although some had black wraps draped casually over their shoulders, only a few covered their faces.

I paused at a cluttered souvenir shop window stacked with brass and dusty pottery. There were long robes on a hanger inside. "I need to buy something," I said, thinking of Derek's request.

Marwan, however, urged me on. "I know a better place." Several minutes later, he indicated a shop. "You'll find good things in here."

He seemed to know the shopkeeper who served us tea as we browsed through the merchandise. I fingered the *gellabias*, simple cotton ones for men, embroidered ones for women. My hands slid over the smooth coolness of the fabric and the prickly gold filigree. An hour later we emerged with a bag full of clay pots, silver chains with Nefertiti heads, gilt sandals, a *gellabia* for Derek, and three scarabs the storekeeper gave me as a gift.

Now, Marwan led me deeper into the market. Through a maze of narrow streets we came to a row of old, multi-level homes with latticed balconies that hung over the road like those in downtown Abu Samra. But unlike the simple craftsmanship of the Abu Samran woodwork, these balconies resembled dense honeycomb.

"Mamluke homes," Marwan said, opening the doors of one of the houses as casually as if he lived there. I followed him inside and down a hallway to a sunny courtyard. There was a shabby garden filled with rose trees and jasmine bushes and surrounded by high walls and more latticed windows.

"The lords of these houses were Circassian mercenaries, originally slave soldiers brought over by the Turks," Marwan said. "They finally overthrew their masters and came to rule Egypt for five hundred years. These houses are museums now."

An elderly watchman emerged from a hallway and sleepily greeted us. He led us up a marble staircase into the main house where the rooms were large and airy with beautifully restored blue and white mosaics on the walls.

The man said something to Marwan.

"He wants me to tell you that this Mamluke home is four hundred years old," Marwan said, indulging the old man although he was obviously aware of the history of the house himself.

I stared at the high ceilings and walls, the arabesque archways. "It's beautiful."

"Mamluke colors," Marwan said pointing to the pink, white, and black marble floors. The glossy stone seemed to have been just polished and I had an eerie feeling that the ghosts living here had slipped away just moments before we entered.

I retrieved my sketch pad and colored pencils from my bag. As

I drew the geometric tiles of the floor, the archways that led into a wide hall, the shafts of light sifting in through the masked windows, Marwan appeared to be explaining to the watchman that I was an artist. The watchman nodded and put out his hands, palms down, as if to tell me to take all the time I needed.

When I was done, Marwan pointed to the latticed windows. "The windows were covered to shield the aristocratic women from the street people. The women could look out all they wanted without being seen."

The old man winked at me. "*Mamluke harem,*" he said, as if he knew what I was thinking. The very air of the room suddenly seemed drenched in sighs of loneliness and passion. I felt my body go weak, wanting Marwan's arms around me again, lifting me onto the bed, wrapping himself around me and erasing the rest of the world with his touch. I wanted him to wake me up each morning with white roses as he had today.

The watchman suddenly ambled over to me, took me by the arm, and walked me to a window where there was a row of tiny, hand-blown glass vials in a case. He looked at me and muttered something, as if he expected me to understand.

"Tear bottles," Marwan translated. "The women of the house used to store their tears in these when their men went off to war. The men always wanted to see how much their women had cried for them when they returned."

I smiled. "Really?"

"That's what the man said."

"And what does Dr. Jassim say?"

He tilted his head. "Dr. Jassim, not inclined to be romantic, thinks that they were probably medicine vials, something to hold a tonic for rheumatism or gout."

"I like *his* explanation better."

"So do I."

When we left the mansions, after apologizing to the old man

that we had no time for tea, we went on to the medieval Cairo citadel.

"Home to Egypt's rulers for seven hundred years," Marwan said, as we stood behind a line of German tourists waiting to enter through the arched portals. The massive building was immediately recognizable to me from countless Roberts lithographs.

"An ancestor of King Farouk's, Mehmet Ali, massacred the last group of Mamluke rulers two hundred years ago on this very spot and took control of Egypt," Marwan said. He pointed to a narrow passageway. "The Mamlukes were ambushed as they left the citadel on their horses after a lavish feast given by Mehmet Ali. Only one is said to have survived. I've met his great-great grandson. Teaches at the University here. His name is still Mamluke."

"How awful to know your ancestors were murdered!"

He shrugged. "He doesn't seem to mind."

"There was so much tragedy here."

"That's why it's romantic. All romance has tragedy."

"Says who?"

"Shakespeare," he said, squeezing my hand.

After another taxi ride, we were let off at the Sultan Hassan mosque, a sanctuary so large that it dwarfed everything else we had seen until now. We were given paper shoes at the door and padded across the plush carpeted floor and out to the courtyard where men were washing in a fountain, preparing to pray. There seemed to be a purposeful, uplifting manner in the way the Egyptians went about their work, even their prayers. I felt my spirit growing lighter.

"Nothing in Abu Samra compares with this," Marwan said, gazing around the immense courtyard. I thought of Saali's small, quaint mosque.

This was spectacular, the harmonious arches, the tranquil inner sanctuary already filling with men performing the mid-day ritual prayers. I watched them kneel and prostrate themselves, envying their serenity and faith.

"Let's eat," Marwan said, handing me my shoes once we were outside.

He led me to a tiny restaurant off a nearby side street where he ordered us lemonade and fava-bean sandwiches.

I bit into the soft, warm sandwich flavored with cilantro. "You know so much about Cairo," I said. "Aside from archaeology."

"I taught at the University here fifteen years ago while we dug at Karnak. I try to come at least once a year. It's easily my favorite city." His gaze fastened onto me. "I want you to love it too."

"I won't know until I see the pyramids," I replied with playful stubbornness.

"Foolish woman," he said, with a mock grimace. "I told you to be patient." Then he turned serious. "I feel as though I've been waiting to bring you here forever, Gina. And not just to have you to myself. Do you know what I mean?"

I stared across the table at him, at his eyes which turned translucent in the muted light of the restaurant, at the softness his face took on whenever he was talking in earnest or explaining something.

I nodded, settling back in my chair. "I think so."

He looked uncomfortable suddenly. "This is what I can offer you, Gina. This place. My time. My love. Do you understand?"

I nodded.

"I can give you moments with a man who is totally captivated by you. That's what I want you to know."

I was quiet. *Moments?* I was not thinking in terms of moments, I could not afford to. I had to think of my life. Of Forever. "I love you, Marwan. That's all I know right now. But I was hoping for more than a few moments."

"You've got me for as long as you'll have me."

Back at the hotel, there was the abrupt ring of the telephone.

"Did I wake you?" the voice asked.

"Hello?"

"I miss you."

"Derek?"

"Have you forgotten me already?" His voice sounded more hurt than angry. There was a pause.

"Of course not," I said, confused, squeezing the receiver. I turned away from Marwan and sat up. "I'm just a little disoriented. I'm glad you called."

Marwan got out of bed, went into the bathroom, and closed the door.

"You sound tired," Derek said.

"We were out all day. I was taking a nap."

"What's it like?"

"Fascinating," I said, trying to keep my voice level, wishing he had not called now, that Marwan did not have to hear this. "My room overlooks the Nile."

"Seen the pyramids yet?"

"No."

"No? I thought you'd go there first thing."

"We're going to. We saw other things —"

"What things?"

"A citadel. And a mosque."

"Well go ahead and see the pyramids and come home. I miss you."

I felt my heart skip a beat. "How are you?"

"O.K. How about you?"

"Fine," I said. "We're fine."

"Good. I had a cold yesterday. Lhatti made me her special Indian tea. If it gets worse, I'll see a doctor."

He told me that there had been another thunderstorm in Abu Samra, then he told me that Sheikha Mariam had called.

I was surprised. "Did she leave a message?"

"No," he said.

"Did she mention my paintings?" I said, wondering if that was the reason for her call.

"No. She seemed upset that you were gone, though."

My heart raced again. I wondered whether the Sheikha knew

that Marwan was out of town as well.

"I bought your *gellabia*," I said. "I miss you."

"Do you?"

A seed of irritation erupted in me, more at myself than at the skepticism in his voice. "Of course I do."

"Hurry back then," he said, finally.

I looked up at the ceiling and took a deep breath. "It won't be much longer." Then I hung up.

I wondered why he had sounded so edgy when he had seemed resigned to my coming. I was feeling worse than ever about leaving, especially knowing that he had been ill.

There was a sudden, soft rap at the bathroom door. Marwan opened it a crack. "Is it safe to come out?"

"Of course," I said, cheerfully, although I realized that I was not ready to face him yet. Not after Derek's phone call.

"What's wrong?"

"I wasn't expecting him to call."

He stared at me.

"I just didn't expect it," I said, pulling the sheet over me.

He looked away. We were both silent. Then, as if unable to think of a better alternative, he got back into bed.

I was almost afraid to look at him. But he reached out and gently pulled me to him.

"Just let yourself *be*," he said, softly. "Don't bring in the outside, just feel what's between us, here and now."

I tried to do what he said, to forget about Derek's phone call, to be aware only of his hand stroking my ribs, my thighs. I closed my eyes, almost afraid to feel again what I had felt an hour ago when we had made love quickly, a ravenous communion before falling asleep.

I suddenly wanted him to grab me, to take me back to that madness, make me forget everything else but the two of us here, now.

He closed his eyes. "Do you love me?" he asked.

"Yes."

"Then don't worry."

"How can you say that? I've never done this before. I don't know where we're going or whether I can handle it."

He reached over and wiped the tears from my face, carefully pulling me to him.

"Do you love me?" he asked again.

"I don't know," I said, angry at him and at myself, at the entire world. I only wanted him to make love to me now, fast and hard. I was his. Only his. He had to know that.

I felt the tears racing down my cheeks.

17

Pyramids

It was four o'clock in the morning. Cairo traffic had slowed. I stood out on the balcony, a blanket wrapped around me, looking down at the rippling Nile. I tried to think of Derek, tried to miss him. But all I could envision was the cool breeze blowing up from the Saali beach and the distant village lights through the mist. All I could feel was an outpouring of love for Marwan that had changed my life.

We had gone to dinner again at the hotel's rooftop terrace. Marwan had talked about his village childhood in Abu Samra, his marriage after he had returned from the university in England, his life alone for the past ten years. His life had been his work during this time and he had been fairly content, he said, even happy to be able to devote his entire time to dig and study. After his failed marriage, he had even thought of giving up digging and considered teaching at Oxford in order to have more time to write. It had never occurred to him that it would be Abu Samra that would change him in more ways than he expected. When he had seen me that day in Dafna and later at the cocktail parties in October, he said, he knew what was missing in his life.

Marwan confessed that, although it sounded corny, it had

struck him the moment he saw me, that we had known each other in some other lifetime, some place where our current histories had no significance. We simply found each other again in Abu Samra. Then he had met Derek, and had to face the fact that I was married — perhaps happily so despite what he sensed as Derek's and my puzzling aloofness toward each other. He told himself that he had made a mistake, that he had to forget me. Then he saw me at the foot of the *tel* in Saali that day and knew it was no mistake. He knew that it was inevitable that we be together, that he had summoned me in some way and that I had responded.

I heard his words over and over in my head as I watched him sleep in the dark bedroom, knowing that my life would never be the same either, that I now faced a new horizon with no clear guide-posts.

Next morning, we headed toward a village on the outskirts of Cairo.

"Few tourists get to see this," he said. Noting my interest in fabrics in the bazaar the day before, Marwan had arranged for me to buy some Egyptian cloth directly from a well-known weaver.

I pointed out the Cheops and Kephren Giza pyramids in the distance, the outline of the Sphinx. A mysterious smile played on his lips. "Don't worry, we'll get to them," he said.

"I'm beginning to think they don't exist," I said, "that they're some mirage."

"They're real, all right, you see them back there."

"If I'd been here with anybody else, I would have seen them right away," I said.

"I know. And you wouldn't have seen much else. There's a right time to experience everything. Remember what I told you yesterday, just let yourself *be* in this moment. We'll enjoy the future when we get to it."

Suddenly the car was veering off the highway along a different road, cutting into a field of pastel houses. The driver pulled up to a

green one with an azure door and a half-dozen children on the door
step. Lavender and orange bougainvillea bloomed along the walls.
Inside, looms were set up in each room, operated by young women
weaving cloth. Marwan and I sat in the foyer with the lady of the
house, a middle-aged woman in a magenta colored shift, the fabric
of which, she told us, was made by her children. She asked me in
halting English, how I liked Egypt.

"It's wonderful," I said. Then remembering the expression
Egyptians seemed to use for all things spectacular, I added.
"*Biganin.*" It drives one crazy.

The woman laughed in approval. A little girl served us tea.

Bolts of fabric were brought out. Stripes, bright solids, prints. I
selected three and Marwan told the woman to have them wrapped,
insisting on paying for them himself.

"She gives me a good price," he said. "Her oldest daughter
was one of my students."

While he chatted in Arabic with the woman, I went and stood
at the open front door, amazed at how easily Marwan seemed to fit
into any milieu he chose. He seemed as comfortable in a local Cairo
village as he was in Saali. In the distance, rose-colored clouds dipped
below the tops of the pyramids. I was still mystified that he was refusing to take me to them.

In a little garden off to the side, several young men sat on cane
stools, smoking. One of them shook a tambourine while a young
girl danced, her loose shift tied at her hips with a sash that bobbed
up and down. She shimmied her shoulders and hips as Sheikha
Mariam and the Abu Samran women dancing at the Sheikha's tea
had. But theirs had been a subtle, veiled sensuality. This Egyptian
girl seemed openly triumphant in hers.

I hesitated at first, then brought out my sketch pad and began
to draw quickly, just a line or two for the men, the angles of the
girl's arms and head as she moved swallow-like, and the pyramid
beyond. When the girl noticed me drawing, she stopped, as though
shy. One of the young men extended his pack of cigarettes to me. I

215

smiled and shook my head, then turned to go back into the house. Marwan was standing behind me, also watching. He handed me the wrapped bundle of fabric.

"They're great, aren't they?" he said.

"I can't capture it on paper, but I don't want to forget a thing."

I was suddenly filled with the aching knowledge that in a few minutes I would be gone from this place and would never see it again. For a moment I imagined us starting a life together right here in this village, Marwan and I, him digging and me painting — with no other care in the world except each other.

On the way back to the hotel Marwan told me that he had made dinner reservations at a restaurant a short way out of the city. He had canceled a dinner engagement he had with a colleague at the museum to be with me.

"You should have gone," I protested. "I don't mind."

He squeezed my hand. "Tonight is for *us.*"

The telephone rang just as we entered the room. I looked at Marwan. "I don't want to answer it," I said.

He was silent.

The rings stopped only after the tenth one.

He sighed, as if in a delayed reaction of relief or frustration to my not having answered it. His face had an edge I had not seen before.

"I'm going down to buy a newspaper," he said. "If you need to call home, do so."

I heard the door click shut and was grateful. Knowing that Derek would be at the office, I dialed the house. Lhatti answered but immediately put Derek on the line.

"Derek? You're home from work?"

"Yes."

"Still sick?" I could hear his labored breathing. "I'm sorry."

"I'm O.K.," he said.

"I bought you a surprise," I said, trying to sound cheerful.

216

"When are you coming back?"

"Day after tomorrow."

"Tomorrow?"

"Day after," I repeated.

"O.K."

"Derek?"

"What?"

"Is there anything else you want from here?"

"No," he said. "Just enjoy yourself."

"I love you," I said, sensing that he knew it was a lie.

There was silence. Then he hung up.

I stood before the mirror, gazing at myself. I would not let myself feel bad. I had come of my own will to be with Marwan. Even if we never had more than these few days, they were ours. Nothing would change that.

There was a knock on the door. Although he had the key, Marwan presumably wanted to give me warning if I were still on the telephone.

He came in and put a newspaper on the dresser. "There's trouble in Iran," he said.

I tried to absorb this, switching quickly from my inner world of guilt to the oddly comforting one of politics "What sort of trouble?"

"The Mullahs want to get rid of Akbari."

"Wasn't he just elected head of the Parliament?" I said.

"Yes. But he wants reforms. If they decide he's too pro-West, he'll be kicked out. It'll cause trouble in the Gulf."

We were both silent. Finally, Marwan looked at his watch. "We should leave soon." Then he came and gave me a hug. "I'm sorry I've been impatient. It's just — suddenly you have a family. I didn't feel it in Abu Samra."

"Marwan, the first time we met I told you I was married. Almost immediately I told you I had been pregnant. What did you think?"

He released me and went over to the dresser. "Of course I

217

knew it, I just didn't *feel* it. And I'm not referring to your pregnancy. I thought your marriage was incidental. I didn't have to deal with your husband before."

"But he's *there,* I can't pretend he isn't. Even if our marriage isn't what it should be, or what I want, I can't ignore him. I'm not exactly free, Marwan."

"You're as free as you want to be. You came here with me, didn't you?"

"Yes."

"Why did you?"

I took a deep, excruciating breath, not believing he was asking me this. "Because I *wanted* to."

"Would you have come if you were happy with your husband?"

"Of course not."

"Then, why did you come here if you're not planning to leave him?"

I stared at him. "You're asking me to divorce."

"Are you?"

"I don't know," I said. "Don't ask me that, Marwan."

"Why not?"

"Because I'm not ready."

"Then, what's all this? What am I to you?"

I felt my head reeling. "Don't ask me now."

He smiled gently. "When, then? What is it you want?"

I took a deep breath. "I want you."

"How?" he said, turning around to face me.

"I don't know."

"Well, you're life's a bit crowded at the moment," he said, calmly. "You seem to want us both."

"I don't want both of you. I'm only happy when I'm with you." I sat down on the bed and buried my face in my hands. Then I looked up. "You make a decision early in your life, when you don't know who you are or what you want, and you have to live with it forever. That's where I am now."

218

"It doesn't have to be like that. Life is *change*. If things don't change, they die. You, like the rest of us, can change whatever you want. Change your perception of things and *you* change. Nothing's holding you back but yourself. *You.*"

"I can't just think about me. There are others I'll hurt."

He was silent. Then he looked away, picked up the newspaper and went out to the balcony. Although I could feel his frustration, I did not follow him.

A few minutes later he returned. "There's something I have to tell you," he said, softly.

I looked up at him from where I was sitting on the edge of the bed.

"I have a heart condition."

"What?" I said, as if he had just told me a startling joke.

"I had a heart attack at thirty nine. Luckily I was in London and not out on a site somewhere. It seems to be heredity. My father died in his mid-fifties."

I stared at him.

"All they can do is monitor me. Medication. Diet and exercise."

I thought of his lunches of yogurt and bread and rarely drinking anything but water and fruit juice despite John's passion for lager. I caught my breath. "Why didn't you tell me before?"

"I try not to think about it. I do what I'm supposed to and go on."

"Are you at risk for another one?"

He shrugged. "Atherosclerosis doesn't just disappear. I'm not a candidate for surgery though, nothing's blocked enough, although sometimes I feel like a bloody time-bomb."

"How often do you get checked?"

"Every time I'm in London."

"And?"

"I'm O.K. Just have to be careful. I've been meaning to tell you all along, but each time I was afraid you'd change your mind about me."

"Because you had a heart attack?"

He shrugged, "I have heart disease."

I felt a crushing in my own chest, like silent gasping. I stood and went to him. He looked both sadder and more wonderful than I had ever seen him. I put out my arms and held him, gently at first as if I might break him. Then I relaxed and squeezed tighter, afraid I might lose him in the next five seconds if I let go.

He had made reservations at *l'Auberge*, near the pyramids. From the highway, I got my first close look at the Sphinx, magnificently lit by floodlights. Even from a distance its bold features were clear.

The tension that had consumed us earlier had evaporated with the unexpected revelation of his illness. I suddenly wanted more than anything to be with him and make him happy.

The restaurant was intimate and already full of people. They were smartly dressed and I was glad I had brought a black cocktail dress that seemed to suit the glamorous Cairo nightlife far more than the restricted one of Abu Samra.

We ordered wine and Marwan, usually limiting himself to fruit juice, raised his glass. "To us."

I raised my glass, smiling, ignoring the throbbing in my chest at the thought of the danger he was in. The memory of my mother's death suddenly invaded every part of my body, the pain as fresh and grating as if we had buried her yesterday.

There was a small dance floor near our table where a group of tight-vested young men were setting up equipment. After adjusting their instruments, they struck up a rumbling, Latin beat. Marwan turned to me.

"Dance?"

Before waiting for me to answer, he eased out of his chair and helped me up. We passed the waiter bringing our appetizers. "Maybe we should wait," I said, seeing that we were the only ones on the dance floor and that I had not danced in years.

220

"Why?"

"The food will get cold."

"Come on," he said, reaching for me.

Derek did not particularly like to dance although he was fairly good. Not having danced together before, Marwan and I moved together uneasily, barely touching, his hand holding me in an almost-caress. Yet I sensed that he liked to dance, without being overly conscious of how good or not he was.

"Are you happy?" he asked, suddenly.

I nodded.

He smiled. "Be with me?"

I could barely believe his words. All of a sudden it hardly mattered in what capacity he meant them. Only that he had said them.

"Well?" he repeated.

I shook my head. "I don't know."

He chuckled, looking surprised. "Why?"

"It may not work."

"Why not?"

My previous fear, that he was unobtainable and that I must stop loving him, was gone. Now, I was afraid of what would come next. After the initial passion, the possible loss. The thought was too much to hold.

"It's working now," he said, his voice rising above the music.

I could feel the despair knot in my throat. "What if we get on each other's nerves? All the things wrong with my marriage will re-surface with you," I said, although I was unable to imagine my life now without him.

"But I'm not him."

I was silent, clinging to him, barely aware of the floor beneath my feet. *No, he was nothing like Derek.*

After the appetizer of Egyptian pastries, I watched as the waiter served our fish which had been grilled in grape leaves. The white flesh was tangy from the leaves and delicately spiced with fennel. When the waiter left I said, "What if we're wrong, Marwan?"

221

"Wrong about what?" He looked me in the eye, then smiled. "We're not," he said.

It was late when we left the restaurant. When we got to the clearing overlooking the Sphinx, Marwan told the taxi driver to pull over to the side of the road. This late, only the car's headlights shone on the phantom half-lion, half-virgin colossus.

Marwan pointed to the triangular shadows further off. "Look. Cheops and Kephren." Then he threw open the taxi door and paid the driver. "Come on."

"Now?" I said, totally baffled.

He pulled me after him. After waiting for some cars to pass, he gripped my hand even tighter, and like children doing something forbidden, we hurried across the dark highway to the other side where we stood face to face with the Sphinx. I leaned against him, trying to discern the features of the crumbling giant, hearing the sounds of the vehicles rushing along the highway behind us.

I gripped my jacket tighter about me from the chill, yet I could feel Marwan's warmth, as if his blood was suddenly scalding his veins at the sight. We were practically in shouting distance of them all!

"It was the Egyptians' unique vision of the cosmos that sustained their civilization for so long," he said. "Victorian travelers used to spend the night on this very plain just to witness the sunrise over these pyramids."

I stared at the shadows. In the dark, the Sphinx seemed strangely placated.

"I told you I'd bring you here," Marwan said, his jubilant voice reaching out to soothe me. "I just wanted you to see it like this first, to *feel* their presence before seeing them in daylight."

I was silent. I traced the calm, eroded face of the Sphinx and suddenly wanted to demand that it solve this riddle for me: Now that I had found the man I wanted, why was he so far out of my reach? Why had he been sent to me now? Why?

"Gina?"

"I love it," I said, tracing the tip of the Sphinx's broken nose, trying to drown my fears in the mesmerizing grandness of what lay before us.

"When you see them in daytime after this, you'll find them entirely different. Your imagination will help you now, and you'll see what you never would in the light. You'll even draw and paint them differently."

"How do you know that?" I asked, surprised at his words, yet immediately struck by the same notion myself.

"I read about it. Some Italian artist, one of the Orientalists. Even though he'd seen it all in daylight, the darkness illuminated things differently. Apparently, he never painted them the same way after seeing them at night."

I snuggled close against him. I did begin to see clearly — the sheer height of the distant triangles, the massive paws of the Sphinx. Although I had thought I wanted to sketch them up close, the thought of coming to see them again in daylight after this seemed utterly meaningless.

"Arab love poetry is so poignant," he said suddenly, "because it's inspired by unrequited love."

I smiled. "Unfulfilled desire has fired up a lot of poets."

He stared down at me. "It's the searching that we're all after," he said, quietly. "But love should never remain unrequited. When you find love, take it and run with it."

"If you can," I said. Despair once again wedged itself between us like a giant boulder.

Marwan pulled away slightly and turned to face me. "What would be the ultimate commitment?"

"What do you mean?"

"Take a pencil and paper and write it down. What it is you

223

want from me."

"It's not that simple, Marwan."

"Try it."

I closed my eyes.

"I guess I want to be able to love as much as be loved. Otherwise none of it makes sense. I want to *love*, Marwan."

Despite the dark, I could detect the peace in his face. "Then *do*." he said, softly.

I nodded, resting my head on his chest.

"I can't give you the life he can, Gina, the comforts, the travel. I'm not wealthy. I've no inheritance to speak of. And I'm sorrier for that than for anything else in my life at the moment. Because in a way, I feel I've no right to expect anything from you."

"I don't want anything."

"I just feel I have to be honest with you."

I shook my head. "I don't expect any of those things."

I knew his financial situation, knew from the first time we met. He had never hidden it from me. But I did not care. I wanted to shout into the cool, desert air that I did not expect Marwan Jassim to offer me material wealth, never did.

"All we have together is this moment. All of this around us was simply a moment. Like Zulaika. A moment. Long gone."

A moment. I shut my eyes. If only I could see it that way.

"And now you know about my health."

"That doesn't matter either," I said.

He smiled slightly, as if in gratitude.

"I just don't understand any of this, don't even understand you. I'm so tied to him now."

"You're not tied to anybody. Don't look outside of yourself to anyone or anything. What about you? What do you want for you?"

"I never think of only me," I said.

"You're the only one who can," he said, firmly.

I pulled away again. "Marwan, you expect me to break apart my life, just like that."

"It was already broken. Long before you met me. I'm suggesting you do something with the pieces. Remember. Flow with the will of the world. Be at peace."

I did not know what to say, but I knew he was right.

18

Derek

I flew back to Abu Samra, alone.

I had not told Marwan that I had rebooked my flight to leave a day earlier. The previous night after dinner, I had asked that he sleep in his room, that he understand that I needed to be alone. I would meet him the next morning so we could go to the pyramids together, see them in daylight as he had promised.

But next morning, I was on an airplane.

I left him a note at the front desk informing him that I had to return home, not to worry, that I would see him when he got back. *I love you*, I had signed it, amazed by the words on the paper, realizing how long it had been since I had written these words to a man and meant them so honestly and intensely. By now he would have undoubtedly read them. I imagined his face, angry or puzzled, perhaps thinking that I was playing some game with him, that I was running home to the safety of my healthy husband.

My eyes began to burn. Of course he would think that he had scared me off, that I was unable to handle the threat of his illness, of what it would mean to the hope of a viable future for us, of what it meant to any woman who came into his life. I lay my head against the airplane window, almost nauseous with fear. I could not think of losing him, of a world without him. I was far beyond ever returning to my old life. Yet, I did not imagine that he wondered much about his own mortality. He would simply accept it, as he accepted his life. The state of things at any given moment.

Approaching Abu Samra from above, the Gulf waters began to unfurl in a jigsaw of shapes and variations of color — limpid aqua, green, and yellow again where the coral shoals and sandbars rose up from the deep, cobalt water. According to geologists, some 20,000 years ago this Gulf had been a mere river through which the Tigris and Euphrates poured into the Arabian Sea. It had taken 15,000 years for the river to turn into the present Gulf, still saltier, shallower, and warmer than most of the world's seas. I had read about this back in New York, before ever glimpsing the Gulf or swimming in it. In my other life, before ever meeting Marwan.

A slender line of sand now appeared to the right of my window. Then came the dark clumps of palm forests, the variegated limestone hills on the beaches, the scattered villages, each with a mosque's lone, piercing minaret. I tried to locate Saali among the clusters of seaside houses, then Dafna further inland. Soon, we were flying over a collage of roads, cars, and concrete and gypsum buildings. Hundreds of flat rooftops slid past below, their metal water storage tanks and solar panels blinking up at us as we swooped lower and lower.

I felt an involuntary thrill at the sight of the downtown. I tried to remember how Abu Samra had looked to me from the air the first time I arrived last summer — so utterly foreign, practically extraterrestrial. Now I seemed to have known it forever. I had not expected the comforting feeling of being home that washed over me. I had not considered myself attached to Abu Samra in that way yet, but in the few months that we had lived here, the sandy peninsula had bored its way into me more deeply than I would ever have thought possible. I had even missed our dull brown house with its

228

high, cement wall. But it was Marwan who had ignited this passion for the peninsula in me, not Derek. Marwan who had made me see the potential in everything, the beauty beyond the surface banality, so glaring at first.

Dafna was still a new residential area and thus not on any official map, so I had to explain to the taxi driver how to get there. I was surprised that he did not seem to know that 'Dafna' referred to the crematorium.

The damp winds swept through the taxi's windows as we approached town. Scraps of brittle mud lined both sides of the road, and there were undrained puddles along some of the smaller streets where a few cars stagnated in brown water.

"It rained a lot?" I asked the driver.

"Much rain," the driver said, curtly, "very bad."

A short beard covered his cheeks and chin and his red-checkered winter *gutra* headdress fell in austere folds on either side of his face. He pointed his finger out the windows, right and left, a pained frown drawing in his lips. "All streets bad."

"Rain is good for the farmers," I said.

He tilted his head from side to side, as if considering the validity of this. "Yes, good," he said, sounding unsure.

The two days that I had been gone made me see the landscape anew. This road with the barren sand on either side was so different from the highway that led from Cairo airport into the city through the cluttered City of the Dead. Although there was nothing of visible magnificence here to startle anyone at first glance, none of the timeless, durable layers of history of Cairo, there was an endearing quality to the porous sand, a tenderness in the open spaces of the landscape and small, low buildings that faded into one another like lumps of soft clay. And there was the awareness I now had of the riches that lay buried beneath it all. The peninsula's magnetism lay in this very mystery, in what rested below the surface of life and the precarious, crumbling palaces, beyond the villages shielded by palms and the inlets of turquoise water. The idea that one could so easily

229

pass through Abu Samra without ever realizing what lay underground made it seem even more elusive, like the women behind their black *abayas* or village shawls. Nothing was what it seemed from the outside.

Staring out the window, I wondered how I would feel when I saw Derek, how I would explain my early arrival home. Then, I thought of Marwan. I could still hear the urgency in his words the night before at the restaurant: *Be with me?*

The taxi driver was listening to the news on the car radio. The static was deafening, but he persisted in trying to get clearer reception, impatiently twisting the tuning knob from side to side.

"Iran bad," he said, suddenly, shifting to yet another station.

"What's happened?"

"Mullahs."

"What Mullahs?"

The driver did not answer, continuing to adjust the radio.

I leaned forward. "Has something happened to Mullah Akbari?"

The driver swept his finger across his throat.

I pulled back. "He's dead?"

The driver vigorously shook his head. "Mullah Akbari, go," he said, flinging his arm toward the window as if to throw out a banana peel.

"He's left the country?"

The driver nodded.

Ayatollah Akbari, one of the most powerful Iranian clergyman who had been well liked by Ayatollah Khomeini, had lately been trying to initiate certain reforms. For this he had come under attack by several of the more conservative Mullahs contending for power in Iran's government.

So now Akbari, regarded as one of the most powerful leaders in the Gulf, was gone? Had he been gotten rid of so easily and quickly? I had not kept up with the riots on the Teheran streets shown nightly on the news; the pictures of angry youths, of black-*chadored* women clutching pictures of the deceased Ayatollah Khomeini. Akbari had advocated stronger ties with other Arab Gulf states instead of the rivalry for control of the Gulf as had some of the other Mullahs. I wondered whether this stance had to do with his ouster. I wondered, also, how much of this would incite the Abu Samra *Shia* villagers. When the Shah was overthrown, the peninsula had apparently been in political turmoil for nearly a year because of the villagers' sudden awareness that if the masses in Iran could over-throw the Shah, surely the masses in Abu Samra could rid them-selves of a small ruling family with no real ties to the peninsula.

When Marwan had read of the Iran problems in the paper yes-terday, I had forgotten it soon afterwards. There had been a televi-sion in the room that we had never turned on, not even to hear the news. The outside world and its occurrences had faded into insig-nificance in that insular refuge where only the two of us mattered. But now, echoes of the *Muharram* marchers seemed to explode in the taxi. I sat back, not sure how to feel about this news.

Some small blond children I did not recognize were playing in the road in front of our house. Outside our gate, the ground ap-peared to have finally been cleared of all the builder's debris of the past months. Open crates with pieces of furniture, still wrapped in plastic, sat in the front yard of the new house next door. The poign-ant awareness that the house had been rented sliced into me. The smells of fried onions and cumin from the workmen's lunches were gone for good, as were the sounds of the men's singing or the clink-ing of pots and spoons as they assembled their pungent curries.

The Buick was not in the garage. Obviously, Derek had been well enough to go to work today. Several small flowers had bloomed inside the front gate, on either side of the speckled tile walkway. A few reddish marigolds and some purple buds had also appeared on the bushes that I had bought from the garden club. Inside the front door I could hear Lhatti upstairs vacuuming.

231

We had nicknamed this foyer 'the ballroom' because of its vast size compared to the smaller, formal living room. But now something was different about it. Against the main wall where the cherry desk had been, was a large, rectangular shape that glimmered in the light of the open front door like some pirate's treasure.

I stared at the shiny, brass nails in disbelief. It was the wooden chest that we had seen in the market the week before, the one that Derek had described as "gaudy."

"Derek," I gasped.

I caressed the rich wood that I had admired in the cluttered shop. It was spectacular. Derek had bought it, even though he had not cared for it.

"Derek," I said again, almost daring someone to hear, although I knew he was not home. "It's too late."

Almost before realizing what I was doing, I was in the Renault driving away from the house. At the major roundabout I started to take the road to Saali, but knew I could not face the *tel* without Marwan there. Instead, I continued around to the carriageway that led to the swimming beach. Finally, I drove off the asphalt into the desert toward the burial mounds.

Pulling my jacket about my shoulders from the stinging breeze, I climbed up the mound I had sat on the very first time I had come with 'Abbas. It had been a month since I had been here. As usual, my eyes followed the rippling vista, the way it rolled away from my feet toward the horizon in huge, sandy waves. This spot always filled me with a curious sense of renewal, as if our unknown future was somehow determined by all that had transpired in the countless lifetimes that lay under the sand.

I sat down and stared off to where the necropolis met the sky in soft billows. Somewhere, I knew there had to be a plan for me. I pulled my legs in to my chest, wrapped my arms around them, and rested my head on my knees. I closed my eyes, wanting desperately to cry, to ease the pain inside me. But no tears would come.

Derek and I sat at the dinner table eating the chicken curry and lentil *dahl* that Lhatti had prepared.

"She makes great rice," Derek said, spooning more of the fluffy *basmati* onto his plate. It was tinged gold by the yellow turmeric that Lhatti put in everything she cooked.

"It's delicious," I said.

"She made an Indian omelette the other day," Derek went on, describing the coriander, cauliflower and onions that Lhatti had fried into the eggs.

"Sounds wonderful." I had been miserable since sitting down to dinner with Derek, trying to keep the conversation on Cairo, the food, or on the current situation in Iran. I had quickly relayed some details about the pyramids and the Sphinx, enough to sound convincing, and explained away my early return to my concern for his flu.

"I still can't believe Akbari left. I thought he was well supported," I said.

"It's not as if he had a choice," Derek replied. He had looked bewildered and tense since he got home from work. "It's bad, any way you look at it."

Although the initial shock of the overthrow had worn off, I could not begin to contemplate what might happen as a result, what it would mean to us in Abu Samra. What it would mean, specifically, to Marwan's dig.

"Do you think he'll come back?" I asked.

"Nobody's strong enough to keep him out for good."

"Will there be more trouble?"

"If some dictator takes over there will be," Derek said.

I took a gulp of water, aware again of the slight salty taste. I thought of the delicious sweet water of Cairo. Marwan was still drinking it, still bathing in it. I imagined my fingers sliding along his back in the shower, rinsing away the foam, saw again the color of his skin change from the deep brown of his arms where the sun hit, to the lighter olive color of his back and buttocks.

233

"How do you think it will affect us, here?" I said, forcibly steering my mind back to the present moment, as Marwan always urged me to do.

Derek leaned back in his chair. "Iran's always had its eye on the Gulf. The Mansours are upset as hell. They're more nervous than they normally are, which is already pretty bad. I just hope they don't try to please these people too much."

"Please which people?"

"Radicals. They could start evicting foreigners, especially Americans."

"Now?"

"Of course."

We watched the English news. There were crowds **in the** streets of Teheran celebrating the departure of Akbari, angry youths, screaming, *chadored* women. Scenes that had become commonplace over the last few months suddenly took on a grave, new dimension in light of what they had led to.

I wondered whether the Abu Samran women could become like the ones on the television, their modest, protective *abayas* becoming warriors' mantles.

"Derek, could it become dangerous for us, here?"

He changed the channel. The same scenes were being played on the two Arabic ones. "People get jittery. All foreigners are at risk."

"But it's nothing like Iran, here," I said. Yet, my words seemed hollow. If the processions were any indication, the Abu Samrans could get as passionate, perhaps even as violent, as anyone else. "What would we do if things got bad?"

Derek switched channels again. "We'd leave. At least *you* would."

I inhaled, suddenly feeling as if he had cut off my blood supply. "How can you say that? I wouldn't leave you here." I was terrified at the prospect of being separated from Marwan. I certainly could not leave.

"Let's not worry about that, now," Derek said, setting down the remote control. An old *Bonanza* rerun was playing on this channel. He leaned back on the couch with a smile. He had rarely watched television in New York with all the paperwork he used to bring home, but things were different here. In an office where he was in charge, nobody asked anything of him each morning. I wondered, briefly, how Derek would ever be able to return to the politics and bureaucracy of the New York office. I tried to concentrate, like him, on the soothing *Bonanza* domestic scene, the family of men gathered around the table in the old West. It was peaceful, even funny.

"Feeling homesick?" he asked, suddenly.

I turned to him and saw that he was watching me. "Why?"

"Maybe you should go home for a while. Spend a month with your father."

"I'm fine."

"You don't look fine."

I tried to smile, to appear wholesome like the actors gathering around the table. "How do I look?"

"You look depressed. You haven't been your old self in weeks."

Months, I wanted to scream. *Ever since I met him I haven't been the same. I can never be the same, now. And anyway, what was my old self? Simply surviving, existing for existence's sake.*

"Cairo didn't do the trick, I guess," he said.

I looked at him, expecting some accusation in his eyes, some hint that he knew. There was only a smug complacency that made me draw myself up. "I guess not," I said, in no mood to argue.

A few minutes later he asked, "Any ideas what to do for Thanksgiving?" He was smiling as if the topic of preparing for the holiday would cure me of what he saw as homesickness.

I shrugged. "I haven't even thought of it." This was true, although at my visit to the supermarket the week before I saw that they had received a fresh supply of frozen American turkeys, cans of

235

cranberry sauce, and even boxes of *Pepperidge Farm* stuffing. I suddenly envied Mary's foresight in baking and freezing her pies during *Muharram*.

'Shall we invite people over?" he said.

"No," I said, suddenly revolted by the idea of pretending in front of guests that we were a normal, loving couple.

"How about Mary and Frank? What are they doing?"

"Mary's having guests. She invited us, too. If you want to be with people, we could go there."

"What do you mean if *I* want to be with people? What about you?"

I was silent.

"Well, I'm shutting the office since New York is closed. The Sheraton and Hilton are having special dinners. We could go there."

"Whatever you want."

"Well, I'd like to have *some* sense of Thanksgiving."

"All right."

"So, shall I book at one of the hotels?" He persisted, making no attempt to hide his frustration with my indifference.

"Yes," I snapped, suddenly feeling like a fire-cracker about to go off if Derek asked me one more question or asked me to make a decision.

"I could bake a turkey here, if you want, Gina. Just give me your mother's recipe. I don't mind cooking."

Suddenly, the mention of my mother, of her Thanksgiving dinners which we had always gone to in Norwalk right up until she had gotten sick, was too much. I started to cry.

Derek touched my shoulder. "I'm sorry. I know it's a sensitive issue for you," he said. "We had great times with your parents at Thanksgiving. It won't be the same, but we can try, Gina. We'll have to start a new tradition. For *us.*"

He brushed away my tears and I reached for his hand. I held it tight. Deep inside me I knew that even when he had been aloof, impossible to communicate with, always planning ahead so that we

were never quite able to enjoy our present lives, he had always protected me. Even his stolid, practical approach to life had pressed
around me like armor to shield me. How could I leave the man who
had known my mother, knew my family, my past? With Derek I
could discuss the time when my mother was alive, the Thanksgiv-
ings when we would all sit around the table tasting some new recipe
she had found in a magazine, debating whether or not to include it
in our Thanksgiving menu the next year. Derek and I had so many
shared memories in our twelve years together. Marwan and I had
none — no past together, barely a present. *You are not your past,* he
always said. *You are not your yesterday.* Yet how, I wondered, would it
be to start over and build a future with someone new who had no
real knowledge of my traditions, of my roots or childhood? Nor I of
his? A man who did not even regard the past with any reverence
except as revealed history? As appealing as it sounded, I had no idea
how to begin to live my life with no use for any time but the present
moment.

Something inside me desperately wanted to tell Derek of all
that had chewed away at me since we had come here, since the day I
first met Marwan. I wanted to completely purge myself by confess-
ing. But, I only lay my cheek against his hand in silence.

He put his arms around me. "I know," he said.

I lifted my head. "Know what?"

"Everything."

I pulled back, slightly.

His eyes penetrated mine, as if I were a slate he were decipher-
ing. He ran his hand over my head. "I know how unhappy you've
been here, Gina. How alien all of this is to you. I know how hard it
is for you to paint, how you hate having to entertain and go to all
the functions. It's a different life from what we had in New York.
But it won't last forever. I promise you. It won't be much longer."

I let him stroke my hair, pat my stinging face. He squeezed my
arm affectionately, as if in gratitude for all that I had gone through
because of him, for all that I had done for his sake, for all that I

237

would still have to do for the sake of his work. For our future. This pattern we had gotten ourselves into the last few years that put him in charge of our lives and relegated me to being the necessary, if sidelined, accessory was only now becoming clear to him, apparently. I thought of how hopeful I had been when I had left New York, how certain I was that years of established behavior and feelings could be turned around by a simple change of scene. But deep inside I must have known that I needed more than just a change of location. The first night that we had walked down Abu Samra's streets, and earlier that morning when I had stood on the roof, I had sensed that something drastic was in store for us. Derek, it seems, had never felt this.

"Derek, don't you ever want more?"

"More?" His eyebrows shot up.

"Out of life."

"Sure."

"But are your hopes being met? By me, by our life together?"

He shrugged. "Most of the time." He paused, "You?"

I finally shook my head. "Not really. Sometimes I seriously think of a trial separation."

"Trial separation?" he started to chuckle. "What are you talking about?"

I could not bring myself to answer.

He moved closer to me. "Let's make it better then." He peered into my eyes as if he were trying to explain something complicated to a child. "It *will* get better, Gina."

I stared back at him, amazed that he could be so blind.

Yet, a part of me still wanted to believe that by some miracle he could erase all traces of Marwan in my mind and in my body, that he could somehow kill all memory of how Marwan and I had clung to each other in luscious desperation only a day ago. I wanted to be free of this madness, free of Marwan and the pleasure and pain that loving him had brought me. If only Derek could do that, I would do anything for him. If he could make me forget, protect me from the suffering that being away from Marwan brought, I would *be* anything for him.

"Derek," I said, drying my eyes. "I need to go to bed."

He rose up from the couch, looking happier than I had seen him all evening, and pulled me up, folding me into him.

He had misunderstood me. I was too tired and too alienated to make love. Intimacy was the last thing on my mind. Yet I worried that he would begin to suspect something if I pulled away.

Later, as I got out of bed to retrieve my nightgown, I noticed Derek watching me in the dark. I slipped on the gown and returned to bed, pulling the blankets up around me as if were he to look at me too closely, even in the dark, he would see through me to Marwan. He would not have known this during love-making. We had always been good partners, even when the passion had gone out of it. Perhaps simple repetition had made it easy to enjoy physical pleasure with Derek. But that was all it was for me now. My shell lying with his.

"Why did you do it?" he said, suddenly.

I froze. "Do what?"

"Why did you go to Cairo?"

I moved further to my edge of the bed, feeling suddenly numb where he had touched me, unsure whether to deny it or admit it. He seemed like a total stranger now, someone who might hurt me if he chose to, if he knew. My fear of what he might do made me want to bolt from the bed, from the room, the house. Instead, I lay still as a corpse, as if I had just been lowered into a grave.

"You went without me," he said, his voice flat. "You've never done that before."

"Why didn't you object?"

"Would it have done any good?"

"I wouldn't have gone," I said, knowing, in some small way that this was true.

"Do you love me, Gina?"

"Why are you asking me that?"

"You keep wanting to run away," he said. "Now you bring up a 'trial separation.' Things have changed between us. I don't know."

I let out a slow, soft sigh of relief that he did not seem to know anything about Marwan.

He turned away from me and covered his head with the blanket.

I felt I would suffocate if I stayed beside him in this thunderous silence. I had to move to the next room, even the floor, anywhere to get away from him. I thought of his having made love to me only minutes ago. He had hidden any resentment or unhappiness then. How could he behave so differently from one moment to the next? My pretense at being connected to him these past few months, while involved with someone else, had taken its toll on me.

I did not move from the bed, however. I lay quietly, as he did, until I recognized the steady flow of his breathing that meant that he was finally asleep.

Yet, I wanted something better for Derek, something more than what I could offer him now. It occurred to me that it was time to make a break, for him as much as for me. He deserved more than my pretense at love. He deserved, indeed I *wished* for him, the passion I felt for Marwan. Although he had scoffed at my suggestion of a trial separation, I knew that it might be the only thing that would liberate him from his hold on me.

I lay awake, aware of the tiniest sound in the room, of my thoughts ticking by one by one.

I wondered whether Marwan was lying like this in bed or was out having dinner with somebody on his last night in Cairo. I wondered whether he was thinking of me, whether he was angry.

My body seemed to suddenly expand inside my skin. How I wanted him with me at this very moment! How I wanted to share the life of this man who had given me back my own life in all its fullness, tumult, pain and joy again.

19

Zulaika

Three days later, I drove to the *tel*. Marwan had been back for two days but I had not been able to bring myself to go immediately. Neither had I told Derek that I was going to the *tel* this morning, although I suspected that he knew that I would soon enough.

It was the first week of December and there was a bite in the breeze, like the ominous, cold silence that used to hover above New York just before a snowfall. Crystalline swathes of sunlight blew across the green farmland between the black, water-soaked road and the gray sea, clear as if the air had finally been siphoned of all the dust and contaminants of the previous summer. The palms shook in the breeze above the sea rolling ashore in great salty curls of foam. Nearing Saali, I lowered the window. I was wearing a sweater and a heavy rain-jacket, the first time I had dressed for winter in Abu Samra.

Marwan had called me the morning he got back — something he had only done once before. "What happened?" he said, as soon as I picked up the telephone. He sounded more intrigued than upset, as if secretly impressed that I had abandoned him without warning.

"It was too hard being there," I said.

"It was too hard being there," I said.

"I thought you were happy."

"I was."

There was a long pause. "Are you all right?"

"I'm fine," I said.

"Come to the *tel* today."

"I can't."

"Come to me, Gina."

The thought of meeting him in the privacy of some hotel room, of feeling him in my arms again made me practically shout into the receiver that I would be right there. But where? All of the hotels were in town where we might be seen. I would not have the luxury of that kind of anonymity again.

"I'll try and come to the *tel* tomorrow," I said.

"Or next week," he said, barely concealing his disappointment.

"I have to be careful," I said, wishing I did not have to impose my other life on him, yet expecting him to understand why I had to. More than that, I did not trust my emotions in front of the workmen and John Reese at the site. How could I stand among them and pretend that nothing had changed between us these past few days?

"I love you," he said. "I just want to see you."

My mood suddenly lifted. "Me too."

The dourness of Saali contrasted starkly with my memory of the flower-filled Egyptian village where we had bought cloth. The maroon and green paint of the houses here, already dulled by too much heat and humidity, could do little to detract from the unsightly metal beams and cinder blocks left to weather away on the side of the road. Yet, having been away for the first time, I felt sentimental as I drove through the village, as if I finally understood that rising above its own plainness was too much to ask of Saali.

Even the *tel* from a distance looked small and pathetic after Cairo's imposing ruins. It was sad to think of all that Marwan had invested in it. I tried to conjure up his face. I wanted to look into his

242

eyes and read what lay ahead for us, as if it were mapped out there for all to see. I was so different from the person he had first met. I could barely recall the conflicted feelings of attraction and disquiet that had filled me then, my giddy annoyance at his approaching me so audaciously. Now I knew only the delight that he brought me, the knowledge that with him I could be the person I really was, the Gina I could never be with Derek, able to say anything I pleased, any way I pleased, without being misunderstood or judged; able to feel pleasure in every moment without constantly having to think ahead or even look back. For the first time ever, I wanted to hold time at an absolute standstill, to experience again and again each moment's glorious fullness, savor each delicious nugget of peace and contentment he seemed to place inside of me.

Marwan's white jeep was parked on the beach. Beside it, however, instead of the blue workmen's pick-up, was a luminous black Range Rover.

I was disappointed at the intrusion. Marwan knew I was coming. I had expected that he would not have wanted any strangers at the *tel* this morning. With only John and the workmen around, we could find moments of privacy, even if only for a short time to dig together. This vehicle changed that.

I sat in my own car, watching the whitecaps surge to shore, and considered going home and returning later. Perhaps the next day. But I could not bear to leave without at least seeing him!

I got out, locked the car door, and started up the *tel*.

A small tent had been erected. The workmen, their soft tunics whipping out from under their sweaters in the breeze, stood in a cluster as if awaiting orders to embark on some harrowing mission. Marwan and John Reese stood by the tent where Marwan was holding open a large sheet of paper. A woman wearing a yellow shirt and blue jeans stood with her back to me. A red scarf was wrapped round her neck and her hair blew toward the sea like a black tangle

243

of seaweed. Beside her stood a man in a gray *thob* and a red checkered *gutra*.

Marwan looked up, his face changing the instant he saw me. The woman turned round. It was Sheikha Mariam. The man in the *thob* was Sheikh Ahmad.

The Sheikha nodded to me, then looked back to the paper Marwan was holding.

As if aware of my apprehension, Marwan suddenly called out to me. "Gina!"

I waved and walked over to them slowly, giving them time to continue their business. Finally, they rolled up the paper.

The cool wind stung my eyes, drying my throat each time I took a breath. I remembered the loose, cold sand beneath me and Marwan's cheek on my face, his hands cushioning my head where we had lain together that night just a few feet away.

"Good morning, Your Excellency," I said, practically blurting out the words as I extended my hand to Sheikha Mariam and then to Sheikh Ahmad. I smiled at Marwan and John, hoping my face would not give me away, that I would not blush or show how suddenly stranded and out of place I felt.

Sheikh Ahmad smiled. "It's good to see you, Mrs. Monroe. How's your husband?" He looked dapper as usual, the snug grey collar at his throat held shut with a gold pin. I remembered how impressed I had been when I had first seen him with his brother in the lobby of the hotel. Today he seemed to look even younger, more boyish, his black hair as glossy as his black shoes, now filmy with dust.

"Derek's fine, thank you, Your Excellency."

He looked at me reproachfully. "He still hasn't brought you to my farm."

"I'll have to remind him," I said, smiling.

"Now, it's a mess, I'm afraid. I'm having my gardens redesigned."

It occurred to me that this was being done in preparation for his and Sheikha Mariam's upcoming wedding. I sensed, however, that now was not the time to congratulate them on their engagement.

I searched for clues that they were a couple, that they were in love, that they yearned to be together away from this public place and the rest of us. But whatever they felt for each other was carefully buried under the stolid gaze of the Sheikha and the aloof, good natured air of her cousin.

The Sheikha turned to me. Her eyes were neither sympathetic nor unfriendly but she was able, with a single look, to make one feel both important and insignificant.

"Did you enjoy your visit to Cairo?" she said.

I stared at her. She had called while I was away and Derek had told her. I decided to pretend I knew nothing about her call.

"Very much," I said, feeling my face grow warm. Marwan kept his eyes on the trench nearby although I knew that he had heard her.

"I thought you would be at work today," she said. "Have you brought any of your drawings?"

"I hadn't thought about it, Your Excellency." I was confused by her continued concern with my work, almost wishing I had never told her of it. "If I know when you're coming next time, I'll be sure to."

"Bring them to my office at the museum," she said.

I was surprised. "That's very kind of you. I'd like that."

"The day after tomorrow, at two o'clock."

"Thank you. I will."

John Reese glanced at me, then walked over to the workmen and said something that made them disperse and pick up their tools. The friction in the air was stifling, as if something had happened or been said just before I arrived. I tried to catch Marwan's eye to find out what was wrong, but he was studying the map that he had reopened as though unaware of my presence. I put my hands in my pockets from the cold.

"Sheikha, this waterway had to have been the harbor," Marwan said, abruptly, lowering the map. I looked out to where he was pointing, to the wide, shallow bay that separated the *tel's* beach from the strip of land that jutted into the sea beyond Saali.

The Sheikha was silent.

"Is it not too shallow for a harbor?" Sheikh Ahmad said.

"Not really," Marwan said. "It just seems that way, now."

It was the first time I had heard Marwan talk with the Sheikha or with Sheikh Ahmad, and it occurred to me that without John Reese they would naturally be speaking in Arabic. It felt odd to hear them all conversing in English — the universal technical language, I supposed.

I had no idea what they were talking about. *A harbor?* Twice each day, at low tide, when the sea seemed to drain away, the sand bars were high enough for donkey carts to cross over the waterway from the trees on the beach a short distance away to the jutting land in the distance. I remembered being amazed by this the first time I had seen some villagers crossing and the sand which disappeared underwater a short while later. But this small beach certainly did not resemble anything like a harbor.

"It was deep enough once, and it was probably dredged. It's the ideal location for a bay," Marwan said, looking from Sheikh Ahmad to the Sheikha. His voice had an adamant edge to it.

Sheikha Mariam gazed out at the water without commenting.

There was a stirring behind us. "Excuse me, Sir."

Everyone turned. I had not noticed Pardi come up. He looked uneasy, strained.

"What is it, Pardi?" Marwan said.

"Sir? Do you know what the villagers say, Sir?"

Marwan stared at the workman. "The villagers?"

"They say that we are digging in the wrong place, Sir."

It was surprising to hear Pardi voice an opinion so openly, especially in front of the Mansours. He was usually one to listen and

246

obey, not propose theories.

But the Indian went on, calmly. "The man at the petrol station in the village told me that this *tel* is nothing. What we are looking for is closer to the beach. That is where the palace was."

Marwan sighed. "What palace?"

Pardi inclined his head. "Five hundred years ago, Sir, there was a palace there."

"The villagers told you that?" Marwan said, not hiding his skepticism.

I imagined that it was not common for the villagers to volunteer any local lore to outsiders. They had never before shown an interest in the *tel* or in Marwan's activities.

"They said that a very strong man once lived there who kept many pigs in his palace," Pardi went on. "Whenever he would quarrel with the villagers, he would send his pigs to defile their village and eat everything in the fields. The villagers prayed to Allah to avenge them and, one day, the evil man disappeared. The earth swallowed him up. Only the pigs were left in the palace, living like kings."

The Sheikha glanced at Marwan. "Pigs?" she said, with obvious Islamic distaste for what was considered a filthy animal.

"That's what they said, Madam."

The Sheikha looked amused.

"Allah works in mysterious ways," said Marwan.

"Sir?" Pardi's eyes clouded.

"We're not looking for anything like that, Pardi. Just keep on with your work."

I watched Sheikh Ahmad lift the hem of his *thob* off the sand as he made his way around the gaping trenches to one side, obviously more interested in them than in the present conversation. Marwan had told me that Ahmad had once been his assistant for several seasons, having been a student at Oxford when Marwan was teaching there. But he had never been the serious digger that

Sheikha Mariam was, nor as talented. He now worked in the Ministry of Education and it was he, apparently, who had managed to get Marwan a grant of an extra five thousand dinars to spend on the excavation this year.

Pardi went to rejoin the other workmen. Although he had always been a hard worker, lately he had shown an almost spiritual interest in the dig. I thought of his evening meditations facing the sunset.

Sheikh Ahmad returned to us. He shivered slightly. "This must not seem cold at all to you, Mrs. Monroe. Not like New York."

I smiled. "Not like New York for sure, Your Excellency."

Sheikh Ahmad turned to Marwan. "How can you work in this cold?"

"We have to work when we can, Excellency," Marwan said, a note of impatience in his voice.

Sheikh Ahmad seemed not to notice, but stroked his chin and smiled, the same disarming grin that I remembered from the first time we met. I was struck by how perfectly symmetrical his features were. Derek had remarked, once, that the Sheikh and his twin brother, Saleh, had reputations as ladies men among the European women on the peninsula, particularly among the British air stewardesses who jetted into Abu Samra several times a week. I wondered whether Sheikha Mariam knew this, whether or not she cared.

The Sheikha now moved away and began inspecting the trenches, scraping with her fingers and gently sifting the sand through them as though the crystals themselves held the answers she was looking for. Watching her, I understood why Marwan talked so admirably about her digging. She seemed to be at one with the earth, with the sand and various strata of civilizations that lay buried on this sterile-looking tel. The secrets of those who had existed hundreds and thousands of years before us seemed to lay waiting to manifest themselves to her intuitive fingertips.

"You're missed this year," Marwan called out to her, fondly.

A faint smile molded the Sheikha's lips beneath her concerned,

248

intense scrutiny. I glanced at Sheikh Ahmad. He was smiling too, obviously enjoying watching her. I wondered what he would say if he knew that Derek had called her the most beautiful woman in Abu Samra.

Sheikh Ahmad now turned to Marwan with a mild scowl. "As I said earlier, you aren't supposed to be working here. You need to go up north as you originally planned."

Marwan looked surprised. "You knew I'd be doing work here before the north. I'm going there in a day or two."

"What is so promising here?"

"I don't know, yet. I've wired Paris for a specialist in Islamic coins and Chinese porcelain. Just in case."

"Portuguese?" Ahmad said.

"Maybe 'Abbasid."

Marwan had told me that up until the Portuguese period in the sixteenth century, this coast had been a trading post between the Muslim metropolises of Iraq and Syria, and China. A substantial number of Ming china fragments had been found over the years.

"What else?" Sheikh Ahmad asked.

"You know what I'm looking for. The problem is I won't know for a few days. We found a Helenistic jug and we're at the ramparts of a Portuguese cement wall going five feet down to bed-rock on the other side. But I'm betting on more."

I guessed that what Marwan meant was that neither six-teenth-century Portuguese, nor Medieval Islamic, nor even Helenis-tic remains were as significant as what he hoped to find. Even someone who had not done field work in a while, like Sheikh Ahmad, would understand the importance of a Zulaikan discovery.

"Let me show you around," Marwan offered, obviously realiz-ing that the Sheikh was taking in the site, the workmen, the survey-ing tools, as though looking for something.

But Sheikh Ahmad suddenly turned to Marwan. "You cannot continue here, Marwan. Permission was given for you to work only at the Portuguese fort."

"I am going to the Portuguese —"

Go now. Today." Sheikh Ahmad drew himself up, as if bracing for an attack. His voice was unpleasantly cool.

Marwan looked confounded. "Why?"

"The Ministry's orders."

"But we've been here for three months. Nobody's said anything to me. I'm simply doing preliminary investigations," Marwan said.

"But things have changed, you understand. The villagers are upset by your presence. They've demanded that the site be closed."

I stepped a few feet away, not wanting to be part of any imminent confrontation.

It was high tide and the water was murky from the waves. I could smell the salt, the fish, and the faint scent of oil from the tankers docked at the jetty several kilometers away.

"Closed?" Marwan's voice rose in anger. "What for?"

Sheikh Ahmad turned to face him. "This area has to do with the electrical plant. The station has to be completed before summer. The villagers want the electricity."

I felt my stomach contract. The Sheikh knew that Derek was in charge of this. Mercifully, Marwan did not look at me.

"It seems, also," the Sheikh continued, "that somebody from the village has disappeared."

"What do you mean?" Marwan said.

"Two men from the village came to the Ministry yesterday claiming that a young girl is missing. They said it has to do with your workmen."

I brought my hand to my mouth.

Marwan seemed unperturbed. "My men are supervised all day. They're taken home before I leave. Either John or I are always the last ones here."

Then they did start to speak in Arabic, lowering their voices, although I was the only one still within earshot of what the two of them had to say.

I wondered how to excuse myself without being too obvious.

"When the French team was looking around this area the villagers warned us against allowing them to move in," Sheikh Ahmad said, reverting to English.

"The French were here *last* year," Marwan said. The French team was his major competitor.

"A German team was in the area several years ago when a child disappeared. The villagers object to any more digging here. They've been tolerant until now," Sheikh Ahmad said.

"Look," Marwan said, his voice suddenly calm. "People don't just disappear. Nobody from the village comes over except occasional fishermen to sell some of their catch. My workmen are too busy to do anything but dig and sift. You know how I work, Ahmad."

I glanced at the workmen still digging.

Marwan pointed to them. "Do they look like they'd harm anyone? It's all we can do to get them to lift a shovel. And how do you know the villagers aren't making this up? They're upset by the Akbari thing, but my work has nothing to do with politics."

The Sheikh sighed. "Those are the orders."

Marwan gazed at Sheikha Mariam, who had just stood up after examining the trench. "Does she know about this?"

"Of course."

Marwan was silent. I could sense his feeling of betrayal. The loyalty of the Sheikha to archaeological interests had probably shifted now. One could not expect her to act against the orders of her husband-to-be.

I could feel Marwan's anger resonating through the air, could hear Pardi's voice recounting what the villagers had told him about the earth's swallowing up a man with pigs.

"Let me show you something," Marwan said, suddenly, beckoning Sheikha Mariam to the tent.

Sheikh Ahmad nodded to me. "Come, Mrs. Monroe," he said, looking irritated. "Let's see what Dr. Jassim has to show us."

I reluctantly followed.

Inside the tent was warm and still, shutting out the breeze. Fragments of potsherds were carefully laid out on a table. Also on the table were two small, transparent plastic bags. Marwan picked up one and emptied its contents into his hand: several triangles of dirt-caked blue glass the size of large coins. The glass glowed dimly from the light squeezing in through the tent's open flap.

"Islamic," Marwan said, matter-of-fact. In the silence, everyone seemed to agree. Sheikha Mariam held out her hand and Marwan let the fragments slide into her palm as if they were nothing more than cheap marbles.

From the other plastic bag he removed two dull, amber-colored beads. He tilted his hand, rolling the beads around his palm as he glanced at the Sheikha, then at her cousin.

"Helenistic?" Sheikha Mariam said.

"Probably part of the same necklace," Marwan said. The beads seemed to grow brighter, as if the open air had suddenly allowed them to breath. I remembered when Pardi had found them. Marwan had immediately suspected they were Zulaikan from both the strata where they were found and the style.

"Not Helenistic, though," Marwan said, "although I suspect that the graves were robbed during the Helenistic period, possibly around 200 B.C."

The Sheikha looked skeptical. "Zulaika?"

Marwan raised his eyebrows. "Fragments of a Zulaikan necklace. I'd place a bet that it's around 2,500 B.C."

The Sheikha was silent.

Sheikh Ahmad looked at him. "Has anyone seen these?"

"Only us. Myself, John, Pardi. She drew them," Marwan said, nodding toward me. "Think what else is down there."

He handed the beads over to Sheikha Mariam. "At first I thought they might have been Neo-Babylonian. But in the last two days we've found sherds of pot lids with Zulaikan symbols. It looks like a kitchen and a small honey-date area." Again, Marwan looked at Sheikha Mariam and then at Sheikh Ahmad. "They're Zulaikan, all right. The only thing I'm not sure of is whether these walls are of a palace or of an entire town. This is our history. *Our* history."

The tension that had pervaded the tent seemed to have consumed itself. I felt relieved, even encouraged, by the Sheikha's sudden attention to the beads.

"And," Marwan went on. "There seems to have been a fire around this entire area. We've found old ash. Probably a massive fire that burned a hell of a lot. Any clay tablets will have been hardened to rock. If we find any, they should be perfectly legible. *Invaluable.*"

Sheikh Ahmad seemed to weigh all of this. Then, with no detectable emotion he said, "You must leave today."

Marwan's mouth opened.

"Cover it up," Sheikh Ahmad said, an apologetic tremor in his voice. "You can resume some other time. I promise."

Marwan sighed. "I can't cover it up yet."

"I'm sorry," said Sheikh Ahmad.

"But we're just starting to make progress."

"Nobody else will be allowed here, if that's what you're afraid of," the Sheikh said dryly. "The area will be off limits, period. There are other *tels* in Abu Samra. This area has been designated for something else. We already know enough about it. It's been documented to death."

"That's crazy," Marwan snapped.

I bit my lip. A minimum of decorum was always observed here, even between old friends, but most especially with the Mansours.

Marwan, however, seemed unconcerned with protocol now. His voice was hoarse. "There won't be anything left here in a few weeks. You know those cables will be running all through here. This is going to turn into a mass of electrical spaghetti once they're done. They're going to bloody devour it. Remember Matoor?"

Marwan had told me about Matoor village where, three years

253

ago, construction workers had dug up some earthenware remains. He had been called over from the Portuguese fort where he and Sheikha Mariam had been working. After further digging in Matoor, they found that the sherds were from Helenistic infant burial pots, each with an infant's tiny skeleton. They had managed to salvage seven complete pots which I had seen encased in glass in the museum near the airport. Everything else had already been destroyed by bulldozers before Marwan had even been notified.

"This is not Matoor, Marwan," Sheikh Ahmad said, seeming as sorry, suddenly, as he was impatient with Marwan. "The decision has been made. It isn't mine, but it's final."

"This *tel* will be destroyed. Can't you explain that to the Ministry? I'll tell the villagers myself. Leave them to me."

"There are other factors to consider. We have to respect the people's wishes."

Marwan let out another angry sigh. "Just give me a few days. Time to obtain more samples. We can't let them dig the place up. Believe me," he said, his voice cracking, obviously knowing that he was begging and probably hating himself for it, "it's important."

Sheikh Ahmad rubbed his forehead beneath his headdress as if he were considering this. Then he said, "These villagers have been promised the electricity for two years. You know our delicate situation here. We can't afford this."

"You mean, Iran? You're worried about that, aren't you?"

The Sheikh obviously expected Marwan to understand the 'delicate situation', the game of politics that had to be constantly played. Villager versus townsman. Villager versus ruling family. Poor versus rich.

But although Marwan obviously understood, he was not relenting. *What did it all matter?* I could hear him thinking. *Some day there'll be a change here, a revolution like there is everywhere else, like Iran, and the 'delicate situation' will be over with. But this — history — is immortal. A find like this will live on long after we and all the rest are dust.*

We can wait a few days," Marwan said, almost speaking to himself. "We can go to the fort and then come back. We won't be so conspicuous when things return to normal."

The Sheikha spoke up, suddenly. Her eyes seemed anguished beneath the determined gaze. "Marwan, we must let this go. For now."

Marwan's face was suddenly a mask, the hollow look in his eyes making him almost unrecognizable to me. "Tell me one thing," he snapped, his eyes following Ahmad as the Sheikh left the tent. "Who told you to do this?"

Sheikha Mariam looked puzzled. "What do you mean?"

"Forget it. It's not important," Marwan said. But I knew that he had meant to ask whether U.S.A. Electric, or even Derek, had anything to do with this. Had I not been there, he might have asked it outright.

I felt myself flush. A sour odor of perspiration seemed to pervade the tent despite the cold.

Outside, Pardi and two others were squatting in the trench. They were about ten centimeters deep, brushing at a cleared area of some two square meters. I watched them, thinking I saw images take shape in the sand beneath their tools. There seemed to be a faint crescent like a circular staircase, then squares, like a walkway of stones placed next to one another. A floor or perhaps a garden.

"Found anything?" Marwan asked Pardi when we emerged from the tent, although there was obviously nothing beneath the brushes except the uneven indentations of the dirt.

"Not yet, Sir. Shall I dig near the water?"

Marwan shook his head. "We're in the right spot. Just do your work."

I watched Marwan escort the Mansours back down the *tel* to the black jeep. I could not believe that they would force him to stop digging. Yet, it was obvious that whatever it was that bothered them was more than they were willing to discuss here.

The Sheikha climbed into the jeep beside her cousin and Mar-

255

wan closed the door behind her, carefully, the same way that he had closed the door for me that night that we had been here together.

"They expect me to sign my own death warrant," he said, when he returned. "We have to go to the northern fort if we want to dig at all. The workmen are to go there tomorrow."

"What about this?" I said.

"We have until tonight." He looked around at the unfinished work. "Then they want us to fill up the trenches with sand."

"What?" I wanted to cry out. Rebury everything? Practically a season's work?

John came up. "Something's really eating them," he said. Although he was usually better able than Marwan to conceal his anger, he made no attempt to hide it now.

"They're scared," Marwan said. "They're out to preserve their own skin. Even the Sheikha won't listen. She's a Mansour first. They say the villagers are rattled over that missing girl."

"Christ! What does that have to do with us?" said John.

"We have workmen. They attribute everything to strangers. This thing in Iran is going to fire up a lot of hotheads who hate the Mansours. That's the issue. The Mansours are trying to buy out these villagers, pour money into the area, more electricity, water. Get them fat and happy so they'll forget their old grudges against their overlords."

"Do they really need the extra electricity that badly?" said John.

"Maybe someone's getting a kickback," Marwan said. "Sheikh Ahmad, maybe."

I felt the bitter accusation aimed at Derek as much as at the Sheikh. John was staring at the ground. His red hair stood stiff as a Viking's from the wind.

Marwan finally looked at me. "You shouldn't be here. Not until we straighten this out." He reached out as if to caress my arm, then seemed to catch himself. He walked me down the *tel* to my car.

I was silent until we reached the bottom, hoping he might say something now that we were alone. Reassure me. Touch me. Say how much he loved me. Remind me of Cairo. But I could not ask him what I most needed to know — what would happen to us?

"What'll you do now?" I said.

"They'll come round. They just need time. I'll dally at the northern fort a few days, then I'll speak to the Sheikha."

Although his words were bold, his voice was less sure. I was suddenly worried about the effect this unexpected obstacle would have on him, on his health. All the stories of people dying from sudden heart attacks brought on by anger or shock began to course through me.

"Are you going to be O.K., Marwan?"

He looked at me. "Of course. This is nothing."

We stood together near the car, the turbulent froth swelling near our feet. "What about us?" I said, suddenly.

He stared at me. "You ran away."

"Marwan."

He smiled, quickly. "We can always go back to Cairo."

I looked away. "Come on, Marwan."

He was silent. Then he said, "We *will* go back." But inside I knew he was also feeling, *I can't think of that now.*

"What will happen here?" I said.

"I don't know. I'll just have to keep talking to them. I'm not going to bury it, that's for sure. I won't let them destroy this." He patted my hand. "Go on." His voice seemed to reach around me as his arms could not. "I'll get word to you somehow."

I suddenly felt my shoes sink deeper into the cold sand. "Where will you be tomorrow? How will I see you?"

"I'll call you," he said.

"At home?"

"Yes."

"I don't want to leave you."

He stroked my hand. "You never leave me. That's an illusion.

257

I'm always with you."

"But when I go, I'm alone. You *aren't* with me," I said, impatient with his faith now, with his ability to suddenly separate so easily because he had more pressing issues at hand.

"We're always together, Gina. Being alone is only an illusion. Remind yourself of that."

"That's so hard."

"But you can do it. Just keep reminding yourself."

"You're not going away, are you?" I said

"Going away? Where to?"

I felt helplessly out of control. "You won't leave Abu Samra?"

He threw back his head and laughed. "I'm only going as far as the northern fort. They can't get rid of me that easily, no matter how much they may want to."

He let go of my hand then, his voice coaxing, gentle. "Go on, darling."

When I was in my car, I watched him leap back up the *tel* like some mountain goat, eager to get on with work. For a moment I thought he was Derek, then was shocked at having made the comparison. Yet in that way I could not deny the similarity between them. Despite Marwan's belief in simply *being*, of living in the moment, he was very much aware of the future importance of his work. Of course he would not feel our separation. I suspected, with a quick catch in my stomach, that for the next few days I would not be anywhere near the vicinity of his mind, nor his heart.

20

Fog

It was only later that I recalled seeing, as I drove away from the *tel*, the lone figure of Pardi walking along the shore toward the shallow bay that Marwan had earlier insisted had been the harbor of the ancient Zulaikans. A workman in khaki walking along the beach. I had not paid much attention, even when I recognized him to be Pardi.

I had been too shocked by Sheikh Ahmad's insistence that Marwan rebury the site to focus on anything else. Nearly a season's digging was going to be scrapped because of unexpected political troubles in Iran. Most of all, I had been worried that Marwan would leave Abu Samra if he was not allowed to continue, that he might *have* to leave if he did not do as the Mansours told him. The thought froze in my chest. I could no longer conceive of a time when I could not be near him.

I had not connected the item in the newspaper the next morning either: the stabbed body of an Indian male had been found on a beach in the south under some palm fronds. It had been a short announcement, four or five lines in a section of the newspaper filled with local events.

259

I woke up late, after Derek had gone to the office, so I had spent more time than usual reading the paper. It was unusual to hear of a murder in Abu Samra. I could not fathom why a workman had been killed. The Indian laborers seemed to keep to themselves, not to get embroiled in something that could lead to a fight, much less a murder.

What had also surprised and pleased me was a short news article on the Saali dig itself. It briefly described the few finds that had been unearthed and ended with quotes from both Sheikha Mariam and a Mrs. Bateson of the Abu Samra Historical Society about the dire need to preserve as much of the site as possible before electrical cables were put in the following month. I was encouraged, wondering whether this meant that the work would be allowed to continue longer than previously agreed. There was a single quote from Marwan as an "expert", but nothing more on his theories of a major Zulaikan find in Saali.

The telephone rang. It was Derek telling me that there was a dense fog outside causing traffic problems across town. He did not want me to drive. He had arranged for 'Abbas to be available to me if I wanted to go anywhere.

I could see the moisture on the glass of the kitchen window, but I did not want 'Abbas taking me anywhere. I could certainly drive myself to the *tel*.

Then the telephone rang again. This time it was John Reese. His voice was perfunctory. Marwan, he said, had instructed him to warn me not to go to Saali or to the *tel*.

I squeezed the receiver. "Is something wrong?"

"The *tel* is off limits to everyone," John said. "Including us."

"Where's Marwan now?" I said, not caring what John would read into my concern.

"He's at the police station."

"Police station?"

I could hear John exhale at the other end. "He might get to the northern Portuguese fort later. I'm heading out there."

260

"What's going on, John?"

"A matter," he said, abruptly.

I wanted to shake him through the telephone wire, to make him shed his stubborn carapace and tell me all he knew. I wanted to go to the north, too, if that was where they were working!

"Will they let you go back to the tel."

"Not this year."

"Oh, John," I said. It had been his father who had initially started the first of the excavations on the beach.

"Well," he said. "Marwan told me to give you the message."

I hung up only after he did, hoping that if I stayed on the line he might volunteer another morsel of information.

I went upstairs, continuing up the last flight of steps to the roof. The fog had settled around the house and I could barely discern the outline of the shanty that was still left behind the crematorium. The crematorium itself was so blurred that I could barely see the platform. The sounds, too, were muted, the echoes of the few cars swallowed into the solid air. I strained in vain to see the horizon, as if I might detect some sign to indicate trouble at Saali. For a moment there was a break in the fog, and some of the heaviness lifted. I could see the remaining shanty clearly now. On the newly-flattened earth where the other shacks had been torn down, a gray-green stubble of grass had spread like an epidemic after the recent rains. Beyond that the fog made a barrier.

Something bad had happened. I sensed it from the tone of John's voice before he had said anything.

I had to find Marwan, although I had no idea where the northern Portuguese Fort was. Even if I did know, I was not sure I could get there from the fog.

I called the office for 'Abbas after all. He would surely know where the northern fort was. But first I would go to Derek's office. I knew, instinctively, that he would know something about whatever was happening at the *tel*.

Derek. The sharp edge of his name echoed inside me like a slap.

The town emerged from behind the fog in layers, like the gradually unfolding plot of a mystery. First the tall, white-washed gates, then the sand-colored buildings, then the overhanging balconies swimming through the mist. A few black *'abayas* could be spotted from a distance but the lighter *thobed* men were practically invisible until they were a mere few feet away. Twice, I gasped as 'Abbas rounded a corner, each time nearly colliding with a man who suddenly materialized in front of the car.

The tailors in the shop of Derek's building were seated cross-legged on the floor, surrounded by stacks of unfinished trousers and jackets basted with bright white thread like carefully traced directions on a road map. The tailors nodded to me as if they recognized me, although I had been in the shop only once when Derek had been measured for trousers. Today, there was a pot of steaming tea on the floor beside them and the men were dressed in sweaters and jackets over their tunics as though the temperature was below freezing instead of a mere 50 degrees.

When I entered the office, Derek was discussing something with the secretary at the front desk. When he saw me, his face seemed to slide into the deliberate frown that I had come to see more and more often lately.

"Can we talk?" I said.

"I'll be in my office in a second," he said, glancing away.

I went down the hall, pausing at the room with the two engineers. I inquired about their wives and children. I had not seen them since the dinner party and hoped that they had forgotten about Pete's vulgar advances. The taller one, whose wife, Awatef, worked with delinquents, had stopped by one night when Derek and I were out and left a plate of sweetmeats on our doorstep. I had been touched by their consideration and had written a note of thanks, even though Derek had insisted that such notes were not expected here.

Derek came into his office carrying two cups of coffee. He shut the door, handed me a cup, and sat down at his desk across from me.

"You haven't been here in a while," he said. "I didn't want you driving in the fog."

"Abbas drove."

He nodded, as if approving that I had heeded his warning. "We nearly turned back several times this morning it was so bad."

"It's still bad. The buildings jump out at you, like they've suddenly been unveiled."

He smiled. "You notice things I never do — I didn't think of anything but getting through it to the office." But he looked totally defeated, as if suddenly convinced that his limited artistic vision is what was finally destroying what we once had together.

"You're more practical than I am," I said, hoping to cheer him up. Yet, I now saw his obsession with the practical as more of a limitation than a strength.

He sighed, as if relieved that I understood him. "You have no idea how tiring this all is, Gina. The red tape we go through every day just to get a damn plan approved."

His eyes changed, revealing the disappointment that Abu Samra had brought him — never enough time to do all that was needed in so short a time, never enough man-power or the expertise he had been used to in New York. I felt sorry for him suddenly. He had not had the opportunity, as I had, to gradually integrate into this new rhythm of life at his own pace. It must have been a nightmare to be dropped into Abu Samra, as though onto the moon, and be expected to function as efficiently as he had in New York, to undertake a complex technical project within an allotted time without first coming to terms with the limitations of the environment.

"You've done well, Derek," I said. "Everyone recognizes that."

"Have I?" He said, finishing his coffee.

"You know you have. You get things done. Your reputation's strong. You're a deal-maker."

A wretched smile drew back his lips. "And what's it all for? What do *I* get in the end?"

"What do you mean?"

"I can't wait to get out of here, Gina."

I stared at him. He had never expressed such acute frustration before. "What are you talking about?"

He got up and took my empty cup from me and put it on his desk. Then, he took both of my hands in his. "Just what I said. I want to get out of here. I want *us* to get out."

My hands were icy in his warm ones. I tried to find something in his face to cling to, something to confirm that I loved him. Yet I felt pity suddenly instead of love, and found myself shrinking away. I pulled my hands out of his. "But how can we go? You're not done here."

He turned away. "Everything seems different between us. You've changed. You weren't this way before we got here. I don't want to continue like this. I don't want to bring a child into this atmosphere. I want to go back to New York and start our family there."

I stared at the back of his head, amazed. Whenever we had this sort of discussion about our relationship he brought our plans for a baby into it. I felt revulsion. I could no longer imagine him as the father of any future child of mine.

"But I don't want to go back now. Not yet. It's just taken me time to adjust here, like it has you. But I'm happy now. A lot happier than I've been in New York in a long time."

He looked surprised at first, then turned to stare out the long glass window that overlooked the *souk*. Usually you could see all the activity in the market from this window, anybody coming to the office, women and children dawdling before store windows, office boys crossing the road from the cafe carrying trays with glasses of tea for store customers. But today the windows were coated, the fog insulating us from all that was outside.

"Derek," I said.

He turned to me.

"Are you going ahead with the plans to build the electrical

264

plant in Saali? On the beach?"

He seemed to be translating what I had just said as if I had spoken in some unfamiliar language. Then, he said, "Don't you know about the trouble?"

"What trouble?"

"Someone's been killed there." He nodded toward the newspaper on his desk.

"In Saali?"

"Yeah."

"Who?"

"A workman."

"At the tel?"

He seemed to flinch at the mention of the site.

I tried to look calm. "Who — who did it?"

He shrugged. "The police think someone from the village. Nobody knows much, and we're not likely to."

"What do you mean?"

"Murders aren't disclosed, here. That's what I'm told. They'll hush up the whole incident and nobody'll know any different."

I felt as if a brick had been dropped on my head. So, this is what John had refused to tell me.

"But Derek, those workmen are pathetic. They just work for the money to send home to their families. Who would attack them?"

"Well, somebody in Saali thinks differently. The workers are being blamed for the disappearance of that girl."

Again, the girl that Sheikh Ahmad had mentioned. "But why do they think somebody from the site did it?" I could hear my voice rising.

Derek stared at me, looking surprised by my anxious tone. "The police aren't saying anything. They want to smooth things over with the villagers after what's happened in Iran. A foreign worker's nothing to get too excited about."

"They're *human* beings!" I was furious to hear him talk like that.

265

There was a thin workman at the site with a pock-marked face who always wore a maroon tunic. I suddenly pictured him lying in a sheet of blood and wondered whether he had been the one killed. I liked him the least because he was always so sullen.

Derek shrugged, obviously choosing to ignore my outburst. "The government won't even let us send surveyors out now."

I felt something set free inside me and hoped that this meant that the site would be left alone, at least temporarily.

"In fact," Derek went on, "I've been thinking of finding a new route entirely for those cables. It means starting from scratch."

"A new location?"

He nodded.

"Why would you do that?"

"It'll make things easier. This whole thing's been a headache from the beginning."

I tried to look indifferent to this news.

"Gina," he said, his voice dropping, "I can recommend a new location. But on one condition."

I stared at him. His face was hard. In that instant I realized that he knew. *Oh, God! He* knew. "It's got to stop, Gina. Do you hear me? You've got to stop."

"Stop what, Derek?"

"Stop seeing him."

I opened my mouth to say something, to protest his accusation, but I could only hear his grating voice. "Stop this nonsense. I've watched enough."

I felt dizzy. A hollowness as thick as the fog outside was sucking me into the floor.

"Don't make this harder for me than it already is, Gina. I'm giving him a chance. It's up to you."

I stared at him, trying to disguise the rage in my voice, the anger burning my eyes. "Why does any of this have to involve me? You're telling me you'll destroy an archaeological excavation if I don't promise to stop going there? You make it sound as if I'm asking for some huge favor. The entire peninsula is a carpet of wonders if you'd only look. You'd know that if you came out to the *tel*, those mounds —"

"I've seen them," he said.

"Oh yes. *One* time. You were more interested in the price the worked flint would bring back in New York. You don't appreciate any of it at all."

"Well, maybe if I had some seductive woman to lure me into digging with her, I'd spend as much time there as you do!" He glared at me. "Stop playing games, Gina. I *know*. I wouldn't be surprised if everyone in Abu Samra knows. My wife God damn it — I just want it to stop!"

I felt my face go rigid. He sounded ill, suddenly, as if he did not have the strength to continue. But rather than feel pity for him now, I felt completely detached.

I stood up, slowly. I did not, at this moment, want to find out just what he knew or how much. I could not stand hearing it from him.

He turned and stared into the fog outside the window. "'Abbas can take you home," he said.

"I'm not going home," I answered, opening the door of his office. I walked down the hall, past the engineers and the Indian secretary in the entrance. I could hear 'Abbas heating water for tea in the small kitchen near the door.

I started down the stairs, knowing that Derek would not be able to see me from his window from the fog for more than a few seconds once I got to the street. But suddenly, my arm was pulled back.

I tried to free my arm from Derek's clench. "Stop it! Let me go."

He tightened his grip.

"I need to be alone, Derek," I pleaded.

"You're destroying your life, damn it. *My* life. Don't you see that?" His voice wavered as I shook my arm to free it. He began to twist my arm, as if to immobilize me. Pain shot up my shoulder.

Behind him, 'Abbas had come out to the hall at the top of the stairs. The older man's face, usually so impassive, now looked ashen. He stepped cautiously down the steps, clicking his tongue as if trying to split up a fight between two rowdy children.

"Let me go, Derek," I pleaded, trying to keep my voice low, afraid to spark some further yelling on his part.

"You bitch!" He raised his own arm as if to strike me and I watched him, too stunned to move out of his reach.

It was 'Abbas who stopped him, grabbing Derek's hand and muttering "*La, la,*" no, no, in a soothing tone, as though to quiet some rabid animal.

I yanked my arm out of Derek's grasp and backed away down the remaining few steps, sure that Derek would now turn round and strike 'Abbas. But he only stared at the driver in surprised silence.

I ran across the road into the pedestrian alley of the copper shops, grateful for the shielding fog.

My heart pounded, contracting in the cool, watery air. I understood, now, the peculiar reticence of the Abu Samrans, their need to cover up, to be private, to hold back in a place where there was little that was not known to everyone, where life was lived out in a glass case, each person vulnerable to scrutiny. I longed, suddenly, for an *abaya* to make me invisible to curious eyes. I wanted the anonymity of New York, the ability to disappear into the thick crowds where nobody would think twice about a woman hurrying down the street with tears streaming down her face.

But most of all I needed Marwan, needed his arms to reassure me that it would be all right. That *we* would be all right. *I'm always with you.* I tried to repeat his words to myself as I stood at a corner looking for a taxi. *Remind yourself that separation is an illusion.*

I arrived home in the taxi barely in time to dress to go see Sheikha Mariam. With all that had happened this morning, I had almost forgotten our appointment at the museum. By now the fog had lifted enough that I could drive myself there with my sketch books and watercolors. I wanted to escape the house in case Derek followed me home. But I suspected that after what had happened on the stairwell, Derek would be in no hurry to get home anyway.

When Sheikha Mariam had asked to see my work it had sounded like a command performance. I should have been flattered by her interest, but now I dreaded it and had the feeling that she was looking for something that the paintings would reveal about me.

I had been to the museum once before, and vaguely remembered how to get there from the airport. It was an attractive, simple white-washed structure built like an old Arab fort with rounded turrets, wind towers, and carved, arabesque windows — how the former Mansour palaces must have looked when they were new. Since the building closed to the public each afternoon at one o'clock, its wide teak doors were shut. But a black sedan and another smaller green car were parked at the side of the building near a door with a sign posted in Arabic.

Inside was an oblong room with several empty desks and a collection of maps and diagrams tacked to the walls. A young woman sat at the desk near the door. She immediately rose and welcomed me when I entered, as if expecting me. She led me down a hallway, past poster-size photographs of the burial mounds and the various Portuguese and Omani forts on the peninsula. There were also detailed aerial photographs of the *tel* and other digs. At the end of the hall was a closed door. The young woman knocked and pushed it open.

Sheikha Mariam stood up and reached across her desk to shake my hand. "Mrs. Monroe."

"You did mean for me to come this afternoon, Your Excellency?"

"Yes, of course. I've lost track of time," she said, nodding to one of the chairs across from her. "Please."

Her hair was pulled back in a tight bun at her neck, the way it had been the first time I had seen her, and she wore a plain khaki shirt tucked into a navy-blue skirt. Although she was as attractive as ever, today she appeared more official than glamorous, as though her beauty was a safely sheathed sword. She removed the glasses she was wearing and rubbed her wide, dark eyes. There were faint circles below her lower lashes, the only sign of fatigue.

"You have been to the museum before?" she asked, pleasantly.

"Only once, Your Excellency."

"It's two years old. Unfortunately only a third of it has completed displays," she said, with a brisk sweep of her arm. "There's so much to catalog and study before we exhibit. Too much building going on and not the time needed to properly examine things. If we don't excavate quickly we will lose much of our history."

There were plastic bags on her desk with labeled potsherds. A small box lined with cotton wool held more sherds and some blue-green bits of glass. I felt guilty, as if the mere fact of my presence as an expatriate contributed to the flood of building on the peninsula and the ensuing ravaging of its heritage. Her heritage. Marwan's. Too many things were constantly threatening to destroy precious evidence just below ground.

"There's bad news at the *tel*," she said, drumming her slender fingers on her desk.

"I know," I said, trying to keep the distress from my voice.

"This is not a good time for Abu Samra."

I could not tell whether she was referring to the new political developments or to archaeology.

"I hope everything's going to be all right," I said.

"*In sha Allah*," she said, God willing, as if to reassure herself even more than me.

I nodded. "*In sha Allah*."

She sighed. "The will of the world is all-powerful, and all of us are swept into it. Even a scientist has to admit that."

Glasses of tea and a plate of cardamom cookies were brought by the young woman who had led me in. I thought of the *henna* party, the flowers and perfume and incense at the end, the Sheikha's dancing. I was amazed at her ability to slip between the opposing roles of exotic hostess and driven professional so easily. Even now, as she straightened up several stacks of paper and cleared her desk, her presence had a mystical quality that made me think of Marwan's belief that the Arabs were one of the few peoples left still possessing true spirituality.

"I heard the good news about your engagement, Your Excellency. Congratulations."

A slow, weary smile touched her lips as she continued to sort through her papers. "Thank you Mrs. Monroe."

"Sheikh Ahmad is extremely nice," I said.

She nodded. "His father and my father are brothers, we are first cousins," she said, then paused as if to gauge my degree of shock that Arabs still deemed such marriages acceptable. But by now I knew that Arabs married cousins, so I was no longer surprised. The Mansours — especially the women — married into the family almost exclusively.

"You must have a lot in common," I said.

"We've known each other since childhood. He's two years younger than I am."

Again, she seemed to wait for my reaction before going on.

"Have you always known you would marry him?"

She laughed, suddenly. "Not at all. It used to be that way. Marriages arranged in childhood. But these days most women marry whom they wish. Ahmad proposed to my father, but only after asking me. We've always been good friends."

"I hope I wasn't rude," I said, embarrassed by her candor.

"You're curious," she said, eyeing me. "You're wondering whether or not I am in love with him?"

I smiled, flustered.

"I *am* in love with him, but I'm more concerned with respect and caring. I've had the other kind of 'love', as it's called. It isn't very reliable."

I listened in disbelief to her stoic remarks, partly envying her apparent mastery over her emotions. It was evident by her voice and manner that what she felt for her cousin was a great deal more than just "caring." I could not see how he, in turn, could not adore her. Being so beautiful and bright, she undoubtedly could have had any man she wanted. Yet she was professing to be basing her marriage on common sense rather than passionate love, something I could not imagine for myself. Certainly not now, after what I had experienced with Marwan. I could tell that she sensed my bewilderment and could not help wondering whether she suspected my own predicament. But as usual, her face was an oblique mask.

"My field was originally Arabic literature," she said, pointing to the gold-lettered volumes on the shelf behind her desk.

"Not archaeology?"

"Not at all. I wanted to teach literature at the University in Baghdad where I studied. But the summer that I graduated, there was a dig at the Portuguese fort here in the north and I volunteered to help. That's where I met Dr. Jassim. But he was not in charge then. Dr. Reese was."

"John's father?"

She nodded. "The government had just established the National Historical and Archeological Society. After digging a few months, I got interested in what they were doing. Dr. Reese helped create the Society and he was looking for Abu Samrans to run it. I went back to Baghdad for a year to dig and take archaeology courses. Then I studied at Columbia, in New York. When I returned, I suggested the government create a Ministry of Archaeology. I got a job there, but I wanted to dig, not work in an office. Finally, this year, they made me Minister, so I have no choice but to see that the business of the Ministry and museum is run efficiently."

"Isn't it unusual for a women to be appointed Minister?" I asked.

She smiled. "I'm the first. It wasn't considered a critical job since not many are aware of the extent or importance of archaeology on the peninsula. But also, I think they realized that I was serious."

By "they" I guessed that she meant the patriarchs of her own, Mansour, family.

"But, you have come to show me your art," she said, abruptly. "Marwan tells me you sketch beautifully."

I felt giddy, suddenly, as if I were about to reveal the most intimate details of my life. I unzipped the portfolio case and carefully removed a few of the watercolors — the Saali mornings after the rains, the field of burial mounds with the large, smoking mound in the distance, the 'tree of life' surrounded by the yellow and purple desert, the crumbling houses downtown with the wind-towers, the views from our roof overlooking the shanties. There was even one I had forgotten: 'Abbas leaning against Derek's car, arms folded, eyes closed in abject boredom, on our first trip to the mounds.

She carefully looked at each one without commenting. "You like blue," she said, finally, pointing to the doors and windows of the village houses.

"I love the constant use of turquoise here. It reminds me of New Mexico. Santa Fe. It's an important color to American Indians."

"It protects against the evil eye," she said, matter-of-factly.

"Evil eye?"

"It's a color that attracts. When exposed to that color, your eye is automatically drawn to it rather than to the thing or persons you might envy. A blue door, for instance, will absorb ill will or harm that an envious person might intend for the occupants of a house. Superstition, of course."

"Do you believe in it?"

She smiled. "I don't exactly believe in it, but," she held out her wrist on which she wore a gold bangle dangling a small, turquoise stone, "I don't take chances."

I chuckled, intrigued by the fact that she seemed to find no

273

conflict in integrating her scientific background with ancient cultural beliefs.

"It's also the color of the Gulf," I said.

"Yes," she said, "the sea is beautiful." Then she pointed to a sketch I had made of the Mamluke home in Cairo. "This is not Abu Samra."

I felt myself blush. "No," I said. The Mamluke walls and windows. I had forgotten to take them out. The gritty voice of the old man as he had led Marwan and me around the Mamluke sitting room drummed in my ears, *these bottles were used to catch women's tears.* I felt my stomach contract at the memory of our hotel room, of our entwined legs and breaths, of Marwan inside me. I took a deep breath, hoping that the Sheikha would not notice my discomfort.

"This is Cairo?" she said, glancing at another drawing detailing the Mamluke black and white and pink tile archways.

"Yes, Your Excellency."

She nodded and smiled, scanning the others quickly. "You have no paintings of the tel?"

"I only make drawings, Your Excellency," I said, immediately detecting her disappointment. I brought out some sketches of the strata of one of the trenches. She looked at those closely. There was a drawing of the jug with the handles, the one Marwan had pronounced Helenistic.

She said nothing else about them, however. Finally, she came to the last watercolor — the study for the oil, the two men sitting on a bench under the Indian almond tree in Saali.

"I would like to buy this one," she said, putting it aside.

"Let me offer it to you, Your Excellency."

She smiled. "Never give away your work."

"Just knowing you like it is payment enough."

She did not protest further. "Just this time, then. Thank you. I hope you'll exhibit your work in Abu Samra. It's quite unusual."

"Do you think so?"

"Most people, even our Abu Samra artists, see only the obvious. You have gone beyond that."

"I try to," I said, flattered that she thought so.

"So many paintings of Abu Samra are beige or brown. In your work there are pinks and purples in the browns, depth most people who have been here only a few months never find. Perhaps it's the digging. I'm impressed."

I looked at her. She seemed to know more than she was saying. "But the colors are here, Your Excellency. If one only looks."

"Most foreigners stay only a short time, though. So many hundreds pass through Abu Samra that we hardly notice when they arrive or leave. We don't even make an effort to know them anymore. I, myself, am guilty of that. They're gone too quickly. Everyone is temporary." There was a wistfulness in her tone. I felt that she was talking about me, as well.

"But, you're so generous, Your Excellency. You attend the parties and entertain expatriates in your home."

"We like to show people our lives, to let them leave with a good impression. Otherwise, they would see only a barren desert and crumbling houses. Black-covered women."

We both laughed.

"Foreigners take the *abaya* to be a form of exclusion, of oppression, to make women invisible," she said, suddenly sounding annoyed. "They never think that it is a woman's way of being *herself*, of being private. It is a misconception about women that we are always forced to address."

She looked at my *tel* sketches again and her tone shifted. "So what is it Marwan is searching for at the *tel*? Something to do with Zulaika, obviously. Once, and if, he proves that, he will go on to bigger and better things. He will even leave Abu Samra."

I was surprised by the sudden attack and by the irritation in her voice. "But this is his home. It's in his interest to stay and promote his finds, isn't it?"

She raised her eyebrows, looking skeptical. "He is not like Dr. Reese. He hopes this *tel* will make him famous and he will take the knowledge back to London."

I felt she was waiting for me to say something, to tell her something I knew. But I was shocked by her assertion. There was nothing I could tell her. I realized that I knew nothing of what Marwan intended to do with the information he dug up except what he casually mentioned at the site.

"But he cares about Abu Samra and I know he wants to share his finds with you," I said, trying to sound impartial. "He regrets that you aren't digging now. He told me how you used to dig together."

"Actually, I think he's relieved that I'm here, instead."

"But he told me himself that he doesn't like to be the one to theorize about Abu Samra's prehistory."

She smiled. "I doubt that. There is a temptation for an archaeologist to become a treasure hunter and this is dangerous because you risk distorting history to suit your own theories. Even without meaning to. I think Marwan falls into that trap more often than he likes to admit."

"If you have doubts, Your Excellency, can't you do something about it? Can't you make sure the sites are analyzed objectively, no matter who's digging?"

There was a hint of sarcasm in her smile, now. "Our history, like our oil, is no longer in our hands. Where is Abu Samra's oil, today? Almost gone. We Arabs don't control our destiny. Our oil, our history, like our incense millennia ago, draws others to control and use us. Marwan wants to be the first to find Zulaika. But more for himself than for Abu Samra. He will do all he can to get that result."

I could see my hand tremble. I remembered his kisses all over again, felt his lips and tongue nuzzling mine, tasted the warmth of his body. Was all of that for his own benefit, for some ulterior motive?

"I hope, for everyone's sake that's not the case, Your Excellency," I said. "I'm sure that Dr. Jassim has only good intentions."

"His conscious intentions are one thing," she said, slowly, as if deciding, suddenly, that I was not on her side. "But his ego seems to eclipse everything else."

I stared at her, at a loss at how to console her or myself at this point. But it was she who reached out and picked up one of my drawings as if to change the subject and soothe me at the same time. "I hope I am wrong. Marwan is a good man," she said, softly. "But even good men have their own agendas. Sometimes I think that his illness has made him desperate. He is always pushing himself. Pushing, pushing. Maybe he thinks he has too little time left."

I could barely taste my tea, wondering how she knew that I was aware of his medical condition — unless he had told her himself. I swallowed the rest of the tea as quickly as I deemed possible without seeming rude. Then I gathered up the watercolors, putting aside the one she liked.

"The one thing in the West you have that we don't is freedom," she said suddenly, as if musing in the privacy of her own mind. "Freedom of thought, of actions. You aren't bound by the cultural cage of tradition like we are." She looked me in the eye, wistfully. "Don't waste that precious gift. Always remember that you are free."

I fumbled with the zipper of the portfolio case, my confusion mounting every second. What was she referring to now? My freedom to leave Abu Samra? To leave Marwan? To leave my marriage which, if she and Marwan discussed intimate things as they obviously did, he might have told her about?

I straightened up and extended my hand calmly, despite my furious heart beats. "I hope your history is preserved, Your Excellency, I really do. I understand how important it is." Then I smiled, both grateful to her and wary. For, all at once, I sensed that she had issued me a stern, personal warning.

21

Qamar

Rarely are things the same underneath as they appear on the surface. I quickly learned this in Abu Samra. Not the tranquil mounds on the horizon, the necropolis that at first glance looked merely like peculiar land formations; not the crematorium, not the placid villages. Marwan had taught me this much as we brushed at the sand, hoping to dislodge some kernel of proof, some reckless signal propelled through the millennia from Zulaika such as a scrap of bone or a potsherd with particular ridges. Always, the unexpected brilliance lurking just below the stale surface.

It was two weeks before Christmas and a warm breeze was blowing across the peninsula. Thanksgiving had come and gone, celebrated privately by Derek and me at the Sheraton despite Mary's protests that she wanted us to spend our first Thanksgiving in Abu Samra with them. Mary was much too considerate to argue with me when I declined, but tried to remind me that celebrating with others would be less stressful than spending a holiday alone with Derek in my current frame of mind. She had hoped, I knew, that we could resurrect our cozy evenings together playing bridge. In the end, however, dinner alone with Derek seemed the best way to avert additional tension between us, and the Sheraton turned out to be an adequate option.

Derek had not apologized for his behavior at his office, nor had I expected him to. It was obviously something that he wanted to put behind him, to obliterate, as if it had been someone else threatening me on the stairwell. But I also sensed that he was satisfied that an essential bit of information had been driven home to me that day — the fight that he could wage if I were foolhardy enough to leave him.

Although it was hard to get into a Christmas mood with so much sun and sand outside, we had bought an artificial tree and I placed the wrapped gifts I had bought earlier for Derek under it. I began to miss the holiday lights on Fifth Avenue, the frigid evenings during Christmas shopping with bell-ringing Santa Clauses on the street corners. Three days ago, Santa had apparently made a huge impression on the neighborhood children here by arriving in a shiny, red fire truck to distribute gifts at the American school. A fire truck seemed appropriate enough given the arid, desert surroundings of Abu Samra.

I had continued to search the newspaper for fresh news about the site, but Derek had been right. There was no further mention of a murder in Saali. It was as if it had never happened. There were no further details on the missing girl, and since my last visit to the *tel* I had had no contact with anybody who might know something — neither Marwan nor John.

Two days after my fight with Derek, I got into the car and began to drive north along the carriageway that became the airport road. The Portuguese fort was at the far north of the peninsula. I would drive toward the airport and somehow find my way from there.

I had only been north of the airport a few times with Derek when we had first arrived. More barren than Dafna and Saali, the ground on either side of this northern road this morning was still riddled from the rains, with chunks of dried, caked mud fitting together like warped pieces of a jigsaw puzzle. Once past the turnoff for the terminal, however, the sand became loose and porous, more like the fine gravel of a terrarium, leaving hardly a trace of the flooding that had plagued the downtown and its surrounding neighborhoods.

The water desalinization plant appeared in the distance, under some clouds, its metal towers glimmering like platinum in the pale sunlight. This plant was the oldest in the Gulf after Kuwait's. Except for the southern villages like Saali and a few of the town's suburbs like Dafna, which still drew water from the natural brackish wells, most of the water now serving the peninsula's needs had to be desalinated from the sea. The efficiency of the desalinization operation was a source of pride for the Ministry of Public Works.

The land suddenly narrowed to a thin strip of sand on either side of the carriageway, flanked on either side by shallow, yellow sea water. Then it broadened again, the sand deepening to a dusky gray as if tinged with oil. A few date palms began to appear, followed by larger clusters like the palm forests of Saali. Suddenly the trees spread out on either side of the road, besieged at their bases by yellow-green saplings. Now they stretched so thick that the sea was no longer visible, only the deep, green mystery of palm fronds crowning slender, brown trunks. Then they disappeared again and the view opened up to the dry sand and sea.

The road sign announced the town of Qamar, 'moon' in Arabic. A quaint row of shops lined the main street where alleyways branched off the sides in mysterious tentacles. There was a remoteness here, as if things had been frozen in time from some former century. The two main towns of Abu Samra were barely twenty-five minutes away from each other, yet were galaxies apart. Here, wind towers topped each of the roofs of the sand-colored houses; myriad donkeys lazed in the shade of the walls. Even the streets, at first glance, seemed devoid of foreigners. No visible British or Americans, no Koreans, nobody in a sari or *Kamis* tunic either. Qamar seemed totally insulated from the modern and foreign intrusions in the rest of the peninsula. I parked in front of a grocer's stall, bought a small can of apricot juice, and asked the shopkeeper for directions to the Portuguese fort. Another five kilometers north along the main road, he said somewhat reluctantly, as if he were imparting illicit information.

Beyond the town the carriageway ended, becoming a narrow, barely paved road. I had never been this far north, even with Derek. Most of the vegetation now appeared to be haphazard, with only a few plots of plowed land like in Saali. Occasionally, amidst the palms on either side of the road, I spotted low, circular walls of mud ringed by pink oleander bushes. I wondered whether these mud walls were remains of the fresh-water wells thought to have been built by the Greeks thousands of years ago that Marwan had described to me.

A tall, run-down structure appeared ahead. For an instant, I thought it might be the fort. Then I saw that it was not one but several large, abandoned dwellings with tall windows and gaping, roof-less rooms. They looked as if they had been gutted by bombs, although one house still had two intact wind towers and an entire wall with arabesque windows and engravings above the doors. Delicate sculpted half-moons ran along the top rim of an outside wall and the bricks had been plastered over with mud which had mostly worn away. Lacy walls had been left to decay as if superfluous.

From what I now knew about the longevity of Abu Samra buildings, I guessed that these were not more than fifty years old. I was baffled anew at how things were allowed to rot like this, that transience in all things was so unquestioningly accepted. A chill slid through me. I saw in the crumbling buildings my own marriage which now seemed briefer than ever. Even more, I was faced with the possibility of the impermanence of my relationship with Marwan. Despite his passion for history, he seemed to deal with the present as something one enjoyed and then let go of easily, without looking back. Was this how he saw us and our relationship? Something that need not be lasting, that had a natural life that would inevitably end, and which he would come to accept as the way things simply were?

Feeling a sudden urge to preserve the eerie buildings, as if on my way back the walls would have already disintegrated, I parked on the side of the road and began to sketch the flowing lines — the porous plaster and exposed brick innards, a wooden beam, the decorative etchings above the windows.

Back in the car, I sensed I was approaching the end of the peninsula. Then I saw it. A single massive wall with half of a turret left overlooking the sea. Marwan's truck was parked nearby and I could see workmen digging at the foot of the wall. Unlike the walls I had just drawn, this one looked like dark, eroded sea coral rather than something once built by man.

I could see the tip of John's flame of red hair where he was kneeling beside the workmen. Further off, Marwan was walking up toward them from the shore, his shoulders stooped as he stared at the ground. As usual, he was wearing short sleeves, as if reserves of heat protected him from the December chill. I parked some distance away from his truck and waited. Almost immediately, he turned in my direction.

When he saw me, he hurried over to me, his eyes shining. "God, it's good to see you."

Although we kept a discreet distance from each other, I felt as if I were straining toward him through invisible bars.

"Marwan, what's going on?"

He moved closer to me suddenly, reaching for my hand with both of his. "Gina," he said again, and something in the high pitch of his voice this time frightened me. I felt a shield form around me, a mask that screened my face against him as it had instinctively done the first time I had spoken to him outside my house, a reflex against the pain my body seemed to know, even back then, would one day come.

283

"What happened?" I said.

He ran his hand through his hair, dulled by the wind and sand.

"Well, we're here, as you can see."

"John said you'd been to the police station, yesterday."

"Yes."

"Is everything all right?"

As if it had just occurred to him, he said, "Pardi's dead."

"Pardi?" I said, barely able to form the word. "My God! It was Pardi?"

"He was stabbed."

I caught my breath. Despite my shock, I realized that I had dreaded all along that it was Pardi who had been killed.

Marwan shook his head. "He was rummaging around Saali. I told him to stay at the site. I don't know what got into him."

Pardi's voice that night in town when I had given him the message for Marwan now lodged in my head as if it had been engraved: *Yes Madam, I'll tell him, Madam...* I recalled his stubborn insistence that morning, the last day I had seen him, that the *tel* was the wrong place to dig. It had been so unlike him to confront Marwan, especially in front of Sheikha Mariam and Sheikh Ahmad.

"He didn't have anything to do with that girl's disappearance, did he?" I said.

"Of course not. No. But the police won't even release his body until they've done a complete investigation."

"Pardi." I took a deep breath. I wondered suddenly whether he had been trying to prove Marwan's point about the shallow bay having once been a harbor.

"The villagers have all been on edge," Marwan said, his voice anguished, exasperated. "Stupid bastard. I warned him not to go wandering off on his own."

I had never heard him use such brutal words about anyone before. Yet I felt they were not aimed at Pardi so much as at himself for not protecting one of his men.

"I don't know what to say," I said, staring at the dreary, gray sky. It seemed to press down on us like a hollow, metal drum.

"Nothing any of us can say or do. He's gone."

"But why?"

"A scapegoat. People have no sense. They've grown bold after the Iran thing. Brings up all the old grievances."

My stomach tightened. "But kill him?" I still could not believe it. "How could they kill him? Without proof, or a reason?"

"We're all at risk," he said, abruptly. "Gina, even you shouldn't be here."

"What about you?"

"Don't worry about me. You need to go, though."

I stared at him, helpless. He obviously wanted me to leave. I glanced beyond him to where John and one of the workers, the one I liked least and whom I thought had been the one killed, were lifting a boulder off the ground. "Can't I stay for a while, help out or something?" I asked.

"This is nothing. Just something to keep the Ministry quiet. They want me to follow up on the French team's work of last year. Sheikha Mariam insists there's an 'Abbasid settlement under this fort. We've turned up some Ming China pieces, but not much else."

"What do you think?"

He sighed. "Ming's not my specialty. I want to get back to the tel. But they won't let us go yet." He ran his fingers through his hair again, as if trying to brush away all that had happened. Some gray was now visible at the temples. The yearning in my fingertips moved up my arms. I wanted to touch him, hold him, to stroke away his bitterness.

"I want to stay, Marwan," I said. "I want to be with you. I need you."

He stared at me, his eyes soft. Then he suddenly stiffened. "Don't ever need anybody."

"But —"

"Everything will be fine," he said, firmly.

I took a deep breath again, feeling I would suffocate, yet trying to stay composed. "Derek told me that he might have the cables laid somewhere else," I said. "He's willing to redo the initial surveys."

"There's no chance of that being done. At best, they'll delay laying them."

"At least you *can* go back to the *tel*," I said, trying to sound hopeful. I tried to be happy for his freedom to continue his work despite the condition Derek had set. "At least you won't have to *bury* it, Marwan."

He nodded, but his eyes did not change.

"I thought you'd be happy. I know you're upset, now, but you can go on with your work. With Zulaika."

I watched his face. I wanted to be back in that muted hotel room in Cairo, to breath in his skin. I wanted to lose myself in his arms. "Marwan, You're happy about the *tel*, at least?"

"I am," he said. "Of course I am."

"I want to stay here for a while. With you."

He shook his head.

"But I could do some drawings."

"Gina, you have to go," he said, gently.

His voice was flat, suddenly. I felt as though I were disappearing before his eyes. What was the matter with him? He had shared his dream with me, had rattled off names of ancient civilizations as if we had lived there together, had led me into his life so fully I could not imagine myself anywhere else. Why was he pushing me away when we had become so much a part of each other?

The sun emerged again against the gloom of sky, casting a few pallid rays over the fort and gray sand. But it was gone, dragged back into the clouds before it could warm the air.

"Marwan, you know you can trust me. If there's something — I won't tell anybody. I just want to help."

"Look," he said, again running his hand over his head as if to take control of himself, "I can't risk anything, now. Thanks for talking to your husband. I'll be grateful, always."

Thanks for talking to your husband?

286

I shivered. I wanted to know whether he had longed for me, whether his body felt shredded to bits at the thought of me these past few days as mine had every minute we had been apart.

"I have to go back," he said, absently, glancing back at the other men.

I closed my eyes. When I opened them I touched his arm. "You're not happy about the *tel?*"

"Gina, you know I am."

What is it you want from me, I could still hear him say, *take a pencil and paper and write it all down. Remember, separation is an illusion. I'm always with you.*

"Sheikha Mariam called me," he said. "She told me they agreed to delay laying the cables."

"Agreed?" I said, surprised. "Who agreed?"

"She had told me that if we could get the company to put the plant elsewhere, we could save the *tel.*"

"The company? USA Electric?"

"Yes."

"You talked to Derek?"

"Yes."

"You convinced him?"

He was silent.

"That's wonderful, Marwan," I said.

He did not react, but simply looked at our feet.

I felt my throat catch. "Is everything alright, then?"

He put out his hand. "Gina," he said, slowly. "You know how important this dig is to us. To Abu Samra."

I nodded.

Again, he was silent.

Then something occurred to me. "You told Derek about us?"

"Gina — he already knew."

I could hardly grasp what he had just said. "What do you mean?"

287

"Gina."
"Did he threaten you?"
"Gina, listen."

A million thoughts jammed my head. I stepped back from him, almost stumbling. He quickly reached out for me, but I pulled away.

What I had said to Derek came back to me: *You've always been a deal-maker, Derek. Everyone knows it.* Had Derek struck some sort of deal with Marwan? Had he agreed to give Marwan Saali if Marwan gave me up?

Marwan started to say something but I put out my hand as if to defend myself. I did not want to hear it. "I don't believe this," I said, more to myself than to him. I tried to push it all from my mind, our bodies locked together that first night on the *tel*, my heart dying at the end of each day when I had to leave Saali. And Cairo.

I took a deep breath. "What about us?"

He was silent. Then, something unthinkable occurred to me. It seemed ludicrous, but I had to know. "Marwan, did you use me to get to Derek?"

"What?" He stared at me. He seemed shaken, as if he had received a blow.

"Is that what I was — *am* to you? A channel to Derek? To USA Electric?"

"Don't be ridiculous! How can you say that?"

I swung round and groped for the car door. I pulled at it roughly but it would not open. Marwan was behind me, holding me, trying to stop me.

"Gina, listen. Gina!"

I turned around. "Is that why you — all those parties where we met, you wanting me to help you, to learn to dig, do your drawings?"

"No. Damn it, no!"

"You were so persistent. Why were you even outside my

288

house that first day? You were thinking of how to get to Derek, weren't you?"

"Of course not! I didn't even know about him then."

I felt a heaviness in my eyes, my neck. "The Sheikha was right about you. You don't care about anyone but yourself. You used me. God! You kept after me – for Derek." I looked up at the sky. The sun was peeking out of the dark clouds in phosphorescent ribbons. "What about Cairo? Was that in the plan too?"

He grabbed my shoulders. "Gina!" Then, he sighed and shook his head. "I admit, in the beginning I hoped you'd convince your husband to abandon the location. But I swear I wasn't devious. I just thought you could help."

I thrust off his hands and pulled open the car door.

"Gina, listen!" he shouted, trying to turn me around, but I jerked away and sat down in the seat. He held onto the car door to stop me from closing it.

"I love you! Nothing I did with you was ever planned. Or for some other purpose," he persisted.

But I had heard enough. I desperately wanted to bring my hands to my ears to shut out the sound of his voice. But they hung down limp, refusing to move.

"I did meet with your husband," he said, urgently. "But only about the *tel*. It was he who brought you up. He looked so pitiful, I was afraid for you. Afraid he might hurt you. I had to agree not to see you — for *your* sake, damn it. But it's only temporary."

"*My* sake? Who are you to decide for me? You're playing with my life. Both of you!"

"Look," he said, sternly. "He seemed *crazy*. I was worried about you."

His words swam in front of me like objects I was watching on a screen. I could not imagine Derek in the irrational, love-sick state Marwan described. Not now. "Don't lie to me," I said.

"Gina, nothing's changed for me. If anything, I love you even more. I just can't fight him on this. What's going to happen to us will happen between two *free* people. You've got to leave him first."

"Go to hell!"

I thrust the key into the ignition.

At first, he made no motion to stop me. Then, as the car sputtered forward, he lunged at it, grabbing my door handle as if to hold the car still. "Gina," he called, as I pressed hard on the pedal, veering down the road.

I saw him in my mirror, standing with his hands at his sides, a timid frown of resignation on his lips. Soon, he was a solitary stick on the horizon. Then, suddenly, he was gone.

Marwan.

My head throbbed. *Had* I been used to get to Derek? Had I been traded for a mound of dirt? *The will of the world.* I could not get those damn words out of my head. They sounded so banal, suddenly.

The pounding in my head grew deafening. I passed through Qamar, past the store where I had asked directions to the fort. The streets were still quiet, even the grocery store was closed now, presumably for lunch.

There was a heady stirring inside me. I put my hand to my stomach, feeling nauseous, but I kept driving.

When I passed the airport, a crashing noise suddenly shook the car's windows. My hands slid to the right, turning the wheels sharply toward the sand. I quickly steered back into the middle of the road, glancing in both mirrors for a sign of the source of the noise. But except for what looked like a puff of smoke or a tiny cloud in the distance behind me, the road was empty.

When I reached home, Mary was walking away from my gate. She started to wave and hurried back to me.

"Where have you been?" she said, anxiously, when I got out of the car.

"Nowhere." Then I saw the troubled look on her face. "I'm sorry, Mary. What's wrong?"

"It was on the radio right now — the distillation plant was just bombed. Police cars are headed out there right now."

I stared at her. "Distillation plant? That's not possible."

She nodded, vigorously. "Were you in Saali?"

"No, I was there — in the north, in Qamar."

"My God! You were there?" she gasped.

"I passed the plant twenty minutes ago. I *heard* a bang, but I didn't see what it was." My thoughts raced to Marwan. "Was anybody hurt?"

"All I know is there's a fire. I came over to tell you to stay away from Saali. Anything could happen anywhere."

"Who did it?"

She shrugged. "Militants. What were you doing up there?"

"I went to the fort," I said, barely hearing my own words. My hands shook as I unlocked the front door.

I wanted to get into the car and drive back immediately. *Marwan!* But the fort was ten minutes away from the plant. If Marwan had remained at the site he would not have been affected.

"Gina," Mary said, gently. "What's wrong?"

"Nothing." Then I gave in. "Oh Mary, everything. *Everything.*"

"Let's go inside," she said, putting her hand on my shoulder. I could feel my trembling under her palm as she walked me into the kitchen. "Sit down," she said.

While I sat at the kitchen table, she rummaged through the cupboards. "Do you have any sherry, Scotch?" she said.

"I don't need anything."

But she persisted opening the cabinets until she came to the pantry next to the refrigerator. She brought out a bottle of Sheffield and poured some into a glass and set it before me.

I took a sip. It's sweet bitterness tasted awful. I started to cry.

She sat down across from me, reaching over the table and patting my hand. "Let it out."

I took a deep breath to bury the flood of bewilderment and anger. "Ever since I got to Abu Samra, my life's been a mess."

"Derek?" she said.

I was silent.

"Somebody else?"

I stared into her balmy eyes. Their calmness told me that she knew everything I felt, had sensed it from the start. This sudden awareness of her knowledge made me weep uncontrollably now. "I never knew how unhappy I was until we got here, Mary. I can't go on with Derek."

She nodded.

"I thought I could have something with Marwan. Something to show me I could still love, still be loved." It was the first time I had talked openly to Mary about Marwan, or even called him by his first name. I no longer cared who knew.

"What happened?"

"A long story." I wiped my eyes. "I'm amazed how foolish I've been. Derek threatened him I think. Made him promise not to see me. And Marwan agreed." I knew, even hoped, that none of this would make sense to her.

She made me take another sip of the sherry. "Why?"

I glanced about the kitchen. A small gecko was crawling above the window. I watched it scurry behind a cabinet. "I think Marwan used me to get to Derek, to make him change his mind about the electric plant's location. He admitted as much to me just now. He asked Derek for time to dig before they lay the cables and Derek agreed to do it if he stayed away from me. And Marwan said yes. I was simply *used*. By both of them."

Mary gave me a horrified look that softened to a quizzical grimace. She settled further into her chair, then sighed and shrugged. "You don't know the whole story."

"I was never more than that to Marwan, Mary."

She was silent.

"I *hate* Derek. I never want to see him again. *Either* of them."

"Well, you sure as hell are miserable," she said. "But I think you're wrong. I saw the way that man looked at you that day on the roof, as if he needed you simply to breathe. That part's real. Whether or not he agreed to what Derek wanted is something else. And Derek loves you. He'll try anything."

I shook my head. "He doesn't love me. He just thinks he *owns* me, Mary."

She looked sad. "You've seemed unhappy since I first met you."

I looked away from her and nodded. She would have seen through my relationship with Derek the first time she saw us together.

"What's stopping you from getting a divorce?" she said, suddenly.

"A divorce?"

She nodded. "A divorce."

I felt my mouth contort and more tears slip down my face.

"Seems like the only way out — if that's what you want."

I was silent.

"*Is* that what you want?" she asked.

I shrugged. I did not know anymore.

"Are you afraid to leave him?" she said.

"Of course I'm afraid — we've been together for so long. We were going to have a baby."

Mary sighed again. She was childless, but she always seemed to revere pregnancy and children.

"Derek thinks he's a great husband. He wants to start a family. But it's too late for us. We can't start over. He'll never change. He *can't*. I don't want to be married to him anymore. Not him or anyone else."

I wiped my eyes on a paper towel. "I might have gone on another ten years with Derek if we hadn't come here. I put up with unhappiness for so long in New York I hardly noticed it anymore. Derek organizing our life as if we're on some five-year plan, marking progress every few years depending on how he's doing at work, putting off whatever I want to do until he's accomplished one more thing at work. *Just one more.* Our entire life has been on hold to suit him. He hates my painting. Although he'll never admit it, he thinks that since I don't support us on it, it's a waste of time. For a while I even thought he was right. But coming here — Mary, I can't tell you how wonderful it is to be with a man who wants to live each moment of life. Who thrives on just getting up in the morning. None of this waiting, waiting, all the time."

"It happens," Mary cut in. "People leave their familiar surroundings and start seeing and doing things they'd never do back home."

"What do you mean?"

"They find themselves."

"You once said they go crazy."

She laughed. "Just a little — maybe they find the courage to do things they never dared before. Being so far from home brings things into focus."

"Is that good or bad?"

"Depends on how you look at it, on what you do."

"Well, look at me, Mary. I've made a wreck of my life."

She put up her hands as though to halt me. "You *changed* it. But you weren't happy anyway, so why feel bad about it?"

I went to the sink and washed my face. The cool water made me shiver. The sherry was still warm in my throat, but it had already calmed me. "I don't know, Mary. You're right. I guess I'm afraid of life without Derek."

"Why?"

I shrugged. I heard Marwan's voice in my head. *Don't ever need anyone. Not even me.* "I always thought I *needed* Derek. Needed his love."

Mary closed her eyes as if to consider this. "Well, obviously his love hasn't gotten you what you want. Without it you might not be any worse off than you are now."

"I know I don't need Derek's love anymore, but a divorce

would devastate him – would devastate my father."

Now Mary chuckled. "Well, I can understand your concern. But Derek and your father will handle things as best they can. Think about yourself. The rest of *your* life. If you're miserable, he will be too. So will any children you have together."

I braced myself against the sink. "I'm scared Mary, and I hate myself for it."

"We're all scared of change. Of the unknown."

"I'm scared of hurting everybody, my father, my mother — at least her memory. Her last wish was for me to fix my marriage. She kept telling me what a fine man Derek is. Now I feel I'm letting her down."

Mary was silent a minute. Then she said, "Derek *is* a fine man, Gina. But he may not be the man for *you*. And you may not be the perfect woman for him, either. Think of *that*. Maybe he'll be better off without *you*. But only you can decide whether to fix your life as it is or start over."

I nodded. "I know. I've only been thinking of myself. I was always afraid I couldn't be safe or happy without Derek."

She shrugged. "Maybe. But life sure as heck will be different."

I stood staring down at my hands on the edge of the sink, then went over to where she was sitting at the table. I took her hand and brought it to my cheek. I was stunned by her insight and nonjudgmental attitude, and more than ever grateful for her friendship.

"Just calm down a little," she said, finally. "Then do what your gut tells you. You can do it Gina. Remember that."

I nodded, but the tears started again. The finality of it all was still terrifying.

"Get on with your life, Gina."

I nodded again, although I was more uncertain than I had ever been on how to do this.

"You'll know how," she said, as if reading my fears, a vague smile settling on her lips.

There was not a hint of wavering in her gentle voice.

295

22

Pardi

Derek did not deny threatening Marwan when I confronted him that evening. Although he seemed shocked at first that I knew that he had done so, he insisted that he had the right to do whatever necessary to keep his family intact.

"I'm not some commodity you can barter when it suits you, Derek!" I snapped.

Derek's laugh came from some unfamiliar, sterile place inside him, like a dull slap. "You bartered yourself, Gina. As far as I'm concerned, this whole damn thing can be forgotten."

I opened my mouth to scream, but my voice came out limp and pathetic. "It's not a *thing*."

It was just like Derek, at least the man he had become, to dismiss something important to me as fleeting, temporary, to be gotten over like the chicken pox or the flu.

His eyes, like his voice, seemed vacant. "I won't allow some fool with nothing better to do than grope my wife ruin my marriage, Gina."

My anger coiled in my chest. "We're all fools to you, Derek. And what marriage are you talking about? We haven't had anything resembling a marriage in years."

Derek stared at me as if I were some lunatic spewing non-sense. But he said nothing. Although I knew I was meant to feel relieved that I had been forgiven, his cold declaration of love re-volted me.

Since our quarrel in his office four days ago, I had been sleep-ing in the spare bedroom, getting up only after Derek left for work in the mornings and going to bed before he did. For all his claims of wanting our marriage to work, he had not asked me to rejoin him in our bedroom. We barely spoke to each other now, moving about the house like logs drifting over thick, cloudy water, each careful to maintain a safe distance to stay afloat. In our earlier, better days to-gether, we had never let a disagreement fester, one of us always call-ing the other to apologize or simply clear the air. Sadly, the need for that contact no longer compelled me to reach out. I no longer knew how.

Meanwhile, the newspaper was suddenly flooded with articles on the Saali tel. Since I had been nowhere near Saali in more than a week, any information I got about the excavation was from the newspaper, which was doing quite a thorough, almost frantic, job of reporting on it. Just as Marwan had predicted months ago. Pleas had been issued anew by the Abu Samra Historical Society and by Sheikha Mariam herself, for volunteers to help salvage the remains of what might turn out to be a Zulaikan palace buried under the *tel*, before construction destroyed it. Volunteers were needed because of the lack of enough trained laborers, and shifts had been set up. The Ministry of Education was paying for a complete photographic survey chronicling every wall, grave, and potsherd found. There was even a quote from Marwan about the probability that Abu Samra's known history could now be stretched back at least a thousand years earlier than had been previously thought — to 3,500 B.C.

I did not know what had happened to change the Sheikha's mind about Marwan's hunches. I wondered whether Derek's agree-ing to delay or reroute the work on the cables made her feel that it was safe to continue the dig. Once the dig was no longer a threat to Saali's getting electricity, and hence the goodwill of the villagers assured, the problem was most likely resolved.

Yet, I could not bring myself to ask Derek whether the location for the cables had actually been changed and why. It was naive to think that could be done. But it was clear that running them through that particular location had been delayed. USA Electric had even paid for the surveyors sent by the Abu Samra Electric Department to help chart the area that had to be dug in conjunction with the archaeological work.

Reading the newspaper, I tried to picture what the trenches now looked like, what had been uncovered, drawn, photographed before the sand crystals tumbled back in, erasing whatever secrets had been unveiled. I climbed to the roof and listened to the cars and trucks along the carriageway that led to Saali, imagining Marwan explaining to some new volunteer how to brush, how to move from the wrist, how to scrape and then gently sift for overlooked sherds or slivers of glass, any cryptic messages from Zulaika. Then I would wrestle my mind to some other thing, away from the torment and euphoria that had been my life these past few months. Back to the present without him. I set up my easel and paints on the roof and, driven by some maniacal energy, dashed colors on the canvas — turquoise, sun-dazzled amber, ecru, and vermilion that began and ended each Abu Samran day.

Mary brought Ellen by one afternoon to show her my work and Ellen, seemingly impressed, suggested I contact some of the hotels to set up an exhibition. My scenes of Saali were dramatic yet authentic, she said, subtle enough to have been painted by a local artist and yet filled with the wonder of an expatriate. Coming from Ellen, a veteran resident of the peninsula, these compliments were doubly reassuring.

Several days later Marwan called. It was the first time I had heard his voice since that day in the north.

I instinctively hung up. As if I were suddenly lifted outside of myself, I watched my hand replace the receiver without my uttering a single word. I immediately regretted it. Although my initial anguish had worn down to a blunt throb, the sound of his voice now, the knowledge that our breaths would suddenly connect through the flimsy telephone wire, brought me to life. Yet I could not speak to him. Even as my pulse raced, demanding to know why, *why* he had so heartlessly abandoned me, I was not able to talk.

I could not help wondering which of them had won. Derek, now so generous with U.S.A. Electric's time in allowing the excavation to take precedence over the engineering work, or Marwan, who was now being permitted to dig his *tel* after all. I thought of the hurt in Marwan's eyes the last time I saw him, a boy's pain reflected in the soft green-brown. But I could not allow myself to dwell on that or to care anymore. I was numb from the realization that I had been foolish enough to fall into such an age-old maze, leading nowhere.

There were few reported details on the bombing of the distillation plant, partly because it had done little damage. Instead, there was an extensive interview with the Minister of Interior who was quoted as saying that during the next few months all foreigners entering the peninsula would be closely screened for any political dealings with Iran. He also asserted that the government would act ruthlessly, carrying out mass arrests if necessary until all guilty parties were apprehended. Troublemakers who thought they could destabilize Abu Samra's government by cowardly bombings, he warned, had better think twice.

However, a news article on the missing village girl did finally appear in the paper. It was a mere few lines: The body of a little girl from Saali had been discovered, apparently drowned in quicksand.

The villagers were alerted not to go into the sandy stretch of barren land beyond the village which would from now on be enclosed with barbed wire and warning signs. It was a miracle hundreds had not drowned there before, the article said.

Quicksand. Near the tel? Pardi had tried to tell Marwan some story he had heard from a Saali villager about a cruel man long ago who had been swallowed up by the sand. A scrap of local lore. Practically a fable. Dismissed even by Marwan as such. Sheikh Ahmad had even reminded Marwan of another disappearance several years ago that the villagers had blamed on the workers with the German team.

Quicksand? An innocent accident? As in so many news accounts in Abu Samra, the absurdity of it hit me, like the drowning of the women and children in the *dhow* a short way from shore because they could not swim. Quicksand. And nobody knew of it all these years? Pardi had been murdered because of some bizarre mistake? I went over the lines a dozen times or more, hoping each time to find that I had misread the words jumbled into the article in the corner of the page. *Quicksand?*

A week later I went into the spare bedroom upstairs that overlooked the crematorium. To Lhatti's horror, I began to unfasten the drapes that I had once pinned to close off the view.

"But, it's not good to see," Lhatti protested.

"They only burn in the mornings, Lhatti. We never pay attention, anyway. The room needs sunlight."

As Lhatti watched, I removed the pins from the fabric, forcing the heavy panels apart. The light shot in as several months of accumulated dust rose from the window sills.

"We can't keep hiding things," I said, more to myself than to Lhatti. I pushed impatiently at the cloth, exposing the view that I gazed at from the roof each time I painted.

Not convinced, Lhatti stared out at the crematorium a moment, then dropped her hands to her sides in obvious disapproval, and went off to finish cleaning. I fetched some paper towels and a bottle of spray cleaner and started to wipe the windows and sills myself. My need to protect my home, or myself, from the outside world was mostly what had kept me with Derek these last few years, even after the hope of any tangible closeness between us was gone. But now I had to learn to deal with the reality we faced. Opening this window was a start. People died and were buried, burned in this case. People got married and sometimes left each other, forever. It would be the end of Derek and me as a single entity, but not of all the other wonderful things in our lives. I had to make sure I never again settled for less than my own real happiness. Mary was right. I had to start living. For Derek as well as for myself.

The view outside had changed. On the empty land beyond the crematorium that had allowed us the wide sweep of horizon and sea, three tractors wrestled sand into a mound, preparing the foundations for yet another new house. There was a cock's crow from the lone, remaining shanty. It occurred to me that time itself was alarmingly speeded up in Abu Samra, that we could actually see the evolution of civilization in the span of a few short, furious months.

I was thinking this when the ice-blue truck pulled up to the crematorium wall. I quickly shut the window panes and started to leave the room. Then I realized that I knew the truck. It was one of the pick-ups that brought the workers to the site. I went back to the glass.

Three men got out of the front. The driver and another were Marwan's workmen. They went to the back where several others were leaping out of the open cab. I felt ashamed to see the pock-marked workman among them, at how I had wished him dead for no reason. Together the men heaved out the slender, white-wrapped bundle.

Pardi? It had to be! The police must have finally released his body.

I turned away. I could not watch. This time I did leave the room.

Yet despite my dread, a few minutes later I returned in time to see the men piling wood into a waist-high pyre. After carefully adjusting the bundle on top, they paused a moment and then, almost

302

half-heartedly, began to throw matches at the wood. They lit one match after another and tossed them like orange butterflies, not so much aiming, it seemed, at the wood of the pyre itself as at the air, the ruthless new void between them and the body.

Perversely, I felt a surge in my chest at the thought that Marwan would surely be coming to oversee this ritual, that I would finally see him, even if only from the bedroom window. I *expected* him to appear, or John. Someone else to see Pardi put to rest. But no other vehicle drew up to the wall.

All at once, I hurried to my bedroom and pulled out a shawl from my drawer. I went downstairs and out the front gate, draping the shawl around my head. At the back of the house the crematorium door was ajar. I carefully peered inside.

The fire had ignited and was beginning to grow, looking smaller from here than it had from upstairs. I remained just outside the entrance, hidden from view, yet wanting to be there for Pardi. I felt a throb of guilt for the times when I had taken up Marwan's attention, the hours when Pardi could have been the one learning from him instead of me. Perhaps I should have taught Pardi to sketch, spent some of my time there developing in him another tool he could use on the site. He had been so dedicated and eager to learn, more than any of the other laborers; developing ambitions and thoughts not expected of him. Again, I remembered the night downtown when I had entrusted him with the message for Marwan: "Just tell him yes, Pardi." *Yes Madam,* he had agreed, never asking what I meant, always willing to do what was asked, and more.

The flames finally broke loose, rising up and out of the wood like thirsty serpents. The men moved back, giving the fire the space to do its work. I could almost hear Pardi's voice patiently explaining to Marwan: "They say that we are digging in the wrong place, Sir."

I thought of his meditations on the beach each evening. Perhaps now he knew the secrets that lurked beneath the tel. As the fire ripened, the white shroud receding within the flames, I felt Pardi breaking loose, becoming light as the crisp, winter air.

I suddenly envied him his freedom.

303

Christmas passed quickly and without any more confrontations with Derek. We attended a Christmas Eve party together at the American Embassy where Santa, arriving atop a double-humped dromedary, passed out bottles of Champagne. After opening presents at home Christmas morning, Derek and I went for an early dinner at Mary's. She and I baked the turkey using my mother's recipe. Even Derek had seemed more relaxed lately as if these traditional celebrations together meant that we were reconciled. He had opened no more personal discussions with me, apparently hoping that by forging a truce and avoiding the subject of the past, our present would resist further deterioration.

Then, between Christmas and New Year it happened.

First, the bombs went off. Two in the north, near the airport. Then one outside the new *Alfredo's* Pizza restaurant in town, which injured ten pedestrians.

Police and soldiers immediately took up positions at the entrance of town, and army tanks appeared at the major round-a-bouts on the carriageways. The oil refinery in the South became a virtual military base.

The familiar, relaxed mood of Abu Samra which greeted us when we first arrived, evaporated. Expatriates were now cautioned to keep a low profile and to stay away from public areas like the downtown market and cinemas lest they become targets for irrational rebels. Even Khalid, our gardener, not wanting our grass to die without the layer of sand needed each winter for new growth, had to smuggle himself from his village to Dafna in the back of a truck to avoid detection by police looking for *Shia* villagers sympathetic with Iran.

Coinciding with the bombings, came my equally sudden bouts of nausea and vomiting.

When the nausea persisted for several days, I took an appointment with Dr. Mustapha, whom I had not seen since he had diagnosed my salt deficiency months ago. Now, the soft-spoken doctor offered a sympathetic nod and said my stomach upset, barring food poisoning, was likely due to an attack of nerves in reaction to the past weeks' upheavals. He prescribed an antidepressant, which had apparently helped several other patients recently, and he also took a blood sample.

The next day, however, a follow-up call from his office directed me to stop the medication at once. I was pregnant.

I became aware of my silence, for the nurse repeated the news, adding a cheerful, congratulatory *mabrook*, before setting up another appointment for me to see the doctor.

My shock at this news was abruptly followed by a heady, involuntary thrill. Even a month ago I would not have been able to fathom another pregnancy, not after having just lost the baby and my growing alienation from Derek. Yet now, it was almost as if I had willed it upon myself, as if I had even suspected it. For sifting back through all that had occurred during the past weeks and months, I suddenly knew that the onset of symptoms at this time could only mean one thing.

I had not been intimate with Derek for several months until that night after returning from Cairo, much too soon to result in any signs of a conception. Although in Cairo I had been careful to use birth control, I had not been prepared on that initial, spontaneous night in November on the tel. Was it possible? Those first intense moments in the cold sand with Marwan — those moments that I had wanted carved into my memory forever — had planted themselves far deeper inside me than simply in my mind?

At first, I told myself over and over not to grasp at straws that would connect me to him. What had been between us was over. Of no use to either of us anymore. Yet, there was also something so undeniably *perfect*, so comforting in the thought that I was carrying Marwan's child.

I stood dumbfounded and silent, taking in a long deep breath and caressing my stomach. My eyes began to fill with tears.

Then, the world began to shrink again. This was not news I could celebrate, despite the nurse's enthusiasm. How could I tell Marwan? I could not begin to imagine how he would react if I told him I was pregnant with his child. I could only think that he would be horrified. And if not, what could he possibly do about it at this point? It would only complicate matters even more.

And there was Derek. What would I tell *him*? The thought of Derek's reaction, however, saddened rather than frightened me. I decided that he should not know. He was no longer involved. This was between Marwan and me now. Nobody else.

My hands rested on my belly again, as if to calm a vast sea of fear. I *had* to stay calm. I had to stay sane.

On New Year's Eve, Derek came home from work with the news that 'Abbas had been arrested along with dozens of other men and boys from his village.

"'Abbas?" I gasped. "What on earth for?"

"For consorting with whomever it is making those bombs."

I stared at Derek in disbelief. "But he's an old man. He wouldn't get involved in that."

Derek looked annoyed, as if I were questioning the validity of what he said. "I called up the Ministry of Interior. So did Sheikh Ahmad. Nobody's in a hurry to do anything."

"But they can't just round up innocent people."

"They will until the dissidents give themselves up."

"Well, we've got to *do* something, Derek. We can't just leave him in jail."

A frown of defeat elongated Derek's face. "I've already been down to the police station, but they won't talk to anybody. Sheikh Ahmad tells me to be patient."

"But —"

"You try something if you can," he snapped.

"Could he—" I was almost afraid to ask what I was thinking. "Could these people be executed?"

306

"Damn it, *I don't know!*" Derek was pacing the foyer now, look-ing unsure whether to go out the front door or retreat back to the kitchen, or burst into a fit of outrage, cursing the day he set foot in Abu Samra. But all he said was, "The Embassy's just issued an evacuation order for women and children."

"The American Embassy?"

"Yes."

"Why?"

Derek seemed not to have heard me, stopping his pacing sud-denly and going to stare out of the living room window at the front yard as he did each morning to check whether 'Abbas had arrived to take him to work. I followed him, half expecting to see the driver pulling out a rag from the trunk to wipe the sand off the car's hood and polish the outer mirrors. I sensed that Derek still resented 'Abbas for his betrayal of him that day on the office stairs, when he interrupted our argument.

"Can't we at least find out if he's all right?" I said.

Derek looked offended by my obvious ignorance of these mat-ters. "They're keeping them in the prison near the oil field. You can't get anywhere near it."

"All this because he's a *Shia*?"

"I told you. It's a scare tactic."

"Then why is the Embassy worried?" I said.

"They need to ensure our safety, Gina."

"Well, what if we don't want to go?"

Again, Derek acted as if he had not heard me. He picked up his jacket and said he was leaving for the office.

All at once I could barely contain my urge to drive out to the Saali dig. If *Shias* were randomly being purged, was it not possible that Marwan could be targeted? There was no way to call him at this time of day. I would have to wait until he returned to his home at night. He had once given me his home telephone number. But I had never called him there and did not want to now in case his mother or sister answered the telephone. I could not allow myself to drive out to him any longer, but I wanted to know he was all right. I needed that, at least. Especially now.

Again, I felt I had to tell him. After all, it certainly was his right to know.

Yet, I could not! I could only wait and see whether I would sustain this pregnancy for any length of time or whether I would lose it as I had the other one. If I lost it — but I did not want to think about that. Not another loss. Nobody could know anything. Not yet.

When Derek returned several hours later, I was waiting for him in the sitting room. I stood up. "I could visit my father until things calm down."

He looked puzzled.

"You said the Embassy wants us out of here," I said.

He stared at me a moment. "No."

"But you said —"

He looked as if my leaving had never entered his mind. "This'll all blow over."

"But what if it's not safe?"

"What happens to everyone else will happen to us."

I bristled at this quick change of attitude. Only a few hours ago he was completely focused on our safety. Perhaps he now suspected that my abrupt willingness to leave was my first step to separating from him for good.

"Are you saying you won't let me go, Derek?"

He seemed unfazed. "I'm staying and you're staying."

I watched him a moment. He could not have known then that I had already made up my mind.

23

Night Sky

I packed my suitcase with my winter clothing and booked a ticket on a TWA flight to London and on to New York. It was obvious that I would have to leave without Derek's knowledge or consent.

I was angry that he had decided to make it more difficult on us both, although I suspected that the idea of any amicable separation was still unthinkable to him. But I could not return to my old world or fit myself back into the narrow tunnel I had squeezed out of. I had changed, expanded like the unruly dandelions beyond the crematorium that strained recklessly toward the horizon. Yet Abu Samra had taught me that even weeds were beautiful and of value if we chose to see them as such. With Derek I would be crushed. It was not necessarily his fault, it was simply the one way he knew to treat anything wild and uncontrollable. Dandelions were weeds to be destroyed in order to preserve the cultivated green lawn. In his mind, my independence would have to be stifled to preserve our marriage.

I would not allow that.

The next morning I gave Lhatti the day off. Although she was certainly loyal and trustworthy enough, I did not want to burden her with the knowledge that I was leaving. I finished packing the last few items I was taking with me, then picked up the telephone.

I had not seen nor spoken to Marwan in nearly two weeks. A glacial numbness engulfed me as I listened to the ringing of his home telephone. I was wondering what to say if a female voice answered. I could not get further than a 'hello, how are you?' in Arabic, although I remember Marwan telling me that his sister spoke good English. I was equally afraid of betraying my feelings to *him* in case he answered himself. I had no idea what to say to him and probably would be overcome by the need to tell him about my pregnancy. Even more, I dreaded learning that he had already put me out of his mind. But I did not care anymore. I simply had to hear his voice one last time.

I imagined him lying on his bed still in his work clothes jotting down notes, diagrams, completing one of his careful, somewhat clumsy sketches of a potsherd or bead. He would be missing me for this chore. But I wanted him to miss more than my help. I wanted his voice to echo with his need for me, his need and faith that we would one day be together. *What would be the ultimate commitment?* I had been a fool in Cairo to have doubted that he was right. Too afraid of change and of the possibility of being wounded in any way. Choosing the safety of a defunct but familiar union with Derek rather than the unknown had, only weeks ago, been the only way I knew how to live.

I counted the rings, both fearing and hoping that Marwan would leap to answer, as though he were innately aware that it was me on the other end. But there was no reply. Nothing. He was probably at the *tel.* The women were obviously not at home.

My only option, it seemed, was to ask Mary to inform Marwan once I left. I had told her of my condition and, to her great credit, she neither acted surprised nor pushed me to tell him. She had merely asked whether or not I was going to keep the baby and, if so, if I felt equipped and ready to raise a child alone. None of which I knew for sure just yet. I did know, however, that asking her to inform Marwan after I was gone was a cowardly way of dealing with the matter, but for now it was the only way I could manage it.

"Are you sure about this?" she said when I telephoned, not attempting to hide the dismay in her voice at my abrupt decision to leave.

"I can't stay here anymore, Mary. And it's not fair to Derek."

She was silent a moment. "I'll miss you, Gina."

"I'll miss you, too. I don't know what I would have done without you."

"Let me at least drive you to the airport."

"No. But thanks,' I said, wiping my eyes. "It'll make it harder with you there. I'll take a taxi. But promise me you'll tell him. And promise that you'll pass by New York to see me."

"I'll tell him,' she said. 'And if things get any worse here, you might see me in New York sooner than you think."

"Will it get seriously dangerous?" I asked, hating the idea that I was running away and suddenly wanted her to verify that for safety's sake — at least for the baby's safety — I was doing the right thing.

As if reading my thoughts she said, "You can't tell."

"Take care, Mary," I said, trying to swallow the lump in my throat.

Soon I would actually be gone. It would all be over. All of this would end.

I had to get out of the house and to the airport before Derek got home. He had been driving my car to work since the Buick was in the garage being repaired. I also suspected that he had arranged things so that I could not drive it. Although I was not about to disregard the embassy directive to Americans not to frequent public places, Derek seemed to think I would do just that.

I was about to call a taxi when the doorbell rang. Hesitant, I opened the front door.

" 'Abbas!" I exclaimed, lunging to embrace him in my surprise and relief to see him. Then, remembering local custom, I pulled back and shook his hand instead. "Thank God, you're safe. Are you all right?"

"Yes. Good," he said, his brow wrinkling in confusion at my outburst, although he seemed just as happy and relieved to see me as I was him. "No work today? No *tel?*" he asked.

"Not today, 'Abbas," I said. Then I saw his glance fall on the suitcase behind me. He looked up at my face.

"I'm going to New York," I said, hearing the sound of my own voice drifting about the room. The house felt so alien to me now, as if it had never really been mine, but rather a part of Derek, a shell I was finally shedding. "Mr. Monroe doesn't know," I added, my voice low.

I felt ashamed, suddenly. To 'Abbas, it would probably be inconceivable for a woman to abandon her husband simply because she did not love him. I thought he would look away, or else simply leave to avoid getting involved in some feud between his boss and his wife. But he kept his gaze on me, like a patient sage trying to determine which of two roads was the less treacherous to pursue.

Finally, he said softly, "I take you."

"Mr. Monroe might need you. I can take a taxi."

"I take you," he said, gruffly. "Taxi is dangerous."

I was not sure whether or not to accept his offer. Although I knew 'Abbas could get me wherever I needed to go safer than anyone else, I knew it could also cause him trouble if Derek found out.

" 'Abbas, you'd better not."

But he was already moving behind me, resolutely picking up my suitcase.

When the flight took off that first night of the New Year, the danger in Abu Samra was suddenly clear, for all of the plane's lights were extinguished to make us less conspicuous to any would-be saboteurs. The sudden hush enveloping the passengers seemed to override the deafening thunder of the plane's motors as we soared like an invisible missile into the night sky. A reassuring full moon coasted alongside us, and as I peered out of the window at the twinkling lights of the town, I thought I also recognized the *tumulii*, the giraffe-like oil pumps, and the Saali Portuguese fort in the shadows. I half expected to see a fire lit on the crematorium platform in Dafna, although there had never been a burning at night since we had lived there.

This night sky, this void, would now be my new life. I had given up everything — my marriage, Marwan, all that I had built these past years.

I leaned back in my seat, keeping my face to the window to hide my tears. It felt sad and yet oddly soothing to plunge into the sky in total darkness, as if our destination were a mystery even to us.

"Ask yourself what it all means, why I was put in your life now," Marwan had told me in Cairo.

"Does there have to be a reason?" I had asked, impatiently.

"I believe things happen when the time is right."

"Don't we control anything? Can't we just decide to fall in love?" I had pushed.

He had smiled. "Look. Zulaika revealed itself to me at the time it wanted to. I had no more control over it than a doctor can control the birth of a child. I was simply present when it wanted to be found."

It had struck me then that this was just the irksome sort of thing Madame Shams would say as her voice sifted through the scent of saffron from a pot of *basmati* rice cooking on her stove.

I tried to see us this way now. What if Marwan had been put in my life for a reason that did not entail our eventually being together. Would it make this awful ripping apart from him any easier?

24

New Life

I stayed with my father in Connecticut for a month before looking for a place of my own. It was only then that I told him that I had left Derek for good. To my utter surprise, he did not seem as upset by my decision as I thought, nor did he argue with me about it. He even seemed to have suspected it.

I enrolled in a sculpture course and called Derek to let him know that I would not be returning to Abu Samra. He was silent for a moment, then said he understood my need to be with my father a bit longer. But it was only when I told him that I would be teaching at the Arts League in New York that he seemed to grasp that I was no longer thinking of a life with him. All he said, however, was that it was best that I was away because the situation in Abu Samra was still unsettled. I did not tell him about the baby.

By February I was painting every day and was able to move up my exhibition to the fall, after the baby's birth. To my surprise, I was enjoying being pregnant, despite the fact that I no longer thought of the child as anyone's but my own. The few times I had spoken to Derek, he had asked how my financial condition was, but I could detect no need on his part to be near me, although he made it clear that my needs would be met. I never mentioned being pregnant even when he discussed money. There was no need.

By March I felt the baby's first kicks, small, random hiccups in my abdomen that began to occur more regularly until I realized what they were. It was exhilarating to finally feel the new life being created within me, to imagine its features taking shape and a personality molding!

Since I wanted to be free of any obligations or work at the time of birth, I painted furiously in anticipation of the self-imposed break: scenes of Abu Samra from my sketches of the villages and the *tel*, and even some of the Mamluke homes in Cairo. I made abstracts of the sketches of the mosaics and delicate woodwork, of the fanciful geometrics. I even showed my new work to the gallery downtown.

I still had the watercolor of the Saali sunset that Marwan had forgotten to take from me, along with the ones Ellen had liked. I made variations on them, showing the sea at different times of the day, with the bold, crisp sun of morning and with a hint of icy, evening moon. I was painting differently now, not as driven to achieve the finished canvas as much as to find what the color and form would reveal as each canvas grew, evolving from the initial sketch to a full work.

Some days, I would insert myself into the canvas, perhaps as a bit of froth from the sea, the shadow of a bird flying over the water, or the frond of a palm tree. Sometimes I would be invisible, imagining myself as a verse, a piece of unfinished poetry that had yet to be completed.

Just let yourself be, I could hear Marwan say. *Enjoy the present moment without looking to tomorrow to offer more than it can.*

I went into the city and wandered in the galleries, often in the Metropolitan. I would go for the art, but I always ended up downstairs in the Egyptian exhibit and thought of the night I had stared the Sphinx in the face in the dark, with Marwan. *Arab poetry is so poignant,* he had said, *because it's inspired by unrequited love.*

316

After a morning in the city at the Met or the Guggenheim, I would have lunch alone in a small second floor Madison Avenue restaurant. I watched people go by in the street below and would think of the view of the shanties from our rooftop, of the Abu Samra market street scene from Derek's office, of women in black shimmering alongside men in moon-white *thobes*. Vendors selling burnished figs or unripe yellow dates.

I missed Abu Samra in more ways than I thought possible. I missed the wonderful people I had met and the genial lifestyle that the Abu Samrans were striving so hard to preserve from the intrusions of the more manic, Western world. The faces of Sheikha Mariam, with her confident smile, and of Awatif describing her delinquent boys, still haunted me. I could see Khalid nursing the new grass that would be emerging from the layer of sand he had risked getting arrested to spread, and 'Abbas's composed sulk each morning as he stopped by the house to ask if I needed anything from the market.

I awaited Mary's letters like a homesick child. It was she, rather than Derek, who told me that Abu Samra was calming down, that most of the rebels had been let out of jail and the government had reverted to its benevolent policy of turning a blind eye to the remonstrances of its disgruntled *Shia* majority. She wrote that she had invited Derek to dinner several times but that, although he seemed to appreciate the company, he appeared to want to spend as little time as possible with people who had known us as a couple. They no longer played bridge together, even though Mary had offered to find him a partner. Instead, Derek had joined a group at the new tennis club soon after I left, and Mary said she often saw him on a Friday morning driving out of the neighborhood, a white cap on his head, on his way to play.

But it was Marwan that I missed most and on whom I focused the countless times each day that I thought of Abu Samra. How keenly aware and susceptible he had made me to my surroundings, how open to new ways of looking at life.

He had gotten my address from Mary and wrote me a long letter in January.

At first I did not want to believe it was his writing on the envelope. I resisted even looking at it for days, knowing how it would unleash the agony and wonder of the past months buried deep in a place I did not want to excavate. Finally, I tore it open.

My beloved — it began. My hand started to shake as I read, hearing his voice inside me relay news of the new findings on the *tel* that were being confirmed as Zulaikan. There were cooking utensils, bits of jewelry, a platter, and the most important finds, which were the graves — Helenistic, neo-Babylonian, and Zulaikan. There would be several teams there next year, the French and Danish along with him and John. The electric cables would be moved a solid five hundred meters away and the *tel* would be off limits while they worked to anyone but members of the teams. It would be enclosed with wire, just as the section of quicksand near Saali was now closed off to protect people. He had several more months of work there, he said, before new conclusions could be drawn for his next book.

He ended the letter by saying that he knew that his instincts about us were correct, too. *We belonged together.*

I dropped the letter on the floor. I did not want to fall under his spell again, did not want to let his words ensnare and imprison me again. Then I picked it up, unable to resist reading it over and over, trying to envision him on the *tel*, wondering whether he wished I were there with him.

Although I did not answer, he kept writing, almost daily now, asking me to understand him, to forgive him. In each letter he declared his love anew, proposing that we see each other just once so that he could explain himself. Although the letters upset me and I often tossed the pages onto the floor, I never threw them away. Finally, I got a letter mentioning 'our' child.

Mary had told him.

25

Epilogue

None of Abu Samra seems real, now. Not Marwan, not Saali, nor Cairo. They appear as within the frame of an unfinished canvas. This is the only way to contain it, to be at peace with it. As I finish off the sky of this small canvas that has given me such trouble today — sometimes a sign that the painting is better than I realize, sometimes that it is simply not going well — I imagine that the bell rings.

In his last letter he said that he would be arriving on the 16th of May, at three in the afternoon, and that he would take a taxi from the airport. I had been skeptical. But as the days went by, it sank in. At first I had not answered a single one of his letters, although I memorized each one, going over the words as I tossed in bed at night. And although I had not replied, his letters continued, as if by my very silence I was responding, letting him know that I was listening, that if he kept writing I might one day answer. Finally, I sent him a postcard, a copy of my watercolor of Saali that he had wanted to buy.

Now I imagine him standing before me in the chill of an after-noon in May, dressed too lightly, as usual, for the weather. His boy-ish demeanor is back, so different from the man I last saw in the north, preoccupied and focussed on his hunches and theories. He has the ease of one who has safely reached a long-sought shore, grateful for the air he breathes and the curl of the chill on his back. There is the twinkle in his glance that I rebelled against the first time we met, the black, smooth hair shades darker than any black I know, the golden olive skin with its ruddy glow from hours of work in the sun. I am amazed how much I have actually forgotten, how much I have dreaded seeing his face again, and how thankful I am to see it now.

"You found me," I say, choking back my terror that this may all be a dream.

I see us again on that hot day in Dafna when I suddenly knew, despite the glaring sun and my nausea from lack of salt, de-spite being wary of inviting him into my life, that this man would one day be a part of me. I remember a November day in Cairo when I had spotted him waiting behind the airport glass, waving en-thusiastically, ecstatic that I had made this journey to be with him.

We now stand for what seems like an eternity, trying to decide where we are, what this shift in locale means, whether we have changed since our last meeting. His eyes slide down to my belly, still several months away from giving birth. He appears to be in awe of it, as if it is some fanciful work of art I have produced. He seems about to compliment me. Then, instead, he slowly retrieves something from the large duffel bag at his feet. It is a small, clear plastic bag.

"*Greetings from Zulaika,*" *he says, with a smile, his eyes lighting up mischievously.*

I take it from him, softly kneading the familiar sand through the plastic. All at once I glimpse the rumpled terrain of primeval desert graves, inhale the scents of incense and coconut oil, and of frying onions and cumin from the workmen's cooking fire next door. I suddenly feel weak.

He seems to sense my yearning. "I need somebody to sketch," he says, somewhat shyly. "I can't afford you though. Unless you'll work for lager."

I take a deep breath, already feeling the change in each of us and in our association. We are standing on firmer ground now, on rock instead of porous sand.

"Australian lager?" I ask, finally, moving toward him.

He smiles. "It's the best."

End

About the Author

Kathryn K. Abdul-Baki was born in Washington D.C. to a Palestinian father and an American mother. She grew up in Iran, Kuwait, Beirut, and Jerusalem where she attended Arabic, British, and American schools. She attended the American University of Beirut, Lebanon, and earned a BA in journalism from George Washington University in Washington, D.C. She has an MA in creative writing from George Mason University, Virginia.

Her books are taught at schools and universities in Multicultural Literature, Women's Studies, and Arab Studies departments, and she is a frequent lecturer on these subjects. She currently resides in McLean, Virginia.